THE RELUCTANT SIREN

Other Books by Lexi Blake

ROMANTIC SUSPENSE

Masters and Mercenaries
The Dom Who Loved Me
The Men With The Golden Cuffs
A Dom is Forever
On Her Master's Secret Service
Sanctum: A Masters and Mercenaries Novella
Love and Let Die
Unconditional: A Masters and Mercenaries Novella
Dungeon Royale
Dungeon Games: A Masters and Mercenaries Novella
A View to a Thrill
Cherished: A Masters and Mercenaries Novella
You Only Love Twice
Luscious: Masters and Mercenaries~Topped
Adored: A Masters and Mercenaries Novella
Master No
Just One Taste: Masters and Mercenaries~Topped 2
From Sanctum with Love
Devoted: A Masters and Mercenaries Novella
Dominance Never Dies
Submission is Not Enough
Master Bits and Mercenary Bites~The Secret Recipes of Topped
Perfectly Paired: Masters and Mercenaries~Topped 3
For His Eyes Only
Arranged: A Masters and Mercenaries Novella
Love Another Day
At Your Service: Masters and Mercenaries~Topped 4
Master Bits and Mercenary Bites~Girls Night
Nobody Does It Better
Close Cover
Protected: A Masters and Mercenaries Novella
Enchanted: A Masters and Mercenaries Novella
Charmed: A Masters and Mercenaries Novella
Taggart Family Values
Treasured: A Masters and Mercenaries Novella
Delighted: A Masters and Mercenaries Novella
Tempted: A Masters and Mercenaries Novella

Masters and Mercenaries: The Forgotten
Lost Hearts (Memento Mori)
Lost and Found
Lost in You
Long Lost
No Love Lost

Masters and Mercenaries: Reloaded
Submission Impossible
The Dom Identity
The Man from Sanctum
No Time to Lie
The Dom Who Came in from the Cold

Masters and Mercenaries: New Recruits
Love the Way You Spy
Live, Love, Spy
Sweet Little Spies
The Bodyguard and the Bombshell: A Masters and Mercenaries New Recruits Novella
No More Spies
Spy With Me
Love and Let Spy, Coming March 24, 2026

Butterfly Bayou
Butterfly Bayou
Bayou Baby
Bayou Dreaming
Bayou Beauty
Bayou Sweetheart
Bayou Beloved

Park Avenue Promise
Start Us Up
My Royal Showmance
Built to Last

Lawless
Ruthless
Satisfaction
Revenge

Courting Justice
Order of Protection
Evidence of Desire

Masters Of Ménage (by Shayla Black and Lexi Blake)
Their Virgin Captive
Their Virgin's Secret
Their Virgin Concubine
Their Virgin Princess
Their Virgin Hostage
Their Virgin Secretary
Their Virgin Mistress

The Perfect Gentlemen (by Shayla Black and Lexi Blake)
Scandal Never Sleeps
Seduction in Session
Big Easy Temptation
Smoke and Sin
At the Pleasure of the President

URBAN FANTASY

Thieves
Steal the Light
Steal the Day
Steal the Moon
Steal the Sun
Steal the Night
Ripper
Addict
Sleeper
Outcast
Stealing Summer
The Rebel Queen
The Rebel Guardian
The Rebel Witch
The Rebel Seer

LEXI BLAKE WRITING AS SOPHIE OAK

Texas Sirens
Small Town Siren
Siren in the City
Siren Enslaved
Siren Beloved
Siren in Waiting
Siren in Bloom
Siren Unleashed
Siren Reborn
The Accidental Siren
The Reluctant Siren

Nights in Bliss, Colorado
Three to Ride
Two to Love
One to Keep
Lost in Bliss
Found in Bliss
Pure Bliss
Chasing Bliss
Once Upon a Time in Bliss
Back in Bliss
Sirens in Bliss
Happily Ever After in Bliss
Far from Bliss
Unexpected Bliss
Wild Bliss
Brooke's Bliss

A Faery Story
Bound
Beast
Beauty

Standalone
Away From Me
Snowed In

The Reluctant Siren

Texas Sirens: Legacy, Book 2

Lexi Blake
writing as
Sophie Oak

The Reluctant Siren
Texas Sirens: Legacy, Book 1

Published by DLZ Entertainment LLC

Edited by Chloe Vale
ISBN: 978-1-963890-31-0

Sign up for Lexi Blake's newsletter
and be entered to win a $25 gift certificate
to the bookseller of your choice.

Join us for news, fun, and exclusive content
including free short stories.

There's a new contest every month!

Go to www.LexiBlake.net to subscribe.

Acknowledgments

As I work my way through this new generation, it's a little like connecting with old friends. There are some I see all the time like Ian and Charlotte, but it's been a while since I really checked in with the threesome from *Siren Unleashed,* and I was surprised at how much I missed them. In a lot of ways Chase Dawson was my first foray into writing characters who think differently than the rest of us. Like many people I deeply love, Chase is neurodivergent. Natalie was one of my first heroines who dealt with trauma in some self-harming ways. Ben was…well, he was Ben. What I learned from that book was I can and should write characters who are different. Who struggle. These characters can connect us, can teach me the way the people in my life have. So getting to write Chase and Ben and Nat as parents felt lovely. Even when Chase is obnoxious. Happily ever afters look different for some characters, too. Chase is still worried about getting sniped. Natalie is still an artist. Ben is still Ben.

And this first series I wrote is morphing into something bigger, bringing in new characters and new windows to this world I love.

I hope you enjoy Harlow's story and this visit with family.

Chapter One

Harlow Dawson sat on the bench in front of the locker that had been designated as hers since the day The Hideout opened and wondered if she should even be here.

Maybe instead of shoving her body into a corset and making sure her butt floss was properly positioned she should be at home, drinking tea and questioning all of her life choices. Beginning with the decision to hire Daisy O'Donnell. Sweet girl. Funny. Nice to have around. Cursed.

Firing her had been an excellent decision, but even weeks later everyone kept staring at her like she kicked a puppy.

A puppy who inadvertently sicced a hellhound on her.

"Hey, you okay?" Chloe Lodge-Taylor looked like she'd come straight from work, which given the fact that the club didn't even open until nine said something about the young woman's work ethic. She worked for one of her father's companies as a junior executive, but Harlow often wondered if the job wasn't making her friend utterly miserable. "I heard there was some trouble a couple of weeks ago. Sorry. I was in New York last week when Hurricane Daisy really blew through this time. Then I was in London and Madrid."

Which all sounded lovely if she thought for a second Chloe was taking some time to smell the sangria. She wasn't. She wouldn't have done touristy stuff. She wouldn't have taken a spa day or found new friends. Harlow was worried about her.

But wasn't she doing the exact same thing?

"Is there a worse storm than a hurricane? Like what if a hurricane also threw bombs all over the place. Shit. I know where they got the idea for *Sharknado*. That writer met Daisy." Ruby Lockwood poked her head around the corner. Her locker was on the next row, but it wasn't like she couldn't hear everything that happened in this part of the lounge. "Get this, Chloe. On her very first day…"

"First hour," Harlow corrected because this was a story they would tell for all of time.

"On her first day, in the first hour of her employment, our brand-new admin not only sicced the deranged Dawson dad on us, but also managed to become a material witness in an ongoing drug investigation. Big Tag was forced to hire a bodyguard, who Daisy promptly fell in love with. They had to hide out in Sanctum because there was a cartel hit on her. They shot up Nate's new truck and everything."

Chloe sat down with a sigh. "Oh, dear. Tell me everyone's alive."

Harlow waved off the fear. "She distracted the assassins with her boobs and her dad turned the cartel on itself and all the bad guys are dead. Mostly. And did I mention the fall in love part? I've been told I'll receive the save the date soon."

It was how things tended to go on *that* side of the club.

The Hideout was made up of what Harlow liked to think of as two weird cults. There was the one she belonged to, which consisted mostly of young men and women who grew up with parents who played at a club called—sigh—The Club, owned by Chloe's father, Julian Lodge. And the spy kids whose parents founded a club called Sanctum, watched over by a man everyone called Big Tag, who was a spy. The corporate kids, as Seth Taggart called them, mainly worked in fields like finance and law. The spy kids, well, there was a reason they had a conference room that sometimes was filled with people who went by names like Mr. Black or Ms. White.

Or Ms. Magenta, but at least she knew what to call those two.

Sometimes she worried she fit better on that side of the club.

Opening a private investigations agency apparently wasn't on the same level as Chloe's junior executive or her own sister's budding art career. Sometimes her dads acted like she was rebelling when they literally made their living as detectives. Well, outside of the massive trust fund they came into when they were younger.

"Daisy O'Donnell is getting married?" Chloe huffed. "I did not have that on my bingo card this year. Her cousin getting a venereal disease was, though. Did you see his latest… Do I call them girlfriends?"

"And I'm out." Ruby disappeared again. "Let me know when we've moved on to new material."

Harlow groaned, facing her childhood friend. Ruby had a point. They'd had this talk before. A lot. "I don't think he has girlfriends. But then it's not like you have boyfriends."

Chloe had been circling Seth Taggart since they were teens, though it didn't reach the level of enemies who would almost certainly end up as lovers until they opened The Hideout. Chloe had rejected Seth's advances since the first night when he offered to top her and she told him she needed more than he could ever give her.

Sometimes she wondered what would have happened if Chloe had been brave enough to give him a try. If she hadn't let being burned by some other guy before hold her back.

Like Jensen was holding her back from giving Niall a chance.

Big, gorgeous, sweet Niall, who every sub in The Hideout thought was absolute forever Dom material. Niall, who had let her know any time she wanted to play, he was there.

He had joined the club a few months before, and in all that time she was almost certain he hadn't slept with a single sub. At least not here. He'd never once signed up for a privacy room, and he definitely hadn't been having sex on the floor. She would have heard about that.

"I have a boyfriend, thank you," Chloe announced.

And Ruby was back because this was definitely new material. "What? Who? The last guy you were with was your college boyfriend, and you broke up because you knew you didn't love him."

A weird smile came over Chloe's face. A kind of still, expectant smile. A smile that held zero humor and let Harlow know she was masking some unnamed emotion. If she was interrogating the other woman, she wouldn't believe anything that came out of her mouth next. Oh, the basics would be true, but Chloe was hiding something.

"Tom," Chloe said with a brisk nod. "Yes. We actually broke up because our career paths diverged. He went to New York to work for a start-up, and I settled in at Lodge Corp."

Which was killing her. Oh, she said all the right things, but Chloe wasn't happy being the heir apparent to her father's massive conglomerate. All the money in the world wasn't going to take the place of Chloe shoving down her creative dreams because she felt a responsibility to her family.

Unlike her own deranged dad, who had done his absolute best to ensure Harlow didn't follow her dreams, she rather thought Uncle Julian would understand.

"So who is the new guy?" Ruby asked.

Harlow put the pieces together. Chloe hesitated because she didn't want to admit the truth. Because Harlow knew the real story. No wonder she'd been spending so much time in New York. "It's the old guy. She ran into him while she was working in the New York offices. He felt safe and warm and right in line with her new life plan, which is to stay safe and warm and never go for what she truly wants."

Chloe's eyes flashed with a bit of the fire she'd had as a teen. "Oh, really? Is this judgment of yours about Seth? I should follow my lust and forget everything I know about him? Maybe get my heart broken? You want to talk about the new guy and how you make doe eyes at him and never say yes to him?"

She was being too harsh. "I'm sorry. I don't have a right to judge. But it is Tom, isn't it?"

Harlow remembered him being a "nice" guy. Said all the right things. Mostly did the right things. Something had felt off to Harlow. He was a bit self-centered, but he could turn on the charm when he needed to. He had definitely liked the idea of being attached to Julian Lodge's daughter.

Chloe sat up straighter. "As a matter of fact, your detective skills are excellent. We met up at a conference and now I see him when I'm in New York. It's getting serious."

She could see so easily what Chloe was doing, but it wouldn't do anything but start a fight to argue with her. Chloe could be extremely stubborn. "If you're happy then I'm happy. Are you going to bring him to the club anytime soon? I would love to see him again."

She would love to take the man's measure now. She glanced over at Ruby and knew she was already mentally prepping the thorough security review they would be conducting on Chloe's new/old boyfriend.

Chloe grimaced. "I'm not ready for that. If I bring him to Dallas, then he gets on my dad's radar. I'd like to be engaged before that happens. If I've got a ring on my finger, I think my papa will rein Dad in."

Like Harlow herself, Chloe had two fathers. The corporate side of the club was heavily invested in the ménage lifestyle. Harlow and her sister, Greer, had a reasonable dad named Ben, a deranged dad who went by Chase or Asshole, depending on who was talking to him, and a ridiculously cool mom named Natalie. Chloe had a scary dad named Julian, a cool dad named Finn, and her supersmart mom, Dani. "You're that serious?"

Chloe shrugged. "It's time. I'm not getting any younger, and I don't want to wait until I'm forty to start a family. I'm well established at Lodge Corp. All I'm missing is a husband. Tom fits the bill."

"Chloe, this is a marriage, not a corporate merger," Ruby said and then shook her head. "Sorry. I'm just… Is he in the lifestyle? Does he know you're in the lifestyle? How does he feel about two dads walking you down the aisle, and it's not like a blended family situation?"

Oh, Julian and Finn blended. Often and intimately, but she got what Ruby was saying.

A flush crossed Chloe's delicate features, answering the question before she did. "I'm easing him in. He comes from a conservative family. They don't know about Papa yet. I mean, Tom does, but we're figuring out how to tell his parents. Anyway, that's not happening tomorrow. So Daisy's getting married. Are we taking bets on what natural disaster will strike?"

This was a mess but one that would have to wait because if she pushed too hard, Chloe would shut down.

Or point out what a hypocrite you're being. Again.

Because she was.

A vision of Niall in his leathers flashed across her brain as Ruby talked about how the betting book they kept in the bar was getting full of all sorts of apocalyptic possibilities for the O'Donnell/Carter upcoming nuptials. Given no one had guessed a helicopter filled with assassins would buzz the last wedding they'd all gone to, the bets were getting wild.

She'd thought about asking Niall if he would be her plus one to the wedding of Aidan O'Donnell and Carys Taggart. She'd wondered what he would look like in a suit. Wondered how it would feel to dance with him.

Now she was thinking about whether or not he wanted to witness the apocalypse that would surely be Daisy's wedding. If she got an invite. She had fired the bride.

But that had led to her getting a superhot bodyguard and this whole wedding thing. So when she thought about it, Daisy didn't get Nate without her. She should totally be invited to the wedding, and it would be a shock to everyone if she came with someone other than Ruby.

There it was. She could say it was all to win a bet. Maybe Niall would be into that and then, well, as long as they were there, she might as well become his sub for the night.

Then she remembered the last time she took on a Dom and how she ended up in jail. Not that he'd put her there. He'd simply left her in a situation where she had to call her reasonable dad to save her, and naturally he brought his insane twin and she now had a watchdog.

You're going to kill yourself with this job. You can't expect me to stand by and watch it happen. Can't you see how worried your mother is? This is not what we wanted for your life.

Her father had chased her down to the café where she and Ruby had been planning strategies to grow their private investigation business, and to say he put a damper on the meeting would be an understatement.

After a moment Chloe stood and gave them a smile that didn't reach her eyes. "I think I heard your sister. We're going to dinner at Top to discuss her doing a series for the new London office. You know my dad thinks having Dawson originals hanging in the place is lucky. You two have fun tonight. I'm going to pause my membership for a while. I'm spending a lot of time in New York.

Gabe and John will be thrilled since they refuse to play on nights when I'm here."

Oh, they refused to play at The Hideout when their sister was in the house, but she was pretty sure they went to Sanctum on those nights. Harlow sometimes went, especially when a new crop of Doms was released into the wild.

None of them affected her the way Niall did. Not a damn one.

"I don't have to have super investigative skills to know that is a bomb waiting to go off." Ruby kept her voice down since they weren't exactly alone.

In the distance she could hear her sister greeting Chloe. Greer Dawson was pretty much the perfect big sister. Gorgeous and friendly and loving and unbelievably talented. She inherited their mom's artistic skills and had already had two well-attended showings of her works here in Dallas and another in Austin.

Greer Dawson made her parents so proud. They didn't worry about her at all.

"Chloe doesn't explode," Harlow replied as she pulled her T-shirt over her head. "That's the problem. She stays as far as she can from big emotion. Honestly, her sniping at Seth is one of the healthiest things she does."

Ruby went quiet for a moment, and Harlow had the worst suspicion her BFF/business partner had been making the same connections she had. But then the other woman sighed. "So are you watching or participating tonight?"

She always came in ready to participate and then something would happen and she would think about Jensen's big, strong, lying hands on her body and she would offer to work a shift in the bar or help out the Doms with their scenes. Today had been a lot. They took a new case that connected to the one Daisy had started. While they had shut down the cartel that had come after Daisy, they apparently weren't the only ones using the system put in place to move drugs through the city.

"I don't know," she replied honestly.

"Is it about the Falls case? It's reminiscent of the case you were working when…" Ruby let the words trail off.

Harlow's first instinct was to ask what she was talking about. The case that led her straight into Jensen Wiley's arms and then to a jail cell had nothing to do with the case they were working for Miranda Falls's mom.

Except they were both missing persons cases where a daughter got caught up in a dangerous world.

"I suppose it brings back memories," she admitted because she needed at least one person who knew what she was thinking. Her parents knew what had happened, though she hadn't given them the name of the man who had sold her out. Jensen Wiley. After she fell in love with him and gave him everything and planned a whole life with him. "It's another young woman who is in trouble because she followed a guy into a bad situation."

"Are you talking about Miranda or yourself?" Ruby asked.

"Both, I suppose, and Sarah Gains. She was…"

"The woman you went to California to find." Ruby sat down beside her. "I know it was before you took me on, but I do my research, bestie. I've always thought it was interesting that she got out even after you ended up in jail from the raid. Two weeks later Sarah was on a plane home. You know she says a guy helped her."

A guy who she described as looking an awful lot like Jensen.

"If he did save her, it was out of guilt for giving me up. He had his own agenda," Harlow said with a sigh. "And it was years ago. I was a kid."

"It was two years ago, and you were twenty-four. Look, I don't know everything that went on with the case in LA, but I do know this new case is similar and might be too much of a reminder of what happened there. If you don't want to pursue this we can talk to Big Tag," Ruby offered. "Honestly, we should anyway. He told us if we ever need muscle, he'll give us a good deal. I actually think the big bastard meant that. Like free bodyguards if we're going somewhere dangerous. This case has the potential to get dangerous, and it's going to be you on the line since I'm glorified tech support."

Sure she was. "You're a brilliant hacker. It makes no sense to send you in. You need to be on the outside watching me. Besides, I have way more lifestyle practice than you do, and it's an underground club. I agree about talking to Big Tag." She took a deep breath because she'd also been thinking about this all day. "I'm going to need a partner."

Ruby grinned. "You mean a top. Wanna go the girl route? I've been watching Kala and I think I can totally whip your ass."

The thought made her laugh. "No. We're not going the lesbian route. I meant what I said. You're going to play tech on this one. I need a big bad Dom the other tops will open up to because they think he's one of them. I know Big Tag could assign one, but that guy will inevitably report back to my dads. It's why Big Tag is so very willing to not charge the competition. It keeps psycho dad off his case."

To say Chase Dawson had been against his daughter opening her own private detective agency would be another one of those understatements. He'd forbidden her to work outside the agency he and her other dad formed when they were way younger than she was. So she'd asked the owner of Sanctum to allow her to not only join the BDSM training class—her dad objected to that, too—but also to allow her to train with his bodyguards. Her father had been all for the training since he'd thought she would quit. Ian Taggart had offered her what she liked to call the Kill the Girl class.

It had been a rough six months, but the man knew how to ensure his people could survive.

Ruby winced. "You're probably right. And he'll freak if he knows we're following up on a case that got our admin put on a hit list. So who do we ask? If the twins are around for a while we might be able to get Cooper or that Zach guy to do it. Although he's a little scary."

"He's a CIA operative and I would say Cooper McKay could be our guy but if we get him scratched up, we have to deal with Kala and I just can't. No. I was thinking of someone else. Someone who's ex-military and owns his own business. Someone who knows the lifestyle but didn't grow up with everyone, so none of the dads can guilt him into talking." It was a terrible idea. An awful idea. The first idea she'd had that made her excited. He was the best choice. It only made sense. Her rational, professional self was going to have her emotional scaredy cat in a choke hold.

And then her horny, curious self could finally play.

Ruby's eyes widened. "Niall Griffen? The dude you have the worst crush on but you're too scared to even play with? You want to go undercover with Niall Griffen?"

It sounded…not so bad. This could work. "I don't know. He's a solid guy. He passed all the background checks, and Gabe thinks he's great. I mean we've only known him for a couple of months, but I can say the same for anyone Big Tag would assign to us, and he won't feel the need to tell my father everything. Also, Big Tag would probably assign someone who wouldn't end up trying to sleep with me, and that means a married dude, and it would be awkward."

"I agree. If you're going in, you need to look like you're really a Dom and his sub. That would be hard if the guy can't touch you in an intimate way. You would have to get super comfortable with him. Physically." Ruby nodded. "I like this plan. It feels like a backdoor route to getting what you want. You don't have to admit you like him. You need him and you're going undercover as a Dom and sub, and oops, there's probably only one bed."

Her friend read way too many romance novels. But then so did she. "Fine. Maybe I want to push myself, and I know if I don't have an excuse I won't do it." She glanced down the aisle and caught a glimpse of Chloe, who was still talking to her sister, but they had been joined by the infamous aforementioned Daisy O'Donnell, who was showing them her engagement ring.

Daisy was happy. A complete wreck, but happy.

Didn't she deserve some happiness, too?

She caught Chloe's expression before she smiled. There was a blank look like she was thinking of someone she shouldn't. Like she was wondering what it would be like to get a ring from Seth.

Or to follow her real dreams.

"I'm going to ask him. I'm going to walk right up to him and ask if he'll help us." She stood, unclasping her bra.

She didn't have to let what happened with Jensen Wiley wreck the rest of her life. She didn't.

Of course she also didn't have to go into this very practical "work" relationship with the delicious Niall Griffen wearing her heart on her sleeve either. She could use the mission to see if he was the kind of man she could trust.

"We're doing this?" Ruby asked with a smile that told Harlow she was on board.

"We're doing this." She pulled out her corset and gave her bestie a wince. "But I'm going to need you to get me into this thing."

Ruby stood. "That I can do."

Harlow took her last deep breath for a while, but she was suddenly optimistic.

It felt good.

* * * *

Jensen Wiley stared out over the dungeon floor and wondered what Harlow was doing tonight.

Was she sitting at home watching TV and eating her favorite takeout? Or was she at another club much like this one?

He wouldn't know until he got the report in the morning, and that bugged him.

It was odd to be back in Texas. He spent the last several years of his life undercover, finding the man who killed his brother. Taking down the entire organization only to find out the last man he needed to get revenge on was building a network in Dallas. Where Harlow lived.

He was so fucking close to her and he couldn't reach out and touch her, couldn't call her and hear that voice that always got his motor going.

Couldn't beg her damn forgiveness. See if there was any way she would take him back.

"Hey, Master J." Lila winked his way as she walked toward the bar.

He gave her a nod. The pretty sub who worked the bar—and did some other things for the organization—had made it clear to him that she wouldn't mind having him for more than a temporary play partner. They'd run a few teaching scenes in the months he'd been here, but he always explained he didn't sleep with his coworkers.

He didn't sleep with anyone. It was one sin he would not have on his soul when he finally made his way back to her.

He took a long breath as the music thumped through the club and the lights fluctuated along to the sexy beat.

He would get her back. He would do this one last thing for his brother and then he would show up on her doorstep when it was safe and he would do whatever it took to get her back.

Because she was the one.

The trouble was he'd found the "one" in the most dangerous place he could have imagined. The woman had two fathers and still ended up walking into a sex club looking for a missing person.

One day he would have such a talk with Ben and Chase Dawson.

Quietly. Where she couldn't hear because his baby could be fierce.

"You know she likes you, right, J?" The manager of Decadence was a forty something who looked like a suburban dad when he wasn't in leathers. Then he looked like a suburban dad in leathers. Like every kid's absolute worst nightmare of how they would find their dad someday. Phil Jackson seemed like a nice guy. He was excellent at his job. The only trouble was his job was moving drugs and money for some of the world's most dangerous people.

"I'm afraid she's not my type," Jensen replied.

Phil watched Lila's hips sway as she carried her tray of drinks away. "She's everyone's type."

She wasn't a gorgeous woman with a sunny smile and a sarcastic wit that could flay a man alive. He would bet Lila had never watched a man's back while he snuck into a drug dealer's office to gather evidence on him.

He had a very specific type.

"I also think it's a bad idea to fuck around with employees I'm supposed to manage," he pointed out.

Phil sighed and ran a hand over his balding head. "You're probably right about that. It causes a lot of drama, and we don't need that now. How is it going?"

He managed to get hired on as the dungeon monitor for this underground BDSM club because of his close ties to other groups Phil worked for. When his old job had been decimated by…well, by him, but he'd done a damn good job covering his tracks…all the higher-ups getting murdered or going to jail, he offered his services here. He had an excellently faked criminal record going back to time spent in juvie. No one knew him as Jensen Wiley. They knew a criminal named Jay Wilson from Los Angeles, California.

The trouble was the bad guys figured out he had a weak spot, so he'd been forced to prove she wasn't.

"Quiet night," he reported back. "I haven't even had to kick anyone out for going too hard."

What you have to remember is that the submissive is actually in control. She only gives the Dom what she's comfortable with. It's the Dom's job to figure out if that's all she needs or if they should push some limits. Consensually, of course.

Just the thought of her with her husky voice and absolutely no hangups when it came to sex could get him hard. He'd learned so much from her. So much about the lifestyle. So much about life and what he wanted from it.

He needed to remember why he was here. To avenge Tommy. To protect Harlow.

His revenge seemed so much less important than protecting Harlow.

Once Cliff Hamilton was dead, there would be no one left who could come after her. No one left to care that he loved her more than his own damn life.

Loved her so much he'd been willing to give her up to save her.

"Good, because you need to know something." Phil moved in, putting a hand on the wall behind Jensen. The leathers were all for show. He'd never seen Phil once play with any of the subs who came through the club even if he would give them all once overs. Decadence was a front for Hamilton's criminal operation, but it was a working club. Mostly tourists, from what he could tell. Which is why he had to break things up. Phil also didn't have the super-sane rules good clubs had.

Two drinks max when you're playing. Usually one before and one after. Or if you're my friend Seth, it's one before and then a shit ton after, but he's not playing at that point. After hours, The Hideout pretty much becomes a bar and we all sit around gossiping and Seth plays some songs and one of the twins tells some insane story no one quite believes. It's my favorite place.

He had never gotten to see her home club, hadn't gotten to meet her friends and sit in that bar with her cuddled up on his lap. Their entire time together had been adrenaline and anxiety, and yet he'd known he could find peace with that woman.

Would find peace with her one day soon.

"What's up?" Jensen asked, certain he sounded like he didn't care. He'd perfected the look, the tone, the dead-eyed stare that let people know he had no soul.

He feared he might have given up his soul in revenge for his brother, but he knew it wasn't gone. His soul was simply walking around with a woman named Harlow.

"Hamilton is coming through town next week," Phil said, leaning against the wall. "I want you to check in with the guys in the office. Make sure everything is tight, you know. They're smart kids who run that part of the business, but they don't know how the world works. At least not ours. Sometimes I'm sure those fucking kids are going to get us all killed."

The kids who wrote the code that looked to the world like a gig app. The kind where someone else picked up your orders for a fee. And it ran that way, for the most part. But if you knew the code, it was an excellent way to order drugs and get them dropped off right at your doorstep. To the cops it would look like late-night tacos or someone picking up your kid's meds from the pharmacy for you. It was the perfect cover.

Hamilton found the coders on the Dark Web, outsiders looking for a place to fit in. They probably hadn't intended to become criminals, but soon they were in far too deep to ever get out again.

Most of the employees had no idea what was going on. Like his brother hadn't. His little brother had thought he was making some extra money so he could try to pay off the student loans that seemed to never fucking get smaller no matter how much he paid. He'd been desperate, and criminals took advantage of it.

And then one day they gave him a "special" delivery.

Jensen brought his attention back front and center. He had to focus on the now and not the ghosts that haunted him. Even though he was doing it all for them. The two people in the whole world he ever loved.

Well, three. Three. There was one more, and he counted on that man for everything right now. His other brother. The one he hadn't shared a mother with. The one who had been there for everything, and now he trusted him with his greatest love.

"Yeah, I'll make sure security is tight down here," he promised.

Phil sighed, an audible sound even over the pulsating music. "I need you to take care of upstairs, too. I know it's a lot to ask but I'm in a bind, and I don't trust anyone else."

Jensen managed to not drop his jaw. He was moving upstairs? He thought he would have to wait months, maybe years for this kind of chance. "What happened to Austin?"

Phil grimaced. "He has been…reassigned."

It was everything he'd been waiting for, and he didn't even feel bad since he'd caught Austin about to rape a passed-out club girl a couple of weeks ago. He'd stopped it, but Austin had it in for him ever since. Austin was pretty much one of the top dogs here. There wasn't anywhere else to go unless he was joining Hamilton himself.

So Austin had been reassigned to a shallow grave somewhere.

Couldn't happen to a nicer guy.

"Let's just say we might have found out Austin was taking more than his fair share," Phil admitted. "It couldn't happen at a worse time. The cops are all over us since they identified the Jalisco cartel we were working with here in Dallas. Lucky for us that ditzy broad who caught them doesn't know we're the real force behind the operation, and anyone who could have talked died in the war her dad set off."

He'd been surprised at how easily the cartel had gone down. He wasn't a fool. Someone had gotten them to turn on each other. A pro. "I heard her dad used to work for an intelligence agency."

Phil shrugged. "His daughter's safe. Trust me. We aren't going after that crazy bitch. We're going to stay as far away from that whole group as we can. I think one of the things Hamilton wants to talk about is moving the operation to a bigger city. Now that we know it works here, we can start the business in Houston. In a couple of years we'll be the supplier of choice for the entire US."

It was good to know they had ambitions. He intended to make sure they never reached their goals. "So I get to meet the big boss?"

Phil put a hand on his shoulder, a paternal gesture. "I think it's time. And I'll get you moved out of here in a couple of weeks. I promise you won't be pulling double duty for long. We just need to find someone who can run this club and train him. You'll like it upstairs. I think you're smart, J. You can go places here. I'm happy you didn't get caught up in that mess that happened in LA. You never told me how you started working for the cartel. You don't seem like their type."

He noticed the couple on the main stage. They were playing out a fantasy scene. At least he hoped so or those ears that guy had were seriously deformed. Nah. He had pretend wings, too. Jensen sighed. He was never going to get used to the freaky stuff, and that seemed to come from people who read a lot.

He wondered if Harlow liked those fairies fucking books.

He remembered her talking about her aunt's books. Something about cowboys and women who liked more than one of them at a time.

Not that he would ever share, but it wasn't like he hadn't wondered if it was a fantasy of hers. Something they could play out in a club like this and then go home and be together and it would all have been nothing more than an adventure they shared because they were in love and trusted one another.

Would she ever be able to trust him again?

He needed to focus. It was being so close to her that had him on edge. "They needed someone who didn't mind getting his hands dirty but who also could put people at ease. I can be charming when I want to. They were particularly interested in hiring young women. I made them comfortable."

And managed to get at least one of them out. He wondered if Harlow knew he hadn't completely abandoned her. He finished her case when it was too dangerous for her to continue. He made sure the woman she was hired to find came out of the experience with her life.

It had been the only gift he could give her.

"Well, you're going to have to do that again." Phil gestured to the dungeon floor. "Hamilton wants us to find a couple who can make a run for us. He's got a package he wants to send to Canada. He wants a couple. Someone we can have some control over."

The thought turned his stomach. He knew what control meant. It meant they would get leverage over a couple and force them to do their will. They would get evidence of what they did here in the club and blackmail them with it. They would have to be selected carefully. They couldn't have ties to law enforcement. It was best if they didn't have many ties at all.

Just a few more days. He wouldn't actually have to do it. He would kill Hamilton before this went down, and then he would find a way to be with Harlow.

His debt to his brother would be paid, and he could start his life.

If he didn't wind up dead or in jail.

He nodded Phil's way. "Yeah, I can find someone for us. Don't worry about it. We get new couples in here all the time. I'll be a mentor and then I'll be their boss."

"That's my boy," Phil said and strode away.

It wouldn't be long and then he could see her again. He could try to put the pieces back together.

She was probably going to punch him. She would definitely punch him if she ever figured out that when he'd come to Dallas, he'd brought along his best friend so someone could watch over her while he worked.

If these people ever found out how he felt about her…

It was fine because according to the reports all she was doing was tracking down wayward husbands so the ex-wives could enforce their child support agreements. And gathering evidence for divorce cases and working with some insurance companies to prove their clients were committing fraud. She was staying away from the dangerous stuff. She was spending time with her friends and family.

She was probably going to be at The Hideout tonight, and Niall would watch over her like he had for a couple of months now. He kind of hoped his friend found someone while he was working his mission there. He knew Niall had taken to the lifestyle quickly. His friend talked about how much more in touch with himself he felt since taking that first class, how he seemed to fit in. It would be so cool if Niall fell for one of Harlow's friends. It might help his case if they could double date and hang out and…be a family.

A shout from his left caught his attention and he sighed, realizing those stupid frat boys they let in were causing trouble.

He had a job to do.

But once it was over. He was coming for her. This time he wasn't going to let her go.

Chapter Two

Niall Griffen liked The Hideout. He liked walking in and having the guys around him give him shit and handing it right back to them. He liked the camaraderie.

He was almost certain this club was some sort of CIA front, and he weirdly liked that, too.

Of course what he liked most about the place was the thing he wasn't supposed to like at all.

Maybe *like* wasn't the right word. He was certain Jensen wanted him to like Harlow Dawson. He was also certain Jensen didn't want him to think about her every second of every fucking day since he met her.

"Hey, Griffen," a voice called out. "Wait up."

He turned, still holding both his gym bag and his kit. He usually left his kit here in his locker, but he'd spent the night before ensuring all his equipment was well taken care of. He'd spent time ensuring the leather falls on his flogger were soft and glossy and ready to use in case Harlow decided she needed a session.

Luke Taggart jogged up, carrying his leathers in a garment bag over his shoulder, his knife case in his other hand, and his kit dangling from there as well. It looked like he was coming straight from his job. Which was surprising since it was Friday night and he worked at his father's restaurant as a chef and usually handled the dinner rush. On Fridays and Saturdays he tended to not show up until after midnight, but he often was in early on Thursdays. Luke was a big, muscular man with sandy hair and a smile guaranteed to knock the socks off every sub within a hundred feet.

He also had a bit of a reputation for sleeping with as many of them as he could.

Luke often played with Harlow, and though he knew damn well she wasn't one of his bed buddies, it still made jealousy rise every time he saw them together. Which wasn't a good thing since she was his best friend's girl and he was supposed to watch over her. "What's up?"

"You own the gym on Good Latimer, right?" Luke asked.

He bought the space right after moving to Dallas. He'd always intended to put down roots in a city but hadn't made the decision before Jensen showed up on his doorsteps six months before, and he reluctantly agreed to watch over the woman he loved.

And a whole new world opened for him.

"That's my gym. Why? You looking for a new place to work out?" Niall pushed open the door to the men's locker room, holding it for Lucas. He had no doubt Luke Taggart had a gym. The guy was in excellent shape.

"Yeah, kind of. I've been going to this place close to Top, and it's getting overcrowded, if you know what I mean," Luke explained.

"He means he's slept with too many women at the gym, and he needs a new hunting ground." Gabriel Lodge sat on the sofa inside the locker room. The actual lockers were in the back along with the showers and pretty much anything a guy could need to be presentable for playtime. This space was more like a lounge, complete with a TV and a fridge stocked with soda and mineral water and beer—though they drank it sparingly. If a dude was playing, he better not over imbibe or he could find himself on the street and not welcome back.

It was one of the things he loved about this club. They deeply cared about safety and consent.

"That is not…" Luke sighed. "Okay, it might be a bit of the problem, but I'm not only asking for me."

"But you are also asking for you." Gabriel Lodge was in

sweatpants and a T-shirt, a bottle of water in his hand and a bit of what looked like sawdust on his sneakers. So he'd likely been here for hours, working in the shop on the third floor. Niall thought his latest project was a complete redo of one of the play spaces. Despite the fact that the man came from a ridiculously wealthy family, he loved to work with his hands. "Tell me which one got too clingy."

Luke's blue eyes rolled. "No one got too…"

"It was Sally Eight Pack." Seth Taggart, Luke's cousin and roommate, threw the name out with a big grin on his face. "She showed up at our place three times last week. He slept with her once but made breakfast the next day. His crème brûlée French toast. I told him not to do it. I warned him that recipe is magic. Even I kind of want to hug him when I eat it."

"She's fine," Luke argued and sighed again. "But the truth is it would be better if I get a fresh start, and there's something else."

"Is it the chick who can bench press you?" Seth asked.

"Fine. It's all of them," Luke shot back with a shake of his head as Gabriel laughed. "But beyond that, we have a couple of new guys working the line who are looking for a gym that can meet their somewhat unique needs."

Oh, now he was interested. Top was known for hiring veterans and training them in the culinary and hospitality arts. And many of them were disabled. Niall was interested in physical therapy. After he left the Army, he got his four-year degree in kinesiology, with plans to work on his DPT. Some day. "I'm kind of spare right now, but I'm absolutely interested in working with vets if that's what you're talking about."

Lucas nodded. "I am. There's a physical therapist a couple of the guys have been seeing, and he recently lost his space. The building owner upped the rent on everyone. He's looking for a place where he can work. He has some of his own stuff, but he relies on gyms for the big equipment."

If all he needed was basic equipment, Niall could help. "Sure. Have him come by."

"Thanks, man," Luke said with a grin. "He's a good guy, and he can probably give you a cut of what he makes. Though he's paid through the VA, so it's not a lot."

He believed in some serious karma. "He can use the place for free. You, on the other hand…"

"Can pay a full rate," Luke agreed. "And hey, I heard all of your clients are either dudes or women who play here, so how much trouble can I get into?"

One of those clients was Harlow. When she found out his gym was two blocks from her office, both she and her partner Ruby had signed up. After that a bunch of the women from The Hideout joined. He made sure they had a safe environment to work out in. One of his personal trainers was a friend of Harlow's.

It struck him how comfortable he'd gotten here. How much he depended on these people as his community.

Would he lose them all if they found out why he was here?

It wasn't like he was with Harlow.

Guilt bubbled up. She didn't belong to him. Of course she didn't belong to Jensen either. She had never once mentioned his name, but he knew she still thought about him. It was precisely why she hadn't dated, but he couldn't figure out if it was because she was still tender over what had happened and didn't want to get hurt again or if she still loved him.

And he wasn't sure it mattered since it was so clear to him that Harlow needed more than Jensen could give her. Jensen could give her the dominance she craved. He could be strong and handle the dark shit, but he wasn't tender. She needed tenderness, too.

Lately, he'd started wondering if maybe she needed them both.

"So much trouble." Seth kept ragging on his cousin, but that was their love language.

"Like you're any better," Gabriel pointed out. "You're every bit the man whore he is. You are seriously risking your futures, young men. What woman is going to have you when they find out you have a triple-digit body count?"

Seth's hand came to his chest like he was deeply offended. "I thought we weren't supposed to use words like *whore* and *body count* because we all know it doesn't matter how many frogs you kiss. It's about settling down one day with the right one. At some point, the right one is going to stop running and everything will be fine. Now, while I'm waiting, I have more frogs to kiss. Someday my princess will come and all that." He grinned salaciously. "She will, you know. Come that is."

Gabe shot Seth his happy middle finger. "You are talking about my sister, you pervert."

"I offered you mine." Seth was completely unimpressed. "You lost out on Tash. You escaped Kala. Only Kenz is left. If we were in the olden days, I assure you my father would give you many goats if you would take her off our hands."

"Yeah, well, my dad probably has some things he would love to give to you," Gabe threatened.

"And yet, I still try," Seth replied. "At least I'm not this one. He's not waiting for his true love. His true love is a perfectly cooked branzino."

"Hey, that is a hard fish to handle," Luke shot back.

He walked to the lockers, his cousin still arguing with him.

Gabe sighed as he watched the Doms leave. "I'm afraid his princess is trying very hard to escape her fate."

"We talking about Chloe?" Niall knew he should keep on moving. He shouldn't sit down and gossip with a dude who was rapidly becoming his friend.

It felt good to have friends. For so long there was only him and Jensen, and then he hadn't even had Jensen. It felt right to be in this place, to help out the people around him. To be a good friend and a good Dom.

Gabe nodded. "Yeah, my sister is…I don't even know. She's in denial and trying so hard to please our parents, who don't need to be pleased. I think she's afraid. And she's not the only one. I can't fix anything with my sister. I honestly don't even know if it could work between Seth and Chloe. Seth is a goofball, and I think she needs something else, but I might be able to help *you* out."

"I need help?"

A brow cocked over Gabe's dark eyes. "You think no one notices how you look at Harlow?"

Fuck. He slumped down on the sofa across from Gabe. He was deeply aware that Gabe was on the board. He made membership decisions. Had he found out why Niall joined? Was he about to get kicked out?

Although he had said he wanted to help him. "She's…special."

"She is," Gabe replied with no small amount of sympathy. "She's a cousin to me. Oh, we don't have blood between us, but she's my family. I think you'll find our parents all kind of bonded together. They were the misfits, the left behinds. My dad had all the money in the world but no one in his family cared about him growing up. When he was older he found out his friends could become his family."

"Yeah, I get that."

"I know. I read the background report on you," Gabe replied, but there was no gotcha in his tone.

He knew what they would find. "I got kicked out when I was in my teens. I lived with a friend, but that couldn't last forever. There wasn't a lot in the small town I grew up in."

"You went into the Army to get away?" Gabe asked.

"I went into the Army because I didn't have anywhere else to go," he admitted.

"Yeah, I figured. You did good work there. You got out, got your degree. You take care of the people around you. And that is why I'm going to ask you to be patient with her because she's curious about you in a way I haven't seen from her since we were in high school," Gabe said. "Look, Harlow has a lot to deal with. You know about her family?"

He nodded. "It's like yours. She's got two dads and a mom and everyone is happy."

Gabe's lips curled up. "I'm glad to hear you say that. It's not what I tend to hear. You would be surprised how many people I'm interested in get scared off when I talk about my family."

"There's nothing wrong with your family. And nothing wrong with hers."

"Well, you haven't met my Uncle Chase," Gabe said with a whistle. "He is…incredibly interesting."

"I think she calls him her deranged dad." He listened. It probably made him a pervert, but he sat in the bar and sipped his beer and listened to Harlow talk to her friends, hoping for any tidbits of information she would give them. "From the stories I've heard Chase is the smart but overprotective one and Ben is what she calls her reasonable dad."

"You are not wrong," Gabe agreed. "Chase is one of those people with such a high IQ he sometimes finds it hard to fit in with the regular folk."

Niall nodded. "I've known a couple of people like that. I also know no matter how much she complains, she loves him."

"She does, and I actually think he's going to approve of you."

He wasn't sure Gabe was being realistic. "Uh, she would have to agree to spend time with me before he could approve of me."

Gabe took a deep breath and studied him for a moment as though trying to figure out his next move. "You're not the only one who listens in on a bit of gossip."

"I thought not gossiping was one of the rules of the club." Was it gossip if one simply listened?

Gabe snorted, an oddly regal sound. "Sure. All clubs run on gossip. The rule is there so we can spank pretty subs who get caught. You know there are two sides to this club."

This was a clear truth he'd learned quickly. "Yes, the ones associated with McKay-Taggart and the ones with Lodge Corp, though you all seem to be friends."

"We kind of grew up together, though my side of the family is more spread out than Seth and Luke's," Gabe explained. "Anyway, the other side is known for being involved in the security business, and we all know there's security in information. I've found subs love to gossip, and they also love to please their Masters by bringing them important news."

"You mean you have them spying on each other."

"That's such a loaded word. I rather think of it as keeping informed. I know we have a board, but for the most part our board members are mostly off on assignment for 'McKay-Taggart.'" Gabe put air quotes around McKay-Taggart. "So it's up to me to watch out for any problems that might arise. Do you understand?"

"Yes." Niall nodded his agreement. "You are a control freak."

"Says the man who also wears leathers and tops subs nightly," Gabe said with a chuckle.

He wasn't wrong. "You like to make sure everything is running smoothly and that your family is safe and happy."

"It's probably a bit of both. I think Harlow is going to ask you for a favor tonight."

That was news to him. "You got this from your gossip network?"

"Let's say the walls of the women's locker room bounce sound around a bit," Gabe admitted. "If you're in the shower area, you can probably hear anything going on around the lockers. Harlow and Ruby have taken on a case, and they need someone to go undercover with them."

He tried not to let his surprise show. "I thought they used McKay-Taggart when they needed bodyguards."

He knew way too much about Harlow's business and her practices. At first he'd researched them to be able to put Jensen's mind at rest. Then he simply wanted to know everything about her. He wanted to put his own mind at rest.

Gabe sighed. "Uncle Chase has been on edge since their brand-new receptionist managed to make herself a material witness in a drug trafficking ring trial. To say it went poorly is understating the word poorly. Chase lost his cool, but then something happened to Harlow a few years back."

Niall was so curious about who knew the truth about what happened that day. He only knew what Jensen told him. "Do you know anything about it? All I've heard is a case went bad, and she ended up in jail."

"She doesn't talk about it," Gabe replied. "At least not to anyone who will tell the tale. I suspect there was a man involved, and he hurt her. Not physically. She would have defended herself and told everyone what a fucker he was. I think he broke her heart. She would keep that private. She would think that was at least partly her fault."

It made his gut tighten. "If some asshole hurt her, it wasn't her fault."

The closer he got to really knowing her, the more he thought Jensen might be said asshole. But his best friend had his own issues. It was hard for Jensen to trust anyone. It was definitely hard for him to trust that anything in his world would work out for the best.

"I agree, and I genuinely think she's starting to get over it," Gabe said. "I think watching our friends finally find the right woman for them has her thinking."

"You're talking about the cowboys?" Josh Barnes-Fleetwood and his best friend Grim didn't play often at The Hideout. They were closer to Austin than Dallas, but he knew Harlow had recently attended their engagement party.

"Yes. Josh and Grim and Nicole. You know she almost asked you to be her plus one." Gabe sat back.

It was a night for news. "She did?"

Gabe gave him a nod. "Yeah, and then you mentioned you were going out of town that weekend."

"I would have changed my plans." He had met Jensen in Fort Worth to give him some research he'd found. And to check on him. To make sure he wasn't too far gone.

They'd talked about Harlow when they weren't discussing the case. Jensen wanted every story, every detail about her life without him.

"I might have mentioned that you should have the choice, but she needed more time," Gabe replied. "So are you going to say yes?"

He shouldn't. They were in a perfect position right now. He could watch over her. Club gossip would reveal anything serious. He didn't have to put himself in temptation's way. Going undercover with her… It was a bad idea.

Or maybe it was time to think about what the world looked like on the other side of Jensen's revenge.

He only saw two possibilities. One—he does what he meant to do and kills Hamilton and gets away with it and tries to get Harlow back. Two—Hamilton kills him.

There was a third. Jensen kills Hamilton and doesn't get away with it. He goes to jail.

Two out of three of those possibilities left Harlow alone. And the other he wasn't sure would work. Jensen loved her but he wasn't good at groveling, and that is what she would need. She wouldn't melt for him and forgive what he'd done.

Since they met in the second grade, Niall had softened Jensen. He calmed his friend and smoothed things over. Jensen made sure anyone who fucked with them never did it twice. It had been an excellent partnership.

But partnerships changed. "I'm going to say yes, but I worry she'll want a family like her own."

A brow rose over Gabe's eyes. "You hiding a brother?"

"I might have a friend I'm close to." It was the first time he'd even come close to saying the words out loud. To tiptoeing around them out loud. What he wanted.

At first he'd thought he was completely fucked because he'd fallen hard for his best friend's girl. Then he'd called himself an asshole since she was her own person and Jensen had been an asshole to her, so she didn't belong to him. He'd spent a couple of weeks mentally justifying running away with the woman his best friend was hopelessly in love with because only one of them could have her.

Then he watched a threesome work their magic on the dungeon floor one night. Two men. One woman. Best friends and the woman they loved all of their lives. They were married now and happy. Just recently some of Harlow's friends had come into town. Again, two best friends and the woman they shared. Half the damn members had two dads and a mom.

He wanted that life.

"Is he in the lifestyle? Because I'm afraid Harlow will require that kind of relationship. A soft one, of course. She's extremely independent. She needs…" Gabe began.

He knew exactly what she needed. "A soft top to gently steer her into self-care and relaxation because she overthinks everything. She's excellent at what she does but she can get lost in it. She needs someone to make sure she takes care of herself. And she needs a harder top to put his foot down when she goes too far, and she will. She'll put herself in dangerous situations. She needs a harder top for sex because it's hard for her to give herself permission to enjoy it. It has nothing to do with how she was raised or some trauma in her background. It's simply how she's wired, and a Dominant partner can give her that."

Gabe looked at him like he was pleased at the words. "And which role would you fill?"

"Oh, we both know I'm the soft top. It's why all the subs who need a cuddle come my way. I can spank an ass and I enjoy it, but I hold back on the truly hard stuff and I'll probably give in when I shouldn't."

"You are far more self-aware than I thought you would be. Excellent. You've given this thought because you're interested."

"Very interested. Gabe, I've been biding my time. She's the only sub I'm truly interested in, but I worry her trust issues are going to be hard to deal with."

Gabe stood and stretched, seemingly more comfortable than he was before. "You'll figure it out, and hopefully this friend of yours can see how amazing our Harlow is. Is there a reason you haven't brought him by?"

"He doesn't live in town." A lie but a necessary one. "But he's thinking about moving here. He doesn't have a lot of family. I'm pretty much it now. And yes, he's in the lifestyle. He's the one who introduced me. He's a good Dom."

"I'll need to see that for myself." Gabriel Lodge had pitch black hair he kept longish. He tied it in a queue when he was working, but now it brushed the tops of his broad shoulders. He was a leopard who led his pack with ruthless precision. There was no question he was the head of his half of The Hideout. "Until he's ready, are you going to take care of her? I think her new case is a missing persons, so she's going undercover to ask some questions. You're ex-military."

It wasn't a question. Gabe would know every answer. Well, not every one. "Yes, I was an MP for most of the ten years I was in."

"But you didn't go into law enforcement?"

"I want to help people. People who want to be helped," he clarified. "I didn't find peace in what I did. I do managing my gym. For a few years I saw the worst of what people can do, how they behave. In the gym I see people trying. Sure, some of them are narcissistic douchebags who only care about their abs and getting the right shot for their Insta. But some of them are fighting to get their health back. To take back their mobility. I don't run one of those shiny gyms where everyone looks perfect. I kind of seek out the ones who don't feel comfortable in those kinds of gyms. That's my purpose, but don't think I've forgotten how to protect someone. I'll take care of her."

Gabe nodded and held out a hand. "Good. I think I might like to check out your gym. I'm always looking for a new investment. I was blessed with a ridiculous trust fund. I view it the same way you do that gym. Sometimes the best investment you can make financially is to give money to people who will put it to the best use."

Niall shook it. He wouldn't mind taking Rich Boy's money, especially since some of the vets he served could use specialized equipment. "I won't turn you down."

Gabe held his hand. "And I'd like to meet your friend soon."

That could be a different story altogether. One he would have to step around but then he'd known this was a dangerous game he was playing. "I'll see when he can come up."

As Gabe walked off, seemingly happy with the outcome, Niall had to wonder if this was how it fell apart.

Or if this was a real chance at putting it all together.

Harlow needed him. He could show her how good they could be together and maybe figure out how to soften her heart toward Jensen.

Or Jensen would kill him.

Or Gabe would kill him.

Or honestly, Harlow would kill them both.

Any way it went, at least he would know.

* * * *

She wanted to know. That was what it came down to. Her curiosity about Niall Griffen was bigger than her fear that he would turn out to be another version of Jensen Wiley.

She needed to know if they could have any shot because she was so deeply attracted to him.

"Do you want me to go in with you?" Ruby stood beside her, waving as Brianna Dean-Miles walked by. "I know we don't normally take business meetings in corsets and heels but hey, we're going with the flow."

If she brought Ruby with her to talk to the gloriously sexy man standing near the main stage wearing leathers that showed off his every muscle, she could pretend this was all business.

Or she could be brave.

"What if this is one of those situations where the reality is way less than what I have in my head?" This scenario had been playing through her brain ever since she made the decision.

Ruby frowned her way, arms crossing under her breasts, which were impressively being shown off in her sapphire blue corset. "Are you changing your mind? Because you told Miranda Falls's mom we would have an initial report by next weekend. As far as I can tell that club is only open Thursday through Saturday. You have to figure out if our girl is even going there, much less which night she plays."

Which meant they should go in tomorrow and Saturday. "I'm not changing my mind. I'm worried it's not going to be as good as I hoped. What if I get performance anxiety? What if I'm thinking so much about the case, I can't properly respond to him as a top?"

"No." Ruby's head shook. "You don't get to shrink back and not say what you are actually scared of. That shit might work with your sister, but it's not flying with me. Say the problem out loud."

Sometimes she wondered why she loved this woman. She wanted to growl. But Ruby was right. "Fine. What if I kiss him and I feel nothing and I've gone through all of this for a big old nothing burger? Also, what if he says hey sure, Harlow, I'll watch your back and then I find out he has a girlfriend or he doesn't like me that way and then all my manipulation will have been for nothing. I think I should tell him I'm planning on manipulating him into seeing if a relationship can work, and then he can make the choice."

"We're going to talk about the word manipulation and how it's supposed to work, but we can do that later. For now, this actually sounds fairly healthy, and I like that for you. It's a good look." Ruby gestured to Harlow's clothes. "This is a good look, too. Okay, you go and plant your freak flag and see if he responds to it and I'll talk to the Taggarts about a backup plan."

Harlow stared across the dungeon at that hot hunk of man. One of the newer subs was approaching. Lisa, Lana, something L. She was probably twenty years old and looked all shiny and new.

Harlow was twenty-six and definitely didn't feel shiny. She had a big-ass scar on her right thigh and another on her left shoulder. L-whatever had perfectly smooth skin because she'd never taken a bullet or gotten twelve kinds of cut up trying to escape from a house where she just rescued a kidnapped kid.

The younger woman smiled up at Niall. She was in all white, obviously playing up the "I'm such an innocent sub I would never suck your cock like I have something to prove. I'm so innocent no one ever tied me up and slapped my ass until I cried out and begged you to fuck me."

"Are you serious right now?" Ruby asked. "She is an infant. I'm surprised they let her in the club. I think she's still in college. You're going to let that sorority sister take your man?"

"Not my man." But the words did scratch along her spine, making it straight.

"You finally going after Niall?" Her cousin stood on the other side of her. Gigi Dawson was stunning though modest in her skin-tight leggings and a bodice-style shirt that clung to all of her curves. She was a few years younger than Harlow, but they'd always been close. Like her mom, Gigi studied to be a nurse and had recently started working in a downtown hospital in an emergency department. "You should know Leah looks sweet, but she's got some teeth on her. I should know. She works with me. Can't stand her, but the guys all love her. One of the Doms was in for a broken finger and he started flirting and invited her to training class. I hate her."

"I hate her, too," Harlow proclaimed. Because if Gigi, who was literally the sweetest woman in the world, hated someone, she was probably evil. Yeah, she looked like she would kick a puppy to get to a pair of designer shoes.

Leah laughed, the sound cackling Harlow's mind, and put a hand on Niall's chest.

"Too bad he's a softie," Gigi said with a sigh. "If she tried that shit with Gabe, she would get the staring of a lifetime. I swear that man can freeze water."

"Yeah, he comes by it honestly. His dad is scary. All the Lodge-Taylor kiddos learned how to stare at a young age. I think they took a kindergarten class," Ruby quipped. "And yes, Harlow is thinking of going in, but now she's doing that thing where she totally lets the past keep her from even coming close to getting laid."

Niall frowned and took a step back.

Leah looked horrified.

"No, I'm not." She was going to go and see if she got a better result. That was what she was going to do. Because he had never once looked at her like that. Like she was slightly distasteful.

"Oh, the huggy Dom is pissed," Gigi said with a grin. "I like it. Actually, he's way hotter now."

Harlow turned on her cousin.

Gigi backed off with an apologetic grin. "I see you also went to Julian Lodge's school for terrifying stares. Sorry, cos. He's all yours.

Honestly, I'm happy to see it. You go get that man."

Harlow sighed. She should have been more private about this, but she wasn't backing down. Shit. She was starting to come out of it. She was starting to heal because she was thinking more about the future in this moment than she was fearing the past. "Damn it. I think I'm ready."

Ruby stood in front of her. "You are, babes. So it's up to you if you want to hedge your bets. You can make him an offer he's not going to refuse, or you can separate the relationship from work."

"I kind of want both." She wanted to see what he was like in the field. It would tell her a lot.

"Then go for it, bestie," Ruby said. "I'll take Gigi, and we'll go watch her friend for a bit. See if we can get her kicked out of the club."

"I don't…" Gigi shrugged. "I really do hate her. She calls me fat. Not in those words, but she always talks about how I must be an incredible cook. I am, but that's not what she means. She also says I'm brave for wearing the clothes I do."

"Oh, we can fix this," Ruby promised as she led her cousin away. "This sounds so much better than playing tonight. It's been a long time since I took a mean girl down. Tell me something. Is she real clingy? Because we might be able to use Seth."

Harlow took a deep breath. It was time. She was ready.

Ready to put Jensen Wiley behind her. Ready to forgive herself for making mistakes. Ready to see if this gorgeous, funny, kind man was someone she might be able to care about.

Hell, she already cared about him.

Be brave. Say what you mean. Use the word.

Ready to see if she could love him.

Fuck. She was going to do this.

Harlow strode across the dungeon, ready to start again.

Chapter Three

Jensen glanced down at his phone and realized two hours had gone by. He'd broken up two fights, kicked out a dude who had too much, and called an Uber for a woman who had a trauma response to watching a scene. He'd tried to talk to her but she didn't want to be near him.

They needed female tops. That woman might have talked to a Domme, but this place wasn't a real club. It was a front for a criminal organization, and management didn't care about the mental health of its clients. Phil had told him they were a more traditional establishment with what he called stricter gender roles, i.e. men dominated women and not the other way around.

He took a long breath of cool night air, needing to be outside for a moment. And then kind of wished he hadn't since this part of the city wasn't the nicest and this was where everyone came to take their smoke breaks. It was right behind the back room of the club, and it was also where the trash bin was.

A good metaphor for his life.

"Hey, was that lady okay?"

Jensen glanced over and noticed one of the new guys standing in the doorway. Jack Cameron had been hired on as a bartender the week before and seemed to be a good kid. Kid? Hell, Jensen was only a couple of years older than Jack was, but he felt like there were decades between them. According to his "application," Jack Cameron was twenty-two and fresh out of college with a mountain of debt and no job to show for it. He had some bartending experience, so he was falling back on it.

It was the story of so many young people these days. It made them vulnerable to people like Hamilton who told them he could solve their problems, who offered them a different way out. One that led to a shallow grave or jail time.

Jack showed up for work every night for the last three weeks and in a few more, he would be asked to run an errand. That errand would be highly criminal and they would have evidence, and then Jack Cameron would have far worse bills to pay than his student loans.

"She's on her way home. Her sister is waiting for her there. I managed to get her to call home to make sure she wouldn't be alone and that someone is looking for her. The asshole she came with didn't care. He was too busy hitting on some other woman." Jensen looked to the younger man. He was a handsome kid and earnest as hell. This was exactly the vulnerable young people Hamilton liked to screw over. If there was any way to get him out before this went down, he would. "The fire play scene freaked her out."

"Yeah, I can see how. That's an advanced scene," Jack said with a frown, letting the door close behind him. He didn't do what most of the staff did. He didn't reach for a pack of smokes or a vape. He had a bottle of water in his hand. "Given how this is a tourist place I'm surprised it's okay to run a scene like that." He seemed to remember something—likely that the whole place had ears—and held his hands up. "But I'm just a bartender. What would I know?"

Jensen tilted his head, taking in the young man. He had dark hair and green eyes and the kind of lean, muscular body that would ensure he didn't lack for any kind of romantic attention he might want. Likely from women, but there was something about the young man that made him think he might be a bit more sexually fluid than that. Which never bothered him. He'd been hit on by guys before and merely took it as a compliment, explained his own sexuality and thanked them for their interest. Harlow told him watching him handle getting hit on by a dude made her interested in him. "You sound like you know a lot. *Tourist* and *play* and even the word *scene* mean something in a place like this."

It would if this club was legit, but he didn't talk about that to the uninitiated.

"Oh, yeah. I did some research when I first hired on," Jack admitted. "I heard of it, of course. We talked a lot about it when I was in school. I'm interested in the psychology of the lifestyle. I was thinking about maybe making a study of it for my graduate work. I mean when I can get back to school, of course. I have to pay off the first degree, which is surprisingly hard. You know you can't do much with an undergraduate psych degree. Apparently you can bartend."

Jensen hadn't even thought about going to college. He'd gone into the military and scrimped and saved to try to make things easier for Tommy. Tommy was the smart one. Tommy was the one who had a future.

Sometimes he wished it had been him instead of Tommy and that Tommy had met a girl like Harlow and they named their first kid after his fuck-up brother Jensen who loved him the best he could.

What the hell was he going to do after he took care of Hamilton? It was a question he never would have asked before he met Harlow. Now he had to ask what he actually had to offer her if he ever managed to get her back.

"You okay?" Jack asked, studying him.

He had to get his damn head in the game. Again, he blamed being close to her. Seeing pictures of her because he was a weirdo freak stalker. She was starting to look happy again, the smiles reaching her eyes.

It had taken every fucking thing he had to not go to her when he found out she'd been shot while protecting a friend. Niall had to give him secondhand information since he'd only recently joined the club and wasn't in her inner circle. They seemed to be friendlier now, but he would bet they would never be close.

"I'm good, just tired." He didn't even talk to Niall about how hard it was to be close to her. As far as Niall knew he was watching over Harlow because Jensen felt guilty. He hadn't told Niall how much he hoped he would have another shot with her, that all of this was about getting back to her. He had specifically told Niall he didn't want to hear about all the Doms she was playing with.

She deserved to have fun, deserved to have someone in her life who took care of her, and right now that couldn't be him.

Niall would mention it if she was getting serious with someone. Right? Surely it would come up in conversation.

"You seem different than the other guys who work here," Jack said, leaning against the brick wall.

That was good for his soul. Not so great for his cover. Still, he wasn't about to freak out because that might cause more questions. So he posed one of his own. "How so?"

Jack's green eyes stared his way as though he was trying to figure out how much to say. There were times when the young man seemed a little older, a bit smarter than he pretended to be, but that might help him in the long run. "You care more than the others. The other monitors would have booted her without any help. They would have been upset she was causing a scene and have her hauled out. They wouldn't have made sure the dude who drank too much had a buddy who could get him home."

"That was a good call, by the way." Jack had been the one to cut the guy off. It hadn't gone well. "I think he was about to pass out, but not before he did some damage. You were right to refuse to serve him."

"I'm not supposed to, you know." Jack sighed. "I already got a lecture about how as long as the card is processing, I should keep pouring."

"I'll talk to them," Jensen promised, though he knew it wouldn't do any good. He might be able to sway management if he could convince them they would get more attention than they wanted if something bad happened. A lawsuit would get eyes on the club, and that was the last thing they wanted.

"And that is why I say you're different," Jack pointed out. "It's weird. No one else here seems to care what happens on the dungeon floor. I have to wonder if other clubs are like this. If you tell anyone I said this I'll call you a liar, but when I did a bunch of research, I have to admit the philosophy behind this lifestyle kind of called to me."

Jensen shook his head. He felt for the kid since he was in the same position. The philosophy—communication, asking for what a participant wanted, taking sexuality seriously—called to him, too. But he wouldn't find that here. "This isn't a real club. You were right when you called it a tourist place. You need to think of this as a nightclub with a sex theme. There's no real philosophy here."

"But a nightclub doesn't have…" Jack stopped and sighed. "I was about to say women don't get smacked up at a nightclub, but we both know that's not true. I wouldn't use that word if it was a real club since consent would be at the heart of every interaction, but they let drunk people play."

At The Hideout you can do one or the other. Drink hard or play hard. Trust me. There are times when you need to get wasted and hang with your friends, but that's why we put the bar on the second level and toward the back. To delineate the space. And there's always someone ready to set you on your ass if you get out of line. That's what family does.

He wanted to be part of that family. Harlow's carefully culled club family sounded perfect to a man who lost everyone except one friend. He wanted to sit in that bar and take care of her if she needed to shut her brain off for a little while, help his friends out because they counted on him.

"A real club restricts alcohol or any substance that makes consent questionable. If you're interested in the lifestyle, there are a couple of places you could check out," Jensen offered. It fucking felt good to be helpful. So often lately all he felt was how he was dragging other people into his hell.

"Really? There are actual clubs here?" Jack asked, his brow rising.

He looked so young and earnest. He reminded him of his brother, so clearly he couldn't help himself. "Yes. They're quiet though. They don't have a website or social media, but they're there. You should check out a place called The Hideout."

Jack went still as though listening carefully. "The Hideout. I like the sound of that. Makes me think of a bunch of childhood friends starting a club. Damn. That makes me miss my hometown."

"Where are you from?" He wasn't sure why, but he was interested. Or maybe he did know. Maybe he needed to form some kind of connection. Any kind.

"A small town outside of Austin," Jack explained. "I grew up on a ranch, and let me tell you, when you're from a ranching family, you get close to your siblings and your friends. You end up needing them to help out. A lot. My parents had blood family, but their friends were family, too. I learned a lot from them."

"My grandfather had a ranch," Jensen admitted, remembering the home where he and Tommy grew up. "Mom ended up selling most of the land, but I still have about a hundred acres west of Fort Worth."

He had no idea what to do with it. The house was well built, and he'd maintained it. He guessed he always thought he would go back to it someday. Or it was just one more thing that got shoved aside and forgotten in his need for revenge.

"Ours is slightly bigger, but I was not meant for ranching life. I wanted to go to college and not to learn how to run a ranch." Jack smiled like the memories were sweet. "Luckily my parents were okay with it, though I had to obviously figure out a way to pay for it. I have a couple of brothers who will happily take over once the…when the time comes. So The Hideout. Sounds like a place to be. If you could go there, why don't you? You seem like a nice guy and not like Phil. I know he seems real nice on the outside, but he's pretty brutal when it comes to the servers."

"He is? I've never seen Phil be anything but pleasant."

"Because you're on a different level," Jack explained. "And you're a guy. He's nice to me, too, but then I catch him threatening the female servers in the back room where no one can hear him."

Damn it. He was not supposed to have to deal with the other employees. He had one job, and he was so close. He couldn't get involved with this. When he took down Hamilton and his whole organization, those women would be safe. "I'll check it out."

Who the hell was he? That was the question he'd been asking since the day he left Harlow in a prison cell, blowing up her case so his could keep going and she would be safe. Back then he'd told himself it was all about her safety, but did he have the right to make that choice for her?

"I appreciate it." Jack glanced down at his watch. "I should get back to it."

"Hey," Jensen called out as the bartender opened the door to the club. "You know there are other jobs out there. You're a smart kid. You can definitely do better than this place."

Jack's lips quirked up. "Trust me. I tell myself that every day. I've got about a million applications out there, but until one of them hits, this pays the bills. Hey, I have a question. How did you hear about that Hideaway place?"

"The Hideout," Jensen corrected. The good news was he didn't have to lie to a bartender who wasn't anywhere close to the inner circle. "I know someone who goes there. Well, I knew her. She's something of an ex."

"That sounds complicated."

"It is," Jensen allowed. "It was one of those right person/wrong place/wrong time things, but she taught me about the lifestyle. She grew up in it."

"Grew up in it? I kind of thought it was all about sex, so that seems worrying. I don't like the thought of kids being around that." There was a wealth of judgment in Jack's tone.

Was this the shit Harlow and her family had to put up with? It rankled. "It's not. There doesn't have to be sex involved at all. Her parents were in a D/s relationship and spent time in clubs. Obviously, they didn't bring their daughters. They were kind of odd since her mom was…is married to twins."

Jack whistled. "Now that sounds freaky."

Maybe he wasn't as open minded as he seemed. "Forget I mentioned that place. If you think it's freaky, then you should stay away."

"You don't think two men and one woman sounds odd?" Jack asked, his eyes narrowing as though the younger man was studying him. "I've always heard it the other way myself. Most men I know would prefer two women taking care of them."

"I never thought about it for me, but if it works for someone else, who cares? We spend way too much time worrying about what other people are doing. How the hell can anyone be happy if they're constantly policing everyone else's joy?" The discussion was definitely riling him up. He needed to shut it down. This was precisely why he didn't talk to anyone here. He did his fucking job and that was to move up through the ranks until he could get close to Hamilton. There was no place for friendship here. "Like I said forget I mentioned it. It's a real tight-knit group. They're probably not taking applications."

"Hey, I didn't mean to offend. I was trying to understand," Jack said, holding the door open.

The sounds of the club pulsed through the door. It was time to get back to work. Later on he could text Niall via the burner he kept hidden and for five seconds feel close to the only two people in the world he cared about. He needed to remind himself of that fact. Harlow and Niall were the only people who mattered. "No offense taken. Trust me. My family was perfectly normal. One man. One woman. When that one man took off with someone else, the one woman was left to raise two kids and found the real love of her life. Vodka. But hey, at least they were normal. You have a good night."

"Jensen," Jack called out.

But he walked on. He had a job to do.

* * * *

"I don't appreciate the way you're talking, Leah. Brianna is a perfectly nice young lady, and I enjoy playing with her very much." Niall rarely had to use a hard tone when he wasn't in the middle of a scene. But then he didn't usually have subs being so intensely rude about other subs.

Leah's sweet expression went distinctly sour. "You can't think she's hot. She's ten kinds of chunky."

He glanced over where the young woman they were talking about stood with her friends. "She's gorgeous."

Leah's eyes rolled and not in a sweetly bratty way. In a "I don't want to be around her" bratty way. "You all say that about every sub. Come on. You gotta be authentic. We connected the other day. You can be real with me."

His crop had connected to her ass. It wasn't like they talked a lot. He gave her the aftercare she required, and it did not include any sex at all. He hadn't even taken her to a privacy room because the last thing he wanted was for Harlow to hear he was hanging out with subs in privacy rooms. "I am being real with you. She's lovely, and I enjoy her company. She's smart and funny, and if I wasn't interested in someone else, I might pursue her."

Honesty. He'd made the decision to be open and honest. It's what the whole damn lifestyle was about. Being open about what he wanted. He wanted Harlow. He was being honest about that.

It was just the whole why he was here and who he knew he

wasn't being entirely honest about.

"I do not get this place," she said under her breath. She stepped back and then she sighed, and when she looked at him again there was a pout on her face. "Niall, come on. I was hoping we could play tonight. We had a good time last weekend."

"Whoever you are, he's not like most of the other Doms. He's an actual working dude. He owns a gym, and not the fancy kind," a husky voice said. Harlow. She stood there with her fists on her hips and those glorious green eyes narrowed. Now she did sound like a sexy brat. "His monthly fees are like forty bucks, and he lives in a studio apartment. If you're looking for a trust fund, Gabe is in the back. You are barking up the wrong tree with this one. He drinks protein shakes he buys at Costco."

They were pretty good.

"And he doesn't even have a freaking Costco membership. He goes with whoever's on a run that week and pays them back. With cash." She said the last like it was a bad thing.

Leah looked like she'd heard the most horrifying gossip she could have heard. "Eww. He doesn't even have an app?"

"Like his phone is smart," Harlow finished.

Leah ran as fast as she could.

Such a brat. The kind he wanted to spank and then fuck and then cuddle up with. "Just to clear a few things up, I do have a smart phone. I like to keep my gym fees low. My studio is above the gym. It was part of the lease."

"Is it crappy, Niall?"

He shrugged. "Pretty much. And the Costco thing, they let me throw in the protein shakes because I help carry everything. I like cash. What's wrong with cash?"

Her lips curled up. "Nothing. Did I interrupt an interaction you were enjoying, Sir?"

Oh, he liked it when she called him Sir. He fucking loved it when she looked at him with that challenging gaze. "No, I was not. She was being quite rude. I don't think I want to service her anymore."

"That's an interesting word. I would think you would use the word play."

This was definitely something he'd learned over the last couple of months. He was surprised how often the tops sat around and talked about what went on here on the dungeon floor. He would have expected them to brag about the sex or complain, but what they did was discuss the subs and their needs and how to provide for them. He was rapidly discovering being around people who genuinely cared about each other and were open about themselves made him want to be more open, too. He was kind of over the masculine bullshit that said he shouldn't talk about his feelings—shouldn't have feelings at all. "Play is something we mutually enjoy. I have never enjoyed my sessions with Leah. I don't believe she's here for the right reasons."

"She's looking for a rich boyfriend," Harlow surmised. "There are always a few. They're usually allowed in by dumbass men who can't see through the mask. I'm glad you did."

"Oh, her mask is not firmly in place," Niall replied. "But we should talk about shaming other people for not having a trust fund, daughter of billionaires."

She managed a pretty flush, and her eyes turned slightly down. "I wasn't shaming you. I like your gym. You've got some trainers there who actually know how to work with women."

He made sure of it. "So the reason you never play with me isn't because you find my blue-collar status distasteful?"

Her eyes came up, flashing a little fire. "Of course not. I didn't say those things because I believe them. I said them so you would see who Leah is, though now I get that you already knew. How was I supposed to know you're the smart one? I certainly don't care how much money you make as long as you're working hard and trying to be a good person. Which you do."

He knew this was wrong, but he couldn't help himself. Their chemistry… He never felt anything like it. Never wanted any woman the way he wanted Harlow. Maybe he could ignore it if he thought for one second she didn't feel it, too. He could absolutely ignore it, could sacrifice for Jensen if he thought she didn't need him. But she did. The truth of the matter was they both needed him. "So why don't you play with me, Harlow?"

Those gorgeous eyes stared at him, sexy bottom lip disappearing behind her teeth. "You know why."

He reached out and touched her, running his fingers over her jawline and then brushing the pad of his thumb over her lips. “Because you’re afraid of me.”

Her eyes rolled, and he was reminded how much he wanted to slap her ass a couple of times and get her to cry for him. “I’m not scared of you.”

Little liar. She was absolutely afraid of what was between them. “You are, but you have a question for me. You’re going to be brave today, and I might finally get what I want.”

“What do you want, Niall?” The question came out a bit breathless.

He gave her a smile. “A chance to show you exactly how good I can be for you, Harlow Dawson.”

The way she was looking at him damn near sent him to his knees. And then it changed, that gorgeous face frowning. “Wait. How did you know I was going to ask you a question?”

He had an answer prepared because he decided to chuck Gabe under the bus the minute he told on Harlow. Oh, he knew the guy was trying to watch over his kingdom and shit and he liked him. The ladies deserved their privacy, however, no matter what King Gabe thought was true. Niall wasn’t lying to her about anything he didn’t absolutely have to. “Gabe has a whole spy network going. He told me when I came in this evening.”

Her jaw dropped. “That asshole. I thought it was the spy kids. I should have known they didn’t care about anything but the betting book and national secrets. When did you get here?”

“Around nine-thirty.” He saw her car in the lot when he parked. He always checked on her. If she asked her question tonight, it would be far easier to do it since he could stop by her work and bring her coffee or stop by her place to see if she needed anything.

Or wake up in her bed.

She huffed. “I only made this damn decision around nine and fucking Gabe Lodge already knows about it and goes straight to you? Unbelievable. I’m going to kick his ass. I think we’re going to have a fight club tonight.”

Oh, that wasn’t happening. He wasn’t worried about her taking care of herself. She was solid, but he didn’t want to waste time. He reached for her arm, pulling her back. “Slow down, my Valkyrie.”

A brow rose over her eyes. “Valkyrie?”

"I have a thing for warrior women," he admitted. He thought of her as one of the Viking warrior women because her fierce nature was always evident. She didn't simper and pretend to be less strong than she was so she could get some man to do something for her. Not his Harlow.

God, he hoped she was his Harlow.

She frowned. "Well, you're in the right place, but I would think you would want a Taggart."

He shook his head. The Taggart women were lovely and he enjoyed their company, but there had only been one woman for him. "Nah. I walked in and knew exactly who I wanted."

"I don't think I'm a warrior woman, Niall. I'm a PI. I didn't even go into the military like so many people here."

She was playing around with semantics. "What would you call yourself? Let's see, you are absolutely an expert at self-defense."

"Only because Big Tag tried to kill me a couple hundred times. Well, he sent people to. I had some weird training classes."

He'd heard. "You take on dangerous cases for not a ton of money."

"I can fund us for a while," she admitted. "You're right about the trust fund baby status."

"Didn't call you that. Just said you had one. Stop interrupting me when I'm trying to explain how fucking amazing you are in my eyes." She stared up at him and he felt comfortable continuing. "You take care of everyone around you. To the point of putting yourself in harm's way." He glanced down at the scar on her chest. It was slightly above her right breast, and there was no way to pretend it wasn't a bullet wound. "I would love to meet the person who did this to you. You got it on a case, right?"

"Sort of." Her hand came up, absently rubbing the scar. "I was protecting a friend. I didn't do a great job."

"Is she alive? Did she get shot?" He knew the story but he wanted her to say it so she remembered how amazing she was.

"No, she got away," Harlow whispered. "And she's engaged and happy now."

He leaned over and kissed her forehead. Not what he wanted to kiss, but it still felt sweet to connect with her. "Warrior princess. Ask me. I'm going to say yes, Harlow. I've been waiting to say yes to you for a long time."

Her eyes closed briefly, and when she opened them again there was a wealth of wariness there. "You're going to break my heart."

"Not if I can help it." He didn't mean to. He meant to heal it, to open it up so she could take everything they had to give her.

"Will you help me on my case, Niall?" she asked.

He felt a smile cross his face. "I will. But I think you should play with me. Tonight."

"Are we negotiating?" Harlow asked, clear challenge in her voice.

"About the play? Absolutely. About me helping you? No. There are no conditions to my help. I'll go wherever you need me to, do whatever you need me to do, but I thought we should probably talk about how you like to play. If you want to play with me, that is. But you know how this goes. I command and you decide because you're always in control."

She stared at him for a long moment and then her hands came up, one cupping the side of his face. He didn't even fight the instinct. He leaned into her palm, loving the way she touched him. "I'm scared you're too good to be true."

Fuck, that made his heart hurt. He reached up and took her hand in his, brought it to his chest where his heart lay. "I'm only a man. I will disappoint you, but I'll also try to make it up to you however I can. I have promises I made a long time ago, but I'm almost through those now."

"Promises?" she asked.

"To an old friend," he replied. "To my best friend. I have things I have to do for him, but when I'm done with those errands, I need you to understand that I'm going to put any relationship I have with a woman first. As I only have interest in one woman, I'll put you first."

"This errand? Is it dangerous?"

"It's more like emotional support. I might have to answer calls and go meet him and I can't tell you why. I can tell you anything I do isn't criminal and won't put you in any danger." He wanted to tell her, but beyond his promise to Jensen he worried if she didn't get to know him better, she would run as fast as she could. "But that only applies to when we're not on this mission of yours. My house could be burning down and I wouldn't leave your side. Do you understand?"

"I can understand the need to keep a promise, and I can definitely understand that sometimes we have to keep secrets." She nodded as though making her decision. She moved in, getting close to him. "Then let's play, Sir. Let's see if this can work."

He intended to make it so when she learned the truth, she couldn't leave. Because he was pretty damn sure he couldn't live without her.

Chapter Four

Harlow was deeply aware that every eye was on her.

Like every single person in the damn club was waiting for them to stop watching and start playing. Even her sister was back from dinner with Chloe. She was still in street clothes, but she was up in the bar, a glass of wine in her hand as she looked out over the dungeon.

Ruby and Gigi were standing across the floor. Neither of them had played all night, just walked around watching scenes and talking quietly.

She was pretty sure they'd dealt with Leah, who was nowhere to be seen.

Niall stood behind her as Gabe took a flogger to a sub's backside. The young woman wasn't familiar to Harlow, but Gabe often brought in women he met at other clubs. Like her, Gabe held a Sanctum membership. Unlike her, he also played at his father's club from time to time.

As her dad often hung out there, she avoided it as though she would die if she walked through the doors.

"Harlow, do you want to do this? I wanted to watch scenes with you so I would get an idea of what you enjoy, but you've done nothing but get more uncomfortable with every scene." Niall had his hands on her shoulders, a comforting warmth. "I've never seen you play. I've heard you once did, but I haven't witnessed it."

Because she'd been so upset about Jensen. Was she going to allow that asshole to ruin everything for her?

Niall had been lovely. He was everything she wanted in a Dom. He was comfortable talking about his wants and needs and wanted to listen to her. He'd been patient, and she understood his issues. He was being careful with her. It felt nice.

Of course she'd also liked the rough way Jensen had barged in, shoving an asshole aside and telling him to get lost because she was taken.

It wasn't feminist of her, but she'd been all over him that very night.

Was she holding back on Niall because of what Jensen had done? She wasn't telling him what her problem was. She wasn't asking him for what she needed. The truth was she wasn't giving him a real chance.

She turned and took his hand, leading him away from the stage. When they were on the outer edges of the crowd, she turned to him. "I haven't played in a long time, and everyone is watching me. I'm nervous, and I hate to admit that. Honestly, I'm wondering if this isn't a terrible idea."

He took her hand and started to walk away, moving toward the locker rooms.

Was he done with her? Was he giving up the first time she had one worry?

She started to pull her hand away but he pulled her close.

"Go and get dressed. We're going to my place. We'll pick up some food on the way and we'll talk in private," he whispered in her ear. "You're right. This is a lot, and we don't need this kind of pressure. Not on our first night. Don't take too long, princess."

He kissed her forehead and stepped back, a challenging look on his face.

"You want to go back to your place?" Harlow asked.

"If we go back to my place, I don't think your family is going to show up. Even if they do, they won't be able to figure out how to get up to my studio," he replied. "I typically go through the gym. You can tell Ruby where you're going if you're afraid."

That made her eyes roll. "I'm not afraid of you."

"Yeah, we're going to talk about rolling your eyes at me when we're in this place." He leaned in, his voice going low. "I want you to keep doing it because I'll spank that gorgeous ass of yours every single time."

The thought sent a thrill down her spine. Damn it. Her long dead libido was starting to come back to life, and she did not want to stop it. "I'll be quick, Sir. Are we taking my car or yours?"

"Oh, I'm driving. It's a piece of crap but I love that junker. I'll be waiting right here."

She hurried along.

An hour later Harlow was fairly certain this man had figured out the way to her heart.

French fries.

"So you had private tutors because no school wanted to deal with your dad?"

He seemed amused with her stories of Deranged Dad. "Not really, but he *was* a pain in the ass. My dad is a genius. I mean he's so smart his brain doesn't function on the normal level, and that includes being able to handle things in a reasonable fashion. He has an eidetic memory."

"Is that where he remembers everything?"

Harlow nodded. "Everything. It's annoying, and he loves to argue. But it wasn't his fault we ended up with private tutors. My sister caught a lot of hell because of how odd our family was. There was a lot of teasing, and she was kind of an outcast."

"I'm sure that was hard, but it would have been hard on you, too."

She shook her head. "Not the same way. Greer always wanted to fit in. Don't get me wrong. She loves our parents. She would never be upset at our parents, but it had an effect on her when some mean girls put shit on social media about us. There were a lot of gang bang jokes and some guys who thought maybe if Greer's mom didn't mind a couple of guys, she wouldn't either."

His face flushed with obvious anger. "Tell me your dad fucked them up."

"Yeah, one of the girl's fathers was involved in some business with my father's friends. They have this investment group. The Masters Fund. The fund decided to sell their shares in her dad's company, and they were bought in a hostile takeover shortly thereafter. They pretty much lost everything. He was kinder to the parents who were embarrassed. A couple of the parents apologized profusely. I took care of the kids, though. Their parents shouldn't suffer, but they needed to pay."

"Damn, but you are fierce, princess." He stared down at her like he was utterly fascinated. Not like her vengeance was something that was going to scare him away. "But it had to bother you, too. I know you don't care what other people think, but you were a teenager. I think your sister is softer than you are so you shoved your feelings down and concentrated on your sister. Was it hard to change your life so much?"

She nodded. "I had to leave some friends, but I joined some others. We shared a tutor with the Lodges, and with our friends Aria and Dane Roberts. So we were our own class, I suppose. Sometimes we would spend a couple of weeks out at Aunt Dani's spa. Most of the people who worked there were in the lifestyle, and they had a school. We would go for special classes. It was nice, but I always knew we weren't normal." She sniffled. It felt good to get emotional. It had been a long time. "You are a very therapy-forward Dom."

He smiled and stroked her hair. "I've learned that the hard way. First thing the board did when they were considering my application was send me to a psychologist. He offered some sessions. I still see him twice a month."

"Did they make you see my Uncle Leo or one of the therapists from the Ferguson Clinic?" They both did work with the different clubs, vetting new members.

"Ash Rycroft at the Ferguson Clinic. I think they're sending everyone my age his way. He's good at working with PTSD and complex family relationships," Niall admitted. "I like talking with him. I'm about to be out of my board-mandated sessions, but I think I'll stick with him for a while. I've got some things to work out. My father was abusive, to say the least. I'm no contact with him."

Her heart ached for him. They were sitting on his couch, which might also be his bed. She wasn't sure. There was a door and it might lead to a bedroom, but she hadn't asked. She moved closer to him, putting a hand on his knee. "And your mom?"

"Same." Niall huffed out a laugh. "My family was pretty toxic." His gorgeous face went soft. "I did not mean for this to turn into a therapy session."

Oh, but wasn't it always? "I feel connected to you. You have no idea how much I appreciate you being open to me. The last relationship I was in… It was passionate, but there wasn't a ton of connection on an emotional level. It felt good at the time, but this feels better."

"Don't discount passion, Harlow." His eyes heated. "I think you need both, and sometimes you have to go to odd lengths to get it. Like your parents. But that's a discussion for another time. When are we going in? I'm talking job wise. Where are we going in to?"

"It's a lifestyle club, but it's more like a bar with BDSM elements, I think. I haven't gone. Normally I would go in myself or with Ruby and do some recon, but I think I should go in with a partner."

"Into a tourist lifestyle club when some Dom might get aggressive with you? Yes." He stroked his hand over hers. "I know you can take care of yourself, but a gorgeous, single submissive is going to attract more attention than you want."

He was so good at handling her. If he'd acted jealous or like she couldn't take care of herself, she could get offended. But he was one hundred percent right.

So unlike Jensen, who plowed through without giving thought to how to phrase things.

She had to stop thinking about him because Niall was turning out to be perfect. Almost too perfect.

"Yes, hence me asking you. I considered asking one of the spy boys, but they're mostly paired off now, and they could get a call in the middle of my op and have to leave to go save the world or something. The McKay-Taggart bodyguards would likely reach out to my dad and let him know what's going on."

"I do not have your father's phone number," Niall pointed out.

"Which is why you're perfect. I also wanted someone who I do have some chemistry with." It wasn't the insane, off-the-charts, do-anything-to-get-into-his-pants chemistry she'd had with Jensen, but she liked it. It was softer, warmer. It felt like solid ground. "But you know I'm truly asking because I've been interested since the minute we met. It's an excuse."

His lips curled up in the sweetest smile.

That was what time with him felt like. Sweet.

Would sex with him feel just as sweet? She was honest with herself. The chemistry between them wasn't as moth to the flame as she felt for Jensen, but she wanted him. It hadn't been the fall into bed the first night and start planning a life, but it was totally there. A slow burn might keep her warm and not torch her whole soul.

"Why do you think I haven't gotten physical with a single sub the whole time I've been here?"

"Because you were waiting for me." The idea was like the man. Sweet. Filling a part of herself that had been empty for a long time.

"I wonder if I haven't been waiting for you my whole life." He winced. "That was probably coming on too strong. Let me rephrase that so I look way cooler and less available than I actually am."

Nope. She so liked that he wasn't a player. She leaned over and kissed him, a brief touch of her lips to his. "Too late."

"Good, because I don't like to play games," he replied and kissed her back, his hand cupping the nape of her neck and holding her there while he explored her mouth.

The kiss left her breathless and more excited than she'd felt in forever. Like she was going on an adventure, but this time she truly trusted the partner she was taking with her. "No games at all, Sir?"

It had been forever since she really played. Oh, she'd let her Dom friends spank her and flog her and get her to cry, but there had been no sexy touches. No fantasy play. She'd put herself in deep freeze after what happened with Jensen. It was past time to defrost.

"Emotional games," he corrected. "There are other games I'm more than happy to play with you. Why don't we start with you pulling those pants down and laying on my lap. I think we should train before we go in. We can certainly be a new couple, but we should look like we've spent some time together."

He might be new to the lifestyle, but he'd already figured out some Dom tricks. "And the only way to possibly look like we're comfortable together is for you to spank my naked ass?"

His big shoulders shrugged. "I know I'll feel more comfortable."

She had to be honest with him. "I'm not ready for full-on sex, Niall."

He showed no anger at all. He simply nodded. "My cock can stay in my pants. How do you feel about fingers? Can I spank your pretty ass and then stroke your clit until you come?"

And there went all of her resolve. "You know where that will lead."

"Yes, it will lead right to my bed where we're going to go to sleep and talk some more in the morning," he promised. "There's a great bagel place next door. They're actually a donut place, but I'm supposed to be all healthy and shit."

"Donuts," she said with a sigh and she stood. "Niall, forget what I said. I want what you're offering me. It's not fair for me to get everything I want and you nothing because I'm wary."

"Then why don't you get out of your clothes. I'll give you a T-shirt to sleep in after we're done. And Harlow, I'm offering you everything I said I would. If I'm your partner, your needs come before mine." He winked her way, and the sexiest smirk came over his face. "Unless you beg."

She pulled her shirt over her head. "I won't beg, Sir."

"Words to make you eat later, princess." His cock tented his jeans nicely, and she wondered if he wasn't right. He was so gorgeous, and he made her feel safe.

She tossed her shirt aside and unclasped her bra, watching him watch her. One big muscular arm was around the back of the sofa and his body was relaxed, with the exception of his impressive erection. She'd seen the man in leathers, seen him dressed for the gym. Not once had that cock of his made an appearance.

Was he telling her the truth? Was she the only woman he wanted? The idea of having every ounce of this man's focus on her made her nipples peak. He made all the right moves. He seemed to know exactly what she needed, and he made sure she got it. Oh, he would prove himself to be human, but for now there was a magical feel to being with this man. She'd hesitated so much in the last few months that it felt good to follow her instincts.

Which had her shimmying out of her jeans and undies and

standing naked in front of him. She grew up in a family where shame wasn't a word unless it had to do with missing the answer to final Jeopardy. She was comfortable in her skin, and sometimes she wondered if a part of that was because she was pulled out of school before she got hit with the mean-girl shit. Her sister had far more hangups than she did.

"Damn, you are gorgeous."

She had to give him a saucy smile. "It's not like you haven't seen most of it. Fet wear leaves little to the imagination. It's why we enforce some strict rules since we've got so many siblings playing."

"Is that what the zones are about?" Niall asked with a grin. "I can go wherever I want, but I heard someone saying he couldn't enter zone three since it's a Thursday. Also, you don't even understand my imagination. It goes to some kinky places when it comes to you. Come here."

She loved how husky his voice had gotten. She moved toward him. "Yes, Sir. Things are carefully planned. Sometimes it's about days. My cousin Gigi only plays on Thursdays or Fridays because her brothers play on Saturday. But Chloe and Gabe and their brother John don't want to limit their days, so they have zones. John tried to tell Chloe she needed to wear a robe when she walked to her zone, and she punched him. I taught her how, so now John doesn't mention robes anymore."

"Blood-thirsty princess," he said with a grin. "I'm glad you don't have brothers so we don't have to worry about zones. Lay on my lap. I want to get this over with. I want to cuddle. You'll stay with me."

Not a question, but still required an answer. He seemed to get more toppy the more engaged his cock was. She liked it. The truth was she enjoyed being dominated during sex. It was the one place she didn't want to be in charge. "Yes, Sir. But only for the donuts."

She eased over his lap, her skin rubbing against the softness of his jeans. They were old and worn in, like he washed them hundreds of times and now they were perfect.

His hand cupped her cheeks, spreading a warm anticipation through her. "Are you comfortable, princess?"

"Yes," she replied, her whole body softening in response.

What would he be like? Would he spank her softly so she

wriggled and writhed and wanted more? Would he go so hard she called out her safe word? They hadn't talked about safe words, but they weren't truly playing. They were experimenting. If she said no, he would stop.

Would she want him to stop?

Her brain was going a million miles an hour. Her body might be ready but her brain was rebelling.

And then she wasn't thinking about anything but the smack against her tender flesh. She heard it before it registered as pain. He'd gone for it but not too hard. Just enough to get her attention and focus it. On something other than anxiety. Heat flashed over her skin and then sank in.

"Tell me if it's too much. We're learning each other. I don't want any of that silent submission right now. I want you to talk to me."

"It's good, Sir. My brain is whirling. I need this more than I thought I did."

Another hard slap. "I don't want you thinking about anything but this."

Three hard smacks and her eyes were watering, but it worked. She wasn't worried about what might happen. She was completely focused on the here and now. As he continued, his hand smacking and then holding the heat in, she let herself start to float. She let go of worrying she would never get over Jensen. Stopped thinking about getting shot. Didn't care that her deranged dad would likely put one of his employees on Niall the minute he found out she was seeing him. The case didn't even matter in those moments when Niall's big hand dispensed discipline. She let the pain flow over her and sighed as it morphed into something else. She didn't even fight the tears. She might have with a different Dom, but he wasn't going to use them against her. He wasn't going to freak out and make this about himself. He would take them for what they were—much-needed release.

She wasn't sure how long it had been when he turned her over, flipping her neatly like she weighed nothing. He cradled her in his arms, and she could feel his cock against her tender backside.

He brushed the tears off her cheeks. "Feel better, princess?"

She felt a bit limp noodley. It was beyond nice. "I do. I think I might be able to sleep." She should be honest if she was doing this with him. "I have bad dreams sometimes."

"Me, too. If you need me, wake me up and we'll talk," he offered. "Or I'll simply hold you until you go back to sleep. But I think after all that harshness, you need some sugar."

She lay cradled against him as his free hand found its way down her body and between her legs. He leaned over and kissed her, softly this time, with no real intent. But his fingers. Oh, his fingers were on a damn mission.

"You liked it," he whispered. "You're so fucking wet, Harlow."

His fingers slid easily between the folds of her labia, foraging briefly before rubbing her clit and taking her breath away.

This was how he treated her in an experimental mini session? Oh, she could sub for this man. She let her head fall back, allowed him access to everything.

"You are so gorgeous," he whispered against her neck. The arm around her back cupped her breast, thumb playing with her nipple, and she wondered what it would feel like to have his mouth there, teeth rasping on just the right side of pain. He could spend hours keeping her on the edge, tormenting her, and she would love it.

The anticipation she felt for this man was hope after long years of wanting.

It didn't take him long before those talented fingers slid inside her. His thumb worked her clit while he finger fucked her. One and then two and three, stretching her gently and stroking in exactly the right place.

It had been so long since she'd had this kind of orgasm. Oh, she'd touched herself a couple of times, but between getting burned so brutally by Jensen and then getting shot and nearly dying, she'd let go of this piece of herself. It slid back into place forcefully as Niall nipped at her earlobe and hit the perfect place, and she went off like a rocket, her body stiffening and relaxing, pleasure pouring through her.

She was a breathless mess when he shifted and stood, picking her up with an effortless grace she found deeply attractive. He walked the short distance to the door she'd noticed earlier. Sure enough, it was a tiny bedroom that contained a bed, dresser, and nightstand.

"So not a studio," she said as he laid her on the bed.

"I mean it's as small as one." He turned and opened the top drawer, pulling out a big white T-shirt. "I might exaggerate so no woman will pursue me for all my wealth."

She did not need wealth. The circumstances of her birth had taken care of that. But she wanted everything else this man had to offer. "Niall, what I said before…"

He gently put the shirt over her head. "We're sleeping, Harlow. Like I said, your needs are more important than my dick. Get in bed. I'm tired, and someone's going to make me walk miles tomorrow to get her donuts."

"It's next door," she countered, but she was smiling as she slid her arms into the T-shirt and pulled the covers around her.

He got down to his boxers, and she wished there was more light. He slid into bed beside her, wrapping an arm around her waist and hauling her close. "Good night, princess. I'm glad you decided to be brave."

She cuddled against him and fell asleep far faster than she thought she would.

Chapter Five

Six days later Niall looked over the building where they would soon be attempting to make contact with a young woman Harlow hoped was working there.

They had been over the case four times now. He'd gotten comfortable in Harlow's office and liked her partner, Ruby Lockwood. Like Harlow she was smart and capable and funny. Hanging with them and Harlow's cousin Gigi had been incredibly fun. He enjoyed watching the three of them plot and plan while he made sure they were fueled with lattes and croissants from the nearby French bakery.

He was rapidly falling for this woman and the life around her, the life she could offer him. He was damn straight loving the man he became around her. He felt happier, more settled, and focused on the future being close to Harlow.

And he hadn't even slept with her yet.

He was taking it slow, though he rather thought she was going to get frustrated with him and then his Valkyrie princess was going to force the situation.

He had to tell her the truth before he took her to bed.

Not that he hadn't. She'd slept at his place the first couple of nights, and they'd slept at her place last night. He'd stroked her and cuddled her, then slipped out of bed when she was asleep and took the coldest shower in the world.

He had to tell her.

"According to the plans Ruby found, there are three entrances. The main we're going into, one at the back of the building, and one on the east side that leads to an alleyway. It dumps out onto Taylor Street," Harlow said, standing beside him on the busy street. She had a trench coat on, covering the fairly modest fet wear she selected for the evening.

She wore boy shorts and a lacy bra that covered as much as any swimsuit would, and the four-inch heels made her legs look a mile long. It also meant she was almost eye to eye with him since she was tall all on her own. Her hair had grown out since he first met her. She'd had an electric blue bob, and now it was a deep purple and brushed the tops of her shoulders.

She was too gorgeous, and he was a jealous asshole because he didn't want to take her in there. He didn't want other guys looking at her. Not in that place. At The Hideout it was fine because everyone knew how to behave and would treat her the way they should. He had no illusions Decadence was the same.

"Are you okay?" Harlow asked, her eyes wide as she looked at him.

He nodded. He wasn't going to admit that his inner caveman was dying to make an appearance. He had a brief fantasy of tossing her over his shoulder, shoving her in his piece of shit Jeep, and making for Jensen's old place a few hours west of Fort Worth. It was a ramshackle house set on what was left of his family's ranch. Up until a couple of months ago Jensen's aunt had lived there and kept the place up, but she recently moved to be near her daughter and grandkids, so with the exception of needing a cleaning, the place was ready to stay in. More importantly, it was isolated and he could keep her safe forever. He would call Jensen and tell him to finish his shit up and meet them there and they would work everything out.

"Yeah," was his reply because he was a man who knew how not to piss his woman off. "I'm good. A little nervous."

She softened immediately, going up on her toes to kiss him. She did it more and more often now. Like she couldn't help herself. "There's nothing to be nervous about."

He was lapping it all up. Though his dick was definitely complaining. "I don't want to fuck this up for you. What if I say the wrong thing and she runs?"

"You won't say the wrong thing," Harlow assured him. "You don't have to say anything at all. Let me find her and talk to her. I'm going to try to figure out how bad the situation is before I tell her who I am. I might not even do it this time. It might take a few meetings to get her to trust me."

So they would have to do this again. He better get used to it because Harlow loved her job, and he wasn't sending anyone else in with her. "Then we should get to it. I'm going to tell anyone who asks that we're just exploring. I'm not going to give away the fact that we know what we're doing."

He wasn't telling her anything she didn't already know since this was her plan. He was simply reminding himself.

"We're ready, babe." She put her hand in his. "Let's do this thing."

She seemed eager, anticipating the job like it was going to be fun.

See, this was why he got out of the military. He was not the dude who liked an adrenaline rush. As they crossed the street he had to wonder what shit Jensen was up to tonight. He'd been careful about not telling Niall anything specific about what he was doing. He wanted Niall to have what he called plausible deniability.

Because it was almost certainly criminal shit.

They'd talked around the Jensen issue, Harlow not saying much more than she'd had a passionate affair that ended when the guy fucked her over in an unpleasant way. But he had to wonder if Jensen's unique style wasn't more of what truly called to Harlow. Would she wake up one morning and decide Niall was boring and ordinary? He was the guy who made her coffee every morning and watched TV with her. He wasn't the guy who swung in and swept her off her feet and into some wild adventure.

When she saw Jensen again, would she realize what she truly wanted?

And where the hell was the guy? Niall had called the burner number Jensen gave him to use in case of emergencies. This wasn't an emergency, but he would have liked some advice on how to handle himself. Maybe some background on the club. Jensen was excellent at research.

Or maybe he hadn't wanted to feel like he was alone in taking care of her.

He didn't even know where his best friend was living at this point. He knew Jensen was in Dallas and working at a business that was a front for a criminal organization. From context he'd figured out Jensen was some kind of bouncer, so it was a club or a bar, of which there were almost a thousand in Dallas proper alone. When he took in the close suburbs, the number jumped considerably.

"Hey, it's going to be fine," Harlow said as they approached the door. "This is a simple case. If I can't get Miranda to come with me, I have to give her mom all the info I have and let the police deal with it if there's anything illegal going on. She's an adult. I can't kidnap her."

"Kidnap? You've kidnapped someone before?"

She gave him her "what, me" look. "I wouldn't call it kidnapping. I would call it liberating. And it wasn't a person. It was a poodle. My client totally had every right to her dog. Her asshole ex was starving the poor baby. I would leave the human extractions to the professionals. Ruby and I are more like intelligence gatherers. That's what we're doing tonight. Getting a lay of the land."

He could do that. He brought her hand to his lips. "I will follow your lead."

He took a deep breath as the big guy at the door opened it for them.

"Welcome to Decadence. Please check in at the front desk," he said with a nod.

That was when Niall caught sight of the gun in a holster under the doorman's jacket.

Harlow squeezed his hand as though she knew he'd seen it and it made him antsy. It wasn't like he hadn't spent his life around firearms. He didn't like going into a club where they were apparently needed. Oh, he was certain there were a shit ton of weapons at The Hideout, but everyone knew everyone else.

He guided Harlow to the big desk inside the foyer. A pretty woman with hard eyes stood with a clipboard. He gave her their names. Well, the ones Ruby faked for them, presented his card—another fake since Ruby was apparently good at them—and they were shown where to leave their coats and bags. He wasn't sure the lockers they were offered would keep anyone out but they used them. They were allowed on the dungeon floor with no lecture on rules whatsoever.

He was pretty sure there were no rules here. The Hideout required a six-week course, psychological examination, and a vote by the board to get a foot in the door. This place required a hundred-dollar cover charge.

The thud of industrial music hit him first, and then the sound of someone groaning to his left.

There was a small scene space being used, and a sub was tied up and being spanked. Her head was down, and it was clear she was gagged.

Outrage sparked through him because her hands were empty. Her legs were tied down. There was no way for her to indicate she'd had enough. He'd been taught when the sub wanted a gag, there still had to be a clear way for the sub to safeword out. Usually, they would hold something and drop it or squeeze it if it made sounds. Or they could raise a leg.

This sub was given no options but to take whatever the top was giving.

Harlow went on her toes but instead of kissing him this time, she whispered in his ear. "I am begging you not to get us kicked out, Sir. I know you are outraged because you're a good Dom, and I promise we will report this place, but Miranda Falls might be in real, life-threatening danger. Please."

He took a long breath and let it go. She had a job to do and he would wreck it if he protested, and very likely nothing would come of it.

But it made his gut twist to walk away.

"Thank you, Sir," she said quietly. "Let's go and get a drink. If she's working here, she's likely a server. I can already see one walking around."

"They're serving on the floor?" He had to keep his voice down.

She winced but started moving.

Once she found her way to the bar, she selected one of the couches that were placed around the somewhat luxurious lounge. It was where it looked like they'd spent the most cash. There was an open love seat in a corner where they could see out over most of the club.

He sat down and drew Harlow onto his lap. He wrapped an arm around her waist and brought her close. "This place is more dangerous than you made it out to be, princess. What do you know about it?"

A slightly guilty look crossed her face, and she leaned in. "I'm worried it's attached to a group that's running drugs in the city. Don't freak out. We're still only here to talk to Miranda. If we can find her."

"We're going to have a long talk when we get out of here," he vowed.

She twisted slightly so she could look in his eyes. "I didn't want to freak you out. And I'm not scared of whatever punishment you intend to mete out, Sir. I'm way more scared that you're never going to fuck me."

This was not the time nor the place, and a wave of guilt rushed through him. "I promise you I will and you'll be ready for me."

She huffed, a bratty sound. "I am ready. You're frustrating."

A young woman walked up dressed in fet wear, a corset, and what looked to be a thong. She wore ridiculous heels and set a couple of cocktail napkins in front of them. She was definitely not the woman they were looking for. "Good evening, Sir. What can this one get you and your submissive this evening? I should warn you our bartender took a break, but this one has some experience."

"I'm easy," Harlow replied. "I'll take whatever white wine you have."

"I'll have a beer." He wouldn't drink it, but they needed to look like they fit in.

"This creature can handle that," she replied with a smile.

"Tell me they're making you call yourself that," Harlow said.

He thought they were trying to fit in. Wasn't asking questions like that going to get them in trouble?

The young woman's eyes rolled. "It's part of the experience. We're supposed to be like these submissives. I don't know. It was something about us not having names so the clients can fantasize. It was a lot. This place is weird. I'm thinking of quitting. I'm kind of worried it's a cult. But the bartender is heavenly. At least he was until he pulled his disappearing act. I don't even know why I'm here."

"It's so hard to get a good job these days." Harlow was off, sounding soft and sweet and totally girlie, like she was the best friend you always hoped to have.

He sat back and watched her work. Within minutes of meeting, she knew the waitress was named Ashley and this was her part-time job. She also worked for an insurance company, but she was in a probationary period and kind of hated it and wanted to go back to school, but she didn't have the cash and this place paid pretty well. Ashley told her the club was attached to some kind of corporate group, and they often hired people from the club for higher-paying work.

"Like three of the waitresses I trained with are already working upstairs and making serious money," Ashley was saying.

Oh, this was Harlow's superpower. His baby was one of those people everyone opened up to. When he'd first heard the word private detective he'd had a vision of her in gritty situations, playing out those noir scenes in movies, but it hit him that this was the real job. Talking to people, getting them to say more than they should.

She was excellent at it.

"But I will admit the scenery is gorgeous, and I'm not talking about the décor," Ashley said with a knowing wink. "Not that you need it. Your guy is hot, but I will say the new bartender is chef's kiss hot, and he has that oh, shucks cowboy thing going for him. But the hottest guy here is the dungeon monitor. I'm not joking, that man is heaven. Master J. If you get a chance, take a look at him." She turned Niall's way with a rueful grin. "Again, not that you are not superhot, Sir."

He had to chuckle at that. "I appreciate it, Ashley, and my girl there is welcome to look as long as she comes back to me."

Ashley looked to Harlow. "I changed my mind. That attitude alone makes him the hottest. Girl, run. The guys here are mostly possessive jerks. But there are some fun things to do. I can take you to one of the playrooms. There's some wild stuff in there."

"Is this one bothering you, Sir?" a deep voice asked.

He looked up and a middle-aged man in leathers stood there. "Not at all. I find her amusing, and she's being incredibly welcoming to my sub. We just got here and we already like it, thanks to that one. She's an excellent sub and a good server."

He had to hope this obvious authority figure hadn't heard everything.

"Well, she's supposed to be working not talking, but I'm glad she's made you comfortable. Go and get their drinks," he said to Ashley, who scurried off to do his bidding.

Niall held out a hand, and Harlow sank down onto his lap. "It's a nice place you have here. My sub and I are new to the lifestyle, and this is exactly what we've been looking for." If they were hoping to play in a hellscape. He didn't say that part out loud. "I'm Nate."

It was the name they'd agreed on. Ruby had told him it was Nate or Nolan. He'd made some snarky comment about the name Nolan that earned him a hearty glaring from Ruby, who apparently liked baseball or something.

"Phil," the other man said and shook his hand.

Harlow cuddled close, her head down like she was slightly afraid of the big guy.

Or she was playing her part to perfection.

"Nice to meet you," Niall replied. "We thought we would have a drink or two and then watch some of the scenes. Kind of ease in. I think it would help a lot if you would let some of the subs talk to mine. She's on the fence but I'm invested. I want this to work."

"I'll see if I can send over one of our more experienced subs," Phil offered. "This kind of lifestyle can offer a lot for a man. It takes us back to when things were good, if you know what I mean."

Sure. When women couldn't have their own bank accounts and couldn't leave a man who abused her. Fucking asshole. This guy was why the lifestyle caught so much shit. He took something that was personal and individual, that demanded communication and understanding, and turned it into gender wars. But he smiled and agreed. "I do indeed. So if you would help me convince her, I would be so thankful."

Harlow cuddled in closer, her arms tightening.

"Will do," Phil said. "I know exactly who you should talk to. I'll see if she's around. Hopefully she's not taking an unexpected break like my bartender. You can't fucking find decent help these days."

He stomped off.

"You are so good at this," Harlow said, her hand coming up to caress his cheek.

He breathed her in because he could feel the tension in the air. "I can handle the Doms. I spent enough time around my father and his friends to know how to act like an abusive prick who thinks he needs to control women."

She kissed his cheek. "I know this is hard on you, babe. I can't tell you how much I appreciate it. When this is over, let's go to The Hideout and play in a place where you feel safe. I know we've talked about keeping this relationship quiet, but I don't want to. I want everyone to know."

Fuck. She was ready. He had to talk to Jensen, but didn't he owe her more? "I think that sounds perfect." He caught sight of a woman striding into the bar area. Phil stopped her and pointed back their way.

A familiar-looking woman. "Hey, I think you're about to get lucky."

Harlow looked up and managed to keep her expression perfectly calm even though she was looking at Miranda Falls. Miranda wore fet wear very close to what Ashley was wearing but in a different color. She took the tray from Ashley, who stayed behind the bar.

Miranda plastered a big smile on her face as she approached them. She had her blonde hair up in a high ponytail and a hard look in her eyes that told him she didn't want to be here, and it wasn't merely about not enjoying her job. She walked with a bounce in her step like she'd been taught how to make those breasts move in a way guaranteed to get some great tips. Everything about the young woman screamed affectation.

"I'm going to convince her to take me to the ladies' room," Harlow whispered. "I think she'll talk more freely there. Stay here and I'll be right back."

"Sir, I have your beer and a glass of wine for your lovely sub," Miranda said too brightly as she set the drinks down. "Master Phil has asked that I show you around a bit."

Harlow sat up and gave the sub a smile. "That sounds wonderful. Could you show me to the bathroom? We don't know our way around, and I don't want my Master to lose this seat. It's perfect since we can see everything and figure out what we want to do this evening. I have so many questions."

He watched Miranda's shoulders come down slightly, as though relaxing under Harlow's brilliant smile.

"I like your hair," Miranda said quietly. "I used to have pink hair. I'll show you where the ladies' room is."

He waited until Harlow disappeared behind the door and then took his phone out of his pocket and texted the number Jensen left him.

Need to talk. Tonight. I'll call later. Answer the phone.

It was all he could do because at some point tonight, he was going to tell Harlow everything.

* * * *

Harlow stepped into the women's restroom and frowned at the lack of amenities. Not that she expected the lavishness of The Hideout. Even when they hadn't had a ton of money for the budget, the Doms had insisted on making the women's locker room a luxurious space.

There wasn't even a shower in here. It was literally two stalls and a sink that had seen better days. And the lighting sucked.

So no one got ready here. There was more to getting ready to play at the club than simple convenience. Sitting around joking with friends, helping them do their hair and makeup, formed community. A lot of serious discussions happened in the locker room. Many a problem was talked out and solved by her fellow subs. The subs here would be isolated.

Anyone who wanted to play at Decadence had to come in fet wear under their street clothes, or in her case a trench coat that made her think she was in a noir film trying to solve a mystery.

The real mystery was why Niall hadn't slept with her yet. At first it was kind of sweet. He cuddled her and got her off, and then she would fall asleep in his arms. And now she was wondering if he wanted her at all. There was something he wasn't telling her. Some secret he was keeping, and she was worried she knew what it was.

And that was why she intended to talk to him tonight about how she could be his friend without the sex.

If he wasn't sexually attracted to women, that was okay. No one at The Hideout would blink an eye. Well, some of the bi guys would definitely start looking his way.

Except he always got hard around her.

It was a mystery for later. She had to get her head in the game. "So why did you change your hair? I bet you're a cutie with pink hair. It's the one color I won't use, though. It's kind of my mom's signature color, and my dad calls her Cotton Candy and it's gross."

Miranda watched as Harlow "fixed" her hair and redid her lip gloss. "Oh, it was a lot of work."

Harlow smoothed down her own hair and wondered if Niall liked the deep purple color. She'd kept her blue bob for a long time until she'd realized it was a connection to Jensen.

I love this color. So bright. Like you, baby.

She'd gone straight to the salon and changed the color and started growing it out. "I like going to the salon. Sometimes it's my only me time. It's my self-care time."

"I like it, too," Miranda said with a smile. "I guess I do miss it. I liked to color coordinate my hair and nails. But then I got this job, and they don't want us to stand out like that. Natural colors only. I could go red if I wanted to, but I don't like the way I look with red hair, so this is my only other option."

"They tell you what to do with your hair? I kind of thought subs were supposed to stand out."

"How much do you know about the lifestyle?" Miranda asked.

Pretty much everything since her parents didn't think shame was a real word. But she wasn't about to talk about her unusual upbringing. "I read a lot. Nate is more into it than I am. He wants to give it a try. I like the way it sounds in the books. It seems like a nice way to live."

"Oh, this place isn't like the romance books. I don't know what other clubs are like because this is the only one I've ever worked in, but it's not like that," Miranda admitted. "I've read those, too. I thought it would be…more like a family. I guess that's part of what I was looking for."

Oh, Harlow would bet that was exactly what the young woman had been looking for since she knew what happened with Miranda's mom. She hadn't held back when she told the story of their estrangement. Miranda's mom was pretty filled with guilt. "Yeah, that's what I like about it, too. I guess I was thinking this place would be like those clubs, but you don't even have a locker room. Where do you get ready?"

"Oh, we have to come in ready," Miranda explained. "We have a break room on the floor above where we can store our street clothes, but it's not easy to get ready there, and there are so many of us we don't fit."

"I guess I thought Doms liked to treat subs like they're princesses." She loved when Niall called her princess. But only because she could hear the warrior part.

Was he playing her for some reason?

"I'm sure some do. It's like anything, I guess. Everyone's different, but I think some of the women who come through here end up leaving because they don't like it."

Was Miranda trying to save her? It definitely felt like she was trying to steer her away, which was not the job she'd been given. "What does your Dom think of this place?"

"I don't have one."

"You're a sub without a Dom? Working in the lifestyle? Do you have any you play with?"

Miranda's head shook. "No. I was seeing this guy before I got the job here, but he wasn't into this kind of thing. Not that I would have done that stuff with him. I don't play yet. I know some of the hostesses do and they get good tips, but I haven't tried it. I think it's one of the reasons Phil gets pissed with me sometimes. It's one of the reasons they don't want us to have boyfriends. They might get jealous."

And it sounded like she didn't want to. Harlow turned. She wasn't going to be able to do this slow. "This doesn't sound like a normal job. If you're not comfortable playing, you absolutely shouldn't play. I know that much."

Niall would flip his shit when she told him what was going on here. She'd been lucky he hadn't freaked out and stopped everything when they'd walked past that completely unsafe scene.

Miranda looked over to the door as though trying to make sure no one came through. "You seem nice. Maybe you should get your boyfriend to take you somewhere else. He seems kind, and I worry if he runs with the men who own this place, he won't be for long. Nice guys don't last long around here, if you know what I mean."

"I don't." She needed as much information as she could get. Harlow was starting to get a bad feeling about this place. A familiar feeling.

It reminded her so much of the club in LA. The one where she met Jensen. Where their two cases brought them together and then tore them apart. Case? His wasn't a case. His was all about revenge.

But that didn't matter. What mattered was Decadence was an awful lot like Club Paradise. The waitstaff there were being slowly transitioned into drug mules and sex workers. Though workers got paid, and Cliff Hamilton didn't pay his girls. He took them for everything they were worth and tossed them aside when he was through with them.

Could they be connected? When they were working in LA, both she and Jensen had theories that there were more clubs. They thought Hamilton was trying to take his business to other cities. At the time there had been rumors Hamilton had some kind of tech work happening. There had been a group of young men who hadn't fit in with the crowd. Hackers, she'd thought at the time, but what if they had been building the app this group was using to distribute their drugs?

Miranda shrugged. "I know I'm supposed to convince you to hang out here, but I think it would be better if you don't. Phil isn't as nice as he seems, and he's always looking for more girls. You would fit the bill. You need to be careful because if he gives you a job offer, he doesn't like it when you say no."

Nope. She wasn't going to be able to go slow at all. "Miranda, are you okay?"

The younger woman seemed to rally, forcing a smile to her face. "Of course. I'm sorry. I'm in a bad head space. Forget what I said."

"I don't think I can. I'm worried about you."

Miranda waved her off. "Nothing to worry about. The money is great. It's helping me pay off my loans, and I'm getting to move up soon and I won't have to deal with the club again. Everyone who moves up seems happy. If you're having second thoughts, you might want to trust your instincts."

"My instincts tell me you're in trouble," Harlow said quietly.

"Well, I'm going to be if I don't get back out to the floor soon," Miranda said with a shaky laugh. "Phil was mad enough that Jack took an unscheduled break."

"Niall will let him know you're with me. We've got time. I would like to talk more."

"I can show you around the dungeon, I guess," Miranda offered.

She was going to lose her. It was a gamble, but she had to take it. "Miranda, your mother is worried about you. She's worried this job is more than a regular job."

Miranda stopped, her eyes widening and hand going to her chest. "My mom sent you? Who are you?"

At least she wasn't running for the door. "I'm a private investigator, and she hired me to find you. I tracked you down to here. I know you had a fight with her and she told you if you left you shouldn't come back, but sweetie, she did not mean it. She's so sorry."

Tears pooled in Miranda's eyes. "She is?"

Harlow nodded. "She would do anything to take it back. You need to understand that this is not normal. I believe this place is a front for drug dealers, and they're going to ask you to do something that they will use against you."

Miranda went still. "I already owe them money. I didn't mean to. Phil offered to buy my uniform and pay my rent when I was behind. I was going to pay him back, but he didn't mention he was charging interest. I owe more than I borrowed."

"That's not legal," Harlow said. "I've got some friends who are lawyers, and they can go over it. I think you'll find your mother will likely pay him off if it means you're out of here. She just wants you safe."

There were other problems. If this was an organization even slightly like Hamilton's, they would care more about the potential for Miranda to go to the authorities than they would the money, but she would deal with that problem another time.

It probably wasn't what she thought it was. After all, Daisy's father had taken care of the situation.

So why was the organization still running?

There was something going on here. Something she didn't understand. But she was going to.

"I think they might come after my mom if I leave." Miranda sniffled. "I don't think I can. You don't understand what they're like."

"I do. Miranda, I don't think this is my first encounter with this group. If I'm right, they used to work in LA, and they were recently caught here, though I think the big guys flew under the radar."

"Are you talking about what happened to the cartel?" Miranda's voice went low. "There was talk of a cartel supplying some of the clubs with party favors, as they called them. I had to serve them when they came in for meetings. That was when I knew we were in trouble, but then this private investigator was looking to track down a wayward boyfriend. He was one of the guys who worked upstairs. The PI caught him in the middle of a deal, and all hell broke loose for a couple of months."

"She wasn't a PI." Harlow fought back a growl. "She was my receptionist. It was her first day. Yes, I know about that situation, but I think the ties go deeper. I think it would be best if we moved you somewhere they can't find you. Do you want out?"

Miranda nodded. "I want out. I'm so scared to stay here, but I don't want them to hurt my mom."

"She'll go with you. I talked to her about what might happen if you were in too deep, and she'll do anything," Harlow explained. "I have to make some arrangements. When is your next shift?"

"Tomorrow. I have to work every day. And I'm supposed to do something new tomorrow afternoon. I'm doing something Phil calls a run. He said it's important that I do it right. I'm supposed to drop something off at an address downtown before I come into work. Harlow, I'm worried it might be illegal."

Oh, it was totally illegal, and she was going to have to work some magic. "If you do that, they will have proof that you're involved in crimes. They will use that to make you do whatever they want. They targeted you, and this is the position they've been working to put you in. We need to move you tonight."

She looked like a deer in the headlights. "Tonight?"

Harlow nodded. "Yes. You are going to work the rest of your shift like nothing happened. Then you're going to go home and I will meet you there, and we'll move you and your mom tonight. Lucky for me a mentor of mine has a couple of safe houses, and he loves to help so he can hold it over everyone's head. From there we'll figure it out, but you cannot go on that run tomorrow. It's imperative they don't get blackmail material on you."

Miranda wrapped her arms around her chest as though self-soothing. "I have to go back out there?"

"I need a couple of hours," she replied. "You can do this. Forget everything and do your job. If Phil asks about tomorrow, tell him you're ready. Pretend like nothing happened. You talked to me and I'm cool with it now. You think my Master and I might become regulars. Can you keep it together?"

She took a long breath. "Yeah. Yes, I can. If my mom can put everything on the line for me, then I can put a smile on my face for a couple of hours."

Harlow slid her phone from its hiding place under her clingy shirt. There hadn't been a rule about no cell phones, but she didn't want to make it obvious. "Put your address in. I'll be there when you get off."

"I usually make it home by two a.m. I don't have much to pack. I can be ready quickly," Miranda assured her, and she added her address and phone number. "You'll be there?"

"I will be there," Harlow promised. "And I'll contact your mom and have her ready to go. It's going to be okay. When you're safe, my partner and I will start looking into how this club works and who's in charge. If we can get enough to go to the police, we will. Until then you need to lay low."

"I'll help you with that. I know some things." She looked to the door again. "I know some people who might be helpful for you to talk to."

Ruby was going to be thrilled. She lived for this kind of shit. She was going to get to hack systems and play chicken with mobsters. She wouldn't care that they weren't going to get paid for this. She would do it for the fun. And that's how Harlow used her trust fund. To keep them afloat while they did good work. She took the phone back from Miranda. "My Dom and I are going to stay for another hour or so and then we'll leave. I'll get everything ready and be at your place at two. Pack light and don't tell anyone."

Miranda wiped away a tear. "I'm going to see my mom."

This was why she did it. This feeling that she was doing something worthwhile kept her going. She wasn't some useless rich bitch. She had a purpose. Harlow reached for Miranda's hand, squeezing it. "You are. You are going to be okay."

Miranda sniffled and checked herself in the mirror. "I'll see you soon."

She turned and walked out.

This was the danger time. She quickly texted Ruby, who would reach out to their client and get everything in place. They would need to move quickly. Ruby would call their contact at McKay-Taggart, who would help them locate a safe house and assign a bodyguard to take Miranda and her mom there.

This was not her first rodeo.

She slid the phone back into its place and checked her hair. She let her expression go slack and peaceful. *Nothing to see here, Mr. Criminal. I'm just a soft, sweet girl who likes to submit to a big, strong man. I'm not about to take down your whole criminal enterprise or anything.*

Yep. She looked like some Dom's plaything, and that was how she liked it. No one saw her coming.

Did she have any right to bring Niall into this? Especially if he didn't truly want her?

Harlow shoved that question aside and started out of the bathroom. She was almost back to the door that led to the lounge when she felt a hand on her elbow.

She turned, ready to punch the fucker, and stopped.

"Harlow?" Jensen stood there, an unholy fire in his eyes.

And she knew she was in real trouble.

Chapter Six

Jensen bit back a growl as he stared down at the one woman he'd ever loved.

Harlow Dawson's hair was longer and she'd changed the color, but he'd known exactly who she was the minute he caught sight of her walking back with Miranda.

She looked like his every fucking wet dream, and his every nightmare since she was in a place where he was absolutely sure everyone in charge was a killer.

He pulled her back to the tiny office he'd been given when he took over as dungeon monitor. Phil didn't particularly like to do things like assign work schedules and duties, so this was where Jensen sat up late or came in early to get done the minor tasks of running the club. It was nothing more than a desk, a chair, and a laptop, but it would have to do.

"What the fuck are you doing here, Harlow?"

Her eyes flared briefly, hurt showing there, but this wasn't some sweet reunion. She was supposed to stay out of trouble. He was going to have such a fucking talk with Niall, who should have been watching her.

Niall, who'd sent him a text earlier, but he hadn't been able to reply. He couldn't call. Not here.

So he definitely didn't want her walking around like the

sweetest treat he'd ever seen.

"I'm on a case." She straightened up, and her jaw went tight. "And now I realize I was right about this place. So the cartel they took out a couple of months ago wasn't the real owner. If you're here, then the real man behind this place is Cliff Hamilton. I knew it."

"You came looking for me? Do you know what a stupid move that was?"

Her arms crossed over her chest, and she huffed out a laugh that held not an ounce of humor. "I was not looking for you. You made yourself clear when you left me to be arrested and assaulted."

The words hit him hard. "What are you talking about? The cops were coming. I had the timing down. I certainly wouldn't have left you there if I didn't know the cops would take control."

"Yeah, well they did, but not before your friend broke my arm trying to get me to tell him where you were," Harlow said with a bitterness he couldn't deny. "Fucker still aches. But that doesn't matter. What does matter is I had no idea you were here, not that it would stop me. I'm on a case, and I swear if you fuck this up for me, I'll be the one looking for revenge. Now I'm going to get back to my boyfriend and you can pretend like you don't know who I am. Good-bye, Jensen."

He slammed his hand against the door so she couldn't open it. It put him in close proximity, so close he could smell her. God, he missed that scent. Strawberries and fucking cream. He was addicted to it. "Harlow, I didn't know about your arm. I…I tried to stay away from you. Even from news of you. I knew your dad came to get you."

"Yeah," she said, not turning around. "Thanks for that, too. He's been up my ass for the last two years over that. You should let me go now, Jensen. My Dom is going to start to wonder where I am."

Oh, he wanted to know about that, too. Niall hadn't mentioned she'd taken a top. All he heard about was her playing with friends who were tops. Nothing serious. Nothing close to permanent. "What is his name?"

"It doesn't matter because we have nothing to do with each other, Jensen Wiley," she replied.

"The fact that you're here tells me otherwise. What is your

case?"

She turned, her back to the door. That stubborn look on her face did something to him. Revved him the fuck up. She was so close, and this was not how he expected this to go. He was supposed to show up on her doorstep with flowers and croissants and pretty much beg for a second chance. He wasn't supposed to be the bad guy in her life. Again.

"I don't discuss my cases with strangers," she said flatly.

He felt a brow rise over his eyes. "Stranger?"

She shrugged. "Well, I never really knew you."

He wasn't letting her off so easily. "Oh, you knew me, baby. You knew me in pretty much every way a woman can know a man."

"I knew your cock, Jensen." She gave him a sarcastic thumbs-up. "Good for you. You know how to work it. But the rest, I didn't know at all or I would have realized what a betraying motherfucker you would turn out to be."

"I did it to save you." He knew she wouldn't understand but he had to try. "Things were getting dangerous, and if you stayed you would have ended up in Mexico with me. They would have used you to manipulate me."

"Oh, that wouldn't have worked. They would have figured out quickly Jensen Wiley doesn't have soft spots to exploit."

She was so wrong. "I assure you the minute they took you into custody, I would have given it all up."

Her purple hair shook. "Tell yourself that so you can sleep at night. I don't care. I have everything from you I ever want. I have a reminder to not trust a man like you again. It still aches every time it rains. I was fairly certain he was going to rape me."

He felt those words like a kick to his gut. It forced him to step back. "You weren't alone with him for more than a few minutes. The cops were coming. I had confirmation they were on the way."

"And you slipped out the back so you didn't have to face the consequences," Harlow accused. She had her tough-girl face on, the one she used when she shut out everyone. "When your friend realized the cops were on their way, he turned on me. He broke my arm, shoved me over a table. I was lucky, but I will never forget that it was my loving boyfriend who left me there."

He was going to be sick. "I wanted you out, and I knew you

wouldn't leave without finishing your case. I got her out. I did that for you."

"You did it for your own conscience. You didn't do it for me. Look, you seem to think you can make me believe you actually cared about me."

"I loved you." He felt his fists clench at his side. "Harlow, I still fucking love you. I know you…"

She put up a hand to stop him. "Don't care. Anything I felt for you died when you left me behind and didn't even give me a heads-up. I don't love you. I don't trust you. I don't think about you. You are a mistake I made and I won't make again, so whatever this is, you can stop. It won't work."

This was his nightmare. She didn't even want to hear him out. "But you have another Dom? I thought you wouldn't make that mistake again."

"I have a real Dom this time. One who truly cares about me."

Oh, she had these little tells. Nothing big, but when she wasn't entirely telling the truth, her brow raised the slightest bit, as though begging him to challenge her.

She didn't know if this mystery guy honestly cared about her.

Or she was worried because her last boyfriend nearly got her killed.

"Did you meet him at your club? It's here, right? The Hideout?" He wasn't about to tell her he knew damn near everything since he'd had someone watching her for months.

He should have had someone watching her every minute they were apart. Then he would have known how much damage he'd done.

Would he have stayed away? Would he have kept his head down and worked if he'd known how much she was hurting?

He wanted to say no.

She took a deep breath. "It doesn't matter because you don't have any part in my life. I have a job to do. Unless you want to give me some intel, we need to be done here. Is this whole club a front for Cliff Hamilton's drug operation? Has he been using a delivery app to run his drugs and possibly launder his money?"

Fuck. She'd put that together quickly. "I'm going to have you kicked out. I don't expect to see you here again."

She stared at him for a moment, eyes narrowing. This wasn't her tough-chick persona. This was her "I will murder you and bury you on some farmland" persona. "And I'll shout to the top of my lungs your real name as they haul me out. I'll make sure you can't work undercover ever again. You're in my city, Jensen. My family owns a nice chunk of it, and that includes cozy relationships with important people. I can have you kicked out of Dallas. Honestly, I might like to see how you handle getting arrested."

He did not like the fact that his cock hardened when she challenged him. "You wouldn't dare."

"I would, and I know you're sitting there stewing in your own misery because how could the sweet, loving woman you idealized in your head ever do something so terrible to you? How could I do it knowing how much you want revenge for your brother? Because I do not care about you, Jensen. You killed the woman who loved you. She's gone and she's not coming back. If it's a choice between your useless, selfish revenge and my client's life, I'll sell you out in a heartbeat, and don't think I won't."

Who the hell was she here for? Who sent her in?

How was she looking at him like he was nothing to her?

Because you dumped her without warning. Because you picked revenge over her when she would never have done that to you. Not ever. She had the chance to get her client out and stayed to help you.

She would have gone to Mexico and given him cover and done whatever he asked because her love was worth something.

His wasn't.

He was in the wrong and acting like a massive asshole. "Tell me what you need, and I'll get it done. Are you here for one of the subs? They aren't really, you know. They got hired with the promise of big tips and were given almost no training and thrown to the wolves. It's not bad right now because the club is pretty new and mostly tourists and couples. But at some point they'll be expected to serve at a private party."

She nodded. "I remember how it went."

She'd taken a job to get close to her target, and only Jensen coming in and claiming her had saved her from being asked to serve at one of those parties.

"Is it one of the girls?" he asked. He was worried about a couple of them. “Please tell me it’s Miranda because she’s getting moved up, and you know what that means. You already know the truth. Hamilton is coming into town, and he wants to expand into Houston. I need a couple of weeks and this is all over. I’ll help you if you’ll trust me this much.”

“I don’t trust you at all, but it doesn’t matter. After tonight I won’t come back. My partner and I can handle it all from outside the club,” she promised. “Now can I get back to my boyfriend?”

There it was again. That hesitation around the word *boyfriend.*

“I want to meet him,” he said. “We walk out into the lounge. You first, and then I’ll follow. I’m the dungeon monitor so no one will think twice about me introducing myself to the new couple.”

“There’s no need for that,” she replied. “Like I said, we won’t be back. I shouldn’t have brought him in the first place. I should have taken a bodyguard, but they’re all close to my dads. The last thing I need is my father showing up here to make sure I’m safe.” She went pale in the low light. “Or worse. My dad bringing my mom here and going undercover. They might actually do that, and Reasonable Dad would come along. Mom always says she would be good undercover.”

He loved when she talked about her family, when she joked and told stories about how weird they were. They were odd but loving from all the stories she told. “Harlow, I need you to let me help.”

“The last time you helped I woke up in a prison infirmary. I think I’ll deal with it myself.”

He had to find a way to make her see reason. “You know I’m the best shot at getting Hamilton. I realize you don’t like why I’m here, but I can take him down and save a whole bunch of people who’ve fallen into his schemes. I can map out the whole organization. But I can’t if you blow my cover.”

“Getting Hamilton isn’t my job,” she said.

But he knew her. “You want to take him down as much as I do. You can’t stand the thought of all the lives he’s ruined, and if you get the chance, you’ll do anything to bring him to justice.”

“You don’t want justice. You want revenge.”

“What if I was willing to do it your way?” He couldn’t quite believe what he was saying and yet he also couldn’t stop. She was here, and while she was upset as hell with him, there might still be a way to save this. She hadn't walked out. She was still standing here and he wasn't blocking the door.

She was unsure of this "boyfriend" of hers. Did this man even exist? If she wanted to save face with him then he had to consider a scenario where she was lying about not caring about him.

"You've been planning on killing Cliff Hamilton for years. You're not going to give up on it."

He moved closer. Carefully. Like she was a deer he would scare away if he moved too fast. "What if I did? What if I agreed to give you everything I have if you'll let me work with you. What if I decided sending him and everyone he works with to jail was enough?"

Her eyes narrowed. "Why?"

A little closer. She refused to cede space to him, and he could use that stubbornness to his advantage. "Any number of reasons. I've been doing this for years, and I'm sick of it. I want to have some kind of life. Because you're smarter than I am and have way more connections. You're right. My plans only work for revenge. If I kill Hamilton, I cut off the head and another one grows back. If I work with you, we can take down the entire organization and save all those kids he fucked over."

"Again with the why?"

He almost had her. "Because if I prove to you I've changed, you might give me another chance. I know you don't believe me but I left you behind to save you. I thought you were in danger, and I knew I couldn't convince you to leave me."

"It's not going to work, Jensen."

But it kind of was because she'd softened. Her shoulders had come down, and she was looking at him, really looking at him. Now that he was here, this felt right. "I'm willing to take that chance."

Her gaze went sharp. "I'll meet you tomorrow."

"No, you're moving tonight. I know how you work. You made contact and if you aren't planning on coming back it's because you don't have to. You're picking her up tonight. Whoever it is, she'll be in danger."

"I was planning on coming back," she explained. "I even told her I would come back so no one would think we were connected, but seeing you here made me rethink because you won't be able to not give us away."

"So you're not moving her tonight?" He stared at her. She gave him nothing. Which gave him his answer. "Where and when? I will give you everything I have, work with whoever you want me to, if you let me help tonight."

She was quiet for a moment and then her eyes closed and they were hard again when she opened them. "I need you to understand that if you fuck me over this time, I won't quietly go away. If for some reason you decide to get rid of me, my family will come after you."

There was the guilt. How could she think that? He loved her. "I would never. Fuck, baby, this is screwed up. Can we please talk?"

"Not about our relationship," she insisted. "That is off the table and has been for a long time. I need you to understand that if you had showed up at my place, I would have slammed the door in your face. But I do want to take this whole group down, and if you give me information, I don't have to get it from my client. I'm moving her tonight at two this morning."

"After her shift ends." He nodded. He believed that she believed she would shut him down, but he still felt the connection between them. He could fix this. "I can leave early. I'll be at The Hideout when the club closes. That will give me time to get together some information. I'll be your partner in this. We can do this together. There will be fallout from whoever you're extracting, but I can handle it."

"It would be better if I came back with my Dom. It might be weird if I spend time with her and then she disappears."

"Please tell me it's Miranda."

She nodded slightly.

He breathed a sigh of relief. This was one good thing that might come out of it. "Good. She wouldn't survive upstairs. I've been trying to figure out how to get her out of here before they sink their hooks in."

"You could get her arrested," Harlow said with an eye roll.

Brat. "How about we concentrate on getting Hamilton."

She took a long breath and sighed. "Yes. I'll give you the address to the club."

"I know it." He was going to have to confess at some point. "I was curious."

But not tonight. He needed to talk to Niall.

"I'm going to go back to the lounge. My boyfriend's waiting. You better be nice to him. He's the best man I've met in forever. It's one of the reasons I'm agreeing to this plan. I'm worried about him. He's not used to places like this. It's going to be hard on him. He's a good man."

And Jensen wasn't. He got what she was saying. He belonged here. The trouble was here was danger, and Harlow was attracted to it. She couldn't stay away from it. She found it wherever she looked and got tangled in it at all times. She didn't need a good man. She needed a man who could watch her back.

Like you let her watch yours?

"We can talk about it at The Hideout tonight." He would be able to get a measure of this boyfriend of hers. Niall would tell him all about it after they had a talk about why he'd never mentioned the man at all.

She nodded. "I'll be there."

So would her whole family. At least the ones from the club.

He would deal with it.

She turned and opened the door. "Hello, Master."

She shut the door behind her.

It took everything he had not to go after her and introduce himself.

He took a deep breath and forced himself to sit down. He wasn't going to go to the security office and look through the cams. He was going to be a fucking adult, one who damn straight knew he wouldn't have a chance with her if he didn't start to show her some trust.

If he could convince her to ditch her boyfriend and come back to the club with him, they would be stuck together for a while.

He would have to mention seeing her tonight. He would tell Phil he'd had a great conversation with the new girl who came in, and he was going to see if she would like to come back for some one-on-one sessions. Lay the groundwork.

He could make this happen.

He just had to have some faith.

There was a knock on his door, and then Phil was coming in.

"Hey, we need to talk," Phil said, a frown on his face.

Well, there was no time like the present.

* * * *

"You did not have to come with me," Harlow said for the three hundredth time.

Niall let his hands tighten around the steering wheel. "Your guy didn't show."

"He got caught up at the club," she replied. She had explained she had briefly talked to the Dom in Residence, who was an old friend of hers. They knew each other from the lifestyle, and he was worried about what was happening at Decadence. "We're going to talk more tomorrow. I've already got Ruby working on a thorough report on him. It's been a while. I want to know where he's been and what he's been doing."

"But you trust him?" He wished he'd met the guy, but he'd gotten distracted once Harlow went off with Miranda. Phil had talked to him about his time in the lifestyle and what he did for a living. He'd stuck to the story Harlow gave him, but something about the man made him uneasy. And then there was the bartender, who had all kinds of questions. The man named Jack had been intensely interested in Niall's sub and how they met, how long they'd been together.

Then the fucker completely disappeared again when he was going to introduce them so Harlow could get a read on him.

The night had been weird, and now there was a vibe coming from Harlow that made him antsy.

She told him he could go home when they left the club. Oh, she gave him the rundown of what happened with Miranda and what they would do next. She hadn't tried to hide her emotional phone call to Miranda's mom or the sarcastic banter with her contact at the big security firm that was going to help out. But he got the feeling she was hiding something.

Niall carefully turned his Jeep down the road that would lead to Miranda's apartment. They had already delivered Miranda's mother to the McKay-Taggart building, and she was meeting with the bodyguard and going over the details of where they would stay.

Now all they had to do was pick up Miranda and get her back to base. Which was a big building in the middle of downtown with a sarcastic asshole who served as the overlord. Harlow seemed to like the big bastard, though, so Niall wasn't complaining.

He had so many other things to worry about, including the fact that the only reason he thought she hadn't fought him too hard was she didn't have her car. It was back at her place. He picked her up. He got the feeling if Ruby hadn't been lost in her computer, he would have been left behind at The Hideout.

"I'm not letting you…" he began and then stopped, realizing how the rest of his statement was going to be taken.

"You want to finish that sentence?" Harlow had been on edge since she walked out of that man's office.

He was on edge, too, since Jensen had been texting him and he hadn't had a minute without Harlow to call the fucker back. Now he wanted to talk? Jensen ignored him all evening and now he was blowing up his phone. It was annoying.

"I don't want you out here alone, princess," he replied quietly as he stopped at a red light. "I don't know why, but I have a bad feeling. I didn't like Phil, and that bartender was way too interested in you. He didn't even meet you. He didn't even show up until you were with Miranda, so I don't know when he saw you. But he obviously did, and I think that one could get aggressive."

For all his twangy cowboy charm, there had been a ruthlessness to the man he hadn't liked. And they'd only talked for ten minutes.

"The hair does it for some guys. I wouldn't worry about him. He was probably told by the manager to get info on the new couple." She reached over and put a hand on his. "Niall, what you're feeling is nerves, and it's normal. You were in a dangerous place tonight. This is not the kind of lifestyle you're used to. You like some peace, and I don't give a lot of peace. It's something to think about."

He didn't like the sound of that. "I don't need to think about it. I need to get back into practice. I wasn't always a mild-mannered gym owner."

"I know." Her voice had taken on a soothing tone. "You've been stuck in potential violence all of your life. First with your dad and later in the Army, and you found some peace and then I come in."

He turned to look at her. "Where is this coming from?"

She shifted in her seat. "I kind of got a visit from an old ghost tonight. The guy at the club. I told you we've worked together before. I guess that's part of it, but I was thinking about why this isn't working before I saw him again."

"What's not working?" She'd been perfectly happy all day. They worked out together, had lunch, prepped for the club, and she'd seemed content. Even excited. Then she'd walked off with Miranda and come back a totally different person.

"You and me." She sighed. "Niall, you don't want me physically, and that's okay. We can be friends. We can have a great relationship, and you don't have to pretend. I'm not sure why you focused on me, but I'm glad you did because I like you. It can be scary to be who we are in public, but The Hideout is a safe place. You can be exactly who you are there."

He was confused. "I know it is. It's why I feel comfortable there. I found myself at that club. Harlow, why would you think I don't want you physically? I assure you I want you. I've slept with you every night this week."

"You've slept beside me," she corrected. "You haven't slept with me."

He should have known this was coming. He'd felt her dissatisfaction. Even when he gave her an orgasm, she wasn't completely happy because she wanted more. "I've touched you every single night. As often as I can. You have to be able to feel how much I want you."

"I know that is a biological reaction that a lot of men can't help when they're in a sexual situation." She turned back to the windshield. "The apartment building is right up ahead. It's the two story. We should talk about this tomorrow. We'll pick up Miranda and you can take us back to the MT office and we can meet up for breakfast in the morning. I promise this is the last time I ask you to be involved in my business. It was too much."

He pulled the car over. "What is going on? Did I do something wrong tonight? I know I came looking for you, but you had been gone for a long time. I was worried. I can't not be worried about you. I knew the bathroom was back there. If anyone asked, I was going to the bathroom. I thought it through."

"It's not about that. You did a great job," she said, putting a hand on his. "You really did, but it's obvious it bothers you, and I don't think what you're getting out of this experiment of ours is worth the discomfort."

"I'm getting plenty out of this relationship." He was starting to feel like they were seriously miscommunicating. "I'm exactly where I want to be, and I don't want you to stop asking me to help." He felt a nasty pit open in his gut. She'd seen an old friend tonight. A guy she knew from the lifestyle. How close had they been? He only knew about her relationship with Jensen, but of course she'd had boyfriends before him. "Is it because of the guy from the club? You never told me his name."

"Because he doesn't matter beyond this case," she assured him.

It wasn't working. "Well, it feels like you saw him again a couple of hours ago and you're breaking up with me."

"We haven't exactly been together long enough to break up. And I assure you it has nothing to do with any other man. You're the only man I've been interested in for years. Not since Jensen Wiley, and I wouldn't go back to him for all the money in the world." She sighed. "I've been willing to have sex with you for days now. You don't want me."

He groaned. He should have known this wouldn't last long. "I do want you. I want you so much I can barely see straight." He chuckled as he realized what she was thinking. "I am hetero, princess. I'm not hiding anything about my sexuality, and I'm not using you as cover. I promise I would feel incredibly comfortable being gay at The Hideout."

"Then I don't understand," she admitted.

Well, he couldn't tell her the whole truth. *Hey, baby. You know the last guy who fucked you over? He's my best friend and I've been stalking you for him so you maybe stayed pure and virginal until he murders a mobster and comes back for you. But I fell for you and will probably be the next person Jensen Wiley wants revenge on.* Nope. He needed a much simpler explanation. And it wasn't totally a lie. "I want the first time we make love to be special."

Her eyes narrowed, and he could feel her suspicion. "Special?"

"All right." He couldn't do this here. She needed to be focused. He knew this was the simple part of her mission, but she still needed her head in the game. "You're right. We'll talk about this in the morning. Should I find a better place to park?"

"We're fine here. I told her to meet us out front. She should be out in a couple of minutes." She stared at him for a moment. "You're not telling me something."

Well, no one said she wasn't smart. "We'll talk about it tomorrow morning. I'll tell you everything, but you should know it doesn't change the way I feel about you. I have some things in my past we need to discuss, and I haven't felt right sleeping with you when you don't know everything."

Her jaw went tight, and all that sweet acceptance was gone. "You've been lying to me."

And this was why he wished he never had to have this conversation. He wished he'd met her in an organic way, without Jensen between them. Just hearing her say Jensen's name made him anxious.

"Not lying, exactly, but I haven't told you the whole truth," he hedged. He wished he had more time. "You don't know everything about my time in the military."

She didn't know why he'd gone into the military. Not fully. It had certainly been about money, but mostly about the deep and abiding brotherhood he formed with Jensen Wiley.

She glanced down at her phone, the suspicion fleeing. "I can handle it if you did bad shit in the military. Half my friends are literal spies. And I'm not supposed to talk about that. If I can be friends with Kala Taggart, I assure you I can handle my boyfriend working some black ops in the military. It does explain why this bothers you. I'm sorry about that. I still don't get what could have happened in your military service that means we need therapy before we fuck."

There were times when he adored her put-it-all-out-there personality. This was not one of those times. "Because I'm serious about us. I'm serious about you."

She softened, looking back up at him. "I'm serious about you, too. But we need to figure out the whole sex thing because it's been a long time for me, and I'm ready to get this train moving. She's coming down. I told her exactly where we are."

He took a long breath and looked out the front window. The

street was quiet at this time of night. There was a light right next to the building Miranda lived in. It was a two-story apartment building set back from the street. They were parked at the front of the building, the parking lot behind them. They were in an older part of the city with big trees and houses and not a lot of traffic.

Harlow looked out over the street. “I still think we should keep business and our relationship separate. You didn’t enjoy this evening.”

“Did I have fun checking out an unsafe club and talking to douchebags who are probably criminals? No. Will I do it again because my girlfriend is a private investigator? Of course I will.” If she didn’t murder him after he told her why he was here.

“I don’t think it’s a good idea in this case,” she said quietly, her eyes on the street in front of them. She was obviously waiting for the moment when Miranda appeared. She hadn’t been this tense with the mom, but then the mom hadn’t seemed to be in danger. “I think there’s a lot going on there, and I probably need a partner.”

“I thought I was your partner. And Ruby. You have two partners.”

“You were cover for me tonight. It’s different,” she corrected. “Ruby is absolutely my partner, but I need her on the outside. Also, despite the fact that we make a gorgeous couple, no one believes our ‘we’re together’ act. We’ve tried it a couple of times, and we always get called out. Even at freaking Costco. I tried to put her on my card. They wanted a marriage license.”

He chuckled at the thought of Harlow and Ruby trying to ensure they got cheap bulk coffee and paper for their office. “I still don’t understand why you suddenly don’t want me going back to that club. I overheard you talking to the big guy. You told him you were going back in. Won’t they be confused about why you’re not with your Dom?”

“I’m going to tell them we had a falling out, but I still want to explore the lifestyle,” she explained. “It will be so much easier for people to talk to me.”

“And to hurt you, to take advantage of you. It’s why you wanted me to go with you in the first place.” He didn’t like the thought of her going into that club all by herself. He’d seen the way the men looked at her. It wasn’t a safe place. It wasn’t The Hideout. He also didn't like the thought that she'd been planning this the last few hours.

"Yes," she said with a bright smile. Like he got it and she was pleased.

She was going to give him a heart attack. "Harlow? Come on."

"Okay, but it's kind of what I need to happen. Look, from what I can tell, nothing really bad goes on until they get shipped to the upstairs business, which I have to believe is the one Daisy sort of took out part of. I think an American group was working with a Mexican group, and we only found the ones with cartel connections, leaving a man named Hamilton to continue his work. I need to take this guy down, and the best way to do it is from the inside."

What had she said? "Hamilton?"

The name hit him like a sledgehammer. Cliff Hamilton. The man who killed Tommy Wiley and sent his best friend into hell. Surely she was talking about another Hamilton. There had to be more than one asshole named Hamilton in the world. There was more than one who had been based in LA and moved to Dallas. That happened every day, right?

Because if she wasn't talking about another Hamilton, then who was the man she met tonight? The one she was planning on working with?

The one she knew from before. The one who sent her into a quiet spiral.

"Yeah," she said with a sigh. "He's a dirtbag. Cliff Hamilton. Former thief turned drug dealer. I can't tell you all the shit he's done. I think that's her. Keep the car going. I'll help her get her case in." She was halfway out the door when she stopped. "Crap. I should have known he would show up. Uhm, you're about to meet my asshole ex. Don't worry. He won't jeopardize our mission. He wants Miranda out, too. Don't punch him. He's a dick, but I kind of need him."

Jensen.

Jensen was the ex. Jensen was the one she met tonight right before she started trying to gently break off their relationship. Jensen was the one she was going to work with. Jensen was fucking here?

He watched as a man stepped out of his truck and crossed the street, making a beeline for Harlow. There was no way to mistake the swagger of the man or the broad shoulders. His hair was longer than it had been the last time he'd physically seen him a couple of months before.

Harlow stopped in front of the car, crossing her arms over her chest and saying something to him.

Jensen. There he was. He was talking to Harlow, his hands out in apology. They both looked ghostly in the headlights. Harlow simply shook her head as though she didn't care.

She was going to care. She was going to care a lot when Jensen took one look at him and figured out what had happened between his best friend and the woman of his dreams.

He should have found a way to call him.

Fuck. This was going to go to hell and fast.

He wasn't sure how long he sat there kind of frozen and wondering exactly what to do, but when he finally took a deep breath and started to get out of the car, Miranda came into clear view.

She dropped her suitcase and started running.

And that was when he heard the gunfire.

Chapter Seven

Harlow wished the man didn't look so fucking delicious. Jensen strode over to her, stepping in front of Niall's Jeep.

I'm serious about us. I'm serious about you.

Niall had said the words and they meant everything to her and yet here she was breathless at being so close to an asshole who betrayed her. Maybe Deranged Dad was right and she made bad choices.

"I'm sorry. I got caught up in some crap at the club," Jensen said. "I knew you were picking her up, and I wanted to make sure everything went smoothly."

"You shouldn't have come. You could freak her out," Harlow said, keeping a careful distance between them. The last thing she wanted was her current boyfriend to think she was going to fall back into her old boyfriend's arms. Which she wasn't about to do. No way. No how. "And you should know my boyfriend is here. I expect you to treat him with respect."

His eyes went soft. "Of course. Harlow, I'm not here to wreck your life. I'm here to help."

"You're here for you." And she shouldn't forget that. She didn't buy his whole "I'll give up revenge for justice" speech. It was bullshit meant to get her into a position where she would help him. Where she would spend time with him. She wasn't foolish. The sex had been spectacular.

But it wasn't worth her soul.

She had to keep reminding herself that she had a good man now. She had Niall. She didn't need a gorgeous asshole who could rock her entire world because that was exactly what Jensen Wiley would do. He would drive her crazy with pleasure and then send her into a shame spiral because he wasn't a man who could love her.

"I'm here to get a job done," he said quietly, his big body lit with Niall's headlights. It made him look like some freaking shadow daddy. "I'm tired, Harlow. I want to be done. I want to come home."

She barely managed to not roll her eyes. "Well, I'll try to help you get out of Dallas as soon as possible. I still think you should go back to your truck. Miranda doesn't know you're in the club under false pretenses, does she?"

"I've never told anyone but you," he replied. "You and my best friend are the only people in the world who know where I am."

"I didn't know where you were, Jensen. If I had I would have sent someone else in," she said, slightly irritated at his poor hot-boy expression. "Now get back in your truck and meet me at the McKay-Taggart building. Look up the address on your phone. We both know you can Google."

"I'll explain it to her," Jensen replied. "She doesn't know your boyfriend either, but you brought him along. Why didn't you bring Ruby?"

"Because Ruby is working on something…" She stopped, a frown coming over her face. "How do you know about Ruby?"

Ruby hadn't become her partner until she got home from LA. They'd seen each other at The Hideout, but they hadn't connected until Gabe had put them in a room together and had them do research on a potential Dom. Ruby had done her computer thing and Harlow had followed him, and they figured out he was a sex offender, called the cops, and saved The Hideout a whole lot of trouble.

And became besties and partners in what her dad called a slow dive into hell.

She wasn't sure if that dive was for her or him, and she wasn't about to ask.

But she did want to know how Jensen knew about Ruby.

He frowned her way. “Like you said. I can Google. Did you think I could walk into this city and not look you up? Not figure out what you’re doing?”

“Well, Jensen, I thought you wouldn’t care.” Since he was the one who had left her to rot in a jail prison where they handcuffed her not broken arm to a hospital bed.

“I told you, I didn’t walk away because I don’t care. I did it because I love you.”

Oh, she was not listening to that. Not for a fucking second. She put up a hand. “Don’t say those words to me.”

“They’re true. I get that you have moved on, but I haven’t. I can’t and I don’t think I ever will,” he replied simply like they were talking about the weather and not a relationship she once hoped would end in marriage and kids and white picket fences.

So unlike the passionate man she’d fallen for.

“I’m sorry. I shouldn’t have said that,” he added quietly. “Seeing you again has thrown me off. Let’s talk about Miranda. You got her mom?”

“Her mom is with a bodyguard, and we’re going to move them both to a safe house.” She should at least let him know what she was doing. She’d decided this after long hours of thinking about how much to trust him. “She’s going to tell us everything she can about the organization.”

“I know more,” he replied. “You don’t need Miranda.”

Had he thought about this in any way? “You know if you are the witness for this particular prosecution, you’re going to have to divulge all the criminal crap you’ve done over the course of the last few years. You aren’t a cop. You don’t have immunity.”

He gave her a smirk that she wished wasn’t so sexy. “Bet I can get it. Besides, I haven’t done a ton of criminal crap. I mean some, obviously, or they wouldn’t trust me. The dude they think I offed for them is living in Oregon now. He’ll be happy to testify that I am a completely terrible assassin.”

The risks this man took. It made her ill. “If Hamilton ever finds out…”

“Then I’m dead and you move on with your boyfriend in there,” he shot back. “All I’m saying is I’m your witness. You don’t need Miranda. She can hunker down in the safehouse. Hamilton is supposed to be here soon and then this can all be over."

"Because you intend to murder him."

"Only if I get the chance," Jensen agreed.

"You won't get immunity for that. The prosecutors won't need you. Do you even think?" It made her crazy, and she needed to be calm. She held a hand out, stopping his next argument. "Just go to the MT building and we'll talk there."

Before he could speak, a huff caught her attention and Harlow turned.

Miranda stood with a suitcase in hand, her eyes wide in the moonlight as she looked at Jensen. "Master J."

Shit. This was about to go south. "Miranda, it's not what you think."

But Miranda's suitcase hit the pavement, and she turned and ran.

"You asshole," Harlow hissed under her breath.

"I'll get her." Jensen took off.

And then she heard the sharp report of gunfire. She ducked down, protecting her head with the Jeep. It had come from behind her, and she thought they were firing at Miranda, not her.

Jensen stopped and turned her way. Harlow already had her weapon out. She shook her head. "Go. Protect her."

Jensen growled but did as she asked. He had a SIG in his hand and had to realize that his cover was probably blown.

All because his ass couldn't think straight.

"You okay?" Niall crawled from the side of the Jeep, joining her. "Should I call the cops?"

That was the least of her problems. "Oh, I assure you someone's already called them."

"Do you think they took their shot and they're done?" Niall asked.

She shook her head. "No idea. You need to get out of here. I'm going after Miranda. If this guy knows the neighborhood at all, he'll know there's a series of alleys he can use to cut her off. I think he panicked when she turned to run. Hamilton always was sloppy when it came to shit like this. He probably wanted to bring her in and the asshole he sent to kidnap her panicked when she started to run."

Whoever Hamilton had sent likely thought Miranda saw him

and ran. But Harlow knew this was about Jensen, the asshole idiot who was fucking up all her plans.

"I know this area. We're not far from my gym," Niall said. "I'll pull around to the west side and pick you and Miranda up there. We can try to get to the MT building. I assume we want to avoid the cops if we can."

He was so sexy right now. Calm and cool under pressure. His green eyes were steady on her, and if it wasn't a terrible idea, she would kiss him. Instead, she nodded. "I'll meet you at the end of the alley behind this street. I'm going to go behind the apartment building and through the parking lot. Hopefully Miranda rounds back to there. The street dead-ends two blocks from here. Call Ruby and tell her to monitor what's happening."

"Be careful," he said, and then he eased back around the Jeep.

When she heard the car door close, she took off running for the entry to the apartment building, quickly getting behind the tall bushes. They made excellent cover. As she thought, the night was quiet around her. Either whoever took that shot was gone or they were after Miranda.

Did whoever shot at Miranda know who she was? Was it random? Harlow doubted it, and that meant they were in trouble, especially if they had gotten a good look at Jensen.

As she moved around the building, she had to recognize that she didn't want the asshole dead and would do what she needed to in order to save his dumb ass. Not because she loved him.

Because once she had. Because she wouldn't be able to live with herself if she didn't save him.

She needed more therapy. Was there a therapy that made a person less sensitive? Oh, yeah. That was called dating assholes.

There it was. It was Niall's fault. Niall was such a good man that he was turning her into some whiny, can't-let-a-dude-die chick. She would have to turn in her tough-chick card. She was morally gray, damn it.

Except she wasn't, and she needed to follow her damn instincts.

Which led her to the pool area of the small apartment building. The pool was surrounded by a metal fence meant only to keep dogs and animals out, so she had an excellent view of the parking lot beyond. It looked like there were a couple of walking trails through the complex, likely leading to the park down the street.

It was quiet, but she could hear someone coming from her right. She stopped before turning the corner, listening. There was no sound of sirens. No people coming out of their houses. Perhaps they thought it was a car backfiring since there had only been the one shot. Dumbass hadn't even used a suppressor. She would have a talk with Hamilton about his hiring practices one day. If the asshole survived Jensen.

"You know her?" Miranda asked.

"Yes, I do. We worked together when I was trying to take down the organization in LA," a quiet voice replied. Jensen's voice.

"If you're going to kill me, I would rather you did it quickly," Miranda replied.

She heard a sigh as Jensen led Miranda around the corner. He had a hand on her elbow. "I'm not going to kill you. I'm literally trying to make sure you don't die or get involved in this crap further. I came out here to make sure they didn't pull this. Come on. She won't have taken off."

"I think I recognized one of those guys," Miranda said. "I think he was the bartender."

"Yeah, I think he was the new guy, too. I suppose that's why he disappeared tonight," Jensen was saying.

She pulled out her cell and quickly told Niall to meet them in the parking lot in a couple of minutes. She slid it back into her pocket, not bothering to make sure he replied. He would be there. He wouldn't let her down because he needed revenge on someone who cut him off or something.

That wasn't fair. She took a long breath and forced the thoughts from her mind as Jensen eased around the corner, watching for anyone who might come their way.

"It's me," she said quietly.

Miranda breathed an obvious sigh of relief. "So you do know him."

Harlow glanced to the side and saw nothing before joining them. "He's an old partner of mine. He's been trying to bring this organization down for a long time. We need to get to the parking lot. We're getting a pickup there."

"I need to get my suitcase," Miranda said. "I can't believe I dropped it, but I saw Master J and freaked out. Even though of all the guys at the club, he's the one who scares me the least."

"I need to work on that," Jensen admitted with a grin. Like a gorgeous Doberman who knew he'd done a good job and wanted a freaking treat.

"We'll get you new stuff. Or I'll send someone to get it. We need to move now." She took the lead. "Why would they send someone here?"

"We'll talk about that when we get her to safety," Jensen replied. "I didn't come because I'm a reckless asshole. I came because I thought this might happen. I stayed behind because I overheard a conversation between Phil and one of the security guys. They have the bathroom bugged. I did not know that, Harlow. I swear I've swept for bugs before. I think it has to do with Hamilton coming into town."

A flush went through her system. "Damn it. That was a rookie mistake. So they know I'm not who I say I am. Do they have them in your office?"

She couldn't believe she'd done that. She'd been in a club, and any kind of recording device was forbidden. Force of habit. She should have remembered it wasn't truly a club.

"If there was, they would have already taken me out," he replied, his voice barely a whisper. "Is your boyfriend meeting us? If not, we should make our way back to my truck."

"Like I said, in the parking lot." She had to think this guy had taken his shot and was running since someone would call the cops. "You said this was the bartender?"

She moved them along the edges, but soon they would have to make a run for it. She could see a big vehicle pull into the lot. Niall. He pulled the Jeep around, and though she couldn't see him, she knew he would be looking for her.

"Miranda said she thought she saw the bartender." Jensen took up the place behind Miranda, though it was clear from the look on his face he wasn't happy with it. "That wasn't who Phil sent after her. After they reviewed those tapes, I overheard Phil talk to Dave. He runs security for the upstairs."

"He's scary. He sometimes plays in the club, and he's rough. Phil won't let him play with the clients, so the staff has to…meet his needs," Miranda explained. "I haven't had to do it. You're not allowed to play until you've been there for six months. Training, I guess."

Harlow sent the girl a what-the-hell look. "They need blackmail material on you. That's the errand you were going to run. Then you would have been Dave's new chew toy. What do we know about this bartender?"

"He's new. There wasn't a bunch of staff working tonight," Jensen explained. "I suspect Phil is using this as a way to get the kid on board a lot faster than he normally would. Jack is… Well, Jack is charming. He's pretty much perfect for Phil's purposes."

He sounded like an asshole to her, but she was going with it.

Niall turned his headlights off, letting her see the Jeep.

Damn but he was good. She was going to take back everything she said earlier and beg him to not hold it against her. He might have been a bit jumpy at the club, but he was solid out here in the field. "That's our cue. Jensen, watch our six."

"Jensen?" a deep voice asked. "I thought your name was Jay. Jensen's a dumb name, but then it fits since apparently you think you can betray us and get away with it."

She turned and then tried to step in front of Miranda. The man behind them had a gun in his hand, aimed right at Jensen's head.

"Well, Dave, you should talk to my momma about it," Jensen replied in a crisp tone. "You have to know you're outnumbered. I don't see your friend."

"He's here. In fact, he's right behind you. Hey, lady. Don't you turn around. Lay the gun on the ground or I will start shooting," Dave ordered.

"Is there someone behind me?" Harlow asked in a whisper.

Miranda nodded and sniffled, tears rolling down her cheeks. "It's Jack. He's got a gun, and it's pointed right at your head."

They didn't know about Niall yet. Or didn't realize how close he was. He would watch and call Ruby. Ruby would know what to do.

Call Taggart, who would call her dad, who would call the US Navy to come and save his ridiculous baby girl.

Shit. Maybe it was okay to die here. It looked like a nice place. It was peaceful. There was a beautiful rose bush her dead body could fertilize, and she would never have to listen to the lecture

Chase Dawson would give her. She could spend eternity listening to the pool.

"Hey, I'm serious, bitch," Dave said.

"Sorry. She's considering whether she wants to die or listen to her dad yell at her." Jensen proved he knew her. "Which way we going, babe?"

Asshole. Unfortunately it would traumatize the hell out of Miranda, and then she would leave her and Ruby a terrible Yelp review. *My mom hired this company and I got the co-owners brains on my favorite sweater. Zero stars. Do not recommend.*

She lowered the weapon to the ground and held her hands up. "Okay, let's talk about this. You haven't actually done anything yet, Dave. You can let us go and I'll get my client back to her mom. You'll never see her again."

Dave had dark hair that needed a cut and eyes that were too small for his face. He was roughly six foot and leanly corded with muscle. She might be able to take him. She knew some nasty tricks, but she would have to get close. She wished she could see the asshole behind her.

"You, too, Master J," Dave said with a chuckle. "Put that gun down or we'll kill the women. I'm going to assume you got a thing going with the PI? Yeah, we figured out you're a PI after you talked to that traitor there in the girls' room. You know we have computers, too, Harlow Dawson. It wasn't hard to figure out your name after we knew your occupation."

Shit. Yep, she had fucked this up on every single level. She deserved the lecture. Of course, peace was good, too. That rose bush was looking better and better.

"Stop it," Jensen said, putting the gun down. "You are not going to die and leave me here. Let's go somewhere and talk because in a few minutes the cops are going to be here. I saw someone looking out their window. You're right in the light, Dave. Whoever that was almost certainly saw your gun."

Dave's expression went dark, and his eyes narrowed. "Then I should get my job done. Jack, take out the traitor. I'll take care of Miss Dawson, and then we'll haul Jensen back. He's got some questions to answer."

She heard Jenson curse and then the sound of a ping in the air.

This Jack person wasn't the idiot Dave was. He had a suppressor on his gun. She looked to Miranda, terrified at what she would see.

Miranda's eyes were wide, her mouth open. But she seemed whole.

"What the hell?" Jensen moved to get his gun back in hand.

That was when she realized Dave was the one with a neat hole in his head.

She turned and then she was the one gaping. "Jack?"

Her cousin Jack O'Malley stood there and gave her a wink. "Hey, there, cos. You wrecked a six-month undercover op. Tell that asshole to put the gun down. I'm a fed, Jensen. And I'm damn near thirty years old, so you can stop calling me kid. Though I know I look good for my age. Hell, I look good for all the ages."

"What the fuck, Jack? You couldn't call?" Harlow asked.

And then Jack's eyes narrowed as he watched Jensen. "Damn it, man. I am not joking. Don't do it."

Jensen was moving, an unholy gleam in his eyes. For a moment she thought he was about to try to kill her cousin.

Then she realized there was another man in the scenario.

Niall jogged up, his face pale. "Harlow, are you…"

Jensen stood there looking slightly psychotic. It was stupidly sexy on him. "Niall?"

"You know my boyfriend?" A nasty feeling was taking root in her gut because she already knew the answer to the question.

He held his hands up. "She doesn't know anything, Jensen. Don't fucking blame her."

Jensen attacked her boyfriend, fists flying in both directions.

Jack sighed and moved beside her. "We're going to get a hell of a lecture from your daddy, you know that, right?"

She felt her heart constrict. Well, at least she knew how Jensen was so up to date on her life. And why Niall wouldn't sleep with her. He wasn't interested in her. He was saving her for his friend.

"Yeah," she replied and thought about killing them both.

* * * *

The big blond asshole slapped the top of his desk again, laughter booming from him. "And then he attacked Harlow's new guy, who is his best friend, who's also supposed to be spying on her? In the middle of the murder?"

"Ian." The woman with the strawberry-colored hair shot her husband a glare.

The man who'd been introduced as Ian Taggart simply continued to bust a gut. Not that he had much of one. Jensen would bet the guy was older than he looked, but he kept it tight.

As tight as Jensen wanted to wrap his hands around his former best friend's throat. Until Niall was blue and that poacher was fucking dead.

Niall sat in a chair on the other side of the office looking sullen and only slightly damaged. He had to admit Niall knew how to block a punch.

Harlow wasn't looking at either of them. She'd been silent, and the only reason she'd gotten into the car with them was the cops were coming.

She'd been ready to get into Niall's Jeep. Not Jensen's truck. He could tell himself it was because Niall's vehicle was closer and Miranda started walking for it, but he knew the truth.

She liked Niall. Niall had spent the last several months stealing his woman.

Needless to say Jensen had gotten his ass in that Jeep, too, leaving behind his truck.

Jack had apparently dealt with the cops quickly and shown up here after Harlow had sent Miranda off with her mom and a check for mental health services since she'd witnessed a lot of shit tonight.

"You got to admit it was pretty funny." Jack was the only one who seemed somewhat comfortable with the outcome. "I was thinking the big guy was about to punch me and he went for the new guy."

Taggart grinned. "Did he have the crazy eyes?"

Jack—if that was his real name—nodded. "It's like you always said. You gotta watch out for the crazy eyes."

"I would like to know what's going on with you." Jensen had been quiet for way too long. "You said you were a fed. At least I think you did. It got confusing."

Taggart nodded. "That's what happens when you lose your shit. Tell me, did you see a red mist or just black out in a jealousy-fueled rage?"

If this guy wasn't so important to Harlow… "I had a normal reaction to learning that my best friend in the world was poaching my girl."

"Not your girl," Harlow said as Taggart's wife sat down beside her and handed her a cup of tea. Harlow managed a slight smile. "Thanks, Charlotte. I'm sorry to get you out of bed. It was supposed to be a simple client move."

"Nothing is simple when you've got two men involved, sweetie," Charlotte replied. "If I wasn't worried about how you're getting home, I would have brought out the vodka."

Jack stood by the big floor-to-ceiling windows that overlooked downtown and all its glittering lights. This building was nice, and apparently Taggart owned it. It reminded Jensen of the difference in his and Harlow's circumstances.

But at least that asshole Niall was as poor as he was.

"I'm FBI," Jack said with a sigh.

"Booo," Taggart called out.

Jack's eyes rolled. "Like the Agency is cooler. Anyway, my team has been following a man named Cliff Hamilton for the last several years, but it wasn't until he crossed state lines and started to build his organization in both Texas and Nevada that we got involved. Up until that point California Bureau was handling things. Then a while back that sweet thing from The Hideout busted the op wide open."

"We call her Hurricane Daisy," Taggart explained.

"And that's when you decided to hire on?" Niall asked. "Did you realize your cousin was involved?"

Jack winked Harlow's way. "Not at all. I mean I knew she got tangled up with his group in California. By the way, we got that stupid arrest thing all cleared up for you, darlin'. She's not actually my cousin, you see. Not a bit a blood between us."

He noticed Niall sat up a little taller. So did he. He might have to kick a fed's ass tonight.

"No, but we do have a whole childhood between us," Harlow replied with a frown. "Don't spin him up again."

Jack glanced at Niall and then back to Jensen. "Which one? Because from where I'm sitting I got a rise out of them both."

Harlow took a sip of tea and then set it down, looking to her "cousin." Who damn well was going to stay her cousin. "Jensen was always a jealous ass. Niall has no reason to be jealous since he was a plant meant to keep me pure while his friend was doing his thing."

"His thing being stupid, get-him-killed revenge on the man he blames for his brother's death?" Taggart asked.

She nodded. "Yup, and now I'm worried that you already know that."

Taggart sat back, not replying at all, simply waiting for someone to take the bait Harlow had thrown out.

"If I was trying to keep you so pure, why did I sleep with you the last several nights?" Niall got hooked.

And was about to receive another one of Jensen's left hooks. What had Taggart said about red mist?

Jack looked his way. Not like he was going to stop him this time. Like he was enjoying the show. "Don't like that much, do you?"

He ignored Jack entirely. "I asked you to watch over her not to take her to bed immediately."

"Was it immediately… What was his name again, baby?" Taggart asked.

"Niall," Charlotte supplied.

Niall ignored them, turning to Harlow. "I think we should talk. Alone."

Harlow snorted. "Did Charlotte give you the good vodka? Because that is not happening."

"Is anyone interested in talking about how the events of the night fucked everything up?" Jack asked, sounding exasperated.

"Nah, it's more fun to watch this completely dysfunctional threesome explode," Taggart replied.

Harlow's eyes narrowed. "We are not a threesome."

Harlow came from a threesome. Her fathers shared her mom. He'd thought it was weird at first, but she talked about how loving her family had been. How her dads always had someone to lean on while they were supporting her mom.

"No?" Charlotte asked. "I mean I agree you didn't realize you were in a threesome because these two are not emotionally mature."

"Hey," Niall said, sounding offended.

"That's fair," Jensen agreed because he was pretty self-aware about some things.

"I've been around several of these types of relationships," Charlotte continued. "Let's see if I'm right. At some point in time Jensen fucked up."

"I'm pretty sure he's the reason Harlow got arrested in California," Taggart added. "I didn't know his name until tonight because she wasn't talking, but a quick search revealed much. I have excellent hackers, even if they get mouthy when I wake them up at three in the morning. They get soft once they're married and have kids."

"Excellent. So Jensen fucked up and sends his bestie in to watch over the woman he thinks he loves," Charlotte continued. "Which sounds like a very threesome thing to do."

"No thinking involved. I know who I love," Jensen insisted.

Niall huffed.

"We'll see," Charlotte replied enigmatically before continuing. "So you sent in your best friend and your best friend… What all did you give up in order to take on this assignment, Niall? I'm going to take it you weren't conveniently located here."

"I suspect you know where I was located and what I was doing with my life six months ago, Mrs. Taggart. I moved to Dallas. Opened a business. I was planning on moving anyway. I was working a couple of jobs, saving money to open a gym. I couldn't do that in the small town I grew up in. I probably would have gone to Houston or Austin if I wasn't needed here," Niall admitted.

"Well, you should feel free to get your ass to either one," Jensen shot back.

Then he was hit with the thought of not being in the same town as Niall. He missed the fucker. Not that he was going to let that sway him now that he realized what a woman-stealing asshole he was.

"I did it all because he was my only real friend in the world," Niall continued. "And then I did it because of her."

Taggart sat forward. "When did you know you were going to go behind your friend's back? Was it early on?"

"Ian," Charlotte said with a sigh. "He wasn't planning on never telling Jensen. It's why he didn't actually sleep with her. Did you?"

"I knew pretty much after my first conversation with her," Niall explained.

"You know we don't have to talk about this. Jack, how fucked are we?" Harlow asked in a crisp, professional tone.

Had Niall really not slept with her? Like sleep sleeping was one thing. Fucking was another. He kind of thought from the way Harlow talked that they were all in.

Why would Niall hold back?

"Pretty fucked since Dave had a chance to take some pictures of you and Jensen and send them back to Phil. We were watching the spot where we thought you would pick her up," Jack admitted. "To say he was shocked when Master J showed up would be to downplay the situation. He was practically giddy. You didn't make friends inside, did you?"

"Did I make friends with the criminals who killed my brother? No." Jensen wasn't sure why he felt judged. "Why the hell would I?"

"Well, I've found when going undercover, it's always helpful to kind of blend into the crowd, so to speak," Jack offered. "Maybe then Dave wouldn't have been so quick to text Phil his golden boy was a traitor. Before you ask, I checked his phone. Phil got the texts, and he's already put out a hit on Jensen and would like to spend some time with Harlow."

"I didn't, Mr. Taggart." Niall was back to the previous conversation. The one Harlow didn't want to have. "I will admit to some intimacy with her, but I couldn't sleep with her until she knew the whole truth and I talked to Jensen."

Harlow kept her eyes on Jack. "So did we blow your cover all to hell?"

"As far as Phil knows, right now I was brought in for questioning by the Dallas PD," Jack informed them. "The official story is I was looking for you on the other side of the apartment building and when I heard the shots, I found Dave dead on the ground. I'm in trouble for letting the cops get involved, but I think I can go back to work."

"What were you planning on talking to Jensen about?" Charlotte asked.

"You were going to tell him to fuck off, the girl's yours now, right?" Taggart prompted.

"You two are the worst," Harlow said with a huff. "I totally understand why Kala is…Kala."

"I was going to tell him that she needs us both and we should gently maneuver her into a relationship where we share her," Niall replied.

Charlotte shot her husband a grin. "You owe me ten back rubs."

Taggart growled. "I do not understand this perverse need to share."

Harlow stood up. "That is never happening. Jack, I'm sorry we caused so much trouble. I promise I'll stay out of your way from now on. As for these two, they can do whatever they like. It's not my problem." She started for the door and stopped as though remembering something. She turned on Niall. "Unless what you want to do is continue to play at The Hideout. You're kicked out."

Niall stood, too, his shoulders straightening and a stubborn look coming on his face. "You can't kick me out."

He wanted to share Harlow?

Niall hadn't slept with her when he could have, when he obviously wanted to because he wanted to share her with him.

For a moment he had a vision of her in between them. She was always so fierce, but she would be small between them.

The pleasure they could give her…

"Oh, I can," Harlow shot back. "You came in under false pretenses. You joined the club to spy on me, and there's no spying at The Hideout."

Taggart snorted.

Harlow frowned his way. "You know what I mean. No spying on actual members of the club. Now I'm leaving."

There was the sound of a knock on the door and then it opened.

"Ian, I told you she was only allowed to do this foolish job if you were watching over her," a big man said. He was dressed in slacks and a button down he'd obviously put on hastily since it wasn't tucked in and one button was off. His dark hair was messy, and he looked to be around Taggart's well-kept age.

And there was a second one of him entering the door. This version of the man wore jeans and a T-shirt. "Chase, we talked about this."

Fuck. Harlow's dads were here.

"You know talking to him means nothing, Ben," a pretty woman said. She had Harlow's eyes but was petite and had streaks of pink in her hair.

Her mom.

Harlow stood still like she couldn't quite believe this was happening.

It was possibly going to be the worst family reunion ever.

Chapter Eight

Harlow wished the ground would open up and swallow her whole.

Or sometimes this building got raided by… She wasn't sure who, but she'd heard stories. Maybe some rival CIA team would come in and kill them all and then she could rest in some peace because she would get none right now.

Deranged Dad pointed Taggart's way. "You are supposed to monitor her."

Taggart sat back, tossing her dad a quizzical look. "You know she's an adult, right? She has all the papers and everything."

"Look, Ian, you might let your girls run around the world blowing shit up, but I run a tighter household," her dad shot back.

"He does not," her mom said, sounding slightly exasperated. She moved into Harlow's space. "You okay, baby?"

She loved her mom. So fucking much. Her mom had been through hell and still stood there with all the love in the world to give and all she really wanted to do was burst into tears and tell her mom everything.

But Deranged Dad was here.

"I'm fine," Harlow told her with a tight smile.

"Even if I were to agree that a tight ship was being run in your household, can we both acknowledge that Harlow no longer lives in that household?" Ian sounded so reasonable. It must be nice.

"Because she's a twenty-six-year-old woman and not a wayward teenager?"

"I believe I made all of these points," Papa said, throwing her a sympathetic look. "I'm sorry, sweetheart. He's been on edge ever since the whole incident with Liam's daughter. When we got the call, he pretty much lost his shit. I would have texted and asked if you needed anything."

"Are you kidding me? She's involved in some kind of drug ring and you're perfectly fine with that?" Deranged Dad was in a full-on panic.

"She's doing a job," Papa countered. "Like we do from time to time. You know happy places and people rarely need to be investigated."

"Well, she's not exactly involved with the drug ring," Ian pointed out. "It's more like she's trying to take them down." Her mentor gave her a thumbs-up. "You're doing great, Harlow. You take 'em down. Only thing you did wrong this time was having these dumbass men around. What did I teach you?"

"Keep sex to the club and the bedroom and don't take dumbasses into the field with me. That means men or women or anyone in between. You were clear that sexual fluidity did not dismiss dumbassery. Yes. I should have remembered that." Sometimes she wondered how her life would have gone if Ian Taggart had been her father. Oh, she would have fought her way through childhood because they were a feral clan, but she might have fit in better. And maybe she would have listened and not tried to take her boyfriend out into the field with her.

Not her boyfriend. Nope. The plant Jensen left behind. She felt like such an idiot.

Her dad's gaze sharpened, and his head swiveled like a predator scenting prey. As though he had just realized there were two other people in the room he could blame for his precious baby's bad choices. Not that he had mistakenly ignored them. Oh, no. The great Chase Dawson would have walked in, taken a single glance, and been able to describe what they looked like, were wearing, and probably be able to discern their chosen professions from clues.

It was hard being the daughter of a genius.

Chase Dawson was one of the world's premiere investigators.

When governments needed a Hercule Poirot, they called her dad. When a murder needed to be solved and quickly, cops had her dad on speed dial.

Niall stood up. Because he obviously had no instinct for self-preservation. He actually held out a hand. "Hello, Mr. Dawson. I'm Niall Griffen."

"Neil?" Dad asked, that judgmental brow of his rising.

"Nope," Ian replied. "It's some weird Irish thing. And the other dude is named Jensen. Like who names their freaking kid Jensen?"

Jensen shrugged, obviously unbothered. "My mom liked *Supernatural* but she had an old boyfriend named Jared, so I got Jensen. I think Niall's mom read a lot of historical romance. It's spelled weird, too. I told him he should go by Neil."

Niall huffed. "Not my name."

Dad turned on her. "I taught you not to date assholes with douchebag names."

She nodded. "And yet you named me Harlow and my sister Greer."

He was good with everything except irony.

Her dad's head shook. "I wanted to name you Mary and Elizabeth. Solid girl names. Your mother has an old-school Hollywood fetish, and since she pushed you and your sister out of her hoo-ha, she got first dibs. And you know we should talk about it. If you were named Mary, perhaps you wouldn't be lost in your own damn noir film."

He could get lost in his own arguments. Honestly, they could go at it for hours, she and her dad. Once they argued for half a day over the validity of the *Star Wars* prequels.

It had been fun.

When had it stopped being fun? Probably around the time he had to pick her up in another state and bail her out and see her in a cast, broken and bruised. He was overly protective before, but then he'd gone into hyperdrive.

"So, you're Chase." Niall seemed to realize he wasn't getting anywhere with the most paranoid of her dads. He turned to her papa. "You must be Ben Dawson. Again, I'm Niall Griffen. I've been seeing your daughter."

Papa shook his hand and gave him a once-over. "It's good to

meet you. How do you and Harlow know each other?"

Dad stood back and rolled his blue eyes. His arms crossed over his chest as he considered Niall. "They met at The Hideout, of course. I suspect she's been playing with him."

Ian sat back. "Oh, he's going to do that thing, baby. I love it when he does this."

That thing was giving a preternaturally accurate rundown of people he recently met.

She should have let Dave murder her. She blamed Jack.

"Does what?" Niall asked, sounding hesitant for the first time.

She could do a little of it, too. She could read Niall in that moment. He was the good guy, the one all parents loved. He was the clean-cut ex-soldier who held doors open and helped old ladies cross the road. He was used to charming moms and laughing with dads. It was disconcerting to him that first Ian paid him no mind at all, and now her dad was looking at him like a bug he was getting ready to pin to his collection board.

Of course she also hadn't figured out he was there to spy on her, so she couldn't be too good at this.

"You're from West Texas but not more than a couple of hours out of Fort Worth. One of the ranching towns between here and Amarillo," her dad began. "You recently moved to town. Likely within the last year. You do manual labo…or you work out a lot." He was carefully watching Niall for any tics as he spoke. Her father was a master at reading micro expressions. He'd taught her humans give themselves away in far more fashions than lying. "You're a personal trainer. Ah, you own a gym. Good luck with that, buddy. You're former military police. Is there a reason you didn't become a cop?"

Niall shot her a surprised look. "Is your dad psychic?"

"He's just really good at reading people," she replied with a yawn because her dad could do this for hours, and it was getting late.

"He knows the MP part from the tat on his arm," Papa replied. "It's not that hard. And it's a good bet that he already knew about you seeing him at The Hideout. He listens in when your sister and Chloe gossip. He's the gossipiest old man I know."

"Hey," Ian argued. "I have that T-shirt, too."

Charlotte waved her husband off. "He prints them himself. Pay him no mind. I want to see what else Chase can figure out."

"Well, I figured out you pissed off my daughter. What did you do to her?" His gaze shifted to Jensen. "You are harder to read. You're friends. You were in the military together, but you had your tat removed."

Jensen's hand went to his bicep. "You can't see that."

"I can see it's a slightly different color. It's been a while since you took it off. Were you ashamed of your service?" Dad asked, his eyes narrow.

Jensen's head shook. "Of course not."

"You have another tat, so it's not that you suddenly didn't like tattoos. You wanted to hide your military service," her father surmised.

Shit. He was going to figure it all out.

Jensen frowned her father's way. "I'm not sure that's your business, sir."

"You tell him, Jensen," her mom encouraged and then shrugged her dad's way. "You can be an intellectual bully about this. And it's obvious Harlow is involved with both of them, so you might want to back off and give everyone some room before you start a fight."

But her dad was merely getting started. "You the one who gave Niall there that shiner?"

"I don't have a shiner," Niall argued.

"You'll have some bruising," her papa agreed with Dad. "Maybe not a full-on black eye, but you got clocked at some point in the last couple of hours."

Jack had taken a seat next to Charlotte and looked perfectly happy hanging out and watching her ruination.

"And *Supernatural* here has some bruising on his knuckles. You taking out bad guys or your friend here?" Dad asked, gaze sharpening. "You were fighting over my daughter?"

This was torture. "I started dating Niall a couple of days ago. Jensen is someone I dated a long time ago. It's that simple. I didn't know they knew each other."

"Uncle Chase, things got heated and confusing out there tonight." Jack jumped in to save her. Finally. The amount of times she'd covered for his ass… "It was a big brawl, and you know it can be hard to tell who the bad guys are in the midst of it. I think they were both trying to protect Harlow and found themselves at cross purposes."

Oh, it had been super clear, and she was glad she'd already gotten Miranda off to the safe house. Jensen and Niall knew better than to argue, but Miranda might have pointed out that Dave got the jump on them, and there wasn't a lot of fight to be had.

Jack really had saved the day.

Her dad looked like he wanted to argue, but he had a new target. He turned on Jack, pointing his way. "And you knew. You knew she was involved and you didn't bother to call anyone?"

Jack shrugged. "I was real busy trying to make sure she didn't get a look at me and give up my entire cover. They tend to know something's wrong when the new girl walks in and starts asking about my family. I wasn't supposed to have one of those since Hamilton likes his drug mules unattached or at least separated from family. I went in as the down-on-his-luck recent grad who happened to know a bit about bartending and has no one in the world to count on."

"She would never do that." Dad sounded offended on her part. "She would not walk up to you in an obvious undercover situation. Harlow knows what you do."

She was confused, but then Chase Dawson often confused her. "Which am I, Dad? Am I an incompetent girl or a professional who should be respected?"

Her dad ignored her, sending a nasty look Jack's way. "You should have called the minute you knew she was in danger. I'm talking to your dads. I'm calling Aidan."

Jack shrugged, looking around like someone could explain it to him. "Again, almost thirty, and my folks are well aware of what I do and what Harlow does. Have you considered therapy, Uncle Chase?"

"He's on all the therapists' no-go lists," Papa replied. "Therapists who see him usually need therapy."

Her mom took her hand. "Baby, are you okay? What happened tonight?"

While Jack and Ian continued to argue with her dad, she turned to Papa and her mom. "Everything was great until I went to pick up my client. I failed to realize the bathroom was wired for sound because we were in a lifestyle club, so I let my guard down and nearly got my client and myself killed."

She didn't want to admit why.

She wanted to run. That was what she wanted to do. She didn't want to consider those words Niall had said.

I was going to tell him that she needs us both and we should gently maneuver her into a relationship where we share her.

That wasn't happening.

She wasn't thinking about how it would feel to be in between them. She'd been in a family where that was the norm all of her life, but she'd never actually thought about trying it. Probably because she had never met two guys she wanted at the same time.

"But you're okay?" Papa asked.

She nodded. "Because of Jack. He was willing to give up his cover to save us, so if you could get Dad off his back, that would be great."

"I get the feeling there's a whole lot of story to those other two, though," her mom said as Jack started to argue with her dad.

"I'm going to get some coffee." Harlow stalked out and moved toward the break room. She knew this building well since she'd trained here. She learned a lot here. If only she'd learned not to have feelings for assholes.

Her mom followed behind her and she heard her mom telling her papa to give them some space.

She took a deep breath when she made it to the break room and wondered where Charlotte kept that vodka she talked about earlier.

"Sweetie, I'm sorry, but you have to know we're worried about you. I know you're competent," her mom began.

Harlow huffed out an unamused laugh. "Oh, I assure you I wasn't tonight. I was everything Dad has always been worried I would be. I was reckless and dumb and a complete fool."

Her mom's eyes had gone wide. "So those men didn't simply get caught up in your case. They're why you were reckless."

She took a long breath and turned, leaning against the sink. "The case was supposed to be simple. I was contacted by Miranda's mom, who like Jack mentioned, she was estranged from. He's right about that. Hamilton likes to bring in people with pressure points and no one to turn to. I realized this was connected to what happened with Daisy O'Donnell about halfway through. The police busted it up, but they only got part of the organization, the part that was the easiest to put a finger on and say this is criminal."

Her mother frowned. "Hamilton is the man you were investigating in LA." Her arms crossed over her chest and Harlow was reminded that her mom might not be an investigator by profession, but she was still a smart cookie. "So Jensen worked that case with you. You had no idea he was in Dallas now. Is he a fed, too?"

At least she wouldn't have to explain it to her dads. "No. He's a civvie. His brother got caught up in Hamilton's web a few years ago. He died. I wish I could believe Jensen is in this to pull down the whole organization, but I think he's biding his time, working his way up so he can kill Hamilton himself."

"He's the reason you cried for a month after you came home," her mom surmised. "Is he the reason you were in jail? I never understood that. You're smart. You would have gotten out if you could. He blindsided you. Did he know it was coming or did he just save himself?"

Damn. Her mom had learned a lot from her dads. She might be an artist, but she listened and knew people. "He claims he did it because it was getting too hot. He was scared I would get hurt. We were getting to a point in the investigation where I was going to be asked to do something that would give them power over me. It was something I had been working toward since the girl I was trying to get out was at that level, and I couldn't get to her unless I was the same."

Her mom paled. "I don't know that I wanted to hear that."

"Please, not you, too."

Her mom shook her head. "No, baby. This is beyond what a PI does. I should know. Your dads have solved plenty of cases, and they've gone undercover for many of them. They go undercover to get information. It's short term. They do not allow themselves to do criminal shit to get a case done. There's no immunity for you. You're not a cop. Jack has a whole department to advise and watch out for him. You have Ruby."

She took a long breath because what her mother was saying wasn't wrong. "I know. I got caught up. Mom, I loved him. I wanted to marry him. I was ready to help him, and I used the excuse of work to convince myself it was okay. I meant to go in and find her if I could and report back to her mother. That was literally all I was going to do. It was one of my first cases, and I hadn't even brought Ruby in so it was supposed to be simple."

"But you met him," her mom said.

"It wasn't just him." She shouldn't tell her mom this, but somehow she couldn't let her think it was all about a boy. It had always been more. "She was caught. They wouldn't let her call her mom or have access to the outside world. I didn't know what was happening to her, and I couldn't stand the thought of leaving her there. I did go to the cops. So did Jensen. They didn't believe anything was wrong. I…I couldn't leave her there."

Tears shone in her mother's eyes. "Because of what happened to me."

She didn't make it a question. She knew. Her mom had been open about what happened to her when she was young. Not when they were kids, of course, but once it was clear both her daughters were interested in the lifestyle, she'd told her tale. Natalie Dawson had once been a curious young woman, having fun and exploring her sexuality, and she'd been kidnapped and raped and forced into a perverted version of the lifestyle she loved. Her mother had saved herself and her Aunt Kate, but Harlow knew there were women who couldn't save themselves. Aunt Kate had been sitting by her mom when she told her tale, had brought her own daughter to listen and learn. She could still remember how her aunt had leaned on her mom, squeezing her arm and lending her strength.

Not everyone got those friends who became family, who would do whatever it took to get you through.

Her mom cupped her face in her hands. "Baby girl, I know you want to be the person who saves everyone, but you have to be careful. You have to remember how important you are, how deeply loved you are, and what a hole you would leave in everyone's lives if you died. Your dad is obnoxious, but it's because he loves you so much, and sometimes being a dad is hard on him. He never thought he would be one. Or rather I think he thought it wouldn't mean so much to him."

She knew her dads and their uniqueness. "You mean he thought

Papa would handle everything, and he could pat our heads and please you by being somewhat present while he did his thing."

Her dad was way on the spectrum, but then she'd learned a lot of people were. Once she got past the word *normal*, she found a whole world of freaky, cool people. And her dads. If she put them together, they would be a whole person. They shared a womb and a face, and sometimes she believed her mom when she told her they shared a soul. According to her mother, it was like that with some twins, and her dad had come out with crazy skills of perception and off-the-charts intelligence and no social niceties whatsoever.

And yet he'd figured out how to love her mom and her and Greer. Her father had extreme anxiety issues, but he loved them.

"He got caught in a trap of his own making," her mom said with a wistful smile. "He thought he could hold himself back, but instead he found a part of himself he didn't know existed, that he thought entirely rested in his brother. He loves you and he recognizes so much of himself in you. Including the arrogance and recklessness."

"I am not arrogant," Harlow protested.

Her mom's brows rose. "You are arrogant and reckless and way too hard on yourself. Baby, I love you. So much more than you can possibly know at this point, but what you did today was dangerous. If you want to be a cop, talk to Jack. I would bet he could get you into an FBI training class quickly."

"I don't want to be a cop." She sighed. "I like investigating. I know it sounds dumb, but I like catching cheating assholes and making things easier for people to get out of a bad situation. I like finding people who've been lost. But I do need to recognize when I'm over my head and need to call in law enforcement. I worry my clients will get left behind."

"What happened to the girl in LA?" her mom asked. "I know you came home and didn't go back."

"Jensen got her out," Harlow replied. "It took him a week. I was planning on finding a way back in but he worked more quickly than I healed. I'm pretty sure he burned those bridges for me, but I would have tried."

Her mom nodded like she'd expected that answer. "So he was worried about you."

"He nearly got me killed," she pointed out.

"Do you believe he thought that would happen? Or did he panic and do what he could to get you out?"

Her mom was being way too reasonable. "He could have asked me to leave. We could have had a discussion."

Her mom snorted. "Yeah, because that would have gone so well. Look, I am not defending him. He hurt you, and at some point in time your dad is going to figure out who he is and he'll lose his shit. But I can also understand wanting to protect the person you love and not quite knowing how to do it. Sometimes the men we love don't know how to communicate, which is when it's helpful to have a more reasonable twin hanging around. Or a friend."

Her mother was not suggesting… "Niall lied to me. He was literally sent by Jensen to spy on me."

"To spy or to watch out for you?"

She wasn't doing this. "Spy."

Her mom shrugged. "There's more than one way to look at things, and I say that because I watched how both of those men looked at you. And you wouldn't be so upset if you didn't care about them both. How long have you been seeing Niall?"

"A couple of days, but I'll be honest I was attracted to him the minute I met him. It was only being burned by his best friend that kept me away. But Mom, he doesn't want me. He hasn't slept with me, and I offered. He was there to make sure I didn't sleep with anyone else."

"Okay, if that's true then they're both assholes and you should walk away," her mother mused. "But you should make sure because if it's not, then you have two men who care about you. One who seems reasonable and easy to communicate with and the other who brings out a passionate side of you. Most people can make one or the other work, but have you considered the fact that you might need both?"

"No, Mom. I have not considered sleeping with the two men who betrayed me," she shot back.

The door came open and Charlotte Taggart poked her head in. "Sweetie, I think your dad is about to explode and maybe take those guys of yours with him."

She gave Charlotte a thumbs-up. "Tell Ian I'll help clean his office and I know some places to hide the bodies."

Her mom sighed. "We'll be right there."

"Yeah, I'm also going to warn you that Ruby called in and she's found a hit on the Dark Web on you and Jensen, so Jack was right," Charlotte said. "Jensen's cover is blown and you're both in danger. Your dad is already talking about moving you home and putting a detail on you."

Shit. She started down the hallway, hoping she wasn't about to get kidnapped by her own parents.

* * * *

Harlow had the weirdest family ever. From the playboy undercover fed, to the big blond definitely ex-Special Forces guy who mostly laughed at everything, to the twin dads, one of whom was like a really pissed-off Sherlock Holmes, these dudes ran the gamut of interesting.

Niall liked it. He wanted in. He could be the quiet one who sat in the back with the twin who wasn't raging and eat chips and drink beer and watch the whole show.

Not that he had an in since Harlow wouldn't look at him. Now she was gone and he and Jensen were sitting here wondering where she went and if she was coming back.

"She's already got one arrest," Harlow's dad was saying.

"One?" Big Blond Guy waved that off. "I can't tell you how many times I've been chucked in jail. The security business is not for the faint of heart, Dawson."

Niall moved to sit beside Jensen, who gave him a deadly look and then turned away.

"Come on. Do you think you can take this crew on alone?" Niall asked quietly.

"I wasn't going to let her get arrested," Jack was arguing. "Why do you think I dealt with the cops? Who I hope are not on Hamilton's payroll or it's going to be a shame to the ladies everywhere that I'm about to die."

Jensen leaned over, whispering. "I'm not taking on anyone. I'm staying because I need to talk to Harlow, you massive fucking ass."

"I'm not going to apologize for falling for her. You sent me in to make sure she was okay. You were worried she was in the same city

Hamilton was attempting to build a base in, and you wanted someone watching over her. Or is she right and you wanted me to make sure she remained virginal and pure so she didn't fuck around while you were off doing what you needed to do?" He wasn't letting Jensen off the hook. He knew he should have talked to him, but it wasn't like Jensen was easy to get hold of these days.

Jensen seemed to stop, the words making him think. Sometimes his best friend had to take a punch to the gut to figure out what he was doing. "I wanted to make sure she was okay."

"So I wasn't supposed to keep all the men off her?"

Jensen sat up, a frown on his face. "Well, I didn't think you would be one of them."

Niall had been considering this all damn night. "Because I wouldn't fall for the gorgeous, smart, funny, tough chick? How many times, man? How many times did we go out to a bar and hit on the same woman? How many times did we argue over who got to go after her?"

Jensen sighed and sat back as the phone rang and the blond guy picked it up while Harlow's other dad was trying to talk Sherlock down. "A lot. I should have known, but I thought you would at least talk to me about it. I guess in some ways, I knew you would care about her. I guess I was counting on it."

But he hadn't been counting on Niall acting on his inevitable attraction. "I did not sleep with her for two reasons, and neither of them were I didn't want her. I couldn't without telling her the truth, and I wanted to talk to you. We have been friends for more than half my life. When you wanted to go into the military, I went with you. When Tommy died and you needed to leave, I gave it up. I would have gone to LA with you."

"It was a one-man job," Jensen said tightly. "I didn't… I couldn't risk you. Like I couldn't risk her."

He'd known it at the time and been forced to honor the decision, and Jensen couldn't possibly know how alone that had left him. Back in their shitty small town without the Wiley brothers. He'd mourned Tommy, too. "All I'm saying is I've never let you down before. Not even once. The truth is if you make me choose between you and Harlow, she's going to win."

Now Jensen's asshole smirk came out. "Back at ya, buddy. And after tonight I don't think she's going to choose you."

"Oh, you think she's running back into your arms?" Something was going on in the background. The big guy was pacing and Harlow's dads were arguing, but Niall was focused. "After what you did? You know she's been healing from that for a long time."

"I know the minute I offered to work with her, she was putting you back on the shelf. She agreed to dump your ass and come back into the club where we were going to make a connection the employees would find believable. She was going to be my acknowledged sub by the end of the week." Jensen studied him carefully. "Yeah, there it is. She talked to you, didn't she?"

He wasn't particularly good at hiding his emotions. Oh, he could, but he never had to with his best friend. A knot formed in his gut. It had been after the meeting with Jensen that she'd talked about how they could just be friends. He'd thought it was about her feeling insecure because they hadn't slept together, but what if there was another reason?

"She loves me. I can fix this," Jensen said with confidence.

"Or you can fuck her up more," Niall shot back. "I can't believe you were going to take her back in."

"Well, it's take her back in or watch her blow everything up," Jensen replied. "With you sitting there. What the hell were you thinking?"

"I was thinking she had a job to do. You never bothered to tell me what club you were working at. You didn't even mention it was a lifestyle club. I thought you were a bouncer at a nightclub or something. Is she not supposed to work? Am I not supposed to back her up? You know I was actually doing exactly what you sent me in to do."

"I did not send you in to fuck her," Jensen snarled.

"No, you wanted her alone and miserable so you could hopefully manipulate her back into a relationship with you. Tell me something, Jensen. What happens to her if this mission of yours kills you? Should I make sure she's alone so she can enter the afterlife pure for you? Same question, but this time you're in jail."

Jensen went a faint shade of pink. "I wasn't planning on doing either."

"You chose your revenge over her once. Why should I believe

you would do anything differently now?"

Jensen's jaw went tight. "I might not have a fucking choice."

"But you're already thinking about how to get back in. So do it and I'll take care of her." It was time to start laying some groundwork because the truth was no matter how pissed he was with Jensen right now, he still wanted this chance. "Or you can accept that Jack and the FBI have this and start giving Harlow what she needs."

Jensen was quiet for a moment. "You would walk away so easily?"

"I'm not walking away at all. I think she needs both of us." There it was. Everything he'd been working through in his brain for the last few months. He knew she loved Jensen, but she cared about him, too. At least he thought she did. He could show her what he had to offer. Jensen might be the big, attractive, over-the-top heroic guy, but he would probably forget her coffee in the morning and also forget that he could get arrested at any moment. Niall could be there, the steady presence in both of their lives.

They needed each other.

Jensen stared for a moment and then opened his mouth to say something, but whatever he had to say was stopped by Dad Number 1 reaching for his throat.

"You little shit," Chase Dawson was saying. "You're the one. You're the reason my daughter nearly got killed in California."

So he'd worked that out. Well, it had only been a matter of time. "Jensen, remember he's her dad."

Jensen stood, facing off with Chase Dawson, who was roughly the same height but leaner in build. "Mr. Dawson, I did what I needed to do to save Harlow. We were undercover, but things were about to get seriously dangerous. So I made the call to get her out. I should have done it myself, but I thought she would fight me. I thought getting arrested would keep her out of an intensely dangerous situation. A cartel was involved at that point, and they wanted to use her. I couldn't let it happen."

"So you left her to get the shit kicked out of her?" Chase practically roared the question.

That was when he noticed the big guy's wife was walking out the door. Likely to go tell Harlow her dad was about to murder her ex.

He needed to calm this situation down. "He didn't realize that would happen, Mr. Dawson. By allowing her to be arrested, he eliminated the chance that the cartel would use her. It's what they did. They used their clubs to identify vulnerable people who could run their drugs for them. Harlow put herself in that position hoping to get picked. When Jensen found out she was next, he stopped it."

"What the fuck were you doing in there in the first place?" Chase backed off slightly but there was still rage in those dark eyes.

Jensen squared off, and Niall knew this was going to go bad. "It's none of your business."

"His brother was murdered," Niall explained. "He loved Tommy. Most of their lives they were all they had. I don't know if you know how that feels, but he was older and his dad was long gone. He felt…"

"Responsible for his brother," Chase said with a long sigh.

"Yes, we do understand what it means to be siblings without parents we could count on," the other dad said. Ben. His name was Ben. "Chase, could we calm down and talk this out?"

"Oh, he's about to explode again." Taggart hung up his cell.

"Or we could not tell him shit," Jack offered. He also had his cell in his hand. There was a text there. "You know technically this is my jurisdiction."

"Hush, you toddler," Taggart said. "I'm not going to hide this, and Ruby found it all on her own, so unless your jurisdiction includes the entire Dark Web, you should brace yourself for Hurricane Chase."

"What?" Chase asked as his brother moved in beside him.

Oddly enough, Jensen took a step back and was suddenly beside Niall, even though he didn't look his way.

"Ruby found a hit order on Harlow and Jensen," Taggart announced. "Those pictures got to the right people, well the wrong people for us. Jensen, unless you're ready to pull whatever crazy shit you were planning on pulling, you're shut down. That's my professional advice."

"Oh, Jensen doesn't look like a guy who takes professional advice," Chase said, his eyes narrow. "He looks like a reckless asshole who won't want to miss his shot."

"Brother," Ben began.

Jensen cursed under his breath.

Jensen's cover was blown. Years of work gone in an instant.

Niall was strangely comforted at the thought. Not the thought of an assassin, but that Jensen couldn't go back. How long had he been in this strange limbo where he was constantly waiting to hear his oldest friend was dead and he was alone? It had been a tension he'd gotten so used to that he hadn't realized it was there.

Of course now he had to worry about assassins. And Harlow's dads, because he was pretty sure that just because Ben seemed reasonable didn't mean he wouldn't stab a dude he thought was hurting his daughter. That was actually a perfectly reasonable thing to do.

Chase growled his brother's way and then sighed. "Fine. We need to talk about where we're going to stash our daughters. I want Greer with us, too. If they find out about her sister, all they have to do is take her and then Harlow turns herself in, so we're all going off the grid. Ian, do you think your cabin in Colorado is safe enough or should we find somewhere else?"

Jensen's head tilted, talking quietly out of the side of his mouth. "Harlow is going to lose her shit. This is her worst nightmare. She'll have to shut down her business, and she won't know when her father will loosen the leash. She'll go crazy."

A bad plan started to form in his head. A plan that would mean Harlow's deranged dad would likely hate him, too. Maybe that was a way to rebond with his best friend. Having their girlfriend's dad loathe them both could be a good shared experience for them. "You hid the house, right? When you decided to go after Tommy's killer, you put the house under another name, right?"

"I was careful. There's no way anyone can trace the house to me. Up until a few weeks ago, my aunt handled the whole thing. I let her live there after my mom passed. All the bills were in her name, though I had to start paying them when she moved out." Jensen looked to Ian, who was busy explaining what he called cabin rules to the twins. "Mr. Taggart, who is the hit on?"

Ian stood, putting his cell down. "According to Ruby it was you and Harlow."

"The name," Jensen corrected. "When I decided to go undercover, I hired a hacker, one I trusted. Niall and I knew her from our Army days. She wiped Jensen Wiley off the books and replaced him with Jay Wilson. That's the name I've been going by for years."

Jack glanced down at his cell. "That's the name on the list. I'll ask my cyber team to dig deeper and see if there's anything out there."

"Please don't." Niall stepped forward. "I would like to keep Jensen's name off the FBI's list. I'm not saying he won't give you all the information he has…"

"Hey," Jensen began.

Niall was going to ignore him for now. "…but I would prefer his actual name isn't searchable on any database."

Jensen huffed but Niall spoke his language. It was a grudging acceptance of the truth that Niall was trying to help him. It was permission to continue.

Jack sighed and seemed to think the situation over. "I would like to see what you have. How long have you been embedded in the organization?"

"Three years, give or take," Jensen replied.

A bullshit answer since he was absolutely certain Jensen knew to the day how long he'd been in hell.

"I'll keep quiet for now, but you have to know it's going to come out," Jack explained.

"I would rather it came out after Hamilton is in jail," Niall admitted.

"Well, it doesn't matter to us what you do since Harlow's name is out there." Chase looked to Jack. "Any idea how that happened? I know she wouldn't have used her real name."

"Of course I didn't, but it wouldn't be hard to ID me with facial recognition." Harlow stood in the doorway, her arms crossed over her chest. Her mom had joined Ben, running her arm through his and leaning on him as though she needed comfort.

Which she probably did since her daughter was being targeted by a criminal organization.

"What matters is they know your name and that means they can get to any of us," Chase said. "So we're going to head to Ian's cabin in Colorado for a while."

Harlow's eyes went wide. "We?"

Chase squared off with his daughter. "Yes, we. I'm not sending you off with some bodyguard when your papa and I can handle it."

"I'll let my friends in town know why you're there," Ian explained, texting on his phone. "They'll keep a watch out for any strangers who show up. It's not high tourist season so it should be fairly easy to do."

"I can't leave my business," Harlow argued.

"You can and you will." Her dad was obviously not giving in. "This is one step too far. Do you know how this is going to affect your sister?"

Harlow flushed. "It doesn't have to. Put a guard on her for a couple of days and we'll sort it out. I'm sure this moves up Jack's timetable."

"Hamilton is coming into town," Jensen said. "It was all going to be over one way or another in a week."

"Well, I'm not actually being paid to murder the fucker," Jack admitted. "I know law enforcement might have some people who say we cut corners, but we haven't lowered ourselves to assassinations yet. Hey, Uncle Ian, what's Kala doing these days?"

"Mostly Cooper," Ian deadpanned. "But they're all married and shit now, so it's to be expected. Chase, be happy neither of your daughters are married because let me tell you they don't care if you catch them. There is no discretion after marriage."

Harlow's mom raised a brow. "You're talking about discretion?"

One side of Ian's mouth lifted in a grin. "I can talk all I like. We all know I do not follow it."

"Well, she's not married, so she's still my responsibility," Chase announced.

"I'm an adult." Harlow looked like she was about to explode.

"I don't know that I believe that," Chase shot back. "Harlow, I love you. I'm doing this to protect you. Ben, I'm going to get the car. You call Greer and tell her we're picking her up in an hour and arrange for a plane with Julian. We'll be at least six weeks."

"What?" Harlow asked in a way too loud voice.

Because her father was pushing all of her buttons, and she needed some calm. She needed some control.

She needed a freaking hero to ride up on a horse and take her away.

Well, at least he had a Jeep. But he would need some help

because her dad was annoying.

They started arguing about how Harlow couldn't walk away from her business, and then her dad yelled about the business being the problem, and then there was something about whether she should have made a living as an uptight debutante, but Niall was pretty sure that wasn't an actual profession. He could be wrong. He didn't watch a lot of reality TV, which was also being discussed as a viable career option that wouldn't get her murdered.

"She'll be safe at your place?" Niall whispered the question.

Jensen's eyes flared, and he leaned over. "I don't think she's being given that option. You know they have your picture, too. You need to find a place to lay low."

Sometimes he wasn't quick on the uptake. "I did. It's your place. Not even these guys should be able to quickly find us, and then we will have saved Harlow from her dad and we'll have her all to ourselves."

"Because you think we can share her." Jensen said the words slowly, like he was tasting them. "You think she needs us both."

"I think we all need each other."

"It probably won't work. She hates us right now."

"You do not get to dictate my life," Harlow announced in a low tone that felt way more threatening than when she yelled.

"I am your father," Chase shot back in an almost identical tone.

"You might not be," Harlow verbally jabbed. "I'm pretty sure it's Papa over there."

Ben huffed. "Yes, because you're acting just like me right now."

"What am I supposed to do?" She turned on her other father.

"We need to sit down and figure this out." Her mom reached for Harlow's hand.

"I'm not going to Colorado. I go to Colorado and he never stops trying to put me in a cage." Harlow evaded her mother's affection.

"You don't get a choice. If you didn't want to go in a cage, you should have been less reckless." Her dad seemed to have an endless supply of poor choices.

"I can get you a good group rate on some family therapy," Charlotte offered.

"Why would we do that, baby? This is some next-level drama right here," Ian whispered in a not-whispering tone.

"I would say fuck you, Ian, but I need you right now. Watch after her until I get back. I want her down in the parking garage in ten minutes." Chase looked to his twin. "I know she won't forgive me, but at least she'll be alive."

Ben's eyes closed and he moved, following his twin. "I'll talk to him. Nat, I'll see you downstairs with Harlow. Don't walk down without Ian, okay? We'll work this out."

He walked out the door.

Her mom turned Harlow's way. "Baby, I'm sorry. He's scared but he's right that you need a safe place."

"You think he's scared but he's practically giddy because it means he can lock us all up and pretend Greer and I aren't grownups," Harlow replied. "I won't let him lock me up. I know that he's seen the worst of what can happen, but I can't live my life like that."

"I can get you in witness protection," Jack offered, looking serious for the first time.

"Another cage," Harlow shot back. She looked at Ian. "I suppose you're going to be my first jailer."

Ian shrugged. "I think it's funny that your dad thinks I'm going to follow orders. Like he hasn't known me for… I don't even want to go into how many years it's been, but he should know me better than to treat me like an employee when I don't have a check in my hand." He turned his gaze on Niall and Jensen. "You two have any plans?"

"Well, I thought I might haul Harlow out of here under her dads' noses and take her to a place that Hamilton will never find, hole up, and figure out what to do from there," Niall replied.

Jensen nodded. "What he said, but I probably wouldn't have said it because now her mom is going to call her husbands or something. He's not good with subterfuge."

"Oh, I disagree," Harlow argued, her eyes narrow. "I think he's excellent at subterfuge. After all, he fooled me."

He was going to work on that. "Are you coming or not? You can come with us or go with Jack or your dads."

Her mom turned to her daughter. "Baby, if you think there's any chance…"

Harlow shook her head. "There's not, but I also don't like the other alternatives, and I'm not dumb enough to go out on my own. Ian, you're not going to stop me?"

The big guy sank into his chair with a yawn that made him look like a sleepy lion. "Like I said, I don't see a check in my hand." And then he pinned Niall and Jensen with an icy gaze. "But if you get her hurt, I won't need a check. I'll help Chase disembowel you just for fun."

"I'm going to get going before Chase disembowels *me*," Jack said. "I'll keep in touch. Hopefully it won't be long. Jensen, I need everything you have. Which is why I might have already sent a couple of agents to your place to grab your laptop and anything that might help."

Jensen puffed up.

Niall put a hand on his arm. "Were you going to turn it over or not? We need to move so if you're going to fight, do it quick."

"I didn't say I was going with you," Harlow said in her brattiest tone.

He was done. They were both so fucking dramatic. He strode over to her, leaned over and had her in a fireman's hold before she could pull any of her self-defense moves on him. He held her firmly by her legs. "Mrs. Dawson, I swear I will guard your daughter with my life and with Jensen's. In fact, I'll try to make sure he dies first because I'm far easier to live with."

"Niall, what are you doing?" Harlow asked, clearly shocked.

Her mom put a hand on her daughter, leaning over. "You use this time, baby girl. See if you can get what you need. I'll try to keep your dad off your back."

"Ian, I will pay you to kill everyone. You don't even have to torture them. Clean kills are fine," Harlow offered. "I can do it. This is the reason I've saved my trust fund."

Ian snorted, an entirely amused sound. "And miss the drama?"

He liked the big guy. "I don't want to drive past her dad. Should we hide somewhere until he's gone?"

Charlotte picked up the landline on her husband's desk. "No need. Go out the back way. I'll have security let you through. Is the other one going? Or should Jack take care of him?"

Jack shook his head as though that was a terrible idea. "I mean, Jensen wouldn't like witness protection. I swear the names they give out are a deterrent. Do you think you can answer to something like Mortimer Lackey? Seriously, I saw that one the other day and wondered what the dude did to piss someone off."

"I'm going with them." Jensen moved beside him. "And it's best you don't know where we are. I'll find a way for Harlow to call in when we can. Keep her family updated so we'll know when she can come home."

"Hey, we should talk about this," Harlow began.

"In three minutes your dad is going to come looking for you," Niall pointed out.

She went quiet. He started for the elevator because he knew she wouldn't stay that way for long.

Chapter Nine

Jensen looked around the house he grew up in and wondered why it felt so damn small now. And why it felt awkward and weird being here after all these years.

When he was young it had been him and his brother and his mom and whoever his mom was shacked up with that week.

How the hell was he back here, and what was he doing with Niall and Harlow?

How had it all gone so fucking wrong?

Or maybe right. Maybe this was the first time in years he was actually in the right place at the right time with the right people.

Was he thinking about what Niall had said?

"You want a beer?" Niall walked in.

They'd stopped at a convenience store at the edge of town. It had security cameras but no Wi-Fi. There were still whole parts of Bonnet, Texas, that didn't have Internet, and this was one of them. Like his mother would have paid for Internet. She was far too busy paying for drugs and spending time with the men she brought home.

"It's morning. I think the time for beer is over." The last thing he should do is start drinking. A couple of beers in and he would be sitting outside Harlow's bedroom door, begging to be let in. Hell, if he thought for a moment that begging and groveling would work, he would get on his knees now.

"And I think we're probably going to need one if we're going to deal with the Valkyrie in there."

Jensen huffed. It was an apt description of Harlow Dawson. At least he was aware. Harlow also *seemed* so sweet and kind and nice. She was kind, but he would argue about sweet and nice. "Did she lock herself in? I mean it's nothing we can't get through."

"She slammed the door in my face, and then I heard the sound of her moving something. Probably the dresser," Niall admitted. "Hope she doesn't throw out her back. Although at least then we could be sure she's not going to run away."

"The good news is there's not a lot of places to go to. The nearest town is five miles away. The rest is all ranchland," Jensen explained like he needed to. Niall lived here from tenth grade until they left for the military. Even before he moved in, he had slept in a sleeping bag on the floor on the nights his dad got too drunk and decided to take it out on him. Jensen sighed. It was hard to stay angry at the man who was seriously the only family he had left. "Why did you have to date her? You knew how I felt, man."

Niall had the grace to flush slightly. He popped off the top of his beer and took a long drink. "I didn't mean to fall for her but she's…she's pretty much my dream woman, and I include all the yelling she can do in there. The truth is I want a woman who isn't going to let me walk all over her."

"You've never walked all over a woman in your life." Niall was one of the best people he knew—poaching aside.

"No, but I have taken a couple for granted. Look, I've never felt for anyone the way I do Harlow, and part of it is how fucking fierce she is. Tell me that wasn't what attracted you to her," Niall challenged.

He couldn't. It was exactly why he'd fallen for her. "She was mine first."

"She isn't a possession, Jensen," Niall said quietly. "She's a unique woman who deserves to get everything she needs."

He wasn't going to pretend to not understand what his friend was saying. "She has never once mentioned to me she wants a relationship like her parents have. In fact, I've never seen her flirt with two guys, much less ask them on a date."

"I've seen her with her friends who are in those relationships.

You know her when she's under pressure. I know her when she's relaxed. Your entire relationship with Harlow was about adrenaline and lust. I'm not saying you don't love her. I'm saying the time you've spent with her is incomplete. You know the highest highs and the lowest lows, but you don't know what it means to sit around and watch TV with her. She likes home improvement shows and the worst reality dating crap known to man. But she makes these cookies with toffee chips and then I don't care that I'm watching a bunch of people potentially breed who should not. They should not."

He wanted to laugh because the idea of his manly buddy hanging out watching dating shows with his girlfriend was pretty funny. Except he should have been the one watching with her. Also, she'd never baked for him. Probably because they spent every night undercover, and the days had been about going over and over their case. Or fucking like bunnies.

Was Niall right? It wasn't like there had been quiet dates. They didn't sit around watching movies. They had talked a lot. Way more than Jensen normally talked. "So you think because you watched some TV with her you have more of a claim?"

"I think you need to stop using words like *claim*, brother." Niall sat down on the fairly uncomfortable sofa. "I also think you know a part of Harlow and I know a part of Harlow, and we should team up like in the comic books. Come on, man. Team ups were your favorites. We would save up quarters and sell cans and crap so we could see what happened when Superman and Batman took out a bad guy together. What would have happened if they took down Wonder Woman together? I'm sure it's out there somewhere. Let me tell you in my time at The Hideout, I've seen some crazy shit."

"You liked it? The lifestyle?" It was the first time he'd truly thought about what he'd asked his friend to do. He told himself Niall was doing his part to help avenge Tommy, but what Niall had really done was uproot his whole life and throw himself into another. One he had never contemplated before.

"I fit there," Niall said quietly. "At least I did. I probably will find my membership revoked, and since most of my business is people from the club and their family recommendations, I'll likely have to give that up. Or we can try to save this whole thing. We can decide that she's worth going against the norm."

"Don't you think that's why she doesn't want this kind of relationship? She had to live with it all her life. She had to put up with people judging her and her parents." It was one of the things they'd talked about. How hard it was to be a kid when you called two dudes dad and they were twin brothers.

"It wasn't that hard," a feminine voice said, and Jensen's heart threatened to constrict. "I know my dad is a paranoid asshole from time to time, but he does love me, and I have to admit that sometimes we butt heads because we're a lot alike. I don't like to reveal that truth."

She was so fucking gorgeous. He thought he remembered everything about her, but he'd forgotten how that colorful hair contrasted to her sun-kissed skin and how plump her bottom lip was. How her eyes seemed to glow in the low light.

How she could look at him like he was a walking piece of crap. Well, he didn't entirely not deserve it.

"Can we get you something, princess?" Niall stood, an overly eager Golden Retriever who was not reading the same signs he was.

Or his friend was being optimistic.

"You could get me a ride out of here," she replied sarcastically.

Sometimes he had to deal with her by using logic. "I've got some burner phones. You can call Uber."

She frowned, the light of battle hitting her eyes. "Oh, you want to be cute?"

"Hey, maybe we shouldn't piss her off more," Niall said out of the corner of his mouth. He set his beer down. "Harlow, you know why we had to do this."

Oh, he was opening himself up to some bitchy comments. "Logic isn't going to work."

Harlow ignored him, zeroing in on Niall. "I know why I had to do this. I know why Jensen had to do this. Why are you here, Niall? You are not under some death warrant by mobsters."

"You know why I'm here," Niall tried.

This was going to be a long, drawn-out fight. Oh, hey, Niall might know what TV shows she watched and how good her cookies tasted, but had he not met Harlow's inner bitch? Had he never been flayed alive by her incredibly sexy and sharp tongue? He must not have topped her much. As he watched them bicker…well Harlow bickered and Niall looked mostly confused…he realized he knew parts Niall hadn't met yet.

Parts he brought out in her.

And he didn't know all the parts Niall brought out in her.

She might never have talked about wanting the kind of relationship her parents had, but didn't everyone learn from the people who raised them? Right or wrong, a childhood prepared one for adulthood. Had she learned she could have different parts of her personality and expect to have all her sides fulfilled?

Yes, he was thinking about it. Sharing her. Not in the long term. Maybe in the long term.

He didn't know. He didn't have to fucking figure this out tonight. He didn't have to set the path of his life over the course of one evening. They had all been through trauma and needed to heal, and she was practically begging for one of them to take control.

Harlow struggled to let out her anxiety. It bubbled up and then she shoved it deep, and it shut her down.

"I know I didn't tell you the whole truth," Niall was saying. "But I had to talk to Jensen first."

"I don't care," Harlow shot back.

But she did or she wouldn't be standing here. She would be in her room plotting how to murder them both and where to bury their bodies.

He wanted their first time back together to be tender and loving. He'd envisioned it a thousand times, those dreams of her his only consolation in the last few years.

But it looked like it was going to be hate sex, and he could handle that.

Could Niall?

"Feel free to walk out, baby." Jensen pulled on his bad-boy persona. She didn't want to hear him apologize right now. She didn't want sweet words. She wanted dominance and confrontation. "Town is to the east. All you have to do is follow the road, though I wouldn't expect to get a ride from strangers. There's a prison not far from here, and we're taught not to pick up hitchhikers."

She turned his way. "Oh, you don't think I can walk a couple of miles?"

"I think you'll need to jog because the minute you leave, my vow of silence is over and I'll call your dad," he promised with a nasty smirk. He meant every word. If he wasn't going to be around to watch her, then her dad could do the job.

In some ways he almost hoped she would do it. Then he could go back to stalking Hamilton and likely get his ass killed and it would be over.

Was he thinking that way?

"You wouldn't," she said.

"Try me." Now she needed some honesty, and it was going to make him vulnerable, but it didn't matter. She could tear him apart, and he would let her. "I'm only hiding here because of you, Harlow. If you walk, then I will call your family and feel safe knowing that you're with them. And then I'll go and finish the job."

"You fucking will not," Niall protested. "This is serious."

"You think I care?" Harlow challenged. "I stopped caring the second you chose your revenge over me."

"I chose you over everything else," Jensen shot back. "Do you know how much trouble I got in when my girl got arrested? It set me back for months, and I had to compound it when I got your client out. They thought I might have had something to do with it. It would have been so much simpler to keep you with me. I did it to save you, but I don't expect your forgiveness."

"Good, because it's not forthcoming, motherfucker."

His eyes narrowed on her. "But I do expect you to not run off recklessly and force Niall and I to put ourselves in danger to save you when it's safe here. So that's it for you. Here or with your parents in Colorado. And if you keep cursing me, we'll talk about punishment since that's what you're honestly here for."

"Excuse me?" Harlow asked, her brows rising.

Jensen held his ground. "If you didn't want to start a fight that's absolutely going to end with my hand on your backside and likely two cocks in your pussy at some point, you would be sulking in your room. Or you would already be walking. No. You came out here to start something."

Niall watched them both. "Jensen, she just wants to talk."

Jensen didn't take his eyes off her, and she stared at him. "She doesn't want to talk, man."

"You think you know me?" Harlow asked in a challenging tone.

"I know this much," Jensen said with confidence he shouldn't have. "Niall and I were discussing the fact that we know two different yous, but it's the you I know that's showing up tonight. I know the gorgeous bitch who takes no shit from anyone. She also has trouble with shoving her anxiety and anger and sorrow down. Really any strong emotion."

"You think a cry is going to fix this?" She moved into his space, her face flushing a pretty pink.

She was so gorgeous when she was mad. Maybe that was why he poked her so often. Or he could accept that he didn't always know how to handle her since she was more complex than he liked to admit. Niall was right about that. His relationship with her was born in fire, and it would burn them both if they couldn't turn the flames down.

But not tonight. Tonight she needed the burn, and fuck all, so did he.

He put his hand around her neck, a gentle reminder of who would be in control if she continued down this path. "I think a good cry followed by an orgasm would do you a world of good. It doesn't have to mean anything beyond we're stuck here and both our lives were completely upended today and we need something to comfort us. I doubt you want me to hold you and tell you everything is going to be okay."

She moved closer, pressing her neck against his hand. "It means nothing."

At least she was done pretending.

He tightened his grip, though it was still gentle. He would never hurt her in anything but a pleasurable way, and he wasn't the type of Dom who lived to see his mark on a sub. But then his sub had always been her. He got into the lifestyle for the job, but he lived it for her. "Do I have to rip your clothes off? Or is it acceptable for Master Niall to pull those pants down so I can spank your ass?"

"I'm confused, actually," Niall offered.

"I don't have any other clothes, asshole," she shot back, a dark look in her eyes. "Are you all about sharing now, or are you going to have him do your dirty work and shut him out?"

How little she thought of him. Although it was plainly what he'd been considering a couple of hours ago. The long ride and being back in this place had him rethinking. He should have known Niall would fall for Harlow. Maybe he had deep inside. Maybe there had been a part of him that wanted to know someone would love her after he died.

It hit him so forcibly that deep down he never intended to come out of this mission alive, and he had to find a way to deal with it. He hadn't truly planned on a life after this, and he wasn't sure of anything except that any life without them would be hollow. "I think you require two of us tonight. He doesn't know this part of you. Have you played?"

Niall suddenly seemed less confused. "Light play only. No heavy scenes. We haven't even played publicly yet. From what I can tell she hasn't had sex in the months I've been around her. I think it's been going on since she came back from LA."

"Just because I'm picky doesn't mean anything. Or maybe I needed time to get over some asshole setting me up to potentially die," she said but she didn't move. She didn't walk away because she wanted what he was offering.

His cock tightened in his jeans. "We'll talk about that at another time. I certainly didn't want you dead, but I accept that what I did hurt you. Do you want a sincere apology?"

He didn't think so, but he needed to give her the option. If he could do this with tenderness, he would.

"Fuck you, Jensen, and fuck your apologies."

Hate sex it was then.

* * * *

Harlow felt the moment Jensen decided to take this to the next level. One minute his hand was around her neck in a way that made her heart race, and the next he was picking her up and moving toward the back of the house. Such an odd house. Parts of it were updated with furniture and décor from this century. Parts were like a museum. There was still high school stuff in his old bedroom. A math book on the shelf along with some notes he'd written in a strangely neat hand. She'd been standing there looking at evidence that once this man had been a vulnerable boy, and she hadn't been able to handle it.

The fucker was right. She'd come looking to start a fight she kind of hoped would end like this.

Of course she had to wonder if this wasn't where they'd been heading since the second she walked into his office.

"If you're coming, Niall, do it now. Once I close this door, it's her and me," Jensen announced.

"Yeah, stay out if you're too fucking afraid, Niall. Or maybe if you would rather spend the night reading or massaging your own feet." She couldn't help it. She was filled with bile, and it just came out.

The whole night, her whole life the last few years… It was too much. Far too much.

They lied to her. Niall had pretended to be this good guy who could heal her flipping heart or something, and he'd turned out to be one more asshole.

Her business was likely in ruins, and she was proving to the whole damn world—including her best friend and partner—that she was nothing but one more trust fund baby who couldn't do anything without parental supervision.

Check that. She could fuck things up. She was good at that.

"Set her on her feet."

She was surprised that deep, dark command hadn't come from Jensen. Niall shut the door to the big bedroom. It was illuminated by a single lamp on the side table. The whole room was dominated by a king-sized bed that took up most of the space. Jensen had changed the sheets and put a clean comforter on. It was obvious he'd cleaned up in here. The rest of the house had a coating of dust on it, but the primary bedroom had someone who cared about it.

Or his military training kicked in. Either way, she wasn't going to complain. Not about that. She had so many other things to criticize as her feet found the floor. She wished they were at the club. She would run from them and force them to chase her down and they could do this whole thing with her kicking and scratching and getting all the poison out of her system. In a club she wouldn't worry about Niall being upset. He would know it was play in a club. Jensen was an asshole who would take whatever she gave him.

She turned and stared at the man she thought might be her first real Dom. "I'm surprised you didn't go back to your room and play with yourself. It's what you seem to do around me."

Jensen whistled. "I told you she wants it. If we were in a club, or honestly in any place where she felt safe, she would already be running. She would make me chase her down and tie her up and drag her to bed."

"I want to say that I find that thought distasteful and barbaric," Niall said slowly. "But right now, I might drag her back by her hair."

Oh, he wanted to play? The other thing that would feel good right now was a fight. A nasty, no holds barred fight, but again she wasn't at the club where they had a sparring ring for just such an occasion. "I'd love to see you try."

"Jensen, do you have a kit?" Niall enunciated every word.

"Back in my truck, which should be parked in Taggart's garage by now," Jensen pointed out and then sighed. "I'll grab yours. I'm afraid I didn't keep a bunch of rope and sex toys hanging around when I lived here. Not that my momma didn't, but I got rid of those real fast. And then I needed therapy."

He needed therapy for so many things, but she wasn't going to point that out right now. She was facing off with Niall, and they were at a very important part of this fight they were in. "You don't have to stay. You're free to go."

"Why would I go when there's a gorgeous woman begging me to fuck her?" Niall replied.

"Oh, is that what you need? My enthusiastic compliance wasn't good enough for you. You need it to be nasty?" If any of her friends heard her, she would get pulled into one of the board sessions where they talked about kink shaming, but she didn't care if she wasn't being fair in this moment. He hadn't been fair to her. He'd spent months pretending he cared about her, days pretending he wanted her.

She needed him to show it. In the worst, nastiest way.

And then she could reject him and walk away with no regrets. Walk away from both of them.

"What I needed was a clean conscience, but I'm not going to get that." The words rumbled out of Niall's throat, a deep, husky sound. "I'm starting to believe that Jensen was right and all you've shown me so far is what you want me to see. You've been polite around me, princess."

He understood nothing. "I've been nice to the man I thought was going to be my boyfriend. I treated you the way I would treat a Dom who took care of me, but you aren't that man."

Niall didn't back down. "Oh, I'm that man and I'll prove it to you, but first I'm going to have to clear up some misconceptions. Take off your clothes or I'll rip them off you and I won't care that you don't have more. I'll arrange for someone to shop for you and until they can safely bring them here, you'll be naked or you can wear something of mine. I keep a bag in the Jeep."

"You wouldn't dare." He was supposed to be the reasonable one.

He reached out and took her shirt in both hands and sure enough, it ripped in two. "Do you want to save your jeans? I've got a knife in the kit."

Anger bubbled up. "You asshole."

"No. If I'm your Dom, then I'm going to be in charge," Niall insisted.

"You are not now and you won't ever be my Dom. You might top me because I need it and you're the only one around, but that's all this will ever be. The minute we leave this place, I won't see you again."

"That's a risk I'm willing to take," he admitted. "Are you willing to risk your jeans? It's nothing we haven't seen before."

"I thought you said you didn't fuck her." Jensen's voice sounded deadly from the door. He stood there, Niall's kit in his hand and his eyes on her chest. She still wore her bra, but he was definitely looking at her breasts.

Maybe she could get them to fight. Maybe she could watch them try to kill each other and that would make her briefly feel better knowing they were as miserable as she was.

But a freaking orgasm would be better. The universe was giving her a whacked-out gift and that was time to fuck these two men out of her system so when she got back to the real world she wouldn't have to think about either of them again.

She could move on. Whatever that looked like.

"I didn't, but I did get her naked." Niall frowned his friend's way. "Have you ever been in a real club? One that isn't run by asshole criminals?"

"He has not," she replied and because she believed Niall, her hands went to the waist of her jeans and she shoved them off her hips and tossed them to the side. "He wouldn't know a real club if it bit him in the ass."

She wanted his attention on her and not his jealousy. He had no right to be jealous.

"Baby, you are pushing me so hard." Jensen tossed the kit on the bed and moved in behind her. His hand twisted the back clasp of her bra, and she felt cool air hit her breasts. He pulled off her undies, too, before speaking again. "If this is going to work, we need ground rules."

"We don't need shit," she shot back. "I'm not following rules."

"He wasn't talking to you," Niall replied. "He was talking to me, and he's right. I have more experience as a Dom, but you're probably more dominant in nature than I am. I prefer to indulge her."

"We can't indulge her tonight," Jensen argued. "She won't take it from either of us. You teach me the finer points of this whole thing and I'll share her with you. For now."

What the hell was that supposed to mean? Asshole. She would have a lot to say if they were actually trying to make this work. Which she was not. She meant what she said. The minute it was safe she was out of here.

She might be out of Dallas altogether because while she loved her dad it was getting hard to live close to him.

She had this time and then she would be gone. So it didn't matter what he meant.

"What she needs now is a spanking. I'm going to assume you've disciplined her before," Niall said, his voice tight. "I think she needs to be over your lap and then she needs a hard fucking and some sleep. Harlow, if you do this with us, you sleep with us. That's my only rule."

"I don't want to sleep with you," Jensen protested.

Niall sent his friend a dark look. "Then you can sleep alone, but if I'm fucking her and taking care of her needs, she's sleeping with me. If not, I'll walk and we can spend the next couple of weeks sniping at each other with no real prospect for relief."

He was forgetting something. "I think Jensen will fuck me and he won't give a damn that I'm not his cuddle bug."

Jensen moved to stand beside him, arms crossing over his chest. "We'll sleep in here. The bed's big enough. It's for security, too."

"Hey, I didn't agree to this." But she was the one who was naked, and was she walking out on them when her skin suddenly felt electric?

"Then go to your room," Jensen replied. "Or you can pull some nasty shit that forces me to take you to that chair, slap your ass silly, and then we'll tie you up and take turns because I'm going to assume in all the no sex in the last two years, you haven't been playing around with your own asshole."

She snorted. When had he gotten all forthright about sex? "No, I have not been plugging my own asshole in the hopes that someday I would get two guys. I was kind of trying to avoid it."

"Sure you were," Niall countered.

She didn't like them working together. They were fucking calm when she was a storm of anxiety and rage and fear. And they were standing there like this was some kind of date.

"Fuck you both," she said and started for the door, knowing exactly what Jensen would do.

A big arm went around her waist and she found herself dragged to the small chair in the corner of the room. There was a bookshelf beside it, but she didn't get a chance to look at it before Jensen had her over his lap and the first crack of his hand hit her naked flesh.

Pain flared through her. It hit like a runaway locomotive stopping and focusing her.

She needed this. She could fucking breathe now. "Again."

His hand came down without hesitation. "You know it kind of feels like I'm not the one in charge."

Niall chuckled lightly. "Welcome to D/s, man. The sub is always in control. It's the only reason I was okay with it eventually. When you asked me to go in, I thought I wouldn't be able to handle it. I had a skewed view. Now I know how much I need it. She taught me that."

"I taught you nothing," she shot back.

And got her ass peppered with smacks. At least ten. All in a row, and it took her breath away. The pain flared through her system, sending much-needed heat. She hadn't realized how cold she'd felt before. How still. Like she was stuck, but now the world seemed to move again.

"You have good technique for someone who hasn't taken a formal class." Niall utterly ignored her.

She glanced up and realized he was only ignoring her words. His eyes were on her body, and she couldn't miss the way his pants had tented. Well, she'd felt that big cock against her before but he'd never used it on her.

He might use it tonight. She might get to feel that hard cock thrust inside.

"I was motivated," Jensen replied. "She needed it. I read some books and talked to some people, but mostly she taught me. We practiced a lot. She needs this to relieve stress. She doesn't drink much so it's this or she starts a fight, and I needed her to look fairly normal."

"You asshole." But he wasn't exactly wrong, and it was refreshing to not be treated like she was fragile and would faint at the sight of blood.

He slapped her ass again, this time his hand staying there, holding the heat to her. Connecting them. "She likes a big bite of pain when we're playing and during sex. She likes to have her nipples twisted and the bite of clamps. I've always thought she likes to be watched."

"Oh, I can verify that. She might not have had sex at The Hideout since I've been there, but she likes to be naked in the club," Niall explained. "She'll walk around in nothing but a pair of fuck-me heels and ask if anyone needs help. It makes me crazy because she's not wearing a collar."

She couldn't help it. It felt nice to be naked. She liked it. Sue her. She only did it at the club or the nudist place in Colorado. Actually, now that she thought about it, Mountain and Valley was secure, and her fathers wouldn't come in if they knew she was there. Of course they might send in other people.

"It makes you crazy because she's not wearing *your* collar," Jensen countered.

Niall's collar. She didn't want to think about the fact that it felt like something they were working toward earlier tonight. Nope. She wasn't letting that in. She hadn't talked to Ruby and Gigi about what kind of collar she would want—because it wasn't like Niall would pick one out without her input. That sounded more like Jensen.

"Probably," Niall agreed. "I'm insanely jealous when it comes to her. Current company not included, of course."

She huffed. "Sure."

That brought another round of smacks that took her breath away. Jensen wasn't holding back. "Hush. We are working things out, and honestly, what do you care what we say since you're going to leave the minute you can?"

That was true. "Maybe I don't like listening to whiny men talking about their feelings."

"Don't," Niall said, his tone darker than she ever remembered him using. "You can handle her bratty parts, and I'll deal with shit like this when she crosses a real line."

What the fuck line had she crossed? She was the one laying over Jensen's lap.

And then she wasn't. Niall hauled her up, and she felt herself flush at the hard look in his eyes.

"I understand that you are frustrated with the events of the day, but you have no idea what you just did to him. You sit around and moan about the patriarchy, and then times get tough and you reenforce it for the one person in this room who is utterly yoked by it."

A pit opened in her stomach and she looked at Jensen, who frowned Niall's way.

"She doesn't want to listen to feelings? I get it. I wasn't talking about feelings. I was talking about sex. No feelings involved," Jensen said with that smirk he got when he needed a mask.

Except he did have feelings. A lot of them, and he didn't know how to handle them because he'd been told his whole damn life that he wasn't supposed to feel anything but anger and maybe lust. Niall had found his way out of the mindset, but Jensen hadn't.

"You could cut him a thousand other ways and I wouldn't have a problem with it, but that was too far. That isn't who you are. I understand you're angry. Are you so angry that you would say something that will send him back into that shell of his? He lost a lot tonight, too."

This was why trios sucked. There was always the reasonable

one who made the two dumbasses look at everything in a different light.

"Are we playing or is this revenge? I kind of thought the revenge would be leaving at the end, but you could hollow him out," Niall said in that all too reasonable tone. "You can take every bit of progress he's made, and at the end he won't open himself up to anyone again. Ever."

"What the fuck are you talking about?" Jensen asked.

But she knew. Jensen had been "the man" for so long he sometimes forgot he could be human, too. She didn't want to think about this, but Niall made it impossible. Jensen worked hard for his revenge. He'd given her up, and then in the course of one night he lost it all and she shamed him for talking about his feelings. Not that she wanted to be his freaking sounding board, but she didn't want to be yet another person telling him he was nothing but abs and a good time in bed.

Sometimes it sucked to have to be the bigger person and live the actual lifestyle which required her to be open and tolerant and accepting. She could walk away. She didn't have to be kind if she was locked in her room. In the room where Jensen grew up and she was surrounded with evidence that he'd been a kid with dreams of getting out of this place, who loved his brother and wished his mom could be different.

Stupid fucking empathy.

She walked up to Jensen and put her hands on his cheeks. "Sir, I am emotional tonight and angry, and I still should never have said that to you. I am sorry. Please forgive me."

He stood there, a muscle in his jaw ticcing like a pulse. "I can handle some words, Harlow."

But it was so plain he couldn't. Or rather he would pretend like they didn't mean anything but they did, and they would send him into his shell. She'd gotten him to open up the first time around. Their relationship had been marked with incendiary passion and some spectacular fights, but there had been moments when he talked about his brother and his family and how much it hurt when his mom would bring home some guy and forget he and Tommy existed. How many times had she told him to suck it up and be a man?

She went on her toes and kissed him lightly. "I am still sorry. You should talk. You should get it out and I should put my clothes back on and be an adult about this."

Niall moved in behind her, whispering in her ear. "That's the woman I know. Good girl. And there's no way I'm letting you put your clothes back on. You know your safe word. Use it if you need to."

She gasped as Niall lifted her up and tossed her onto the bed. She barely had time to breathe before he had her ankles in his hands and he spread her legs wide after dragging her down the bed so her ass was almost hanging off.

"Good girls get treats." Niall hauled his shirt over his head and tossed it aside. "You going to safe word on me?"

She was caught between stubbornness and horniness. Not even horniness. Curiosity. Curious horniness. Did she want to go to the grave not knowing how it felt to be with Niall? Jensen damn near killed her and here she was spreading her legs for another asshole who lied to her.

She felt her fists clench around the comforter. "No. I'm not going to use my safe word, but this changes nothing."

"I know," he said, a gravity to his tone. "We have to work for that, and we will."

She shook her head. "It won't happen. I won't forgive you."

"Then you have nothing to fear." He lowered his head down and put his nose right in her pussy.

She fought for breath. He rubbed himself against her like he was reveling in her.

"You smell so fucking perfect," Niall muttered against her most intimate skin.

"That is way hotter than I thought it would be." Jensen stood by the bed, his eyes on the place where Niall's head bent over, his tongue coming out for a long, luxurious lick. "She tastes like honey and sex. I can still taste her on my tongue and it's been two fucking years, man. You should be careful. She's addictive."

"I'll risk it. I don't mind being addicted to her." Niall didn't move his head. He kept up the slow exploration of her pussy as he talked, and every single word rumbled over her sensitive flesh.

It was hard to think while he was doing that. He was being

extremely thorough, and she realized she'd never once had a guy spend that much time down there. Sex with Jensen was quick and rough and exciting. It wasn't like there was never tenderness between them, but it wasn't like this. This was a man who was taking his time, who wanted to spend hours learning her body. He already knew way too much about her soul.

Pleasure coursed through her as he sucked part of her labia between his lips, and she felt the press of his thumb against her clit. She could barely see. Barely breathe. It had been so long. So damn long, and this was way beyond the little pleasures he'd given her up to this point. Those had been delivered with his fingers. This felt like so much more. It was more, and the fact that Jensen was watching heightened the whole experience for her.

She opened her eyes and took him in. Jensen stood there, his dark eyes down. His hair had grown and was slightly shaggy. It looked good on him. His jaw was tight, and there was that impressive cock, tenting his jeans.

Were they really going to do this? Was she going to have them both?

She could steal a couple of nights from them and still get out with her whole heart. She could do it.

"She's so beautiful when she comes," Jensen said. "Make her come, brother. Make her come hard."

The words seemed to work some magic on Niall. His tongue speared her, going deep while his thumb rotated on her clit, pressing down and sending her over the edge.

It felt so good, so fucking perfect. She let go, not holding back. She writhed and twisted on the bed as Niall and Jensen held her down, forcing her to take every lash of his tongue.

Heat bloomed, and she shouted out as she came.

Her whole body felt languid and perfect.

Niall stood, his hands on the fly of his jeans. "Tell me I can have you."

Asshole understood way too much. He was going to force her to say yes, to consent when it was so much easier to fall on top of her and take her. She wouldn't have to admit she truly wanted him, wanted both of them. Would watching her fuck Niall send Jensen away?

Yes, that's why she would do it. To show Jensen she wasn't going to be his perfect sub and come back to him after what he'd done to her.

She nodded Niall's way.

Jensen took his shirt off, tossing it aside. "I'll hold her for you. She likes to squirm."

Harlow felt the bed tilt under her as Jensen climbed in behind her, gripping her wrists and dragging her up the bed with him.

He was right. She was definitely going to squirm.

Chapter Ten

Niall had not expected that level of assistance from his best friend, but he was going with it. He could still taste her on his tongue, still hear all those sweet sounds she'd made as he licked and sucked that sweet pussy of hers. His cock was desperate, but he wasn't about to simply fall on her. He wanted to make this last, and he had something to prove.

Jensen was still in his jeans as he dragged Harlow against him. He sat with his back against the headboard and pulled her close, holding her wrists in his hands and hooking her ankles with his, making her a treat laid out for him.

The picture of the two of them together did something for him. He worried at first that he would have to get used to this, to having another guy in bed with him, but this felt oddly natural. Like they were two pieces that fit together to give her a whole man.

Maybe that's what they had always been.

They looked so gorgeous. Harlow and Jensen looked absolutely perfect together, and he couldn't miss the way his always shut down best friend was kissing the curve of her ears, whispering to her. Telling her how stunning she was, how much he was looking forward to getting inside her.

Harlow's eyes were closed but she was so much more relaxed than he'd seen her since the moment Jensen arrived.

This was what they needed. What they all needed. It had been the roughest of days and they lost a lot, but they might have found something new, something that could work for all of them.

He had to convince them, and he would start by giving that woman her second much-needed orgasm of the night. He ditched his jeans and reached for the kit Jensen retrieved. He'd kind of meant to tie her up, but they'd gotten a little out of control. She'd pushed him and he'd called her on it and responded exactly how he hoped she would—with grace and the love she held in her heart.

"How long has it been for you, baby?" Jensen asked.

Niall came back with the condom in time to see her flush. "It's none of your business."

Jensen needed to stop talking.

Niall dropped the condom on the bed because it was obvious she was going to need more foreplay. Well, he hadn't even sucked on her nipples yet.

"I haven't slept with anyone. Not even Niall, and apparently that's a real possibility now," Jensen murmured. "Twist her nipples. She likes a hard twist."

"I do not." She sounded flustered. "And this is not going to…"

Niall placed himself between her legs and took a nipple between his thumb and forefinger and gave that pretty bud a hard twist.

Harlow gasped, and her eyes went soft and wide.

Oh, she so liked it. He leaned over and licked the abused button and gently sucked on it, feeling Harlow's breath hitch. "I bought clamps. I've spent months buying clamps and ties and toys just for you." He gave the other nipple a nice twist, too. "Every class I've taken has been for you."

"I thought it was all for Jensen," she snarked.

He nipped her, eliciting a soft scream. That was when he realized Jensen had done the same thing to her earlobe.

"Stop with the sarcasm, Harlow, or you'll be over my lap again and you won't get a cock until you apologize prettily and maybe cry. You know you're gorgeous when you cry," Jensen said.

"I know you like to make me cry," she practically snarled back.

This time he reached down and gently pinched her clit.

She nearly came off the bed.

"There is a time and a place for your reasonable anger with us, princess. This is not it," Niall said. He hated the words about to come out of his mouth, but he had to give her the choice. His cock protested his sense of fairness. "Do you want to talk now? I've waited this long. I can handle a therapy session."

"I don't need a fucking therapy session," she shot back, and then her gaze softened. "This is all I can give you."

"Then be a proper sub when we're playing," Jensen offered. "If this is all the time we get, then give us something to think about for the rest of our miserable lives. Be the sub I know you can be. Do you know why you crying melts me every time? Why I'll spank that pretty ass of yours whenever you let me? I'll do it because when you cry in front of me, I feel like I mean something to the world. I feel like I'm not a fucking gun that's pointed and waiting to go off. It's the same reason I've been friends with Niall for most of my life. Because he didn't look at me like I was muscle without a brain or a soul. He gave a damn about me, and when you cried I could pretend you did, too. Earlier, that is. I know you cared about me before. I fucked that up and I accept whatever you decide to do, but if this is all we ever get from the only woman I'll ever love, then I want these days. I want to pretend to be your Dom. And if you maybe want to get rid of Ni…"

She growled.

"And I want to share you with my best friend," Jensen amended.

At least one good thing was coming out of this.

"It doesn't mean anything," she replied but in a much gentler tone. "I can play a part because maybe I need to know, too, but it won't change the outcome. I won't ever be able to trust you again."

He was going to gamble. Gamble that Jensen could be swayed with seeing how good it could be to share her. Gamble that her heart could soften over time. Gamble that they didn't kill each other while they were stuck in this house.

He might lose half his soul because he got the feeling if she walked away, it would also be the end to the most important friendship of his life.

"I'll take that chance." He pulled his body up so he could feel the heat of her pussy on his cock. "Harlow, I want ground rules. I don't want to ask permission for every touch."

"I have a safe word," she replied softly. "I know how to use it. If you're talking about kissing me now, do it. I'm so angry with the both of you that I can't stand it. I'm angry at the world, so mad at myself. Give me something to not be angry about. One thing in this whole wretched day. You and him. I want you both, and then I want to sleep here and we'll pretend like I'm not going to walk away at the end of this."

He could do that since he happened to know that sometimes pretending was a good way to make something real. He leaned down and pressed his lips to hers, kissing her gently before she opened her lips and let him inside. Their tongues slid alongside each other, mingling and mating, while his cock throbbed and he took in every sensation of being against her body. The way her breasts felt against his chest. How he nestled between her legs. How he could feel Jensen's hands moving on her, stroking her like he was a part of what was happening. Because he was. It was the most intimate moment of Niall's whole fucking life, and he wanted more.

He wanted to fuck their girl and then watch Jensen do the same and then sleep with her in between them. He wanted to wake up with them and plan days with them.

But first he had to show them this could work.

He let the thought go because he wanted to live in this moment. To be present as he connected their bodies. He managed to roll the condom on, his eyes on her breasts and the way Jensen was still holding her wrists. His best friend's nose nuzzled her neck and he licked her there, biting down gently and sending tremors through her body.

Then he didn't care because he lined his cock up and started to work his way in. So fucking tight and hot and wet for him. She was ready. Despite the anger, she wanted them. And he had to believe this wasn't merely sex. He had to. He pressed in until she'd taken all of him.

She took a long breath and then her hips rolled. Though she couldn't move much since Jensen was holding her down. It seemed to do something for her because her eyes lit and she pressed her pelvis against him, forcing his cock slightly deeper. "That's what I want."

Then he would give it to her. He pulled out and thrust back in, his eyes nearly rolling to the back of his head from the pleasure of it. His body felt electrified as he began to fuck her. He stared down, watching as her eyes went wide and she dragged in breath. He put a hand around her neck—the way he'd seen Jensen do it. Gentle, with little pressure but enough to remind her he was in charge.

She flushed and then writhed beneath him, her pussy clamping down and sending him over the edge. He lost some of his control, his hips thrusting with wild abandon as they both came.

He loosened his hold and laid himself down on her, kissing her neck and feeling better than he had in months. It was all out in the open and she had still let him in.

For now.

"Feeling better, princess?" He kissed her lazily as he asked the question.

"Yes, but I think we have another problem. There is a huge cock pressing into my backside, and I'm pretty sure if he doesn't get relief soon, he might die."

"My dick might fight its way out of these pants, and then I'm screwed because I don't have my gym bag like Niall does," Jensen complained. "Baby, come on. I need you. I can't stand another second. Niall, get me a condom."

He already had one. He thought ahead. This was the con. The sex was the pro, but having to get his ass up to help his friend have sex was the definite con. They needed to do this thing together so they could all cuddle and go to sleep after. Still, he hauled his ass up and then dragged her with him.

Jensen shoved his boxers down and wrapped the condom around that big dick of his.

"Ride him, baby." Niall guided her to straddle Jensen and watched as she took him inside.

Niall sat back and enjoyed the show.

* * * *

Jensen woke up as the early morning light snuck in through the cracks in the curtains, and it took him a minute to realize he wasn't alone in his bed in Dallas. At first a bit of panic set in. He reached for his gun. It was always close.

He couldn't find it.

"Hey, it's okay," a soft voice said.

A familiar voice. Harlow. He heard her voice in his sleep all the time. In his head. But this time she was real, and she was laid out next to him.

The events of the previous day flooded his brain.

Seeing her again. Knowing something big was about to go down. The fuck-up at the apartment. Finding out Niall was in love with her.

Her dads. Oh, he'd met her dads, and he had not made a good impression. Not at all.

Bringing her here. Watching her fuck Niall.

Fucking her.

Losing everything.

"It's okay," she reiterated, her hand on his chest. She stroked him in a soothing fashion. "Niall's making coffee. He apparently got up early and went into town and got some groceries and picked up some clothes for you. I wouldn't expect much. I think it's probably sweats and T-shirts. Are you okay?"

"I'm fine." It was only a waking dream, something he dealt with a lot. Those nasty worries that struck him when he was waking up. How he would lay there for a moment, wanting to make sure he was alone before he gave away the fact that he was conscious.

She was still for a moment and then turned away. He immediately felt the loss of that hand on his chest. "I'll go see if Niall needs anything."

He was barely awake and already screwing up. After all the sex the night before, he'd lain awake and tried to figure out how he felt about going from hardcore dude, ready to murder for revenge, to confused dude who was suddenly somehow in a threesome. Or was it more technically a throuple? Maybe they were only called that after they were together for a longer period of time. He was pretty sure what happened last night was a devil's three-way since most of society thought two girls and a guy was more like heaven.

Last night felt pretty damn close.

But as he laid there he realized if he wanted any kind of chance with Harlow—with or without Niall—he would have to open up. It was what put her off about him the first time around. They'd fought about his unwillingness to ever admit anything was wrong. Right up until the moment he exploded. Their fights had been spectacular and sometimes his words were cruel, and he wasn't doing that to her this time around.

It was more than simply being with her. It was being in this house and remembering all the crap his mother put up with so she could say she had a man. Always just a man after his father left, never a husband or a real partner. They didn't talk about their feelings.

Harlow had been so open when she'd apologized. He hadn't taken her complaining about his delicate feelings the way Niall thought. Or maybe he had because it shut him down. Maybe his only chance was to open up.

He reached out and touched her back, noting the line of her spine, the softness of her skin. "I'm sorry. I sometimes wake up and worry that Hamilton will have put a dead girl in bed with me. It's one of the ways he solidifies his higher-up men. I've heard he makes some of them kill and some he simply ensures that it looks like they did it. So sometimes I wake up and for a moment I think it's happened to me."

She turned, shifting back into bed and gazing down at him, her hair brushing the tops of her shoulders and her breasts on display. She was comfortable with her body, and it was one of the sexiest things about her. "Jensen, you have to know you would be one of the ones he had to trick. You would never have hurt someone."

And her kindness and generosity was one of the other. Her kindness was the part that made his freaking heart beat like he was an actual human being. He brought her hand back to his chest, laying her palm against his skin and feeling warm again. "I'm glad you think that way. There have been days when I wondered."

She frowned. "I don't want to feel for you."

"You can't help it because you feel for everyone, baby," he replied quietly. "Just tell yourself that it's part of playing the role of my sub. You liked this part. You liked being a comfort."

Her nose wrinkled. "You make me sound all gooey."

He chuckled. It felt so good to be here with her. He should be way more upset. He worked for years to get to the top of Hamilton's organization, and now it was all gone and he wasn't going to get his revenge. And yet he was lying here feeling safer than he felt in years. "You are extremely tough, but you have a gorgeous, gooey center."

She huffed but she laid back down, shifting to her side and holding her head on her free hand. She made no move to take her hand back. "Yeah, there's a reason I chose the career path I did. I thought about going into the military. I thought about talking to some people I know and seeing if the CIA needed someone like me."

He shook his head. "You would have been miserable. You wouldn't be able to deal with the moral compromises you would have to make. What you do is perfect for you. Dangerous as fuck and might get you killed one day, but it's what you do."

"Then why did you push me away?"

His heart clenched because she didn't ask the question with anger. This time there was a wistfulness to the query that made him feel far more guilty than he ever had before. "Because while I know your job might get you killed one day, I couldn't be the reason for it. I couldn't do it. I couldn't watch them come after you. The truth of the matter was I was going to get us both killed. I couldn't let them touch you."

"I want to believe you." She sighed. "Not that I think we should get back together, but I don't want to go on being so angry with you. It's held me back for years now, and I can't anymore."

He breathed for a moment, his hand over hers. "If the only thing that comes out of this whole debacle is you aren't angry with me anymore and you can move on, then it'll be worth it."

He meant it. It surprised him, but he truly meant the words.

"Jensen, I'm not dumb. You have to be pissed off. I marched in and everything you worried would happen came to pass. You got caught because of me," she pointed out.

"That was not my worry." He closed his eyes. When was the last time he felt this relaxed? He'd gotten used to his whole body being tense and having to force his muscles to relax. How long had he lived in a state of anxiety, his whole soul placed in an unrelenting stress position? "My worry was you would die and I would have another person to avenge."

"Or you could have had another person to fight with you."

He opened his eyes and turned so they were face to face. She was so gorgeous in the dim light, the sun peeking in under the curtains making almost a halo around her. "Baby, I never thought I would get out."

Her eyes widened. "What do you mean?"

"I mean I knew when I went in that the only way I got out was in a body bag or handcuffs." He finally admitted the truth out loud.

She was quiet for a moment. "Then why would you send Niall to watch me?"

"I suppose when they moved into the Dallas territory and brought me with them, I thought there was a chance," he said with a sigh. "Or my brain wasn't willing to accept the truth. I wonder if somewhere down there I really did want the two of you to get together. So I would know the only two people I loved who were left on this earth had each other."

"I'm not ready to hear that word from you." She pulled her hand away, but she didn't leave. "And I can't trust Niall any more than I can you."

It was odd. Only last night he was thinking about how the hell he'd gotten himself into this position, and now it felt fairly easy to back his friend up. "But you can. Niall is the most honest person I've ever known."

"And yet he lied to me," she pointed out.

"He might have lied about the whys and hows, but not what he felt." He reached out and brushed back a strand of purple hair. So pretty. "He didn't sleep with you because he didn't want to start what he felt was the real beginning of a relationship with untruths between you. He tried calling me. I ignored him for days because I was getting ready to meet Hamilton, and then you showed up. If I had answered him, none of this would have happened. He would have told me he was going on a case with you, and I would have figured out how they connected."

"But you didn't and everything fell apart."

"It did," he agreed. "It fell apart at the worst possible time. Or you could say it fell apart at the best time. It fell apart before I had to truly make the decision about what I was willing to give up for my revenge."

"You gave up me."

"Not for revenge." If there was one thing he wanted her to understand, it was this. "Baby, think about how much easier it would have been for me if you stayed. I wouldn't have been questioned about whether or not I knew you were a PI. Yeah, they figured that out, and I knew they would."

"I didn't think about that. What happened?"

"Nothing important." Nope. That wasn't going to work. He let his head fall back. She deserved the truth, and he deserved to say all this shit so he had some chance of purging it from his system. He was so tired of carrying this load alone. "They beat the shit out of me. I got my ass sent to what passes for a cartel prison for a couple of days. I told them I discovered you were lying to me right before you called the cops in, and I only barely managed to get away. I think the only reason they didn't kill me was I worked with a supplier who wouldn't talk to anyone else."

"Rick? The guy who made X?"

He nodded. "It was their best seller at the time, and they decided scaring the shit out of him didn't work. The only thing that worked was me. He died, you know. Got caught in the middle of a firefight when he was delivering a shipment." He thought about Rick a lot. Smart. Had everything to live for except a couple of undiagnosed mental health issues caused him to slide into criminality. He could have been a chemist or a researcher if his parents had the money for college, or hell, even a damn doctor. Instead he made money the only way he could, and he died for it. "There was also the fact that I texted my direct superior. I had to let him know or it would have looked bad. I know you think I up and decided to dump you one day, but I carefully planned it once I realized they were coming after you next and you wouldn't leave me behind."

She was quiet for a moment. "You could have talked to me."

"Really? Because I remember several conversations that ended in screaming matches about the subject." Of course those screaming matches had turned into long sessions in bed where they solved nothing but the sexual tension between them. He wondered how Niall would have handled it. Niall likely would have sent them to their corners and said no hot sex until we can leave the word hate out of the mix.

Would they be here if Niall had been with them back then?

"Yeah, I remember that, too. We were always way too passionate. I don't suppose that would have lasted. My dad figured out it was a guy who I got into trouble for and he told me passion like that always either burns out or burns the people caught in it. So the truth of the matter is it wouldn't have worked. You were like a drug to me. I got addicted fast, and I was willing to do anything to get another hit."

His heart ached that she thought of him that way. "I don't remember it like that. I saw you as the only real thing in a world I didn't want to be in. You were… Sometimes I wish I met you before Tommy died."

Her head shook. "You still would have investigated."

"Investigated. Not given up my whole life because I didn't think I had one. Because I know I should have been there for him."

"You were in the military," Harlow argued. "You couldn't exactly come any time he called. We've talked about this."

"Not this way. Not when I'm calm and looking at my life in a different way. It's odd how clear things become when you have no more options. Or I guess I have most of the options now." He sighed. It was overly dramatic but true. "It's weird. Now I have to figure out how to live a whole life. I have to find a way to not feel like I failed. I meant what I said. If your cousin can take down Hamilton, I'll be at peace with it. Even if it means I have to testify and admit everything I've done."

Even if it meant going to jail. Hell, at least in jail he could moon over her without the option of stalking her. Although that was another way to get his ass thrown in jail. Or dead, if her dads got hold of him.

"It won't come to that," she replied. "I get the feeling Jack will work with the prosecutor to get you immunity. You never killed anyone. Anyone you hurt was likely self-defense."

She was leaving out so much. "And the drug running? The deliveries I made that I have no idea what was in the package?"

"Are peanuts compared to what you know about how the organization runs," she replied. "You're not going to jail. You're not going to die. So it's time you figured out how to live. You think I don't know what goes on in your head? You might never have said the words to me because you didn't trust me enough to show me your soul, but I still knew."

"That's not true."

"It is," she insisted. "Or maybe you don't trust yourself. Either way, there's a lack of trust, and that will kill any chance at a relationship. What I was trying to say is even though you never said it out loud, I know you think it should have been you. You think Tommy had more to offer the world, and if anyone could die and have no one notice, it's you."

She'd summed him up perfectly. "It never helps to tell the woman you're in love with that you're a worthless piece of shit. One tends to want to hide the fact."

She laid back, her gaze going to the ceiling. "I can't fix you, Jensen. Thinking you love me won't fix what's empty inside you."

He wasn't letting her off so easy. He'd gotten to know her, too. "Tell me you don't think your sister is more important than you. If something happened to your sister, you wouldn't want to take her place."

She was silent for a moment, and he worried he'd lost her. "Of course I would. Greer is… Well, she's ridiculously talented. She got all our mom's artistic skills. She's smart."

"She's not smarter than you. Maybe she's better at you in art, but she's not smarter. I would bet she can't sit down and figure out a puzzle the way you can. I bet she doesn't throw her damn body into battle the way you do," he replied.

"Yeah, and while Tommy might have been smart, he was naïve and he was stubborn," a familiar voice said. "You told him not to take those loans. You sat him down and found a school you could afford for him. Harlow, did you know he offered to pay his brother's way through college?"

Harlow sat up, the sheet right below her breasts as she turned to Niall, who stood in the doorway. "No. He only told me his brother went to college and took out some predatory loans."

"Which I wouldn't have let him sign if I had been around." He should have kissed her instead of talking. Now he felt weird because he was naked and Niall was here.

Did he feel weird? Or was it weird that he didn't care, and that's what he was worried about. Or not worried about. He wasn't sure, and honestly, he didn't want to think about it right now. Fake it 'til you make it. Wasn't that his motto when it came to becoming walking vengeance? He was such a douche, but it was true. He'd decided to play Punisher and he'd done it by sinking into the role and not coming out of it until he met a gorgeous girl with electric blue hair and eyes that brought him back to the real world. Or showed him that there was another, better world. What if he sank into this role? What if he tried?

"Like I said," Niall continued, "Tommy could be stubborn. He wanted to be a doctor."

"Yes, I knew that. He was smart," Harlow agreed. "But he still got caught by Hamilton."

"He thought he knew what he was doing," Niall explained.

Jensen shook his head. "He was ashamed. He knew damn well something was wrong with his new job. It was why he tried to hide it from me. It took me a while to untangle what happened to him. According to my brother, he was just working to save up money for medical school. What I realized was he was trying to pay off his loans at first, and then he was underwater with the cartel Hamilton was working with. His undergrad degree cost one hundred and twenty-three thousand dollars. I paid fifty of it. So my brother's life was worth seventy-three thousand dollars. I thought my life was worth way less. I meant to stay in the Army until I retired because it was the only place for me. Lately, I've been wondering about that."

"Lately?" Niall asked, moving to the bed. He sat down but not before he laid a kiss on Harlow's forehead.

It was intimate, being in this room alone with them. It felt…right. "Well, since last night. I'll admit that until last night I was very focused. I was close, and I didn't want to think about anything except achieving my goal. Now I kind of question the goal. Turns out I don't particularly want to go to prison or die."

Harlow sighed. "Now you decide this."

"We can talk about this after breakfast. I made some pancakes and bacon and eggs," Niall announced. "Jensen, there's some sweats and underwear and a T-shirt in the bathroom waiting for you."

There was this piece of him that wanted to tell Niall to fuck off. He wasn't in charge here. It was the part of him that liked to start fires just to see them burn.

He wasn't letting that place rule him anymore. "Thank you."

"What about me?" Harlow asked, her chin tilting up in that sexy, stubborn expression of hers.

Niall leaned over and brushed a kiss on her lips. "You don't need clothes, princess."

She growled his way. "I am not wearing your shirt all day. Also, I need a laptop."

Jensen had bad news for her. "Uh, there's no Internet out here."

Harlow fell back on the bed, pulling a pillow over her face and screaming.

So she was going to be fun today.

Niall looked at him. "She's going to be fun."

Damn. They'd always been in synch.

The sound of tires crunching on gravel made every muscle in Jensen's body go tense, and he reached for the gun he'd placed on the bedside table the night before.

"Harlow, get in the…" When he turned to order her to hide in the bathroom, he noticed she already had a gun in her hand, the sheet wrapped around her body.

A brow rose over her eyes. "Get in where, Jensen?"

Yep. That was a trap he needed to stay out of. "I meant Niall. Buddy, you should get in the bathroom. Harlow, watch my six."

Those gorgeous eyes rolled. "You watch my six."

She strolled out.

"I am not hiding in the bathroom." Niall followed her.

He had lost all control.

He hoped they weren't about to lose everything.

Chapter Eleven

Harlow felt the weight of the Beretta in her hand as she eased down the hall.

She wished she had on some undies, at least. She might be about to go into a gun fight with a threadbare sheet as her only clothes. Technically it could be a sheath dress, but it was proof of her shame.

Was it shame? She didn't feel ashamed. She felt…relaxed. Like super relaxed. Muscles that had been stiff for freaking years now felt like jelly. Except for her trigger finger. That was ready to go since they were apparently about to be invaded.

"Who knows we're here?" Niall asked in a hushed tone.

"No one should," Jensen said from the back.

It wasn't like the house was big. It was pretty tiny, so they were close together as they moved toward the kitchen. The smell of bacon hit her nose and then she was pissed because she was freaking hungry, and did she get to eat the delicious-smelling food that she did not have to cook herself? No. She had to deal with potential assassins. And he made coffee. Damn it. She worried about coffee, and Niall had made sure she had it and now she might die.

It felt unfair. She kind of wanted more than one night with them. Oh, she told herself she didn't care and it had been all stress relief, but it had been good. Like spectacular. The absolute best sex she'd ever had, and she wanted more.

It did not feel like she was going to fuck them out of her system. It felt dangerous. Like she was going in the opposite direction and fucking them into her system more.

And last night she'd decided she was going with it. Oh, she was still going to walk away at the end of this, but for the time they were stuck together she was going to play her role and enjoy it.

"We got rid of all the phones," Niall whispered as he followed her into the living room. The place was quiet and dark. He'd opened the shades in the kitchen but kept the living room closed up. "All we have are burners. Is there any way there's a tracker on my Jeep?"

"I would suspect there would be one on mine, but not yours," Jensen replied. "They didn't know you existed until last night."

There was one tracker she hadn't thought about. Damn it. "It's in my upper arm." She lowered her gun. "If that's my dad, I'm going to live in the fields with the cows."

"What do you mean it's in your arm?" Niall asked.

"You let them chip you?" Jensen snorted as he snuck a peek out the window. "Not your dad, but also not anyone we're going to murder."

There was a knock on the door. "Hey, Har. Let us in. We've got your shit, and I picked up some donuts. Gigi is worried, and she wouldn't let me come alone. Neither would your sister."

Ruby. She flicked the safety back on the gun and opened the door. "How?"

Ruby flashed a grin. She was looking fresh and happy this morning in her jeans and T-shirt and leather jacket, her curly hair in a ponytail. "I hacked Big Tag's system, of course. He tried to give me some BS about how if he wasn't giving your dad your location, he couldn't give it to anyone. So I took it. See, guys. She is obviously fine."

Her cousin's eyes were wide, and her sister stood back slightly.

Greer had a suitcase in her hand that hopefully included underwear and a bra. "She obviously has joined the club. Like The Club club. Uncle Julian should have named it better. When I heard who Jensen was, I worried you were going to commit murder. I'm glad you didn't choose violence, sis."

"Do I want to know how you figured out who Jensen is?"

Harlow stood back and allowed them to enter.

"Oh, Dad ranted for hours," Greer explained. "You should know he's got a dossier on Jensen now, and he's pushing Jack to get the FBI involved. When Papa tried to point out that Jensen was doing exactly what you were doing when you got arrested in California, Dad added assault and battery."

"Jensen didn't break my arm." So her Dad had been having fun in the wake of her flight.

"I did put her in the position where her arm was broken." Jensen seemed to realize he wasn't wearing anything but a pair of boxers. "I should…go and put clothes on. And then we can talk about the fact that our position is helplessly compromised and start trying to figure out where to go next."

Greer smiled at him. "You don't have to do that on my account. I'm in the lifestyle. I'm used to hot dudes running around with their dicks hanging out."

"It's not…" Jensen looked down where yes, in fact, his dick was slightly poking out. And he ran back toward the bedroom.

"What exactly are you doing here?" Niall had his Dom voice on. He was all big muscles and broad shoulders and a deep voice that brooked no disobedience.

"Checking on my friend, asshole." Ruby didn't miss a beat.

She could have told Niall that the Dom thing didn't work on any of her friends outside a club setting.

Greer frowned at Niall. "You are a rat-fink lying jerk, and I hope you got the least amount of sex."

Niall frowned as though the morning was not going how he'd planned. Welcome to her world. "I got a reasonable portion of the sex. And I also apologized and made breakfast."

Gigi sniffed the air. "Is that bacon?"

"Yep," Niall replied.

Gigi sighed and walked inside. "Good. My mom has my dad on this low-fat diet because his cholesterol is high. Let me tell you nurses know how to fuck with a diet. I'm starving. They wouldn't let me have a donut. She said you might need to eat your feelings, and she wasn't sure how many feelings you would have."

"Well now I know she fucked her feelings, so we can eat all we like," Ruby announced, passing her the box. "Please tell me there are pancakes."

Greer held back, allowing Niall to follow their cousin and Ruby into the kitchen, saying something about how he hadn't planned on this many people. "I was going to defend those donuts. Carbs are your go-to heartache food."

"My heart doesn't ache." But she still opened the box and sighed in anticipation of that soft, sugary treat. Bear claws. Her sister knew her well. "I had a job go wrong, and now I'm stuck in hiding for a while. Jack will figure it out and then everything will be fine. Now explain to me how Dad isn't riding in on his shiny SUV to rescue me from my own idiocy. He should have a bodyguard on you, and you should be on a plane to Colorado now."

"Oh, according to Mom he spent most of the night harassing Big Tag and then finally passed out like an overly stimulated Rottweiler. You know how he gets when he's that way." Greer looked around the house. "Whose place is this?"

"Jensen's childhood home. From what I can tell they used to own a lot of this land, but the house is what's left." It was odd to see her sister here. She associated Greer with the beautiful places of the world. She looked right at home in their parents' big house in Highland Park. Greer fit there and with all the prep school girls they'd been around.

Harlow had preferred hanging with the Taggart kids. She loved her sister but was surprised she was here. Greer always followed the rules.

"You met him in LA?" Greer asked.

Harlow nodded. "Yeah, when I was on the Gains' case. We were supposed to work together and he decided it was too dangerous for me and put me in a position where I got arrested. He didn't realize I wasn't alone in the building, and the guy who was there figured out the cops were coming and took it out on me. That's how I ended up in the hospital. Why are you here?"

Greer's eyes widened in obvious surprise. "Because you're my sister and you're in trouble. I know I'm not some tough chick and I can't beat the crap out of whoever's chasing you, but I can at least make sure you're okay. Why are you surprised I'm here?"

That wasn't a question she was ready for. "I don't know. I guess I thought you would be helping Mom deal with my latest attempt on

Dad's health and happiness. I didn't mean to freak him out. I was only trying to do my job."

"Mom can handle Dad. She's excellent at it. Sometimes I wish she wasn't so good at it or that they would at least, like, lock the door or keep it to the club," Greer replied with a delicate shudder. "I knew for a fact that there was zero chance Ruby didn't have a way to contact you so I showed up on her doorstep at six this morning with Gigi in tow because she heard the story from one of the Taggarts. The lawyer with the baby, I think. Let me tell you The Hideout's gossip grapevine does not stop for sleep."

Excellent. So everyone knew she'd fucked up. "I'm still surprised Dad let you out of his sight."

"Didn't have a choice," Greer replied. "I knew the minute Gigi told me what was happening that there was probably a bodyguard on his way to my place, so I managed to not be at my place. I went to Gigi's and we went to yours and got you everything you could need, and then Ruby yelled at us for a long time."

"Good, because that was dangerous. They could have been watching my place." She didn't say they could have followed Ruby because Ruby would have made damn sure no one was watching.

"Yeah. Ruby mentioned that a couple hundred times," Greer admitted. "She can yell really loud."

If Ruby was yelling, then she was annoyed, not truly angry. When Ruby got mad she went still and silent and cold as ice. "What you did was dangerous."

"Well, I was taking after my little sis," Greer replied. "Though I didn't consider grabbing some undies and clothes and your makeup to be a walk on the wild side. That's what you did last night. I thought we were never going to marry two boys. We made a deal and everything."

They'd been teens and their parents were weird and obnoxiously in love, and two dads seemed like a lot to put on a girl, so they'd pinkie sworn to be normal. "Yeah, well, we were kids. I suppose we always look for the type of relationship we understand."

"You understand Dad?"

"No one understands Dad," Harlow shot back. She sat down on the couch, taking a bite of the bear claw. It was cinnamony and tasted like comfort. All she needed was a cup of coffee.

"Hey, it's not your usual brand, but it'll have to do in a pinch." Niall was walking toward her holding a mug. "Your partner is bossy. I'm going to check and make sure Jensen isn't suffering the PTSD of having his dick hang out in front of your family."

He turned and walked away.

The man was heavenly. Even after all the stuff that happened last night Niall was looking freaking fine. And he brought her coffee. Since they started dating, he always got up before she did and made a big pot of coffee and brought it to her and they would sit in bed and talk about the upcoming day.

It was dumb because it had only been a couple of days, and she already missed the ritual.

Greer leaned over as though watching him leave. "Tell your partner he has nothing to be ashamed of. It was a good way to start the day." She frowned back at Harlow. "He could have brought me one."

It was petty, but she kind of liked that Niall had only thought of her. Greer was gorgeous and sweet and way more feminine than Harlow, and every single boyfriend she'd ever had flirted with her sister. Greer didn't flirt back. She would never, but it still rankled that they all took care of Greer.

"I'll get you one." It was totally okay for *her* to take care of her sister.

Greer reached out, putting a hand on hers to stop her from standing. "I don't need coffee. I need to know you're okay. I'm joking about the whole threesome thing. I'm actually worried about it because up until yesterday, I didn't know this Jensen guy existed and you were barely dating Niall. It's not like you to move so fast."

"What if I told you it's only sex," Harlow tried. "I had a lot to deal with yesterday and I needed some stress relief."

Greer's eyes rolled. "I would call bullshit. Not because I don't think sex can be casual. It can, and there's nothing wrong with that. But it's not how you work. If you sleep with someone, you care about them. I'm worried you're going to twist that care into something it's not."

"I don't understand."

Her sister's brows rose, her dumbass-said-what expression. "Tell me you're not angry with Niall. I don't know the Jensen situation since you don't talk to me like that, but I do know you've been happy with Niall the last few days. You actually had lunch with me, and it wasn't a three-martini lunch where you show me how much you don't fit at the country club."

Well Greer wasn't pulling punches today. "Sorry. I'll try to keep the drinking down. I wouldn't want to embarrass you."

Greer sighed, a deeply frustrated sound. "Not what I meant. And I blame myself because I always invite you out there because it's close and easy. I should come into your world every now and then. You know the only person who's worse than you at the country club?"

She did, of course. "Dad isn't exactly a country club guy, and you know neither is mom. She goes because of their gym, and she claims they have the only massage therapist worth using in the city. And Papa's golf. I know Dad was raised in that world, but he doesn't truly belong. I'm honestly not sure where he belongs. Maybe some university teaching investigation techniques."

"He would kill all the students," Greer said with a laugh and then she sobered. "I guess the other reason I came was to make sure you don't, like, decide you're done with us."

Harlow put the coffee down. "What is that supposed to mean?"

"It means I know Dad can be a lot, but he loves you. He loves you so much," Greer said. "He worries about you." She held a hand up as though staving off the argument she knew was coming. "It doesn't excuse him acting like an overprotective asshole, but you need to think about how he… Well, how he thinks. It's hard for him to know you're in danger."

This was well-worn ground. "I love Dad. But I can't be someone I'm not."

Greer nodded. "He knows that. The truth of the matter is he doesn't want you to be anyone but you. I know you won't believe this but he's proud of you."

"You're right. I don't believe it." She kind of wished her sister hadn't come along now. She could sit and think about how moronic it was to sub for two men she couldn't allow herself to trust. But no, she now had to think about her relationship with her dad. And her sister.

"He is proud of you. Hell, Harlow, when you're not around

you're almost all he talks about."

Harlow knew that wasn't a good thing. "Because he thinks I'm going to die and he's paranoid. You know he used to spend all his time worrying about people sniping him. I don't know why he didn't think that the easiest way to stop people from sniping him was to not be a massive asshole, but here we are. Now he's transferred that problem to me."

"He goes to therapy, you know," Greer said quietly.

That was news to her. "What?" She figured out what her sister had to mean. "Uncle Leo doesn't count."

Leo Meyer was The Club's resident therapist. He was also one of her dad's closest friends.

Greer sighed. "He's not seeing Uncle Leo, though you know he's always been in that group Leo has with a bunch of the men in our circle."

Harlow waved that off. "They play basketball. He's played for as long as I can remember."

Greer shot her a look that told her she knew something. "It's not about the basketball. Think about who those men are. Uncle Leo, Big Tag, Dad, Papa, Uncle Cole, Uncle Mason. Wade Rycroft. Alex McKay. What do they have in common? It's not a love of basketball."

She thought for a moment, and then tears pulsed behind her eyes. "They always play when Mom has her group. I thought…I thought they just wanted to be where she was so she didn't feel alone."

The one thing all those men had were wives who had suffered horrible abuse. Either at the hands of former husbands or boyfriends, or complete strangers in her mom's case.

"From what I know they support each other and have for over twenty years. It's how Big Tag finally convinced Dad to talk to someone about his problems with anxiety," Greer explained. "He won't take anything yet, but they're working on it."

Guilt swamped her. "And I'm setting him back."

"That's not true, and it's not my point. My point is he's trying. I know he wasn't the easiest parent in the world," Greer began.

"No, I got lectures on how I could die while riding a bicycle. Like he used physics and everything." She sighed. "He also never once told me he was too busy to help me with my homework. He would sit and work Legos with me forever."

"I did puzzles with him," Greer said with a wistful smile. "But it was awful to watch mystery movies with him. Like dude I'm ten. Of course I don't know Goofy accidently stole Mickey's sandwich."

"I did." She remembered that cartoon. Her dad was right. The writers had been asleep at the wheel on that one.

Greer nodded like she'd made her point. "Yes, you were a pain in the ass, too. You and Dad would wreck every murder mystery by figuring it out two minutes in."

They had been a menace to all who wanted a mystery solved at the end. But was that her fault? Most mysteries were fairly easy to solve since the author—unlike real-life criminals—tended to follow some form of logic. So a person with investigative skills could usually figure out a whodunnit. Oh. That's where she was going. "I am not like… Fine. I'm a little like dad, but I can function in the normal world."

"So can he. Mostly. I want you to think about the differences. You are very much like Dad, and I'm Papa."

Of course she was. "I think you're more like Mom."

Greer's head shook. "I might have gotten her talent, but I'm not as fierce as Mom. I'm more like Papa. I'm content to sit back and let things come my way. I'm not the one everyone notices. I'm not the big personality."

"No, you're the one everyone loves."

"Uh, I've been dealing with phone calls all day from our friends and family who are freaked out that you're in trouble. The twins asked if they should look into it," Greer said like she hadn't told her there was a bomb waiting to go off.

"You tell them the CIA does not work on domestic soil." The last thing she needed was to get the twins involved.

"I don't think they know that. I'm pretty sure they run a ton of ops at The Hideout," Greer replied. "But my point is everyone loves you. You like to pretend you're the tough chick who doesn't fit in. The trouble is you got born into a group where tough chicks are kind of the norm, and I'm the one who doesn't fit."

"You fit." She couldn't believe she was hearing this from her always-confident big sister.

"With some, and when I say fit, I don't mean I get left out of things. Our friend group is amazing and diverse, but I always think it's ridiculous when you pretend like no one understands you. It reminds me of…"

"Dad." She felt a flush go through her system. "Because he often feels like he's in his own world and no one but Mom and Papa can be there with him."

"Sometimes he doesn't even feel like Mom and Papa can understand him," Greer continued. "I know it sounds dumb, but it's hard to be as smart as he is."

"And as picky as he is. And as weird as he is about sniper positions and how clean a bathroom has to be before he'll use it." Her dad was a weirdo. And she was a lot like him, which was why they clashed from time to time. It was inevitable, and she probably made it way worse because she wouldn't sit down and talk to him about it. They went right into arguing. She wasn't patient with him, and he had been patient with her for so many years.

How hard had it been for her paranoid, obsessive-compulsive, genius dad to deal with kids? To deal with dirty diapers and getting thrown up on. He had a thing about bacteria, and yet she remembered him sitting with her when she was sick. "I'm sorry. I'll sit down and talk to him. It's the chasing me down thing that bugs me, but I will try to give him some grace."

"I'm not even asking for that," her sister said. "I'm begging you not to go no contact with us."

Harlow felt her jaw drop. "I would never do that. I have never once said that to Dad. He's been reading too many Reddit posts. We need to keep him out of certain parts of the Internet."

Greer smiled and leaned over to take Harlow's hand. "I'm glad to hear that. I know you won't believe me, but I've missed you."

"I've been right here," Harlow insisted.

"You've been in your own world, and that's okay. You need to be from time to time. But the last few years it's felt like you're pulling away. Not in an 'I'm all grown up and having a great time' way. In an 'I'm leaving you behind' way."

She was so self-centered sometimes. All this time she'd assumed Greer was probably happy she didn't have to dole out big sis advice to her fuck-up younger sister. She wasn't giving herself enough grace either, and she wasn't being honest. She never meant to hurt her sister. She'd meant to protect herself, but her family wasn't something she needed to be protected from. "I shut down after Jensen dumped me. I was ashamed I let myself be in that position, and I didn't want any of you to know it. I'm lucky Dad didn't investigate and get involved in this whole mess."

"They had a huge fight about it," Greer informed her. "Right after you got back from LA, Dad wanted to do just that. He knew there was a guy involved, and he had talked Papa into going back out and finding him. Mom put her foot down. Like hard down."

Harlow sniffled. "I didn't mean to cause them problems."

"Mom said you would tell us what happened when you were ready, and if you never were we would love you and help you where we could. You did tell someone, right? Ruby knows." It wasn't really a question. "I want to make sure you tell someone if you can't tell me."

Yep, her sister was making her cry.

"This bacon is excellent," Ruby said as she walked in and then stopped. "Sorry. Is this a sister thing?"

Greer looked up and nodded, but then held out a hand. "It is, so you should join us. You have been the best thing to happen to my sister in a long time, and I'm happy you're part of our family."

"I don't know how to deal with that. I'm feeling things, Harlow," Ruby admitted, a frown on her face.

"Greer does that. It's the artist thing." Harlow leaned over and shouted toward the kitchen. "Gigi, we're about to talk shit about the two men I slept with last night."

There was a gasp and then Gigi was in the room, plate in hand. "I'm here. Did we start? Should I make mimosas?"

Of course Gigi brought champagne to her safe house. Harlow nodded. "We're going to need them."

She turned to her sister and told her the whole story.

* * * *

"You do not want to go in there." Niall sat in the afternoon light and slowly sipped his coffee. He looked his best friend over. Jensen was dressed in the sweats and T-shirt Niall had bought him at the only store within twenty minutes of this place. He did not miss Bonnet, TX. Sometimes he didn't even recognize the place. His tiny apartment in Dallas over his gym felt far more like home. Especially now that Harlow had a toothbrush there.

Jensen stared at the swinging door that separated the kitchen from the living room. No open floor plans here. This puppy was built in the forties when women's work needed to be hidden away so it looked like no work at all.

"We need to have a long talk with the ladies about what it means to be in a safe house," Jensen said. "They are pretending like this is some fun sleepover."

"I think that would be a huge mistake, man."

Jensen turned his way, frowning. "And them potentially leading Hamilton's men right here isn't?"

He knew there was some kind of lecture coming, but he'd kind of already gotten the answers from Ruby. "She made sure no one was following them, and she checked her SUV for trackers."

"Which apparently Harlow has," Jensen replied with a hint of outrage. "They tagged her like she's a dog who might go missing."

"Or like a young woman who works in a dangerous business and wants to be found even if the assholes who might take her steal her phone." Niall was kind of all in on Harlow having a tracker. He wished Jensen had one. He could get an app for his phone and then always know where the people he was in a relationship with were about to die. "Ruby says only she and Taggart know how to turn it on, and Taggart signed an NDA when Harlow agreed. He would only turn it on if she was in real danger. Ruby informed him what she did and where Harlow is, and he feels no need to let her dad in on her location."

"But she told Harlow's sister and cousin, and now we have a family reunion." Jensen started for the living room.

"They're talking about you," Niall explained.

Jensen stopped, his hand on the door. He seemed to listen for a moment and then turned and grabbed a coffee mug. "Tell me they aren't drinking champagne. That sounded like someone popped a bottle of champagne."

"I believe they are calling them mimosas, though they didn't use a lot of juice. There is some. I got orange juice for breakfast."

Niall pointed to the fridge. "It was on sale."

"Maybe they're not the only ones looking at this like it's some kind of vacation." Jensen stared at him. "How are you so fucking calm?"

"I assure you being back here is not a vacation." It was unsettling being here. Tommy was in every room of this house. Damn but he missed that kid. "What should I be feeling, Jensen? How should I react?"

Jensen huffed and ran a frustrated hand through his hair. "I don't know, man. Freaked out. I got us in the shittiest situation we could be in."

His friend was not thinking big enough. "Oh, I can think of shittier. You must have lost your powers of imagination, brother. We could be in custody. We could be arrested and blamed for a ton of stuff. We could be dead because the fed didn't want to blow his cover. We were lucky, you know."

"I don't feel lucky." Jensen pulled out a plate and looked over the breakfast Niall made. "When did you start cooking?"

"When I decided I wanted to eat food that didn't come from a drive through." Niall took a sip of coffee and wondered if he should see if Harlow needed a warmup. Then he heard someone say *no he didn't* and decided to stay right where he was. "After we left the military I found myself eating like we did when we were in high school."

"Turkey sandwiches and frozen pizza? It was pretty much all my momma bought. That and boxed mac and cheese." Jensen frowned as he sat down and stared at the plate he made for himself. "Are these frozen?"

Now Niall was offended. "No, it was not frozen. I can make pancakes. It's a mix, but there are ways to enhance it. I put some vanilla and cinnamon in, and one extra egg. I usually drink a protein shake or eat an egg white omelet, but somehow today my protein intake doesn't seem so important. Pancakes felt like the way to go."

Jensen took a bite. "Wow, that's actually good. Damn, you know I'm pretty sure when I'm not at the club I also still eat like we did in high school."

"Then I'm worried about your cholesterol, brother," Niall shot back.

Jensen put his fork down. "I guess we should talk."

Niall stared at him for a moment. "I've been trying to talk for over a year. Hell, I've been trying to talk since Tommy died." He sighed. "I'm sorry. I don't mean to push you. I've been talking to a guy at the club. He says you'll talk about it when you're ready. I'm worried you're never going to be ready."

A brow rose over Jensen's eyes. "Not to push me? Are you fucking kidding me? We had a three-way last night. I assure you I feel pushed."

He was intentionally misunderstanding. Probably because he wasn't ready to talk about what was actually wrong. "I wasn't talking about that. I was obviously talking about Tommy and why you've spent years of your life in a criminal organization. And don't tell me you didn't enjoy last night."

Jensen sat back, and for a moment Niall worried he would get up and leave the room. Instead he took another bite and sighed before talking. "Last night… I didn't think I would like it. But I'm serious about Harlow. I'm possessive when it comes to her. I did it because I thought it was the only way I would ever get her to let me back in."

None of this was news to him. He knew exactly why Jensen agreed to last night. "Oh, I think that's going to be far tougher than it looks. Last night was nothing but the opening salvo in a war we only have a few days to fight. I worry if we don't secure her and convince her we're good together, she'll walk away. She has a whole family waiting for her, so we can't use the 'we're all we have' argument."

"We *are* all we have," Jensen replied. "You and me, I mean. I know all about Harlow's large, kind of weird family. She talked about them a lot. But you and me, we're it. It's what I've been thinking about all freaking night. I'm trying to not be angry with you. I'm trying to understand why you wouldn't tell me."

This felt like progress. At least he was asking and not throwing punches. Niall would take it. "At first I didn't tell you because I honestly didn't think she wanted to have anything to do with me. She was shut down when I got there. She didn't play much and when she did it felt perfunctory, like she was going through the motions. And then one day she sat down at my table in the lounge and asked me what my story was. We started talking and I realized she was interested but wary. We started something of a friendship, but she still didn't make a move, and I realized she had to be the one to make a move. I wasn't sure she ever would. What would you have done if I told you I was attracted to her?"

Jensen seemed to think about the question for a moment. "I don't know. I didn't have a plan for what I would do after the mission was done because I didn't think I would survive it. At the time it seemed reasonable, and now I realize how fucked up it is. I don't… I don't think this is the life Tommy would have wanted for me. I never considered what he would want even though you asked me a hundred times. I told myself it didn't matter because Tommy was fucking dead and if he wanted a say he should have stayed alive. Why am I mad at him?"

Finally he was asking the right questions. He was seeing through the fog of grief. "Because he was your brother and he died. Because he didn't call you when he needed help. Because we were all we had. You and me and Tommy. For most of our lives we had to watch out for each other, and he didn't let you do your job. Of course you're mad, but throwing your life away, throwing what we could have with that woman away, isn't going to solve your problem. You want to punch me? I'll take it."

A chuckle huffed from Jensen's chest. "It won't help."

"Might make you feel better," Niall offered. "I'll take the punch and I won't hit back. In fact, I might even cry a little."

That got a slight smile from his best friend. "Planning on getting Harlow to baby you?"

Niall shrugged. "I bet it would work. Or she would punch me too and tell me to take it like a warrior. See, the thing is I don't know that I want to be a warrior. I was for a while, and I find I prefer being a caretaker. I like making sure the gym is clean and everything is ready for the next day. I like to sit and make plans for clients. I like to think about them. Everyone's different, you know. Everyone has a place where they're comfortable. I like the rituals of a quiet life."

"And I've lived on nothing but adrenaline for years." Jensen sounded tired. "I don't even know what to do now. If Hamilton doesn't kill us, what the hell do I do with the rest of my life? Shouldn't I know? Shouldn't I have a plan?"

Not if he didn't expect to live out the year. What his friend needed was something to live for. "We can work on that. You would be a good personal trainer. You could do that part time while you figure it out. Or you could work investigations with Harlow."

"I seriously doubt she's bringing me on the team."

"You would be surprised. She brought me on, and she didn't want to." At least he thought she hadn't. She'd been reluctant because of his inexperience. "She would love to have backup that doesn't include the McKay-Taggart team. Her dad might feel better if he knows she's got solid backup. You're ex-military."

"And I've spent the last couple of years doing criminal shit."

This was something he had to be careful about, but they needed to discuss. "How bad is it? Legally?"

Jensen suddenly found his plate very interesting. "I've managed to stay away from hurting anyone who didn't deserve it. Anything physical has been in self-defense, but then I never got to the higher levels. So for me it was all dropping off packages I wasn't supposed to open or ask about. I've absolutely aided in laundering their money."

Niall nodded. "Good. None of this is going to freak out a DA. They'll give you immunity if you can turn over some good evidence."

"I can prove the money laundering beyond a shadow of a doubt," Jensen offered. "I'm sure either Jack's team has my laptop or Phil managed to get it before Jack got there. The good news is the really damning evidence isn't on the laptop. I had to keep it pretty clean in case someone from the organization wanted to inspect it. So I would download the real information onto a thumb drive and it's hidden. They won't find that. I can give it to Jack when the time comes."

"After we find a lawyer for you." He wasn't about to let Jensen give everything up without a solid offer of immunity. "I'm going to talk to Harlow about that. She knows some people."

"I don't have money to pay for a lawyer," Jensen replied. "They give you a lawyer if they arrest you. Turning myself in is an option we need to talk about."

"With a lawyer who will talk to you for free since you're connected to Harlow. Also, our princess is a moneybags. She won't miss it at all. That's the hardest thing. Her parents are filthy rich. It's weird. She doesn't act that way. It kind of freaks me out."

"Yeah, I met what I thought was a middle-class, normal woman with an interesting career and then she's got two billionaire dads, a trust fund that could buy the world, and a mom who's considered a modern master painter," Jensen agreed. "And I came from this." He gestured a hand around the worn kitchen. "I wondered what I could offer her. I worried I was her rebellion."

Niall shook his head. "Nah, that's not who she is. Honestly, from what I can tell, it's not who her family is. And if you think she's rich, I don't even know what to call Gigi. Her dad is the oldest of the Dawson kids, and he apparently was a ruthless businessman. Guess who he married? A nurse from rural Colorado. At least that's where they met. Harlow's mom was a massage therapist when she met Ben and Chase Dawson. They're not some elite family who only hangs with other elites. From what I can tell they're pretty normal with the exception of the money, and she'll pay for your lawyer even if she hates you. She'll do it because it's who she is."

A sniffle caught his attention, and Niall hissed because he had not noticed Harlow had joined them.

Shit and shit. "Hey…"

"You see me that way? You genuinely think I would pay for the lawyer of the man who burned the hell out of me?" Harlow asked, and Niall couldn't figure out if he was in serious trouble or not.

He decided to go with honesty. He stood up. "I think you could hate a person and still help them because you couldn't withhold aid if you had it. I'm not talking about something small. I remember when you refused to help that friend of your sister's fix her corset."

"Well, I heard her call a friend of mine fat, so she could do that herself," Harlow shot back.

"And if she tripped and broke her wrist?" Niall prompted because he was right about this. No matter whether she was upset with him, he would speak truth about her.

"I would do whatever I needed to in order to make sure she got help." Harlow moved into his space, her head tilting up as her hands went to his shoulders. "I want to be mad at you."

Oh, he was so in love with this woman. He put his hands on her hips, his whole body feeling electric because she was close to him.

"I'm going to make it very hard, princess. I'm going to do anything I need to do to ensure you can't be mad at me."

She sniffled again and then went on her toes and brushed her lips against his. "I'm going to try hard." She stepped back. "Sorry to interrupt. We're out of juice."

He grinned and turned to the fridge. It still worked, thank the universe. He pulled out the bottle of orange juice and passed it to her. "Here. You need fuel to trash us."

"I don't think we should encourage her." Jensen had a frown on his face.

She huffed his way. "Yeah, I don't need encouragement. I have rage to keep me strong. And your way smarter friend is right. You are not talking to Jack or anyone else until we get a lawyer. My uncle doesn't do criminal law, but I have a friend who does. Greer will talk to Travis. He's a Taggart, by the way."

Jensen's head shook. "How fucking many of them are there?"

"It's an army," she conceded. "Also, he's a baby lawyer, but he'll know what to do. Now I have some assholes to trash to my friends."

Niall winked her way. "You have fun, princess."

She winked back and then turned and gave them both her middle finger before walking through the doorway.

Damn but she was pretty. "She's asking for it."

Jensen's dark expression turned his way. "I don't like that she kissed you and she didn't kiss me. She should have kissed me, too. Isn't that how it works?"

Oh, they had finally gotten to the portion of the talk he was most interested in. "Nope. We have our own relationships with her, and she is not expected to keep some chart where she divvies out her affection in a perfect fifty/fifty fashion. You want her to kiss you, tempt her."

"What if I sleep with her when you're not around?"

Niall shrugged. "I hope you have a good time, and I will try to tempt her to sleep with me, too. Though I suspect a lot of the sex will be the three of us. I don't intend to let her live on her own for long. I'm going to work extremely hard to get the three of us in an apartment quickly. Think of this time not as a traumatic experience, but rather as a trial run. We need her to never want to be without us."

"I don't think I know how to do that," Jensen admitted. "I'm way better at pushing her away."

"Okay, we're not going to do that anymore. I know you don't think this can work. I know you think you want her for yourself," Niall began.

"I don't know," Jensen interrupted. "I love her. She's the only woman I've ever loved, but I think loving her scares me because I'll fuck it up. I'll hurt her."

"I won't let you. Or if you do, we'll work on it. And she'll always have me, too. Think about that. You can rely on me. Now that doesn't work if you think you can come in and blow her mind with sex and leave everything else to me."

Jensen held up a hand. "I don't want that. If we're going to do this thing, I want to be a fully functional member of the family, and I'll do what I need to in order to be that man. You said you were talking to someone."

He was not going to cry. Niall nodded slowly. "I am. He's an expert at family trauma and PTSD. He's roughly our age and he works at a place called the Ferguson Clinic. He plays at The Hideout, so he's lifestyle friendly."

Jensen grimaced. "Is he another Taggart?"

Oh, he was going to have to get used to those, but at least he could spare him this time. "No. His dad is the head of Julian's security. I think you'll like him."

"And I want to learn to cook, too." Jensen seemed to be building steam for this new life they were facing. "I shouldn't be eating nothing but sandwiches, and I don't want it all to fall on you. Harlow… She's not good in the kitchen."

Oh, he knew. "Yes, but when she gets it in her head to try, we have to smile and thank her. And eat it all."

"All right," Jensen agreed. "Now sit and let's talk about how to take her down. She's going to be stubborn."

Niall took his seat. "Yeah, but we're going to be sneaky and smart."

He picked up his fork. He was hungry again.

Chapter Twelve

Jensen closed the door on Harlow's guests, hoping that Ruby didn't actually know how to use that evil eye she'd given him. It was a powerful stink eye. "She does not like me. She is never going to hire me."

"You'll work on her," Niall promised. "You have some charm when you want to."

Harlow looked so fucking pretty standing there in the yellow sundress she'd changed into after her shower. Her sister and friends had stayed for a late lunch and helped Harlow settle the bedroom the way she wanted it. Luckily, they hadn't tossed him or Niall out. There was now a bathroom filled with all kinds of nice-smelling things like shampoo and conditioner and soaps he'd been told were for different parts of the body. He wasn't sure. He only knew they smelled like Harlow. With the late afternoon light coming in, her hair looked vibrant and her skin practically glowed. "Why would Ruby hire you?"

Niall sank down to the couch. "We spent the day talking about the future. He's going to need a job. I mean if we can keep him out of jail and alive. Alive is important."

Strong arms crossed under her breasts, and she looked at Niall with a clear challenge in her gaze. "You have a business. You hire him."

Niall simply smiled at those bratty words. "I think that's how we'll go at first, but he's so much like you, princess. He needs more than a physical challenge. I think it would do him a world of good to help living people."

Okay, that bit a little, but it was also true.

Harlow looked to him as though he was going to attack. Jensen simply shrugged. "He's not wrong. I liked helping your client get out. It made me feel…worthy."

Harlow's nose wrinkled. "I don't even know what to do with that. I have to think about it."

Hey, she wasn't kicking him out. He would take it.

Niall also looked like that was their best-case scenario. "Did Ruby have any new information? I mean about the case. She has tons of new information about the three of us. The Hideout will be buzzing tonight."

Having a partner did come with privileges. Like having him cover his ass when he said stupid things. "Yeah, has she talked to Jack at all?"

Harlow's eyes narrowed, but she took the seat across from the sofa. It was an old lounge chair that his mom had kept around because the men she dated tended to like it. She always said they shouldn't sit on it because it was a chair for the man of the house.

He liked Harlow sitting there. But he also thought he should get the fuck rid of it and let her completely redo the place. If she wanted to. It was kind of nice out here. He'd sat outside and watched the cows in the distance and listened to the sound of the river that ran through the backyard. It was peaceful here. He could think, and that was weird. He thought coming back here would be awful. He thought every single step here would remind him of Tommy. And it did, but it wasn't in a bad way.

This property was something he could offer. It wasn't too far from Dallas. A couple of hours and they were in the country, away from everything. He might have thought Harlow wouldn't fit in, but she seemed to relax. He'd heard her talking to Gigi about how pretty it was here. The field by the river was lush with wildflowers, and she liked seeing the horses and cattle in the distance.

"Jack is going to be in touch with Ruby if he hears anything. He hasn't gone in to work since last night. He's got a shift tonight, and he's probably taking over Jensen's position," she explained. "He sent a report to her about what happened from his perspective last night so she could understand. I think he also sent it to Big Tag. He'll be there if we need him."

"He's taking my job? Jack's a bartender," Jensen complained. It had taken him years to get to dungeon monitor of a big club. It was rude.

"He's also been in the lifestyle for years," Harlow explained. "He's a member of The Hideout, but he put his membership on hiatus for the last year. I think he was probably concentrating on his job, likely out of town for a lot of the time. I didn't know what he was doing, obviously. But that's why Niall never met him. So we should know more after tonight. How pissed off are you that she showed up?"

That question had been directed at him. Not Niall. Because Niall wasn't the pissed-off one. Niall was the good one.

He had to stop thinking that way. He and Niall had spent much of the afternoon walking around what was left of the property. At one point they'd hauled out their old fishing gear and caught some catfish that Niall promised he could cook and talked about Harlow.

That was fucking nice, too. It was nice to be in it with someone else, someone he trusted.

"I was worried at first, but it's clear to me that Ruby is a competent professional and if she says no one could have followed her, then I believe her." He parroted back what he and Niall had decided would be the best answer to the question they knew she would ask.

Niall nodded like he was proud.

Harlow looked at him with suspicion. She turned her head to take in Niall, who sat back, the smile leaving his face. He took a sip of his beer.

"I thought you two were fighting," she said, her gaze going back and forth between them.

"We've been friends since we were seven, so we almost never fight for long," Jensen assured her. "Niall has been my brother for a long time. It would take a lot to break us. Though I almost managed it."

"So a woman could never break you up. A woman is a bump in

the road," she said softly.

Ah, the danger zone. Luckily, he knew the answer to that one. "No, this particular woman is the end destination. I simply didn't realize I would have a passenger for the long run. We settled this last night. You're not something we fight over. You're the woman we work together to take care of. And dominate. Why exactly are you wearing that dress? Your friends are gone. It's late in the day. I think it's play time."

He needed them on the right footing. He needed her to think about pleasure and how well they could take care of her. She'd had time all day to vent her frustrations. Now it was time to fill that space with caring and attention and love.

Yep. He fucking loved her, and he was going to do this because he loved Niall, too.

Maybe he could start loving himself if he could change his mindset. For them. For himself. For his brother who couldn't be here. Who would want him to have a good life with everything he missed.

Her eyes widened. "I thought it was talk time."

He let his lips curl up slowly. "I can talk while you're naked. Come on, Harlow. You know you like it. You spend most of your time naked."

"She does? I mean I know she does in the club, but she's worn PJs to bed with me," Niall said with a frown.

Ah, Jensen knew this one. "Probably because you weren't actually sleeping with her. I mean fucking her. You made her feel vulnerable so she wore clothes. She honestly feels way more confident if she's had a good hard fuck."

They could navigate her dangerous waters. Together. Like they had done with Algebra, except way better because he liked Harlow. And he'd never had hot sex with an integer.

"I want to say he's wrong, but he's not," Harlow admitted. "And I'm still wearing the dress my sister so thoughtfully brought me because I'm worried about the dust in here."

Niall stood up. "I'm on it. I actually did intend to clean in here earlier, but it was taken over by a lovely group of women who spent all day complaining about me."

"It wasn't just you." Harlow had the most adorable pout on her face. "We complained about a lot of things. Also, we need to figure out how to keep Gabe from kicking Niall out. He's pissed."

"Why would I get kicked out?" For the first time Niall sounded like he wasn't perfectly comfortable. "I didn't lie about anything. I was honest on my application. No one asked me if I was there to watch over someone."

"I don't think that's going to matter to Gabe," Harlow admitted. "He wants to call a board meeting to reevaluate your status. The good news for you is half the board members are off on some kind of international mission now. They left last night, too. So it'll probably be a week or two before he can kick you out legally. We have bylaws and everything."

Niall moved toward the back of the house. "It's good to know I have a little time."

"He loves that club, you know." Jensen hated the fact that he might get his friend kicked out of the only place he'd felt at home in for years. "Although I have to wonder if he'll have friends there now."

Harlow's hands went to her hips. "Am I supposed to go around telling everyone it's okay for him to stalk me for months?"

"He wasn't stalking you. He was watching after you." Jensen sighed. "Although I'm sure you don't see it that way. If your best friend asked you to watch after someone she loved, would you do it?"

She seemed to deflate slightly. "I suppose I would. I probably wouldn't try to date him though."

"I can't blame him. Well, I did, but having genuinely thought about it, I can't. You're quite easy to love," he said.

"No, I'm not." She got a V over her eyes, a vexed expression. "I'm difficult. I'm complex and irritable."

"And you're going to get a spanking because you might be those things, but there's nothing wrong with them. Niall makes up for all of it. He's simple and easy going and rarely causes trouble," Jensen pointed out.

"I can cause trouble," Niall argued as he returned with his kit and a big quilt he'd washed earlier in the day. He settled it across the lounger. "I can also be difficult when I want to be. There, princess, take off your clothes and sit down and we can talk if you like. Or we can start to work on that pretty asshole of yours."

"Excuse me? I did not say I wanted to do that," she replied, though her hands went to the hem of the dress and she pulled it over her head, showing off the fact that she wasn't wearing any underwear.

"But you do." Of that he was certain. Harlow wanted them both. The question was what she would do with them after she got what she wanted. "And that means we need to prepare you. Do you think I don't remember talking about your fantasies?"

She carefully folded her dress. "I remember, but I also told you I wasn't looking for a long-term ménage."

"Because you've seen how hard it is?" Niall asked even as he was opening his kit and laying out what they would need. "It's hard on your mom?"

Her lips kicked up slightly. "My mom is happy, and my dad wouldn't be able to have a relationship that Papa wasn't involved in because they're weird twins who pretty much need each other to function. I mean Dad does. Papa would be far less adventurous. He would have taken whatever came his way. My dad made him wait for the right woman, so I suppose I'm glad they're a threesome. Not suppose." She growled a little. "I love my parents. I love them all and they work. I think maybe my assertion that I would never be involved in a permanent ménage is a strange form of rebellion. Do you know how hard it is to rebel against an artist and two dudes who share a woman?"

Thank the universe they had that out of the way. If he couldn't get her to even agree it was a possibility, he didn't see how they could move forward. "I'm sure it was difficult on you."

She cocked a hip, so comfortable in that gorgeous skin of hers. "I have a rebellious soul, and when I told my mom I wanted to dye my hair at thirteen, she found some non-permanent dye and did it herself. She went to concerts with me. I got a long talking to when I got caught with alcohol at a dance, but it was all about how much they loved me and understood how tempting it was and how it could lead me to make bad decisions. No one yelled at me. Until…" She grimaced. "Shit. Until I decided to work as a PI, and not with my dads. Damn. Am I low key looking for that rebellion I didn't get when I was a teen? Oh, that makes me sad. I kind of wish I didn't know as much about psychology as I do because now I feel pathetic."

He needed her to not feel pathetic. "You want some discipline, baby. I think you should lean over and hold on to the arm of that chair. Niall, do you have anything to torture this gorgeous sub with? I think she needs a little something this evening."

She leaned over and gripped the arm of the chair, her back flat and ass in a perfect position to spank. "I'm only doing this because you're right. I do need something. I hate self-reflection. It's awful. Now I have to be nice to my dad."

Yeah, Jensen was still worried about her dad. She might have had a revelation, but he suspected Chase Dawson wasn't going to have one about him or Niall. It was a problem he would deal with later. "Right now, all you have to worry about is being a sweet sub. I want you to stop thinking about anything but me and Niall. There's no future right now. No past. Just two Doms who want you more than their next breath and a night where we take care of you. This is how tonight is going to go. We're going to play for a while and then we'll have dinner and watch whatever we can get on that old-ass TV of mine, and then we'll go to bed and hold you and kiss and cuddle you and we'll figure tomorrow out when it happens."

A long sigh of relief came from her chest, and he watched as she visibly relaxed. "I think I can do that, Sir."

He wanted to do all the talking, needed to believe there was some kind of future for them, but he pushed it aside because this was what she needed. Niall brought out a small paddle and handed it over.

"How bratty were you today?" Niall asked.

Her head came up. "I thought we weren't talking about the past."

"Then give me another reason to spank you because you don't take it for any reason. You like the play involved. You like to be disciplined," Niall pointed out. "Is it going to hit the same way if he's doing it because you like it?"

Her nose wrinkled. "I don't like how much you know about psychology either. You should never have taken all of Gabe's Dom school classes."

Niall grinned, a wholly happy expression. "Oh, princess, I

learned all of this from Leo Meyer's classes."

He was going to have to take classes. He was going to have to sink himself into this lifestyle, and damn but that didn't sound so bad. "You do like to be disciplined. Even though you know you didn't do anything wrong, you like the idea of it. So tell me how bratty you were today. How much shit did you talk on us?"

"A whole lot, Sir," she replied.

"And you deserve to talk shit on us," he admitted. "You also deserve this."

He pulled back the paddle and slapped that gorgeous ass. Harlow's ass was plump and round, and he loved getting his hands on it. But he also loved the way her whole body went tense and then released when he used a paddle on it. And he adored how pink her skin got. Perfectly rosy. He gave her a rapid ten and then pulled back.

"This is for talking about how difficult you are. Because you are not. You are a reasonable, lovely woman who knows what she wants and doesn't shrink back from asking for it. That is not difficult." He loved the sounds she made when he spanked her. Those breathy moans went straight to his dick, tightening up his whole body in pure anticipation.

He gave her twenty this time, peppering the smacks all across her cheeks and thighs, making her moan and squirm, but she remained still. She held on, her chest moving with the force of her breaths. Her head fell forward.

He let his hand brush over the warm skin of her backside. She moaned slightly and opened her legs, obviously remembering how their sessions used to go. He would spank her and then slide his hand between her thighs so he could test how she was reacting.

She was wet. She always got so fucking wet for him. Her pussy was soft and ripe already. Her arousal coated his fingers, and he brought them to his lips, tasting how much she wanted. He loved her taste and smell and how he felt when they were close. Like the world made sense again.

He passed the paddle back to Niall. "I think she's ready to move on."

He definitely was. The night was going to be a special one.

* * * *

Harlow wasn't sure what they were moving on to, but her whole body was humming with a pleasant arousal.

No future. No past. Just tonight.

She could handle that, but the thought of Jensen working with her played around in the back of her mind.

Was he ready this time?

She could accept that he was a dumbass who thought he was saving her. She could accept that Niall was a dumbass who thought he was helping a friend and got caught up in a trap she had not laid out for him.

Actually, now that she thought about it, Jensen was the one who laid the trap, but he did it in a dumbass way, and now they might all be trapped.

"I wouldn't like what you're thinking right now, would I?" Niall asked, and he was holding a big old anal plug. She was fairly certain it was also a vibrator.

"Not at all, Sir. I was thinking about how nice my spanking was and how we all understand that I have never actually had anal sex, so we should start small," she said in her sweetest voice.

He snorted, but he put that large plug away. "I have a starter. I bought it for you."

"Where?" Jensen asked. "It's not like there's a toy store out here."

Niall shrugged. "I'm an optimist."

Jensen's eyes narrowed. "Sure you are. Let's move this to the bedroom. Don't forget to bring the lube."

She gasped as Jensen's big arms went around her waist and he lifted her up.

No one carried her around. No one except him and Niall.

All of this anger is justified, but I also want you to feel okay forgiving them if you want. I will do whatever you need, sister. I will hate them both or I will welcome them as my brothers and try to protect them from Dad.

Her sister's words whispered through her head. She didn't have to be stubborn. She didn't have to be completely unyielding so she looked tough. Her mom would welcome them. Her papa could be softened up. Her dad could be blackmailed.

Her friends…

Her friends would love and support her, and if they thought she was stupid then she would prove them wrong or not care about their opinions.

Was she thinking about this? She'd thought when Greer and Gigi and Ruby showed up that they would bolster her belief that she'd been treated poorly and could use Niall and Jensen and toss them away like trash. They'd listened to her and agreed with her, and somehow she was still here because she also knew they loved her and would stand by her.

And they would love the Niall and Jensen she knew. The Niall who took care of the people around him and the Jensen who loved so fiercely it was hard for him to ever let go.

But they hurt her.

"Baby, I meant it." Jensen lowered her down. "You don't have to think tonight. You don't have to make a single decision beyond whether or not you want us. You decide you don't want sex, we'll watch some TV or play a game or something. I think there's an old copy of Clue around here somewhere."

He could be so sweet. She'd forgotten how sweet he could be. Somehow she'd reduced their entire relationship to sex and a one-sided love and had totally forgotten how he'd loved her. Fiercely and holding nothing back. It made for some passionate fights, but somehow Niall being here with them cooled off the hottest of the fires that burned between them.

Was this the way it was with her parents?

Eww. She thought about her parents and she was naked.

Jensen stared down at her. "We can do whatever you want, baby."

"I need you to be a rough as fuck Dom right now because I just wondered if this is how it was for my parents and if you don't get that image out of my head, I might never have sex again."

His whole demeanor changed. His eyes got hard, and his shoulders seemed broader than they were before. "Bend over the bed, Harlow. Right fucking now."

She did as he commanded and then fought to breathe because he was right back to smacking her ass. And he wasn't holding back.

"Niall, you want to take care of her mouth while I handle her little asshole?" Jensen asked when he was done setting her ass on fire.

But she wasn't thinking about anything but them now.

She felt the bed move underneath her and then Niall was in front of her. At some point he chucked his clothes, and she got to stare at his masculine perfection.

"I think I can handle her mouth. Do you have any idea how long I've waited to feel those gorgeous lips of yours wrapped around my cock?" Niall's voice had gone low and deep. His hand was on that cock, stroking himself until he was long and hard and impossibly sexy.

How long had she thought about sucking him off? Definitely the last couple of months. She'd had visions of getting on her knees in front of this man, of being his good girl.

Jensen was going to make it hard on her though. She could feel him moving behind her, prepping to play with her ass. Play with it? He was going to work a damn plug in there so she would be ready to take both of them.

Both her men. Her temporary men.

She shoved the thought out. Jensen was right. She didn't have to think about that tonight. All that mattered tonight was pleasing these two Masters.

"I will do my best, Sir," she promised. "It's been a while for me. I haven't…not since…"

"She'll be fine," Jensen replied with a chuckle. "She used to make my eyes roll to the back of my head. You'll struggle to make it last, her mouth is so fucking hot."

That was what she needed to hear. Being around Jensen in this place where he grew up was reminding her of all the good parts of their relationship. And she was discovering how nice it was to belong to Master Niall.

A D/s relationship might work.

Nope. She wasn't going there. She was focusing on the issue at hand, and that was making Niall's mind go wonky like he'd done to hers the previous night. That man had eaten her pussy like it was his damn job, and she was going to return the favor.

She leaned forward. It was difficult because she couldn't use her hands. She had to hold on to the footboard of the bed to balance against Jensen's work. It was a challenge.

She liked a challenge.

Niall's cock was thick and long, and she couldn't wait to get her tongue on the pearly fluid peeking out of the slit. She went right for it, swiping her tongue across it and reveling in the taste of his arousal. A low groan came from her Master's throat, and she could see the way the muscles of his thighs tightened and his hand gripped his cock.

"You're going to make me crazy, princess. Do it again," he ordered, his voice going to that dark, deep place it only went to when they were playing.

It only went to for her.

It struck her that neither of these men were in the lifestyle before her. She was the only sub they'd really played with. Oh, they might have run some scenes, but it was all for work or training. She was the only sub either one of them had prepared and planned for, had known they would take to bed and be there for her in the morning.

She rolled her tongue around the head of Niall's cock. The skin there was silky and smooth, and her tongue found the groove under the head and worked it.

Behind her she felt Jensen's hand on the small of her back. He moved between her legs, making a place for himself there. She licked and sucked Niall's cock and whimpered when she felt Jensen part the cheeks of her ass.

Niall's hand found her hair and gripped her there. Hard. The edge of pain was enough to get her going. Her nipples peaked and her whole body went on alert. "Don't stop. You stop and we'll have to start all over again, and this time I'll tie you up and we'll move to the bigger plug."

She didn't want that. Not at all. But Jensen was right, and the threat of punishment during play made her pussy tighten in anticipation.

They knew exactly what she needed.

She managed to not squirm when she felt the cool lube start to coat her tender flesh. It made her breath hitch, but she concentrated on the big cock in her mouth. Niall had her hair in a tight grip, moving her on and off his dick. Her scalp felt lit up, every slight pain pushing her higher.

And Jensen was working, too. She gasped around the cock in her mouth as she felt the first press of fingers against her. Pressure and heat mixed with the arousal flooding her system.

She was caught between them, and there was nothing she could do but ride out whatever they intended to give her. It was a hot fantasy in her head that fed her soul, and yet she knew it was only possible because she trusted them, because she knew damn well they would give her nothing but pleasure. So it was safe to play out fantasies and explore the boundaries of her sexuality because they wouldn't take more than she had to give. They would honor her boundaries fully. It was easy to give over to the idea that they had her captive and she couldn't get away. She would be forced to give these men everything she had, her body, her mind, her soul.

Her heart.

Jensen was definitely giving her a couple of fingers. She couldn't help the moan that came from her throat as he breached her and rimmed her, massaging the lube in before replacing warm fingers with the cool, hard feel of the plug.

"Fuck, I'm not going to last," Niall said, his tone low. His hands tightened again, lighting up her scalp. "Suck me hard, princess. Let me fill that mouth up."

She wanted nothing more than to be filled with them. She could feel the warmth of Jensen's skin against her backside and knew he'd shed his clothes at some point. He was likely going to give her exactly what she wanted as soon as he was satisfied she'd taken the plug.

She tried to relax because while sucking Niall's cock was exciting, she wanted Jensen's deep inside her pussy, wanted to feel how tight he would be with the plug in her ass. It would be a preview of what was to come.

What she wanted. Both of them, and then even if it didn't work, she could hold on to the memory forever.

She felt a low groan go through Niall and the spurt of his orgasm on her tongue. He held her head there, pumping into her. He wasn't treating her like a fragile doll. He was treating her like a sex toy, there for his pleasure, and it did something for her.

She felt the plug slide home, felt the way it held her open and how she tightened around it.

As she licked the last of Niall's arousal off his cock, she heard the sound of a condom wrapper being torn open, and she had to bite back a cry of anticipation.

"That's right, princess," Niall said soothingly. His hand stroked her hair now, easing it back. He sat there, his cock still on full display. He took her hands and put them around his hips. "Hold on to me while he fucks you. Tell me what it feels like. I want to know how tight you are, how wet you are."

"She's so fucking wet," Jensen said with a groan as he pressed his cock to her pussy.

She could feel the plug riding hard inside her. Like Niall was there. Like they were all together and would be that way for the rest of their lives.

He thrust up inside her and she felt Niall's hands on her body, holding her and giving her something to balance against. "Tell me how it feels."

"So good," she managed to get out. "I love how big his cock is, how it fills me up, and it's the right side of pain."

Jensen's hands gripped her hips, and he slid his cock in and out. "She feels like heaven, but you know that."

"And the plug?" Niall asked.

"Makes her so tight I can barely hold it together," Jensen admitted even as he worked his cock inside again. "I don't know how we'll manage when she's between us and we can… We'll be able to feel each other…fucking her."

"Fuck," Niall cursed. "I'm hard again. Hold on, princess. Let him have you and then I'll get my chance. I love your mouth, but nothing feels as good as your pussy. I can't wait until I'm the one fucking you. Do you have any idea how gorgeous you are right now?"

She held on to him as Jensen worked his magic, each thrust taking her higher and higher. She fought to breathe but Niall was right there, giving her tender words while she enjoyed the primal pleasure of Jensen's cock.

It was overwhelming, and she couldn't deny that this was a place she'd never been to before. She'd never felt this level of intimacy and worried nothing would ever be as good as being between these two men.

"So fucking gorgeous." Niall leaned over and brushed his lips across her forehead even as Jensen's thrusts moved her back and forth. The tender gesture sent her right over the edge. Jensen's cock hit her sweet spot, and the pleasure was overwhelming.

"That's right," Niall encouraged. "Let it all go. Take everything he has to give you."

She heard Jensen groan and then felt him stiffen behind her. His fingers gripped her hips as he lost his rhythm and fucked her with abandon.

She held onto Niall and rode out the rest of the orgasm. She felt Jensen slip from her pussy and kiss her neck before pulling away.

"I'm going to get the shower ready," he said. "Bring her in there when you're done and I'll clean her up."

Niall chuckled. "You won't. You'll fuck her again."

A low laugh huffed from Jensen. "Probably."

Niall hauled her on the bed. "Well, you're mine for now. Squeeze that plug tight. I want to feel it."

He kissed her and started the process all over again.

Chapter Thirteen

Four nights later, Niall sat in the backyard and listened to the sound of the river rushing by.

The days had been oddly peaceful. He cooked, Harlow and Jensen cleaned. They watched some movies and played a couple of old board games that Harlow and Jensen took way too personally. Competitive assholes.

They fucked. A lot.

They'd gotten into a nice pattern. Wake up with her clinging to one of them and kissing her until she was awake and begged them to take her. At night they played. They tied her up and spanked her ass and plugged her. They ate her pussy and got her on her knees so she could suck them off.

He wasn't sure they were any closer to having her accept the relationship outside of this ramshackle house.

He took a long breath, inhaling the night air and turning his head up to the full moon that illuminated the velvet sky.

"Hey." Harlow stepped into the space. There was a small fire pit Niall hadn't lit and four old lawn chairs. She wore PJ bottoms and a tank top that showed off her toned arms. Her purple hair was up in a messy bun, and she looked adorably rumpled.

Of course she'd also looked adorable naked when he'd left her in bed. He didn't suppose it was a good idea to be bossy and tell her to take off her clothes out here.

"I thought you were sleeping. Everything okay?" He gestured for her to join him.

"Can't sleep, and it isn't because I'm sore." She huffed as she shifted to the chair across from him.

They'd moved her up to a much bigger plug earlier this evening after they'd used a violet wand on her and made her cry out. After she'd come three times.

He had to bite back a laugh because she sat down gingerly. Poor princess. "Do you want me to massage you?"

She snorted. "I think I'll pass on the asshole massage. I've had that a couple of times already today." She sat back. "It's nice out here. I guess when Jensen talked to me about this place I got an idea in my head that it was awful. It's beautiful here. The house needs some work, but you can't argue with the view."

She tilted her head up, looking at the blanket of stars spread across the sky.

It was spectacular, but nothing compared to her. She was the most beautiful woman he'd ever seen, and he was worried he was going to lose her. There was a distance during the day. When they were in bed or playing, she gave them everything. But she held back slightly in everything else. Nothing that would make it necessary to talk about, just distance that worried him.

The moonlight played over the river making it look like it was dancing. In the distance he could see the high grass sway. "No, you can't. It is beautiful out here. During the summers there's a pond about half a mile from the house where we used to swim when it got too hot to do anything else. I have no idea how, but the pond always stayed cool even when it was a hundred degrees out. I think when Jensen talks about this place, he's talking about the emotional toll of living here. It's beautiful land, but the town was hard on Jensen. Hard on his whole family."

"He never liked to talk about his mother," she said quietly. "He kind of avoided the subject. He didn't talk much about his childhood, but he wouldn't talk about her at all."

It didn't surprise Niall that Jensen had never gone into details with Harlow. "Well, I knew her. She was… She longed for something more than this place but had no idea how to get out. That's not exactly right. She decided she did know."

Harlow nodded. "Let me guess. She thought a man would take her away."

She was a perceptive woman. One of her many talents. "Yes. She was the only daughter of ranchers, but they died in a car accident a year before Jensen was born. I don't think they prepared her for much more than getting married and helping her husband with the ranch. They never expected her to run it herself. She was supposed to get married to someone they approved of and he would be trained."

Harlow's nose wrinkled. "That sounds terrible but then it's not like my dad wanted me to take over the family business either."

"I don't think it's exactly the same. They weren't worried about Jensen's momma getting killed in the line of duty," he explained. "They simply didn't think a woman could run the ranch."

"She wasn't married when her parents died? How old was she? How did she handle things?"

He was glad she was at least curious. "She was barely nineteen, and she didn't. She spent all her time either helping her mom with chores or going to the church in town. She had no idea what to do. Jensen's dad was their foreman, and he almost immediately married her and got her pregnant, but what he actually wanted was the ranch."

"Did something happen to him? Because I know she sold off most of the land to a big ranch collective," she replied. "I have some connections in that world. Jack's parents own a big ranch outside of Austin, as do some of my parents' closest friends. Selling any land would be the option of last resort for them. The ranchers I know would never sell unless they were going to lose it all."

She did know how to point out a problem. "Jensen's dad might have been a foreman, but ranching wasn't exactly his dream. From what I've heard he mostly wanted to be rich. Didn't care how it happened. What he wanted was the money that came with the ranch. He convinced her to sell off some of the land so they could upgrade the house. Which was always going to happen soon. He kept putting it off. She was pregnant and she'd been taught that a good wife didn't question her husband, so she did what he asked. A little land became a lot of land until they were left with this space and then

Jensen's dad took off with the cash."

"And left her with two kids, right?"

Niall shook his head. He wondered how much Jensen told her. It didn't seem like a lot. "No. Tommy was technically his half brother. When Jensen's dad left, she tried waitressing, but she ended up letting her latest boyfriend move in, and that worked for a while. She got pregnant again and had Tommy and then Tommy's dad left her for another woman. From there on it was a series of men she let move in and out of their lives. Always looking for the one who would sweep her off her feet and take her family away from here."

She sighed, a sympathetic sound. "That had to be hard. I think the worst thing a child can go through is chaos." She wrapped her arms around her legs, hugging them to her chest. "I don't like to think about what my parents went through. It was similar, but it was their dad, and he had a mega shit ton of money. My dads have three brothers and one sister, and they mostly have different moms. I think my grandfather married three times, but the affairs were too many to count. They kind of had to raise themselves. And by kind of, I mean they did. My Uncle Win—Gigi's dad—he was pretty much the father to his younger siblings. Was it like that for Jensen and Tommy?"

Niall nodded. "Very much so. Jensen was five years older than Tommy. He was Tommy's protector. By the time he was eight or nine he was left alone with Tommy while their mom worked or went on a date. It was both better and worse when their mom got a boyfriend and settled down for a while. It depended on the guy. Some were nice. Some were abusive bastards."

"My dad once told me it was like trying to walk through an earthquake. The ground was always shifting under their feet. Sometimes it was good. They liked one of their stepmoms, but he divorced her quite quickly," Harlow explained. "Sometimes they would have a nanny who helped, but Granddad almost always fucked that up by sleeping with her. So my dad and his brothers and sister had to grow up on their own."

It felt so good to be talking, really talking. They'd spent a lot of time joking around and discussing the case and D/s philosophy, but this felt real. "That had to be hard. I'm glad they found someone to settle down with. I know sometimes when you grow up like that, relationships can be difficult."

"My mom is great. Her parents are wonderful people." Harlow's voice softened, love coming through in the tone. "I never met my paternal grandparents. Crazy thing. They are both still alive. They just don't care, but my mom's parents are the best. And you know they prove that you can do everything right and it can all go wrong. My mom…she got kidnapped and raped and pretty much all the bad things in the world."

His heart threatened to hitch. "Your mom?"

She nodded. "I'm not like betraying her or anything. She would tell you the whole story herself because she did nothing wrong. She talks about it so other people…other victims don't feel alone. My mom is, well, she's totally my hero. I think I do the things I do because I want to be there for women like her."

"Have you told your father that? Put it that way?" Niall asked. He knew she loved her dad, loved all of her parents, but he had to wonder if she had truly talked to the one parent she clashed with.

She sniffled. "No. I guess I haven't. I get way too upset that he doesn't think I'm competent. I'm coming to realize that I'm a lot like my dad. I think we spark off each other and don't talk enough. But he can be obnoxious. Is it wrong that I kind of miss him right now?"

He shook his head. "Absolutely not. You love him. You're in a dangerous situation with two men you're not sure of. He's your father and he's been good to you. Of course you miss him."

"You don't talk about your parents," Harlow said.

"I try not to think about them, but I'm more than willing to talk about how I grew up. I think Jensen and I became best friends because we were similar. A lot like your dads, but with way less siblings to count on."

"How did you two meet?" Harlow asked, leaning forward. "You know he kind of talked about you back in LA. Not much, but sometimes he mentioned how he wished he could call his best friend. He called you his best friend and told me the two of you grew apart."

A harsh chuckle came from his throat. Jensen was good at rewriting history. "We didn't grow apart. I can't tell you how hard I tried to keep us together. I got into the Army because I wouldn't let him go alone. I got out because I thought he needed me. I was willing to go along with him. He refused. He lost his damn mind when Tommy died. That's what happened. You know you're not the only one he pushed away because he couldn't handle the idea of his loved one getting hurt. He carries a lot of guilt around."

"He's not the reason his brother died," she said softly.

"I think he's finally starting to realize that. The fact that he's sleeping right now kind of proves it. I don't think he's slept a lot in the last couple of years," Niall admitted. He reached out and brushed a hand over her arm. "Why can't you sleep?"

She shook her head. "Nope. This is my time. When the two of you are together you're coming up with ways to torture me. Now I have the talker all to myself. I want to know how you met."

He thought her curiosity was a good sign. He wasn't going to argue with her. They did spend their time trying to figure out how to get her between them, and he was definitely the talker between the two of them. Though he had some hopes Jensen was coming around. "We met at school. I lived in town so I had seen him, but his momma didn't bring him to Bonnet much. She wanted to pretend like she didn't have kids a lot of the time. She thought it would be better if the men she dated didn't know about the two kids who came along until they were already in too deep. Needless to say that didn't go well for her."

"That must have been chaotic."

And chaos scared her. She was right about the word, but sometimes a person didn't mean to create it. "Mrs. Wiley wasn't a terrible person. She was just always hoping someone would come and save her. She never stopped praying for the dude on the white horse to ride in and pick her up and take her away. But you should know she also opened her home to me when I was in high school."

She seemed to consider his words. "I thought your parents were married. They live here, right?"

"I think so. I wouldn't know. I cut ties a long time ago when my mother chucked me out of my house at the age of fifteen because I dared to step in front of her when my dad was beating her. I threw a punch, and she chose him. She always chose him. He was my dad and he smirked when he kicked me out. He lied to her. Cheated on her. Beat her half to death sometimes, and when he told her to kick me out, she did it. Told me I was temporary and he was her forever. But I thought I would always be her son."

"You were. Even if she loved him, she should have chosen you."

This was a pain he'd held for a long time. It wasn't sharp anymore, but sometimes he still ached with it. "Which is why you should give your dad some mercy. I know he's acting like an ass, but he loves you. I know what it feels like when the two people in the world who should love you no matter what can't find it to even care what happens to you. When I tried to contact her before I left for the military she wrote me back and told me she didn't have a son and never to contact her again."

"Sir, I think I need a hug," Harlow said with a sniffle.

There was his warrior princess. She was strong and tough and cared so damn much. She was a woman who would always stand up for the people she loved, who would risk everything for them. He sighed in pure pleasure as she settled herself on his lap and wrapped her arms around him. He rubbed his forehead against hers, enjoying the sweet affection she offered him. "I'm okay, Harlow. Like I said, I had a place to go, but now that I'm talking about it, I think I know why we both fell so hard for you. You're strong and capable and you would never take shit like that. You will always want to stand on your own two feet, and you'll protect the people you love."

"You would never deal out shit like that, Niall," she whispered. "I'm pissed at Jensen, but neither would he. And I'm not sure he thinks I'm competent."

"He does. I assure you. He knows how smart you are, but Tommy was smart, too."

"Tommy was a student. He did not have the training I have."

How to explain this to her? "No, but he was incredibly smart, and Jensen loved him and lost him. So when he got the news that Hamilton wanted to bring you into the inner circle, he freaked out. He knew what could happen."

She sighed and rested her head in the nook of his neck. "I wish he would have talked to me."

"I do, too, princess. I wish I would have talked to you. If I could do it again, I would have walked up and knocked on your door and laid it all out for you."

She chuckled. "I don't know that would have worked. I probably would have told you to pound sand and kicked you out. I definitely wouldn't have allowed you in my club. In this case, Jensen was probably right about how to approach me. When you first showed up, I wasn't in a place to even talk about Jensen. I was licking my wounds."

He brushed back her hair and breathed in her scent. It felt so good to be sitting here with her. "And I was simply trying to get through the days because I think in the back of my head I've been waiting for the call. Waiting for someone to tell me he was dead and then I would be alone in the world. Then I was lost in the club and all these new friends I was making. I felt like I belonged somewhere for the first time in a long time."

She was quiet for a moment. "I want to stay mad."

He felt so much for her. What he'd done wasn't fair, but he wanted to make up for all of it. He loved her and that meant giving her space and time to decide what she wanted. "It's okay. You can stay that way for a while. You can sit and stew on all of the crap we put you through, and we'll talk when you're ready."

"What if Jack can't close this case in the next couple of weeks? What are you going to do? Who's even opening the gym?"

"I have employees," he replied with a chuckle, letting his hand stroke the curve of her hip. "Before we had that long talk with Taggart, I texted my assistant manager. He's going to run the place for another few days. He and a couple of the trainers will keep it open."

"And after? If this goes on for weeks or months?"

He shrugged. Strangely, he wasn't worried. If he lost it all, he would start over. He didn't feel the same way about her. "We'll deal with it as it comes. You're more important."

"You know you weren't included in that assassination order," she pointed out. "You should be able to go back to your normal life. Hamilton doesn't know how you're involved. I can call Big Tag and have him assign you a bodyguard. You don't have to give everything up."

"Or you could convince Gabe to not hate my ass and find a couple of my fellow club members who'll fill in for a while. Like we all do when someone's sick or needs help." He'd worked in a bakery for a couple of days when a sub had her wisdom teeth out and couldn't keep up with her work. Some of The Hideout members had worked shifts for her and gotten her back on her feet. It was what they did. The Hideout was their community. If there was one thing he was afraid of losing beyond Harlow, it was his place in that beautiful found family.

"I'll talk to him," she promised. "I won't let him kick you out. He's being an overprotective big brother. Or he's showing off for Gigi. I can't tell what's happening with those two. But I'm serious. You should think about this. I don't know what's going to happen with Jensen. I think Jack will work a deal out with him, but I don't know how long it's going to take. I also don't know how bad it got after he pushed me out."

"I know he wouldn't physically hurt anyone."

"Do you? Because I watched him get pretty rough with some of the guys in the organization. He had to in order to move his way up. They don't let you hang out and refuse jobs. He's had to run drugs and knock heads together and likely some other things I don't want to know about."

She was giving him exactly the opening he needed. "And he didn't want that for you."

"I know," she agreed. "I know why he did what he did. Personally, I think I could have manipulated the situation in a way that got me out of any rough stuff, but he didn't give me a chance. He didn't even talk it out with me."

"I was scared you wouldn't listen so I didn't even try, and that was my bad call," a deep voice said. "If you did the same thing to me, I would be so angry, Harlow. I was playing a role in my head with you. I was martyring myself to save you from something you might have been able to handle. Or at least you could have understood why I wanted you out. Sorry. I woke up and y'all weren't there."

She frowned. "So you thought we were out here cheating or something?"

Oh, she was prickly. "No, princess. He thought we might be dead."

She growled and stood up, starting for her chair. "Did not."

"Well, it did go through my head that maybe Hamilton got you.

I think I'm paranoid. I could have sworn I heard someone moving around on the porch, but no one was there. It must have been one of you." Jensen yawned and sank down on the third chair. "Also, I'm pretty sure we shouldn't use the word cheating when it comes to the three of us. That's not how it works, right? I thought we were free to fuck you whenever you agree to let us. I'm cool with that."

Miracles did happen. "Yes, that's the general rule. As long as it's the three of us any pairing is fine."

"Really?" Harlow's lips quirked up.

"I will never say never, but I think we're both pretty hardwired in our sexuality," Niall explained. "I think of the two of us, I'm probably the one most likely to enjoy bottoming from time to time. If we want to experiment that way."

Jensen grinned, looking younger in the moonlight. "Dude, I would have told you I would never, but that sounds fun. I do have things I would like to take out on your ass. I still haven't forgiven you for the great food fight of Bonnet High."

"It was an accident." Niall winced. He had let Jensen take all the credit for it though. "I'm only saying it's cool for us to talk about things we want to experiment with in the lifestyle."

"When we can go back to a club," Harlow said with a sigh. "Although you know if we get tired of being out here, we can stay at Sanctum. It's got safe rooms. Apparently Big Tag's people get into a lot of trouble. We could stay at The Club, but then we run the risk of seeing my dads in leathers, and let me tell you, it's disturbing."

"According to Ruby, Jack thinks this thing will be over fairly soon," Niall pointed out. He didn't want to move. He liked it out here. It was quiet, and if they went back to Dallas he was fairly sure she would be at a friend's house.

"Yeah, well soon can mean different things with the feds, and we have to worry that they might decide there's a bigger fish to fry and they make a deal with Hamilton," Harlow pointed out.

Jensen shook his head. "I've studied this organization for years. Hamilton is the head. He's trying to make some deals with other organizations like the one he made with the cartel a couple of months ago, but he hasn't made a ton of inroads. I think he'll have to give up too much control if he goes that route, and that's why he's decided to expand into Houston rather than make a deal with another group."

"But you admit you weren't in the inner circle." Harlow leaned forward. "There could be a lot you don't know."

"I was close enough to get most of the accounting. The real accounting, that is. I managed to hack into Hamilton's right-hand man's system." Jensen sat back like he was talking about the weather.

Okay, even he knew that was bad. Like not morally bad. Jensen was trying to close the organization down. But from Hamilton's point of view, it was a damn fine reason to kill Jensen Wiley. "Does he know?"

"Does Jack have it?" Harlow asked.

A long huff came from Jensen's chest. "No, I did not give up my potential get-out-of-jail-card for free. I keep that information on a thumb drive and no one knows where it is. It's secure, and once I talk to that lawyer you've mentioned and we cut a deal, I'll hand it over. As to Hamilton knowing about it, I doubt it. I think the hit he put out on us was for helping Miranda leave."

"We can't know that," Harlow said with a whistle. "What were you waiting for? If you turned that over, you could have been out. How long have you had those?"

Oh, they were in a dangerous place. He kind of wished Jensen had stayed sleeping. They were in a good space earlier tonight, and now Niall felt the ground shifting. "I think he was trying to find a way to prove Hamilton killed his brother."

Jensen was strangely quiet, almost preternaturally still.

"No, he wasn't trying to prove that. He was trying to get close because justice was never enough for Jensen. Revenge was what he wanted. He wanted…wants to be the one to pull the trigger." Harlow was on her feet again, this time pacing as she spoke. "Is the real reason you didn't mention this because you want to see what the lawyer says or because you think there's still a chance you can get back in?"

"Harlow, be quiet for a minute," Jensen said softly.

"No. I'm not going to be quiet." Her arms crossed under her breasts. "You're thinking about it, aren't you? You want to go back. All of this has been one long play to soften me up so I talk to my cousin and see if you can get back to the Hamilton investigation because you were close, weren't you?"

Jensen stood, a deep frown on his face. "Niall, I think you should get Harlow inside."

"You were going to do it." Harlow didn't seem to care that Jensen had gone super serious. She was pissed and not giving an inch. "You were going to walk right up to the man and pull the trigger and damn the consequences. You were going to kill him, and it didn't matter that you had people who cared about you, people who would be devastated that you died. People who couldn't stand the thought of living the rest of their lives without you."

Niall gasped because that was the moment he saw Jensen's hands go up and the red dot painted on his chest.

"Baby girl, I'm so happy you said that," a deep voice said, and Chase Dawson peeled from the shadows and placed a pistol to the base of Jensen's head. "Because that's exactly how I feel about you, and I'm not going to let this two-bit asshole criminal cost you everything. Jack, I have him. You can come in. Jensen Wiley, I think you're about to find out you're under arrest."

Niall stood and realized his best friend was about to get arrested by their future father-in-law.

* * * *

Harlow stared at her father in the moonlight. "What are you doing? Jensen, get over here. He is not going to arrest you."

"I'm not. Jack is," Dad said as though that was a completely reasonable thing to say. As though it was perfectly normal for him to sneak up on her boyfriend and put a gun to the back of his head while her cousin held a sniper rifle on him. He was in all black. A dramatic uniform for a dramatic man.

Also, hypocrite. "You were going to snipe him? Are you even kidding me right now?"

Her father was paranoid about a couple of things. Germs. Public food. Hospitals. Strangely, rural strip clubs. She did not ask about that. But the thing he was really freaked out about? Getting sniped. How many arguments had she listened to about perfectly nice windows being turned into a killing zone?

"I didn't know if that one would be in on it. I needed Jack to cover my back, and I thought the best way would be him on the roof. If the roof holds him. I think this place should be condemned." Dad nodded toward Niall. "You should keep your distance, Griffen. I'm still not certain you don't have something to do with this."

"Harlow, have I ever told you that your dad is a nut bag?" Jack jogged in, carrying a rifle. "Could we stand down, Chase? I told you I need to talk to him. I didn't say I was going to throw him on the ground and arrest him."

"No. You said you have proof that he's been paid over a million dollars by Hamilton," Dad said.

The whole night seemed to still.

"What?" Harlow asked, the words shocking her. She was pissed at Jensen, but not for a second did she believe he would take a million dollars from Hamilton. No way. Unless he thought it was a way to get closer to him.

But he said he was rethinking his plans, that he had started to wonder if this is what his brother would have wanted.

Would he say all of that so he could soften her up? So she would talk to Jack and maybe find a way to fix the situation she'd gotten him into?

"I would like to point out that I wanted to talk to the three of you on the phone, but when you fled you didn't exactly leave a number for me to use," Jack explained in his slow Texas accent. "Hence, I had to connect with everyone's favorite crazy-ass uncle here. Also, you should know he's pissed off Big Tag, or at least he will when Big Tag finds out he hacked his system to turn on your tracker. Now I did make use of that, but I would prefer that we don't mention it because I would like to stay on the big guy's good side. I've heard he sends his daughters out when he's pissed at a man, and I personally am going to need my balls later in life. It would be a damn shame not to pass on these genes of mine."

"I told you that tracker was going to get us in trouble," Jensen said under his breath.

"That tracker is the only reason you're still alive, asshole," Dad shot back.

Which made no sense whatsoever. "If I didn't have the tracker, we would still be talking this out without my father here threatening to kill my boyfriend."

Dad frowned but that gun didn't move. He was older but he kept in excellent shape, so he could hold that gun up all night long. "He is not your boyfriend. He's the guy who kidnapped you."

Niall raised a hand. "Actually, Mr. Dawson, I was the one who drove the car."

Her father was so obnoxious. "No one kidnapped me. And you're probably right about the boyfriend part. I was using that word to spare your sensitive ears. So let's be honest. He's the guy I'm currently screwing on a nightly basis. So is Niall. Dad, I get it. You're scared. Okay. I'll give you some grace on that, but you are not arresting Jensen."

"I would like to talk about that million dollars," Jensen said haltingly, his hands still up. "Because the last time I checked I was down to four hundred fifty-two dollars and twenty-nine cents. It was definitely not a million. I would not be living in that cramped apartment if I had a million dollars."

"A little more," Jack said with a yawn. "It's one point two million, and from what I can tell it was transferred to your account in the last couple of days. I might have mentioned this to your dad. It's incredibly shady timing for a large transfer of funds. I'm sure Hamilton intended to send some hacker in to make it look better, or this was going to be a payoff so Jensen here doesn't go to the cops, but either way we do have to talk about it. I came because Chase wouldn't let me come alone, and he wouldn't give me the address. He's a big old pain in my ass."

"And you're playing fast and loose with the law, Jack. You know you should arrest him and bring him in for questioning," her dad argued.

Harlow could see the problem with that. "If you haul him into a police station or FBI headquarters, Hamilton will figure out where he is. Do you honestly think he doesn't have a way to get to Jensen inside a prison? Seriously? Are you trying to kill him?"

"It would solve so many of my problems, daughter," her dad admitted.

Niall huffed and shook his head. "I think we should probably pack up and find another safe house since this one is completely compromised."

"I know how to ditch a freaking tail. I've been doing it since long before you were in diapers, son," Dad said with frown. "I'm certainly not going to let some criminal kingpin follow me to where my daughter has been kidnapped."

She stared at her father. "Are you serious right now?"

"Well, you were definitely not in your right mind when you left the safe building to go on the run while assassins are stalking you with only two dumbass boys to watch your back. Harlow, they are not watching your back. They are watching your boobs, and that is how they will get you killed."

"Their eyes are going to kill me through my boobs or someone's going to shoot me in the backside?" She was not following her father's logic. "And they have been extremely interested in my backside. Let me tell you there is a whole lot of watching that part of me."

"I did not need to know that," her dad said, his voice tight, and even in the moonlight she could see how he'd gone faintly green.

"I think that as long as your dad has a gun, maybe we should avoid talking about anything that might or might not have happened earlier in the evening." Jensen proved he actually had some self-preservation instincts.

"Now, see, that is a story I am interested in," Jack admitted. "You joining the ménage life, cousin?"

"She certainly is not. Not with these two," her dad replied. "They are a part of her ridiculous need to rebel. She went out and picked two men she knew would set her parents off entirely."

"You don't even know them." Her father was impossible. "You've literally met them once."

"You think I need to meet them?" Dad asked, but at least he brought the gun down. He frowned her way. "You think I don't have a full dossier on both of them?"

"And what do you object to?" Harlow asked. "Beyond Jensen being a dumbass in need of therapy instead of revenge. I'll give you that, but you should have figured out that he was trying to protect me when he left me behind to get arrested."

"To get the shit kicked out of you," her dad countered.

"I did not plan on that. I assure you I will find that fucker in jail and deal with him," Jensen vowed.

Her dad rolled his cool blue eyes. "Like I didn't already do that."

Harlow felt her jaw drop. "What did you do?"

A broad shoulder shrugged. "He's alive. The Russian mob knows how to shank a guy and leave his ass alive. I think I'll have it happen every three years or so. Like regularly enough that he knows it's going to happen, but he doesn't know when it's going to happen. I want him thinking about it all the time. And before you yell at me for getting into the mob's pocket, I paid them. I'm betting I can get a frequent buyer discount."

"Like a punch card." Jensen smiled like he appreciated the idea.

"I need to point out again that I work for the Federal Bureau of Investigation, and we do track mafia crimes. Including assholes who pay them to hurt people." Jack sounded like he'd been over this more than once.

Her dad ignored him completely. "So I already took care of Jensen's mess. Let's talk about Niall."

"We don't have to," Niall offered.

Harlow waved him off. "Oh, no. I want to hear what shit he's come up with. Do you have a problem with his honorable military service?"

"He was in the Army." Her dad shuddered distastefully. "He wasn't even Special Forces."

"You snob." She wasn't taking that from him. "The Navy is not the only military service worth doing. And what did you expect? That I would let you find a Navy SEAL you could sell me off to? With a dowry? So say it. What honestly bothers you about Niall?"

"He works and lives in a crappy part of town. You're going to end up getting hurt. He runs a gym. Most private gyms fail. So you're going to end up living in a rat-infested hell hole in the middle of a criminal warzone working two jobs to support your unemployed boyfriend and driving to the federal prison on the weekends for visitation time with the other asshole."

He was such a drama llama. "And how have I lost my trust fund in all of this? Or were you planning on taking it away if I don't do what you want?"

Her dad seemed to deflate. "I would never, never do that to you. I would never leave you alone like that. You think I don't remember what it was like? One day Ben and I were overly privileged teens and the next our dad told us we were eighteen and the trust fund from our mom's side of the family didn't kick in until twenty-six. We went from having everything to having nothing. I would never do that to you."

She took a deep breath. Her father was acting out of love, and she wasn't going to get through to him by yelling. "Well, you should talk to Niall. He got kicked out of his house for trying to save his mom from his abusive dad, and he was younger than you. They still don't acknowledge he's their son."

Her dad nodded like she'd made his point. "I did know he has no real relationship with his family. He's looking for a woman to take care of him."

"No." Niall stared her father's way. "You're wrong. I'm not looking for Harlow to take care of me. I want to take care of her. Me giving to her, ensuring she has what she wants and needs and that she has a safe space is important to me. I know I don't come from money, but everything I have is hers."

"Well, that's easy to say when you don't have anything," her dad said, completely forgetting what he'd talked about.

"Uhm, apparently I have a million dollars," Jensen pointed out. "Do I get to keep that?"

Jack looked like he was getting a headache. "No, Jensen. You don't get to keep the obviously criminally attained blood money. Unless you would like to admit to what you did to earn it."

She shot her cousin a nasty look. "He's not saying anything at all. He's getting a lawyer."

"See, never once when I thought about the man you would marry did I think he would need a lawyer," her dad righteously announced.

"Every word out of your mouth is pure hypocrisy. I am trying here, Dad," Harlow pleaded. "You want to tell my guys about how many times you've gotten arrested during a case because you went somewhere you weren't supposed to go? Got mouthy with the cops? Physically assaulted a client?"

"I only assaulted them if they were assholes," her dad replied. "And the job sometimes requires a certain moral flexibility."

She gave her dad a smirk. "Yeah, I know. I do it a lot. The moral flexibility part. I learned it from you."

Her dad's eyes narrowed. "Then you can unlearn it."

"Jensen, how about we go inside and make a pot of coffee and talk this thing out?" Jack gestured to the house. "I still have to be back in Dallas for my shift tomorrow night. Hamilton is coming in, and I need to be ready. I would love to arrest the son of a bitch if I can."

Jensen actually nodded.

And she needed a keeper? "He is not talking to you without an attorney present."

Jack's jaw tightened. "Well, call one up then, cousin. Do you expect a lawyer to appear from out of nowhere? Want a knight with a law degree to ride up on his horse and save your boy there?"

That was when she saw the headlights coming down the dusty road that led to the house.

It was either someone coming to murder them all or it was her other dad trying to save his more obnoxious half from completely decimating his relationship with her.

"Papa's here." The assassin would be more subtle. He probably wouldn't be driving at a breakneck speed in the middle of the night.

"Damn it." Dad frowned and watched the car pulling up. "I told him I would handle this and he said he was okay with it."

Jack had his rifle up against his chest again. "How the hell do they know where we are? Also, we can't be sure it's them. It could be Hamilton's men."

Her dad sighed. "Nope. I can feel him. Lying liar. He never was okay with it. He knew I couldn't be talked out of it, so he agreed and then followed me."

"I thought you knew how to ditch a tail," Jack said, the words tinged with accusation.

"He didn't really follow me. He sent Nat in to ask Big Tag politely for the address so she could save Harlow from my tyranny. Or something like that. If Ian wouldn't give it to her, Ruby would." Her dad started to walk around the house toward the front lawn. "We're about to have a throwdown, my twin and I. He's putting you in danger."

"Don't scream, baby." Niall put his hands on her shoulders. "We talked about this. He's afraid."

"He's an asshole," Jensen proclaimed and then frowned. "I kind of like him. The Russian mob prison thing was a pretty cool move.

You have to admit it."

"I admit nothing except that this is a complete clusterfuck. My dad brought my cousin out here to arrest you and now my papa is going to spend the rest of the night trying to talk sense into him and we're sitting ducks." Did no one understand? "We're going back to Dallas tomorrow. Jensen, if you want to have any shot at a relationship with me at the end of this, you'll do what I tell you."

His eyes narrowed. "I'm talking to Jack. I would think you would want me to cooperate with the authorities."

"She does, but she also knows her cousin is a shark, and she wants you to be protected," Niall tried.

He was the smarter of the two. "What he said. I love Jack but if he thinks turning you over helps his case, he'll do it and tell me to thank him for saving me."

"That's not what he said," Jensen pointed out with a sigh.

"For a man who has spent the last couple of years of his life inside a cutthroat criminal organization, you sound like Suzy Fucking Sunshine," she shot back.

"Harlow, I'm not going to throw your boyfriend to the wolves." Jack stood there listening in like it was his right.

"Sure. Well, I'd still like for him to have a lawyer." She knew all of her cousin's moves. Not only did he believe in the rule of law, he was ambitious. He wanted to move into a better role, and if Jensen's case was a stepping-stone, then those worn boots of his would come down hard.

"I don't need a lawyer." Jensen sounded stubborn. "I'll give him everything I have, and the DA will understand what I'm doing."

"Baby," a feminine voice said from the shadows beyond the house.

Her mom. Her mom was here.

"Are you okay?" Natalie Dawson rushed in, giving her daughter a once-over. "Have they been treating you well?"

She hugged her mom, a deep feeling of relief flowing through her. Damn. She hadn't realized how much she needed her mom. She was a full-ass adult with a dangerous job, and sometimes she just wanted her mom to hug her. "I'm good, Mom, but I can't convince my idiot boyfriend that he should have an attorney if he's going to talk to Jack."

Her mom gave her a big smile. “Well, Papa and I fixed that for you. We found a lawyer for Jensen.”

Jack snorted. “Did you get some yokel up in the middle of the night? Cool. Let him sit in. He can’t pull a fast one on me.”

“I thought I did that when you were four and I convinced you that your horse used to be a unicorn,” a deep voice said.

Oh, her mom was mean. So mean. She loved her mom.

Lucas O’Malley stood beside her dads looking cool as a cucumber. He was dressed in a suit in the middle of the night like he was going to go toe to toe with the Supreme Court instead of his own son.

Jack’s face fell. “Papa, are you kidding me?”

“That’s his father? I mean, he really looks like his father,” Niall whispered. “If we were at The Hideout someone would be popping corn right now.”

The thought brought a smile to her lips. He was right. The twins would be popping corn and Gabe would open the bar even if it was already closed because this was some good drama.

“Yep, but his family is very much like mine, so that’s Papa. His dad is the rancher I was talking about. Lucas is a lawyer and an excellent one, though he tends to stick to corporate law,” Harlow replied back.

“I still know how to ensure that a client’s rights aren’t trampled over in the name of so-called justice,” Lucas assured them. “And I was serious. I made that horn and everything. I hid it in the barn thinking your sister would find it, but you did and decided you were the one with the unicorn horse.”

She could practically hear Jack’s teeth grinding. “I was talking about the case. You are my father. You would be required to recuse yourself.”

“That’s for judges. As long as my client is cool with it, we’re fine.” Lucas held out a hand to Jensen. “Mr. Wiley, I’m Lucas O’Malley, and I’ve been hired to represent you. This is my son, but I assure you I won’t let that affect me in the slightest when it comes to my job. The same way he absolutely won’t allow a familial connection to stop him from ensuring a full prosecution if he thinks justice will be served. And he’ll regret hurting his cousin.”

Jack’s head dropped back. “Fuck this case. I’ll be inside when you decide to talk, Jensen. Wake me up and we can get started. It's going to take forever now because your lawyer is a smartass who likes to shove the law in everyone's faces."

"The term you're looking for is due process, son," Lucas called out as Jack walked back toward the house. He sighed as though deeply satisfied. "This is going to be fun. I love my son but as my husband would say, he's way too big for those britches he's wearing."

"Mr. O'Malley, I don't have the money to pay for more than an hour or two of your time," Jensen began. "Unless I get to keep the million plus my criminal boss put into my account to frame me. Then I might be able to afford like twenty-four hours or something."

"This is what I'm dealing with, Mom," Harlow said. "No one is serious."

Niall moved in beside her. "We are absolutely serious. I think Jensen is on the confused side. It's been a weird, wild ride. But you should understand that we are entirely serious about your daughter, Mrs. Dawson. I know we met the other day, but it was a little chaotic. I forgot to mention that I'm your daughter's Dom."

"Hey," Harlow said because were they just putting it all out there now? "My parents are listening."

"You didn't mind when it was me," her dad pointed out.

"Do I have to be punished?" Papa asked. "I'd like to remind everyone that I'm the half that doesn't cause a shit ton of trouble."

"You did for me, brother," Dad pointed out. "I told you I was handling this."

"By offering up one of her boyfriends to the law," Papa shot back. "Which is why I countered your move. You brought the son. I got the dad."

Her mom sighed and looked her way. "Are you sure you want two, baby? This one seems nice and not that hard to handle."

"I'd like to point out that I'm also her Dom." Jensen didn't seem to want to be left out. "Not the switch. Niall's the switch."

She turned to Jensen. "You need to take this more seriously."

Jensen sighed and moved into her space. "You'll let me find a way to pay you back for the lawyer."

She shook her head. "I have more money than I can ever need. I get to use it how I want."

"I've already been paid," Lucas admitted. "Your mom gave me a five when she picked me up from the airport, so that's handled. I'm doing this for the absolute joy of spending quality father/son time. He doesn't want to come home on a regular basis, this is what he gets. I think he'll also find that his mother is writing some complex characters who resemble him. Not sure if he's the good guy or the bad guy. I won't even go into how worried Aidan is. Jack is great at his job but he's reckless, and he's absolutely certain he knows what he's doing. So I'm here to let him know he can't avoid us forever."

"And to make sure Jensen gets a good deal." Her family drama was going to kill her.

Uncle Lucas's lips kicked up in a grin. "That, too. Come along, Jensen. Let's get this started. My son doesn't do well on little sleep. I might be able to convince him to call the ADA in charge of the case. He's probably sleeping with her. He sleeps with everyone. I wish I could say that wasn't genetic. I had my own…phase."

Jensen stared down at her. "You want me to do this?"

Did he even listen to her? "Yes, I want you to take this lawyer who will make sure you don't say anything that might incriminate you before you have an immunity deal."

Jensen nodded and leaned over, brushing his lips to her forehead. "Then that's what I'll do." He turned and looked at the intimidating men dotting his childhood lawn. "Mr. O'Malley, I'll follow your lead. Mr. Dawson, I hope we have a chance to talk. Unreasonable Dad… Sorry, that's what she calls you when she's not angry. Uhm, I think you're cool and I'd like to help you figure out new ways to torture assholes who hurt her."

Her dad's smile was entirely predatory. "Sure. We can talk about the things that scare you."

Jensen nodded and then sighed. "He's planning to torture me, isn't he?"

"The first smart thing that kid has said all night," her dad remarked. "I think I'll sit in on the interrogation." He turned and walked toward the house.

"I'll make sure he doesn't cause a fight," Papa said, slapping Uncle Lucas on the back. "Come on. Let's get some of that coffee."

Jensen followed the men, and he was halfway to the house

before he seemed to realize something was wrong. He turned and looked to Niall. “Dude, she’s going to want to talk to her mom and she’s going to cry and say a lot of shit about both of us, and she won’t care that you’re listening but later on she’ll feel bad about it.” He winked Harlow’s way. “You say whatever you need to say. She’s your mom. You get to cry on her shoulder all you like.”

Niall kissed her and jogged to catch up.

“Oh, baby, I like them,” her mom said.

“I do, too, and I think I have to leave them.” She turned and her mom hugged her and it finally felt okay to cry.

Chapter Fourteen

Jensen sat in the small kitchen where he'd eaten most of his meals during his formative years and wondered when it started to feel like an interrogation room. Probably when he was surrounded by Harlow's family. He knew the light above wasn't brighter than it had been before, but the damn thing felt like a spotlight on him.

What the hell was he going to do about Harlow? Hamilton was playing hard if he was setting him up like this. If Hamilton was willing to lose a million dollars to make him look bad, what would he do if he realized what Harlow meant to him? If Hamilton figured out that he would do anything for Harlow…

The thought of her in Hamilton's hands made him want to throw up. It would be his fault this time. He had worked his way into feeling like maybe it wasn't his fault Tommy died, but he would be serving up Harlow on a silver platter if he stayed close to her.

His gut clenched. How had his life gotten to this place? Where this man he had never actually met held so much fucking power over him? And he'd been the one to give it to him. He'd been a fool and gotten them all into this mess. He should have done exactly what Niall had advised him to. Become a total pain in the police detectives' asses. Done whatever it took to find justice for his brother. Not revenge. Revenge was for him. Not for Tommy.

"Do you understand what Special Agent O'Malley is saying?"

The lawyer—who looked like an older version of Special Agent O'Malley—had taken the seat beside him while Niall leaned against the kitchen countertop where they used to make peanut butter and jelly sandwiches for their lunches. Sometimes they stole jelly packets from the local diner because Mom forgot to buy groceries or couldn't afford them.

So many memories in this house, and they were all hitting him hard tonight.

Harlow came from a different world. A world he might never fit into. A world she would be safe in.

"Really, Papa? Special Agent?" Jack's eyes rolled. He was doing that a lot tonight. Since his father had arrived, Jack had acted a bit like a sullen teenager.

Lucas O'Malley, on the other hand, seemed chipper even though it was two in the morning. "I'm keeping it professional. You should call me counselor or Mr. O'Malley. Also, we're not agreeing to any data transfer until you give us a deal on paper signed by the ADA handling the case."

Jack's head swiveled, and he looked to Jensen. "He's a corporate attorney, you know. He doesn't do criminal defense. He checks contracts to make sure his brother's company doesn't get fucked over."

"Hey, I have a degree in criminal law. It's called twenty seasons of *Law and Order*," Lucas quipped. "And you know I'm right."

"If this goes any further, we'll hire a criminal defense attorney for you, Jensen. Lucas will liaise with a firm in Dallas to hire someone good." Ben Dawson was a carbon copy of his brother when it came to looks. The only difference he could tell was his hair was slightly shaggier than his brother's. Attitude wise they were polar opposites. Like one was a dark mirror of the other. "But I trust Lucas to manage this portion."

"Since I'm not actually trying to fuck anyone over, I have to ask why the hell you can't trust me?" Jack was disgruntled by the whole evening.

"It's not that we don't trust you," Niall began.

"I'm not paying for this asshole's lawyer." Chase paced at the opposite end of the table.

That was an angry man. It would be slightly funny if Chase

Dawson wasn't his girlfriend's father, and he wasn't the very asshole he was complaining about. Also, it would be way funnier if he didn't need a lawyer.

Damn, but he was tired. He hadn't realized how fucking tired he was until he got to spend these days with his two favorite people in the world. The house needed a lot of work, but if he could stay here with the two of them and never have to go back into the real world again, he would put up with all of it.

Hamilton would find him. Oh, it might take him a while, but at some point he would end up on Jensen's doorstep. There was a bill due, and Hamilton would ensure it got paid one way or another.

"Oh, you should not trust him," Lucas told Niall. "He's law enforcement, and the case is everything."

Jack huffed. "Do you honestly believe I would fuck over a woman I've known my whole life for a case?"

"If we don't pay for a lawyer, then Harlow will." Ben was having a completely separate conversation with his twin. "Do you not understand that you're pushing our daughter away? This is a way to bring her back, to get her to trust you again."

"Why the hell wouldn't she trust me?" Chase asked, making the question sound like an attack.

Jack pointed to Ben. "See, that's a dad trying not to make his kid into an enemy combatant."

Lucas shrugged. "You chose to rebel by going into the FBI. Have you seen my rap sheet, son? I know exactly why you did that."

Jack's head fell back. "I don't need to hear about your cocaine days, Papa. Please don't go into it. You were a rebel. I get it. My rebellion against your infamous days was to never get my face on the cover of a gossip rag. See, rebellion complete."

Ben ignored the other conversation. "She doesn't trust you because you don't trust her. Because you act like a massive ass when she's young and trying to do things on her own. You know we did that, too. We went out in the world and made a shit ton of mistakes and grew from them. Well, I did."

"You're so mature, Ben," Chase said with a huff. "Did you consider for a second that we went through all that crap so our kids didn't have to? Greer doesn't pull this shit."

"Hey, do not compare her to her sister." Niall faced Chase

down. "Harlow is her own person, and she loves her sister. Pulling that comparison shit puts a wall between them. Is that what you're trying to do?"

Chase frowned. "Of course that's not what I'm trying to do. I'm trying to protect her."

"My choice of profession was not a rebellion." Jack faced down the man he called Papa. "It was what I dreamed about doing since I was a kid. You have three other offspring. Why don't you harass them? Oh, yeah. They're the good ones who stay on the ranch so they can spend the rest of their lives punching cows."

Ben pointed to the O'Malley men. "See. Niall's right. Playing your kids off each other is a terrible idea."

Lucas finally turned Ben's way. "I am not playing my kids off each other. And Jack is exaggerating. Only one of his siblings even wants to run the ranch."

"Yes, I have one brother who is following in Dad's footsteps and running a ranch. One in law school and my sister is training to be a vet." Every word was tinged with bitterness. "I'm the bad guy because I wanted out of that small town. Also, he wasn't actually coked up. That would be far too cool for my papa. It was baby powder. That *is* on his rap sheet. The only reason he got arrested was he was drunk and threw a punch at the cop that did not actually land."

"I made him trip with that punch," Lucas argued. "He was trying to avoid me and should have tied his shoelaces, so I don't think that should count as assault. Hah, see—what I needed was a good lawyer."

"I'm not playing my daughters off each other. I remember our dad doing that with us." Chase actually looked hurt. It wasn't much. A softening of his eyes, but he would bet anything the man had his feeling hurt. He looked like the kind of dude who thought of feelings in a singular fashion. Jensen kind of approved. It was easier to deal with the one.

And up until now that feeling had been guilt. If he let this shit happen to Harlow, it might always be guilt.

The last few days had been something else. He'd been…content. Happy. His brain hadn't been centered on survival, and it was nice.

Maybe these few days were all he deserved.

"It doesn't matter what you mean to do, Mr. Dawson," Niall was saying. "All that matters is when you say things like that Harlow hears she's not as good as her sister."

"It's not about being…" Chase stopped and seemed to have a deep revelation. He looked to his twin, and they had a whole conversation through a series of raised brows and tilted heads.

"He's definitely the me," Ben agreed. "He's the reasonable one who sees a lot of the social things you miss. I know you don't want her to grow up but she's going to, and she'll do it with you or without you. You're fighting a battle you can't win. Not without her losing. Do you want her to lose? Do you want her safe so badly you're willing to keep her from the kind of love you and I found?"

Chase's expression said it all. He didn't need to hear psychic words to know that Chase Dawson had questioned whether he and Niall were worth Harlow's love.

The trouble was Jensen was asking the question himself.

"Is there any possibility of us getting back to the actual reason I'm out in the ass end of nowhere in the middle of the night? I know you think this job of mine is a ridiculous rebellion and I'll wake up one day and come home, but I have to be undercover with a notorious drug kingpin in roughly sixteen hours," Jack pointed out.

It was such a weird family dynamic. They were arguing but about something important. Jensen hadn't really known his dad, and when he tried to talk to his mom about anything that wasn't puppies and kitties and how great it was to have that two liter of store-brand soda she had a coupon for, she dissolved into apologies and tears. He never had anyone he could get real advice from. Someone who would argue with him. Even Tommy did what he wanted and hid his problems so no one had to be bothered by him.

Everyone except Niall.

Niall listened. Niall tried to force him to talk.

Niall would be good for Harlow.

"If I go into witness protection, do you think they would still target Harlow?" Jensen asked.

No one was listening.

"Come on, Jack. I'm ribbing you because you haven't been home." Lucas had softened considerably. He leaned toward his son.

"We miss you. Do you honestly think I would be up in the middle of the night if I didn't want to see you? If I didn't worry this might be my only chance to see you? I had to argue with your mom and dad or they would be here, too."

Jack sighed, a weary sound. "I'm not ducking you. I'm undercover. I can't pop down to Deer Run to hang with the family. And I miss you, too."

Chase seemed to lose whatever psychic discussion he was having with his twin. He sat back, hands coming up. "Fine, but can we move them to Sanctum? I would feel better if they were in a secure location. I promise to not visit at any time when our daughter might be pursuing…" He went slightly green. "…whatever she's pursuing with these two."

"Love," Ben said with a sigh. "She's pursuing love."

She wouldn't be pursuing it if she stayed with him. She would be on the run. She would be Hamilton's prey. "This could take a while. I don't want Harlow stuck in some club when she should be out living her life."

Finally, Chase turned his way. "You didn't think it would last this long before? You didn't think bringing Hamilton to justice wouldn't take a couple of years? The wheels of justice move slowly. Apparently you need to watch more *Law and Order*. Lucas can give you a rundown."

Nah, he was an asshole. Jensen could like an asshole, but he wasn't in the mood tonight. He had shitty things to do and his own life to ruin. But at least he could save the two people he loved. Sitting here listening to all the ways Hamilton was putting him in a corner had sent a jolt of reality through him.

He'd made this choice a long time ago. He'd chosen revenge over healing. He'd chosen revenge over her. If he'd walked away with her, he could be out. He could have spent the last two years building something with her and when Niall met her and they all played at The Hideout…they would have ended up together. It might have been hard, but they would have gotten through it. If he'd chosen differently, they might be married by now, and he could sit around with Niall and listen to everyone argue and poke each other and know they were a part of this family.

Niall would be. Niall hadn't made all the wrong choices.

Yeah, he definitely had more than one feeling, and they were all hitting him right now. It had been easier when he was numb.

"I wasn't turning him over to the police," Jensen admitted. "It was going to be an easy job once I got close to Hamilton since I was going to put a bullet through his brain."

The room seemed to go still, and then Chase groaned.

"Damn it. I don't want to like him," Chase said.

Niall turned to Jack. "He wouldn't have done it."

He couldn't let Niall smooth this over. Harlow's life was on the line. Her happiness was at stake. "I would have. I would do it today if you could get me close enough. I could use that sniper rifle of yours, Jack. There's a nice perch on the building across from where he'll meet with his crew."

"Yeah, I know exactly where you're talking about." Chase leaned forward. "The top left corner of the building to the west. You've got a clear view of everyone going into and out of that building. What? Of course I looked into it. Maybe I wouldn't have had time to if I was in Colorado protecting my family, but I was working through some anxiety. So I know the kid is right and we can snipe that motherfucker."

Lucas's head shook. "Do not talk about your crimes in front of the lawyer. Have I not taught you that? And you're literally talking about murdering a man in front of an FBI agent."

"At this point all I want is to clear the case and move my ass back to a desk for a while." Jack stood up. "But if you two are going to live out Uncle Chase's wildest dreams, I think I'm going to grab a nap, and I'll head back to Dallas in the morning. I really do have a shift to work."

Jensen couldn't let that happen. Not without him. He wasn't going to risk Harlow. "I'll take you to my apartment and get you the data you need. Your people didn't find my thumb drive, did they, Jack?"

"No, you won't." Lucas sent him what Jensen was sure was the look he sent all his clients who acted like dumbasses. "We'll give him what he needs when we have the immunity deal signed."

"Papa, I promise I'll get it signed. If I have what I think Jensen has on Hamilton, I don't need to wait for him to come into town. I can have the police in LA pick him up and I'll start the extradition process." Jack looked tired. "This could be over by morning."

"It'll be over for you, but not for us," Jensen pointed out. "I assure you Hamilton will try to ensure I can't testify against him, and some of that data will require explanation."

"Won't he be behind bars?" Niall asked. "I'm not naïve. I know he'll still have connections, but I also assume the feds will freeze his bank accounts."

They would, but he knew Hamilton would have some cash hidden. "He'll still be after me. He only put out the hit on Harlow because she was there when he lost Miranda. He won't care about some woman PI who helped a girl. He'll have much bigger problems, and when it gets out who Harlow is, he'll back off."

As long as he didn't put together one plus one to come up with Jensen being in their threesome. Then all bets would be off. But he didn't point that out because it was rapidly becoming clear that he would have to pull some shady shit to save her from the situation they were in.

He would have to break her heart again. At least this time Niall would be there to pick up the pieces.

He was pretty sure he was going to break Niall's heart, too.

"Julian has connections," Ben affirmed, his tone grave. "I might already have him working on it. I want that part of the underworld to know what will happen if they touch my daughter."

"Okay, I should have thought of that," Chase admitted.

They would protect her, and they would have so much better a chance if they weren't worried about him at the same time.

"So as long as they don't put her with me on a romantic basis, she'll likely be safe." Everything they were saying made him more sure of his decision. "Right now all he knows is I was with her when she helped Miranda."

"He's not wrong about that," Jack conceded. "From what I can tell, they're worried about the fact that she's a PI, but they don't know about the connection between the two of them. Everyone they knew back in LA is dead or in jail, and they're not talking to Hamilton. Harlow has a chance to get out from under this. Especially if some of Uncle Julian's more unsavory contacts put out the word that she's protected."

"Then he can do the same for Jensen," Niall argued.

"He doesn't know me." Niall wasn't thinking. "And even if he did, it wouldn't matter. Harlow isn't testifying against Hamilton. She's not the one who's going to put him in jail. Hamilton has to come after me."

"He also has no reason to come after anyone if he's buried in my backyard," Chase announced.

He was back to liking Chase, but he couldn't put Harlow's dad in the line of fire, either.

"We don't have any room in the backyard," Ben said under his breath.

Lucas stood and sighed. "I'm leaving before this gets worse. I'll go find Nat. Chase, she got a couple of hotel rooms for us. We can leave in the morning. Jensen, take the night to think about this. There's a way forward that doesn't involve you going to jail or dying. Let me help you find it."

But all of those ways led to her being in danger. Led to Niall being stuck in the middle of something he'd never meant to become a part of.

However, he was certain that putting out his brand-spanking-new plan would only end in arguments, and these motherfuckers could argue forever.

It was best to do what he needed to do.

After he had one last night with them.

At least this time he was leaving his best friend with the most beautiful girl in the world. "I don't think I'll be able to think about anything else, Mr. O'Malley."

Jack stretched and yawned. "I'm going to stay here. I need to be on the road in a couple of hours. Uncle Chase, can you catch a ride with my papa?"

Chase nodded. "Yes, though I suspect we'll hang out at least until tomorrow afternoon. I'm sure Nat will want to spend some time with Harlow, and I might need to talk to these two a bit more. I'm pretty sure that one is going to pull something stupid."

Naturally he was gesturing toward Jensen. "I told you I'll think about it."

Chase frowned, and a long sigh went through him. "You've already thought about it. I know because if anything has been made perfectly clear to me this evening, it's that I had it all wrong. I thought you were the me. You see there are always roles in a relationship like this. There's the reasonable guy who smooths things over for the super-brilliant one who struggles to fit in from time to time. There's the super-brilliant one who's good at everything except interpersonal politics."

"We call them relationships," Ben corrected.

Chase waved him off. "And there's the beautiful, damaged one who needs a shit ton of therapy because of all the damage. That one is the dangerous one because she'll make split-second decisions based on the trauma she survived and not what's best for the three of them. She'll martyr herself because that's all she knows to do. Because she thinks maybe she doesn't deserve good things like love and protection, like no one should risk for her."

"Harlow isn't like that," Jensen protested. Her dad needed to get to know his daughter.

"He's talking about you," Niall said and sniffed like he was getting a little…emotional. "You're the one who can't love himself."

Jensen stood. He wasn't going to do some weird therapy thing. His mind was made up, but he was now worried if he tried to plead his case, he would get hauled off. He didn't trust the Dawson brothers to let him make the choice himself. He got the feeling if they decided he was making the wrong one, they would lock him up until he changed his mind. "I'm fine. I'll talk to Jack in the morning, and we'll figure this thing out."

"I hope you're telling me the truth, but this has to be your choice," Chase said, pushing his chair back. "I'm going to go apologize to my daughter. You were right, Ben. I hate that."

"I'm always right." Ben moved to the door that led to the backyard.

"Are not. You suck at *Jeopardy*," Chase bickered. "You can't even answer the *Celebrity Jeopardy* questions. They're softballs."

Ben sighed as his brother walked through the door. "Yeah, so you're the trivia champ and I understand actual people."

"Hey, only one of those things gets a big trophy and a payday, brother," Chase snarked but he also stopped and turned to Lucas. "Thank you for coming out. We'll make decisions in the morning. Niall, you look like a man who can cook. I like my bacon crispy. Jensen, seriously, think this over. You'll come to the right conclusion."

"I thought you wanted me gone." Jensen was confused. He'd kind of thought Chase would drive him to jail if given the chance.

"It's been pointed out to me that I need to let my daughter make her own mistakes. Sometimes mistakes have a way of turning out okay," Chase said solemnly. Then his lips quirked up. "Like Ben being born."

Lucas groaned. "Jensen, we'll talk more in the morning. Jack, I'll be in Dallas on Monday. I'd like a sit-down with your boss."

Jack gave his dad a salute. "I'll look forward to the experience."

Lucas looked at his son like he wanted to say more, but he turned to follow the Dawsons.

"Papa, I'll be way happier to introduce you to my boss if you brought me some of Mom's snickerdoodles," Jack offered.

Lucas nodded. "Oh, I think your mom might bring them herself."

"Good. I'd like to see her," Jack replied. When the door closed he turned to Niall. "Is there a second bedroom or am I on the couch? I won't be here long. I need a couple hours sleep and I'll be out of your hair."

Everyone looked to Niall when they wanted hospitality. He needed to rehab his image. Of course he'd have a lot of time to think about it soon. "It's the second door on the left. We're in the primary bedroom and it's got its own bathroom, so you can use the small one across from your room."

Jack nodded. "Tell Harlow good night for me and that I'd like to sit down and talk with her sometime. I don't want to lose my whole damn family over this. Call me when you're ready to make a deal."

And then he was alone with Niall.

"What are you planning?" Niall asked, a worried look on his face.

He felt like a shit, but this was for him. For him and Harlow. "I'm planning on getting our girl and taking my mind off the fact that her uncle is a lawyer who is going to be a pain in my ass, and her dads are going to be ten times worse. I didn't get to spend time with her mom yet. Was she the super smart one or the reasonable one?"

Niall's head shook. He put a hand on Jensen's shoulder. "We are so lucky you're pretty."

He wasn't sure what that meant.

Shit. Niall was the reasonable one and Harlow was the supersmart, genius one, and that meant he needed therapy.

That might be accurate.

But it didn't matter. When Niall moved toward the backyard, he followed his friend.

One last night and then he would do the right thing.

* * * *

Niall walked into the yard where Harlow sat with her mom, holding her hand as she talked.

"The sex is incredible. That's not the problem. The problem is I'm always waiting for it to fall apart," Harlow said.

Chase groaned. "Does she have to talk about the sex? I thought we agreed to never do that."

Natalie Dawson stood and frowned her husband's way. "We agreed that you're risking losing your daughter. By we, I mean Ben and me."

Lucas raised a hand. "I also agreed."

Nat pointed a finger his way. "Did you fix things with Jack tonight?"

Lucas suddenly seemed fascinated by the trees around them. "I'll be in the car."

"Coward," Chase muttered and then moved toward his daughter. "Harlow…"

She stood up and walked to the man she called Deranged Dad and threw her arms around him. "I love you, Dad. I wish you would trust me to know what I want."

A shudder went through Chase Dawson as he hugged his daughter tight. "I love you, too, baby girl. So fucking much. I'm going to be better. The last thing I want is to make your life harder. If you want those two idiots over there, I'll make sure it happens."

Now, see, somehow he managed to make that sound like a threat. But given the fact that Jensen sometimes made poor choices, maybe having a deranged Dawson around wasn't such a bad idea.

Harlow pulled back with a laugh. "I think I can handle them,

Dad." She moved to her papa and hugged him, too. "Thank you for bringing Mom and Uncle Lucas out here."

Ben hugged his daughter. "You're welcome. We'll talk some more in the morning. Your dad has already put in his request with the chef."

Harlow was still smiling as she stepped back. "Niall is good with breakfast. Maybe we can sit down and talk this all out. Did Jensen fire Uncle Lucas yet?"

"No." Niall moved in. "But he is being stubborn."

"Then we'll work on him." Harlow took his hand.

He brought it to his chest, placing it right over his heart. "It's not going to fall apart, baby. I will do everything I can to make sure it doesn't."

She leaned into him.

"Niall, I look forward to getting to know you." Nat Dawson was a lovely woman who looked far too young to have two grown daughters. Maybe it was the pink hair or the vibrant smile.

This was the woman who hadn't thought she deserved the love she was offered.

She did now.

Could Jensen someday smile like that? Look comfortable in his own skin because he trusted his family?

He held her hand for a moment. "I look forward to it, too."

She told Jensen the same thing, and Jensen was saying all the right words.

"Come on, Cotton Candy," Chase said, taking his wife's hand. "You know you want to get to whatever passes for a hotel in this place so you can yell at me."

Nat gave her husband a grin. "Nah. I'm just going to point out all the things that housekeeping might have missed, and that can be my revenge."

Chase's eyes closed. "A proper revenge. The only thing worse than public buffets? Public beds."

Ben snorted. "Then you can sleep in the car and I'll play out some hooker fantasies with our wife."

"Papa," Harlow protested.

Ben started to lead their wife away. "Nope. If you're going to talk about sex, then we're free to as well. I'll tell you all about what your dad and I are going to do to your mom."

"I'll be silent," Harlow yelled out. She looked to him, a frown on her face. "He's supposed to be the nice one."

She was so freaking adorable. He was madly in love with her. And so scared they were about to lose Jensen. He needed to show Jensen that they were together. They were a team. If he could show Jensen how good it could be, maybe he would be more willing to listen in the morning.

"Princess, I think he just doesn't want to listen to stories about our sex life," Niall pointed out. "And I do not blame him."

"Are you okay?" Jensen seemed to relax when he heard the car doors close and the engine come on.

She put a hand on Jensen's arm, drawing him close. "It was good to talk to my mom. I know it's dangerous, but…"

Jensen's head shook, and he leaned over to brush a kiss on her forehead. "I'm glad you got to see her, too. I'm glad they came. It was good to spend time with them, and I'm definitely happy you made up with your dad."

She sighed and seemed comfortable between them. "Me, too. But it was stressful, and I'm worried and I'm never getting back to sleep. I should talk to Jack."

That wasn't happening. "He's already asleep in the guest room. We'll talk in the morning. For tonight let's see if we can get you relaxed."

"Yes, I think we could all use some comfort." Jensen's eyes went soft as he looked down at her. He put his hands on her cheeks. "I want us to be together tonight. I know we had you earlier, but…"

She nodded. "I'm fine. Yes. I want you. I'm ready. Take me to bed and let me get in between you both. Talking to my mom gave me some perspective. I'm afraid and I'm not being brave. It's easy for me to put my life on the line, but my heart is a different story. I'm going to be brave from now on. I promise."

"You are brave. You are fucking perfect, Harlow. I've always known it. You are smart and capable, and you deserve the absolute best life you can have," Jensen said.

"The best life is with us." Niall wasn't sure what was up with his best friend, but he had the night and tomorrow to work on him. Without Jack around dangling law enforcement promises in front of him, he might have a chance.

Harlow nodded and turned her lips up. “All of us.”

Jensen leaned over and kissed her, practically inhaling her sweetness. Niall watched as his partner drugged their girl with kisses. She was soft and pliant as Jensen picked her up and moved for the door. Arousal started to thrum through his system.

They were going to get her between them and then it would be done. Then their pledge would be made, and Jensen wouldn’t be able to back out. He was being paranoid. Like Harlow, he was letting his fear lead him, and he needed to be brave.

This was going to work because he couldn’t imagine a world without these two people.

He wanted to live this life with them.

He jogged to get ahead of them, opening the door and letting them through. Jensen was focused on the bedroom, but Harlow winked at Niall as they strode by.

He followed them, pulling his shirt over his head as he walked through the living room.

Jack opened the bathroom door and started to walk out and then turned and closed it, obviously not willing to witness his cousin being ravished by the two men who loved her more than life itself.

He prayed Jensen loved her more than his own guilt.

Jensen strode through the door that led to the bedroom they had been sharing for days. He set her on her feet and kissed her, his mouth covering hers, hands pulling her against his body.

Niall moved to the other side. What had been awkward at first now felt normal and natural. He let his hands roam the curves of her body as he kissed the nape of her neck. He breathed her in. He was never going to get tired of this. Of being with them. There was something special about being with the two of them that he wasn’t sure he could replicate on his own. Oh, if anything happened to Jensen, Niall would be right there, taking care of their girl. But he would feel his loss, too.

“Your father is irritating,” Jensen said against her lips. “And I think he might have been planning on assassinating me. He told me he checked out my apartment building, but I’m pretty sure he did recon on the whole area.”

That made Niall chuckle. “A sniper’s perch was mentioned.”

Harlow growled, the sound strangely sexy. She was actually a little like her dad, but it was sexy on her. “He is such a hypocrite. He fears the sniping above all others and yet it’s his first go to.”

Jensen focused on her. “I don’t care what he thinks of me. You’re all that matters, and you need to remember that. Anything Niall or I do, we’re doing it for you.”

“Which is why we’ll talk out any big decisions.” Yeah, that didn’t sound good. It sounded like they would be having a big talk in the morning.

“Of course we will,” Jensen said as though Niall was worrying for nothing.

And he might be. This might be the trauma of the last few years messing with his head and threatening to cause drama where there was none.

He wanted to forget it all and concentrate on what they were about to do.

Make her theirs.

Harlow’s head shook. “I don’t want to talk about this tonight. Tomorrow we can sit down with my parents and my uncle and we’ll figure this out. For tonight, kiss me. I want to be between you. I want to know what it means to have both of my men.”

The request went straight to his cock, blurring any warning signs and pointing him in one completely undeniable direction. Her head turned enough that he could get his mouth on hers. She was sweet and submissive, and every fucking thing he needed in the whole world.

She turned and he managed to draw her into his arms, hands going to cup her ass and pull her against his hardening cock.

“You’re getting both of us. Right now. Tell me where you want me, princess.” He growled the command.

“You’ve spent so much time torturing my ass, I think you should take it first, Niall. And I want Jensen in my pussy. I want to watch his face when he feels your cock slide against his while you’re both inside me.”

“Fuck,” Jensen cursed. “I don’t know that I can handle it when you start talking dirty.”

She was the sweet, filthy, gorgeous sub. He pulled the tank top over her head, exposing her breasts. “I love it. Tell me more about how it's going to feel when we're both inside you."

He reached out and cupped one, letting his fingers find her already hard nipple.

Her breath hitched like she knew what was coming next. "I'll be so full. I won't be able to move because I'm trapped between your big, hard bodies. I'll have to ride one of you while the other gets behind me."

"I'll get behind you," Niall promised. He had to focus on breathing because all he could think about was how tight her asshole was going to be around his cock. He would have to fight his way in.

He twisted her nipple. Hard.

A gasp came from those lips of hers, and her body shuddered delicately. She bit her bottom lip and continued on. "I'll feel Jensen under me, and his cock will stretch my pussy and it'll be so good."

Jensen was the one behind her now. His hand wound its way down her torso to the apex of her thighs. One big finger slid over her pussy, parting the petals of her labia before circling her clit and making her gasp again. "I'll make sure it feels good. I'll hold you tight so you won't be able to wriggle and squirm and fight him. I'll hold your cheeks apart so he can thrust his cock right in."

Another hard twist. This time to her other nipple. Her eyes glazed over with pure need. "He'll make sure you let me in. I won't be kept out. Your ass is mine tonight. Your body is ours always."

Theirs to protect and pleasure and comfort. It was all he wanted to do with the rest of his days. He'd spent so much time trying to tie his life and worth to some career or level of success, but this was it. A man's life could be wound up in serving his family, in building with them. He loved the gym, and as long as it served his family he would probably run it forever, but they were more important than anything else.

"Yours, Niall. I'm done playing around like I'm not going to forgive you," she vowed. "Deep down I forgave you both quickly, but my pride sometimes gets in the way. I won't let it come between us."

He had never heard sweeter words. "And we'll get through all of this, princess. We're going to put our pride aside, too. We'll do what it takes to keep us together."

Jensen kissed her shoulder. "We'll do what it takes."

He had to believe his partner. Niall set aside his worry. He wanted to concentrate on being together. Tomorrow was soon enough. He would sit down with Jensen and come up with a plan to deal with her dad. Her mom seemed to be on board, and Ben would likely give them long lectures on how to treat their daughter.

But he did have to figure out how to keep Chase from sniping them.

He dropped to his knees because those pretty nipples needed more. He leaned forward and didn't care that Jensen's muscular arm was brushing against his shoulder and he could feel it against his chest since his partner was currently stroking Harlow's clit. Jensen didn't move, didn't seem to feel any of the awkwardness they'd started out with. They were getting this whole team-up play down.

He licked her nipple, eliciting the sweetest groan.

"Wait until we get you back at The Hideout," Niall promised. "Wait until we take you on that main stage and tie your hands and ankles down and fill your every hole with our cocks. And they'll all be watching. All the Doms will want to be us, but we would never let them touch you because you're ours."

"Yours," she vowed before he gently bit down on her nipple, and she jerked slightly.

"Damn, she's wet. Whatever you are doing, keep it up," Jensen said.

She was going to come if he let Jensen keep going. He didn't want that. He wanted her desperate for them.

He kissed her nipple, easing the ache his teeth had caused. He could smell her arousal, loved the way her hips were rolling, trying so hard to get Jensen's fingers to apply the exact amount of pressure so she could steal an orgasm from them.

He let his head dip back so he could see her face. "Princess, you're not allowed to come until we're both inside you."

"Sure," she said as her hips rolled again.

Jensen huffed and backed up. "I don't think she's listening."

"Then we'll have to discipline her." He knew exactly what he wanted to do to their gorgeous girl.

It was time for some punishment.

Chapter Fifteen

Jensen felt like the breath was knocked out of him. He was trying so fucking hard not to get emotional, but it was almost impossible. He shoved it all deep. He needed this night. Needed the memory of her to fuel him for the rest of his lonely life.

The idea of being in that club with her, of walking in every weekend and kissing her at the locker room door before he and Niall went into the men's and joked and laughed with their friends. They would get ready together and then play all night and stop for waffles on the way home with her sister and cousin and Ruby and sleep with her between them. Their days would roll on like that, each bonding them closer and closer until they couldn't imagine a life without the other two in it.

They would plan a life together in those quiet moments.

He would not be there.

But he was here now, and he had to build as many memories as he could.

Starting with the way she tasted. He brought his fingers to his lips as Niall instructed her to get on her hands and knees, but only after she'd given him her underwear.

She tasted so good. Tangy and somehow sweet. He sucked the evidence of her arousal off his fingers while he watched her hand her panties to Niall. His cock was about as hard as it could be. He needed a release or he would lose it the minute he got inside her.

"I'm sorry, Sir," she said in her sweetest voice. He loved that she could be both sweet and a righteous bitch when she needed to be. She could put them both on their asses if they required it.

It was one of the reasons he loved her so deeply. She was a woman who could be counted on. She would let herself be submissive here, but she could stand strong when required to. She could be a rock they all clung to.

Niall could. Niall would hold on to her when he needed her to be strong.

"Sure. You're so sorry," Niall teased and then his gaze hardened. "Hands and knees. You should know this drill. I want you to take care of Master J while I teach you a lesson about stealing orgasms."

"Evil man," she said but with a smirk. It was a game, and they were all aware. They knew she would get the orgasms she needed, but it was fun to play.

"Master Jensen. Not J. Not for her." Master J was his undercover name, the one that he could remember to react to, but he could also put some distance between. He needed that distance so badly in the field, but he didn't want an inch of it here. Here he wanted her as close as possible. Physically. Emotionally.

She went on her toes in front of him, the sweetest look in her eyes. "Of course, Master Jensen." She put a hand on his cheek. "I think your partner is going to ask me to suck your cock, Sir. Is that what you want?"

She never needed to be concerned with consent when it came to this. He would give her blanket consent to put those sexy lips around his dick whenever she wanted.

Except he wouldn't be around. He would be miles and miles away.

He brushed his lips over hers, hoping she could taste herself there. "You suck me, baby. Suck me hard. I want to come inside your mouth. I think I'm going to need it because I want to last when we're all together. I think it's going to feel like fucking heaven, and I don't want it over too soon."

He wanted it to never end.

She gave him a wink and gracefully sank to her knees. Her

hands came up and unbuttoned his fly and then soft skin was touching his cock, releasing him from the confinement of his clothes.

"Play with him for a minute. I'm going to grab a few things I need to get you ready," Niall announced.

She stroked him, sending blood straight to his dick. It felt so fucking good. Every pass of her hand had a wave of lust thrumming through his system.

"I love how hard you get for me," she whispered, her palm squeezing around his cock. Up and back. And all around.

Only for her. He was worried he would only ever get hard for her again. "All I have to do is think of you and I'm hard, baby."

Her hand moved over him from the base to his cockhead, where he was already seeping fluid. Her thumb ran over it.

He wanted this. "Lick me. Taste it. It's for you."

Her tongue came out as she leaned forward, and he hissed at the glorious sensation of her swiping across the head of his cock.

His jaw clenched so he didn't shout out.

"Hey, I need access, if you know what I mean," Niall said.

Jensen had an idea. He stepped back and quickly got out of his jeans and boxers, tossing them aside. He held a hand out to Harlow, a vision of what he was about to do to her banging around inside his brain. He got on the bed, his head toward the foot so Niall would have room to work. "Come on, baby. You're going to sit on my face while you suck my cock and Niall plays with your ass."

He wasn't sure it would work, but he was going with it. If the logistics got too tough, they would call an audible and change things up. It didn't matter. Nothing was awkward with these two. They would laugh and change the position and keep right on fucking.

Because they weren't auditioning. They were together, and that made the weirdest things seem normal and loving.

He hoped they were still playing like lovable perverts when he was gone. He wanted all the best the world could offer them. A beautiful life together.

He had the most delicious view of Harlow's ass as she straddled him. She eased down, and he could smell her arousal, see that juicy, waiting pussy. It was a needy, glorious thing, and he welcomed it.

The minute she was close enough, he feasted. He licked and

stroked and thrust inside with his tongue. Her taste poured over him like honey and wine, and he was completely drunk off it. He pulled her hips, forcing her further down so he could fuck her with his tongue.

He felt her gasp and squirm, and then she seemed to decide this was some sort of challenge because she swallowed his damn cock whole.

He almost came right then and there, but he wasn't one to miss out on a challenge. He forced himself to concentrate on her and not what she was doing to him. He tried not to think about how good it felt to be buried inside her mouth, her tongue running along his most sensitive flesh.

Over and over she ran her tongue down the length of his dick and back up again. She hummed along him, making his spine quiver.

He ate her pussy like a starving man. He felt the moment Niall moved behind them. Heard him opening the lube, the shadow of his body falling over him. She quivered and he felt her gasp around his cock. He held her hips, holding her still for his partner.

"Is she fighting you?" He grumbled the words over her flesh before spearing his tongue inside again, laving her with his affection.

"Her little asshole might try to keep me out, but she won't win. I'm getting in," Niall said, his voice guttural. "I won't let her keep me out. This sweet ass belongs to us."

For tonight. In the morning she would be all Niall's.

A low groan went through her, and he could practically see the plug. They had been playing with her ass for days, prepping her for this moment. He loved how she always squeezed tight before letting out a long breath and accepting the plug that stood in place of their cocks. Her back would flatten out and she would make the sweetest moan.

"Let me in, princess," Niall ordered. "Relax and let me in."

He felt her breathe out, and her muscles relaxed.

"That's it. That's what I want." Niall sounded pleased.

Because she was letting him in. Because she was opening her beautiful body to them both.

She settled back in as Niall's plug play gently moved her body back and forth. He let the motion lead him as he found her clit and started to work it.

Her tongue whirled around his cockhead, drawing out more and more arousal. He could feel her milking his dick, and it was everything he had to not fill up her mouth then and there.

"Tell me how it feels to have me fuck your ass like this," Niall ordered.

Bossy dude. It seemed to work for Harlow when it came to sex. She loved to be ordered around when they were playing.

Neither one of them would do it in the real world, though. Their baby was a badass, and didn't take shit from anyone.

Except him. She'd taken his crap and forgiven him for it.

"It feels full, Sir. I don't know how much longer I can hold out between Jensen's mouth and your plug. It feels so good," she said, her tone deep and low. "It feels like I'm caught between you, and there's nothing I can do except give in."

"That's what I want. Give in, Harlow. Give in to me. Give in to us," Niall coaxed. "Let us take care of you. Let us show you how good it can be to have both your men. Tell me that's what you want."

Jensen didn't need to hear the words. He could taste how fucking much she wanted this. She was so wet, desperate. She was likely close to the precipice. All it would take was one more lick, one more stroke over that bud of hers.

"I want it. I want it so bad," she said around his cock.

"Make him come and I'll give you what you want." Niall threw down the gauntlet.

She didn't hesitate for a second. She sucked him hard, taking him deep inside her mouth until he could feel the soft, warm place at the back of her throat.

It was too much. He couldn't handle it. He let his head fall back and the pleasure wash over him as he filled her mouth. He was so connected to her in that moment that the world and the future and everything else fell away.

"That's good, princess. Exactly. Now I'm going to help you up and we're going to get into a better position. Why don't you play with me for a minute while our partner recovers?" Niall offered. "It won't take him long if he's watching you suck my cock."

Jensen watched as that sweet pussy was lifted off him. He felt drugged with the pleasure, the connection of being with them. The intimacy was something he would never have again. Not without them.

He breathed in the moment, savoring it and getting ready for more. When he opened his eyes, Niall was kissing her, their tongues mingling over and over. One hand was on her breast and the other on the cheek of her ass, holding her close.

Yeah, it was sad that he only recently discovered what a voyeur he was. Of course, like most good things in his life, it was only for them. He only wanted to watch them, but damn they were hot together. He forced himself up as Niall sat back on the bed, offering up his cock. Harlow leaned over, giving him a view of her ass and the plug peaking from between her cheeks.

It was not going to take long for his cock to come to life.

But he worried what his heart would do in the morning.

* * * *

Harlow could barely breathe she was so aroused. She licked her lips, taking in the last of what Jensen had given her before leaning over and licking the head of Niall's cock.

His hand came out, stroking back her hair. He looked down at her with those gorgeous eyes of his. They were warm and filled with affection. How had she thought for an instant he'd played her? Niall was open and honest about how he felt. Not so honest about how he got there, but she trusted him now.

And Jensen. It might be a mistake, but she loved him. She'd loved him from the moment she met him, but now she realized it wouldn't have worked in the long run. They needed Niall to ground them and bring them together when they got stubborn. Niall was the bridge between them.

She swiped at it again, feeling her power over this man. She would never abuse it. She would give him everything she had.

Her jaw might ache, but she was here for it. Somchow she thought they would all be better in the morning. Better for committing to each other fully tonight.

That's what this whole thing was. They still had hurdles to jump, but they would do it together. She wouldn't talk about leaving them again.

Being around her mom made her admit what she wanted. She didn't want to compromise. She wanted all the love they could give her, and damn the world if it couldn't accept them. The good news was her parents and their family and friends had built a whole lovely world where no one would bat an eye.

Her friends would ask her questions, want to know that she knew what she was doing, and then they would get on board. Oh, she had no doubt the guys—and Kala Taggart—would have a deep, serious discussion about what would happen if they hurt her, but these guys could handle it.

She licked at Niall's cock, playful swipes of her tongue as she adjusted to the position. If she didn't keep that damn plug in they might make her start all over, and she was so close. Jensen's tongue had felt like heaven, and she'd been desperate to ride that wave, but no, her Masters had to be nasty about it.

"Buddy, is this what she did to you?" Niall asked in a deadpan tone.

She glanced up and Jensen stood right beside Niall. Like their shoulders were touching. These men, who had been awkward as hell about sharing her sexually, stood there like decadent gods staring down at her. If there was any hesitation at watching each other's dicks, she did not sense it. They were all about the sex and the intimacy, and their past worries about masculinity had no place here. They were all masculine. Oozing with male authority, and none of the insecurity they had before.

These men knew she was theirs and didn't doubt it for an instant.

"No. She went all in. She sucked me until I couldn't take another second of it. I was worried, but she's so fucking sexy I'm already springing back to life," Jensen said as he palmed that big cock of his, and sure enough, he was getting hard again.

"Yeah, that was my impression. I think she might need some encouragement to do the same for me," Niall observed.

She shook her head. "No, Master, I can do it."

She used her sweetest, subbiest voice because they were playing and she wanted whatever they were going to give her.

Niall stroked her hair. "But you didn't. Let's see if you can do better now."

Jensen moved and she lost sight of him, but she was pretty sure what he was going to do.

She licked Niall again because if she was getting a spanking, she wanted to deserve it. Niall couldn't stop the smile that crossed his face. He was never going to be the hard-ass Dom. He loved how bratty she could be, and it was hard for him not to show it. He managed to get his affectionate expression under control and look a bit intimidating as he glanced behind her.

"She's a brat who needs some punishment, brother," he said.

She braced herself, and sure enough, the sound of her flesh being spanked hit her before the pain did. The sound cracked through the air, and she clenched tight right before the sweetest ache hit. It made her check her breath before becoming heat that flooded her system.

"Try again," Jensen commanded. "You make him moan. You take him deep or I'll replace that nice plug he gave you with one that's lubed up a little differently."

Oh, he was mean. He wasn't talking about simply re-lubing up the piece of plastic she had shoved up her ass in place of a warm cock. He was talking about ginger lube or worse. Something that would make her burn and squirm, and Niall wouldn't care because he would be wearing a condom so it wouldn't affect him.

She decided to take the threat seriously, and when she took Niall's cock into her mouth this time, she wasn't playing. She sucked his cockhead behind her lips, grazing him gently with her teeth and sending a shudder through her Dom. Jensen's hands went soft on her skin, rubbing where he'd spanked, and then she felt him laying kisses on the curve of her lower back.

She concentrated on Niall. She loved the fact that she could still taste Jensen on her tongue even while she worked it over Niall's dick. She settled in, whirling her tongue around and not leaving a centimeter of his cock left untended. She explored, learning how he was built, what parts were particularly sensitive. He moaned every time she lapped at the slight dent under his head, and his whole body went tense when she gently sucked at his slit, drawing that salty arousal onto her tongue.

"That's better. That's what I need." The words came out of

Niall's mouth on a low groan, and she felt him touch her hair, fisting it in his hand. He pumped his hips, filling her mouth with cock while Jensen kissed her back, and she could feel him get hard again. The evidence was there against her thighs as his hands moved under her torso to cup her breasts.

It was all she could do to not cry out when he twisted her nipples. Instead, she let out a groan that resounded around Niall's flesh and made him curse.

He pulled away, his body flush with need. "I can't. I'll come if she touches me with that tongue of hers again, and I want to be deep inside her ass when I do that. Get her ready for me."

Oh, she was ready. She was so ready. She could feel how wet her pussy was, how her nipples were tight and desperate.

Jensen laid down on the bed, holding a hand out. He was so gorgeous, every inch of him muscled and covered in smooth golden skin. His cock was erect again, brushing up against his abs, and there was a pearl of arousal there like she hadn't recently swallowed him down. His eyes were hot on her as he waited. "Come on, baby, I want you to ride me."

There was nothing she wanted more. She moved carefully, not wanting to lose the plug.

She slid her pussy over his cock, letting it get wet from her own arousal. Jensen's jaw was clenched as Niall passed him the condom. She leaned back and watched him stroke himself and slide the condom on, rolling it over his cock. Then his hands were on her hips, gripping them and guiding her down.

She sank onto his dick, loving the way it felt as he filled her.

With the plug she felt full, but she was still missing something. Niall. She needed them both. In bed. In life. Always. She was in love with both men, and she didn't want to pretend or play around anymore. She wanted this for the rest of her days.

Jensen held her hips even as he rocked his up, thrusting further and then pulling back, rubbing that glorious spot deep inside her.

"Ease down, princess," Niall commanded. His big hand was on her back, and he gently pressed her down until her breasts were against Jensen's chest and their mouths close together.

Jensen's hands came up to cup her face and bring her down so he could kiss her long and slow. His tongue invaded, lazily rubbing against hers while his cock twitched inside her.

She felt Niall pull the plug from her, but she couldn't tense up because Jensen was distracting her. Over and over with kisses and strokes. He lit her body up, and all she could do was whimper when she felt Niall move in behind her, heard him rip open the condom wrapper.

She heard his low groan and then let out one of her own when she felt him start to press his cock against her. Pressure sparked but she held herself still, letting him rim her and then start to breach. She whimpered, and Jensen ran his tongue over her bottom lip.

"Relax, baby. Let him in. Let him in so we can fuck you together," Jensen whispered. "So your men can love you properly."

Together. All three of them. She kissed Jensen again and pressed her pelvis out.

She felt the sharp pleasure of Niall's cock sliding inside.

Jensen's head fell back, and his jaw tightened. "That feels so good."

It felt… She wasn't even sure what she was feeling. It was a jangly sensation that sizzled through her, moving from heat to light pain to pleasure. She felt so alive in the moment, so connected to them.

Niall growled behind her, one hand running up her side to cup a breast. "You feel like fucking heaven."

"I think you should move this train along," Jensen said with a chuckle. "I'm not going to last, and she's on the edge. Her pussy is clamped down so hard on me."

"You should feel her ass," Niall muttered. "Let's give her what she needs because I'm already close to the edge."

Niall pulled back, and Jensen shifted his hips up. The twin sensations sent her reeling. She gave over to them, holding on while they moved her body, riding her and taking her higher and higher with each stroke. They seemed to find the perfect rhythm and she moved between them, rocking to the music their bodies made.

She wanted to stay here, to forget the world outside and never leave this place where she was safe and happy and connected to them. But the feeling couldn't last. Niall seemed to find some spot deep inside her that sent her over the edge. She felt her muscles stiffen and relax as the orgasm hit. It sent her men over the edge, too, each holding her as they found their own pleasure.

She felt drugged as she lay on Jensen's body. Niall slipped out of her and kissed the back of her neck before he headed to the bathroom.

"Love you," Jensen whispered. "Don't ever want to let you go."

She smiled and kissed him, settling in even as Niall eased back into bed. "Love you, too. Both of you."

Niall cuddled behind her, keeping them all close. "Remind your dad of that in the morning. I'm worried he's still got the sniper plan in mind." He chuckled and nuzzled the back of her neck. "Remind him how much we love you. But maybe don't mention this part."

It was her turn to laugh because this moment was perfect.

And she was going to make sure it stayed that way.

Chapter Sixteen

Jensen took one last look at the two most important people in his life. Harlow was in the middle of the bed. He'd lain there for hours with her head on his chest. He'd thought about leaving it all up to fate. If she stayed where she was, he couldn't wake her, and that meant Jack would leave and there was nothing he could do about it. He would stay and talk to her parents and do what they wanted him to do. It would be rude to leave without at least talking to them. Saying good-bye. Of course if they woke up, he likely wouldn't be able to say good-bye and Jack would leave and he would end up letting her parents take over. If he thought for a second her mom and Ben would advise her to let him go, he would do it.

It was cowardly, but he'd considered it.

When she'd sighed and turned in her sleep and Niall's arms had gone around her, he'd known he had to get his ass up and do the right thing.

The right thing was going to kill him. The right thing was breaking his heart, and he would never be fucking whole again.

He was turning himself in, and he was going to request witness protection, and the next time he would see them would be years from now. It would take years for the whole debacle to wind its way through the court system, and then he would have to weigh the risks. He couldn't think about the future. By this time tomorrow he might be in another state. Or on his way to DC, since this was going to likely be handled by the big guys. The two people he loved most in the world wouldn't be kept informed of his whereabouts. They would be told it was classified and that by all accounts Jensen Wiley no longer existed.

They would move on without him. Niall would become her husband, her only Dom. He would be a part of her big family, and he would make himself important to all of them. Jensen could see his best friend charming Nat Dawson over brunch and watching football with Ben. Niall's charm and love for Harlow would eventually bring Chase around.

Would they have kids by the time he was free again? If he was ever free again.

His gut clenched at the thought. He didn't want to leave them. He wanted to stay right here and never leave. He wanted to stay warm and soft with the family he never actually dreamed of because he'd been so sure he would be alone.

He hadn't understood the damn word. Alone meant being without them.

He heard the slight sound of a door opening down the hallway and knew he had to go. He'd dressed in the bathroom but his boots were in his hands because they would make enough noise to wake Niall, and he couldn't stand a big dramatic scene.

Was he being an asshole? A coward because he wasn't facing them? Or was he sparing them a whole lot of heartache by not forcing them to watch him go?

It didn't matter because there was no longer any time left.

Jensen moved as quietly as he could, easing the door closed. He turned and Jack was standing there, his backpack slung over his left shoulder.

"You're up early," Jack said quietly. "Can't sleep? Or are you dreading this morning's meeting with the family?" He moved toward the kitchen. He looked a bit older in the early morning light, with his grim expression and tired eyes. This was the real Jack O'Malley. "Here's the key. Ignore Chase. Talk to Ben and Nat. Especially Nat. You get her on your side and Chase will fall in line. There's a saying in our family. Chase acknowledges no authority but one."

"His wife." Jensen didn't blame him. He kind of thought he would be the same way. Would have been if he'd had a real chance with Harlow.

Jack nodded and yawned and moved to the sink. He pulled out a glass and used the tap. After a long drink he turned to Jensen. "Is there a place that serves coffee at this time of the morning out here? I suspect yes since this is a ranching community and those motherfuckers tend to be up early."

"There's a diner in town, but if you're in a hurry there is a fast-food place on the highway that serves breakfast, and they have a drive through. I can show you," Jensen offered.

Jack waved him off. "Don't worry about it. I'll find something on the way. At least Nat and Ben showing up with my father last night means I don't have to wait for Chase before I go back. He can catch a ride with his family. It's a long drive back to Dallas, and the man likes to talk, if you know what I mean. For a guy who claims silence is golden, he likes to hear himself complain. I won't even go into the lecture I got on using gas station restrooms. Did you know Chase knows all the bacteria? I mean all of them. I'm pretty sure he could list them and what they can do to your junk."

"I'm coming with you." Jensen said the words with a quiet determination.

A brow rose above Jack's green eyes. "I thought you were going to meet with my father and iron out what you want in an immunity deal. I know I said he was a corporate attorney, and he is, but he's also one of the smartest men I know. He won't steer you wrong. He annoys the hell out of me from time to time but if I was in trouble, he would be my first call."

Jensen shook his head. "It would take too long, and it wouldn't solve my main problem."

"Harlow," Jack surmised. "You think you're hurting her if you keep her close. You think if you disappear then her family connections can keep her safe."

Jensen nodded. "Meeting her parents made me believe they'll do anything to protect her. She's better off without me. She'll be much safer, and it'll be easier for them to keep her far away from this whole mess if I'm out of the equation."

The Dawsons weren't like his or Niall's parents. While Jensen knew his mom would have tried, she wasn't as fierce as Natalie Dawson. She wouldn't have walked in and taken control of the situation and helped him figure things out. She would have cried and asked him to tell her what to do. He'd forgotten his father, but he knew damn well he was neither of the Dawson brothers. His father had been concerned with nothing but his own comfort.

Jack seemed to consider what to say. "You know she's actually a smart, competent woman who can make her own decisions."

She was everything. She was all he wanted in the world, and this was the only gift he could give her. "She shouldn't have to make this decision. She shouldn't have to give up her whole life for me. Would she be able to see her family if she has to go into witness protection?"

"We can't be certain that will happen." Jack said the words but there was a hesitancy to them that Jensen pounced on. "You're making a lot of assumptions. Reasonable ones, but still assumptions."

"You know it will. Unless Hamilton miraculously dies this will go to trial and it'll take years. His lawyers will put it off as long as possible in the hopes that something happens to me." Jensen explained, though he was certain Jack already knew. "And then we'll get years of appeals. What is the likelihood that I ever come out of protection?"

"It's good," Jack countered. "If we convict Hamilton on even a couple of the counts we can tag him on, he'll be in jail for the rest of his life. Eventually his organization will either break up or move on. He's not a mafia man, for all he wants to be. When it's clear he's not getting out, they'll divide up anything that's left and move on. You'll be okay because there won't be anyone left who'll be willing to risk their lives for revenge when the boss isn't the boss anymore. But, I mean, best-case scenario is still years, and I won't have any control over where you go or what work they give you to do."

Nothing the man said made him think about changing his mind. "Do you want your cousin stuck in that life? I'm going to admit something to you. If I could do this all over, I wouldn't. I would have tried to get justice instead of revenge. If the shit hadn't hit the fan, I might have been able to slip out of the life with no one the wiser, and I would have gotten a chance with her."

Jack leaned against the counter. “That’s not likely. Once you’re in, you’re in for life. It’s precisely why Harlow has been asked to get not one, but two women out of the organization. But I understand what you’re telling me. I don’t know that her family can be happy without her. I worry my uncle would look for her, and he would find her. But man, this is going to kill her heart.”

Did Jack think he hadn’t taken her feelings into consideration? He had, but her life was more important. “She’ll still have Niall. He won’t leave her. Fuck, man, I’m doing this for her. I wish I had another option, but I don’t. Meeting with your dad in the morning still leads into witness protection, or if I refuse, it leads Hamilton right to Harlow and Niall. I do not see a scenario in which I live with them and they’re not in danger.”

“And what happens when she gets called into another case like this one? Do you think she’s going to stop working?” Jack seemed determined to play devil’s advocate. “Even if we put Hamilton away someone will move to fill in the space and more young women will get pulled in. Harlow won’t stop being the warrior she is. Even if you’re no longer around to watch her back.”

The thought made his stomach turn. Not because of her work. She would always do that, but he wouldn’t be there to help her. But then had he ever? She’d helped him in LA. His “help” had gotten her assaulted and arrested and took years to recover from.

He never deserved her. “I have to hope her family will look after her. If Hamilton ever figures out how much she means to me, he’ll know how to shut me up. But if I walk away, he doesn’t have any reason to believe she’s anything but a pretty girl I followed around one night.”

“I want to argue with you,” Jack said.

“But you can’t. So take me back to Dallas and we’ll get to my apartment and I’ll give you what I have. We can meet with your boss and maybe you don’t have to be a bartender anymore. It seems like you could use some time off,” Jensen pointed out.

Jack huffed. “I could use a vacation, but I suspect I’ll pull desk duty for a while and then go back into the field. I’m good at it. For the most part I like it. Hell, I was okay with this assignment until I realized it was going to break my cousin’s heart and probably turn my whole family against me.”

He did feel for the guy. It was obvious there were some serious family dynamics at work. "I'm not trying to cause trouble."

Jack sighed. "I know, but it's coming for both of us, and I won't be under a protective order. I know you think I'm being overly dramatic, but you didn't grow up with a romance-writing momma who will have her happily ever after if she has to kill everyone to get it. I'm lucky it was Papa who showed up. My mother will be on my doorstep when Nat calls her and tells her what happened here. I'll be lucky if she doesn't walk into the middle of an undercover assignment to give me a lecture and then walk around asking all the criminals questions so she can better write their points of view."

For a moment he worried Jack would refuse him. A bit of panic set in because he couldn't take Niall's car and leave them out here. And there was no such thing as ride share in this rural part of the state. If Jack decided he couldn't take the heat with his family, Jensen was going to be in trouble.

"We should get going." Jack set his glass in the sink and made for the front door, his keys now in hand. "If I know my uncles, they'll be here earlier than you would think. You don't want to get caught fleeing the scene of the crime."

A sigh of relief went through him. "The crime would be drawing her further into my life."

Jack frowned his way. "Then why did you sleep with her last night? Or rather keep her up for a long time. These walls are thin, brother. Why did you give her hope that you would stay this time? Don't give me some bullshit. We both know the answer. You were selfish because you think she's going to shrug it off eventually and you'll be the only one to pay. Because for some damn reason you think you love her more than she loves you, but I'm going to tell you you're wrong. She might move on, but this will kill a part of her."

Jensen tensed at the accusation. He was in a trap, and any way he went he hurt someone. "What the fuck do you think I should do?"

"I think you should have been a damn man and come with me last night. You would have pissed her off, but she wouldn't have felt used." Jack's head shook. "I don't know why I'm arguing with you. I'm going to get what I need, and there's obviously no talking you out of it. Hell, I don't know if there is another way. I'm tired and feeling guilty, and I don't handle either well. Let's go, and maybe we can leave them behind with all the people I care about."

He was going to be a fun traveling companion.

Was he right?

It didn't matter. He stepped out on the porch, and the last time he'd been here flashed through his head.

It's going to be okay, Jensen. I'm going to make something of myself. One day I'm coming back, and I'll bring my wife here and we'll all sit down and talk about the hard times. But then they won't seem so hard. You'll see. Me and you and Niall, we're going to be okay.

His brother was dead, and he was lost.

He prayed Niall would be okay. Niall would help her forget him.

As dawn broke, he got into Jack's car and drove away from the future he wanted.

* * * *

Harlow came awake to the sound of the burner phone Ruby had given her buzzing. She'd slid it into the side table the day Ruby had brought out Gigi and Greer and the much-needed clothing and makeup and skincare.

Ruby had explained she'd toyed with it to boost the signal, but it still wouldn't work half the time out here. There had been a lot of talk about satellites and the position of the Earth and the amount of time she would do if she got caught, so Harlow was fairly certain it was serious.

That didn't mean she wanted to answer it.

It was nice here all cuddled up, and she was pretty sure it was way too early to be awake after everything that happened the night before. Her men had kept her up. Her beautiful, sexy, amazing men.

"Why?" Niall yawned and turned over in his sleep. He looked deliciously rumpled, and she wished she could lay back down and wrap herself around him.

Also, her backside was sore. Turned out when you shoved a big cock up there, one felt it the next day.

She snorted and reached for the handle on the drawer to the nightstand. The phone was buzzing along.

"Is that Ruby?" Niall sat up, yawning. "Or did your dad find a way to boost a signal out here? Tell me he's not already on his way."

She could see her dad striding into the bedroom she shared with her superhot boyfriends if he thought they needed to chat. She fumbled for the phone. It was easy because that side of the bed was empty. "He doesn't have this number. As far as I know he's not aware this phone exists. Though you should know he'll have a new one for me as soon as he can."

He looked around. "Where is Jensen?"

Harlow gripped the phone and brought it out, not caring that her sheet had slipped and she was naked. It wasn't like Ruby would be on a video call. Maybe if this was some kind of work meeting she could get Niall to eat her pussy while she handled it. It would make meetings so much more fun. "Probably starting the coffee. Or trying to hide from my parents."

Niall frowned and slid out of bed.

No fun for her. She slid her finger across the screen and put her best friend on speaker. "Hey, Rubes. What's happening?"

"That's what I'm trying to figure out, but I wanted to give you a heads-up." Ruby sounded so serious it made Harlow sit up and start reaching for a robe.

"About what?"

"There's been a lot of chatter in certain forums that the hit is going down today and everyone except the hired gun should back off. This conversation happened about an hour ago," Ruby explained. "It's like it's a done deal. I don't know what's happening. I've also checked out the sat coverage of your area, and I don't see anything that would tell me there's a problem. Although I did hear a rumor that your dad and Jack showed up. Big Tag is pissed Chase hacked him."

"You hacked him."

"I was polite about it. I know how to handle Big Tag. I sent him a dozen lemon tarts and an apology explaining he didn't understand what could happen if you didn't get your skin care regimen," Ruby explained.

It was so early. She glanced over at the clock and stretched. "Yeah, Dad showed up with Jack. I think they were going to try to convince Jensen to give up everything with absolutely no promise of immunity. I love Jack, but he can be a massive ass sometimes. Although my dad could just have come to try to murder him. Needless to say Dad's plan was screwed up because Papa figured out what he was doing and made Uncle Lucas come with him and mom."

Ruby whistled. "I bet that went well. Are they still there?"

"Jack is probably on the road by now." She found some PJ pants and slipped them over her legs. She hoped her parents slept in. She'd like time to shower and not look like a well-loved and doubly penetrated woman before they showed up. Although her dad would know. He always knew. "If he drank all the coffee, I'm going to have a long talk with him."

They would have to go into town soon. She loved being alone with her men, but worrying about whether they could buy groceries was going to be a problem. And her parents would be here soon.

She was probably in for some complaints of nausea this morning. If her dad started in on her, she would shove a pancake in his mouth. Niall's pancakes were excellent tasting and might actually shut the man up.

She would have to have a long talk with her dad today. It was past time they came to a cease fire. She didn't want to be a point of contention for her parents.

"I tried his cell, but he didn't pick up," Ruby said. "I'm worried something is going down. I think at the very least someone has figured out Jensen might have intelligence on Hamilton, and they're going to move on his apartment today. I have a plan, and I hope you're not upset about it, but I wanted you to have the option. I know he's safe and all, but Jack is going to want to lock down that apartment, and I don't think he knows where it is. Jensen used a fake name to rent it."

"I'm pretty sure Jack knows everything now. Jensen talked to him for hours last night. What he doesn't have is the actual proof. Which I think is hidden at his place, so yeah, we need to get him on the phone. Can you call Big Tag?"

"I did. He's sending someone over to secure the apartment later on this morning, and then if Jensen gives them permission, they'll put in a new security system. My worry is if they get in before Big Tag can, they'll have not only the information Jensen was going to use against Hamilton, but they might figure out where you are," Ruby explained. "But like I said, someone from MT is going over there this morning, so I might have freaked out for nothing, and I hope it's okay that I told them where Jensen was living."

She praised the day her parents became friends with that big bastard. He was a dude you could count on. And now that she thought about it, his son was practically an attorney, with connections to a good firm with a scary defense lawyer. "I'll speak for him. Do it. I honestly think we should come back to Dallas this afternoon. Could you negotiate with Big Tag to let us stay at Sanctum? The Hideout isn't as secure, and I think The Club will be a bit much for my guys."

They would probably prefer the quirky charm of Sanctum to the rich decadence of The Club. The Club was beautiful and filled with powerful people. Sanctum was full of Big Tag's people.

Jensen and Niall were way closer to that. Also, Sanctum had a princess castle room, and the things she could do with her guys and all that sparkly glitter.

"Thank you," Ruby said with a grateful sigh. "I thought I would have to fight you. I think you should come back to Dallas. You don't have real Internet out there. If you're at Sanctum, we can work this case together. It's getting lonely at the office. Gigi came in to answer the phones on her day off, but she is not interested in solving crimes in any way that doesn't involve listening to a podcast."

Harlow snorted and glanced into the bathroom. No Jensen. And it was weird because his razor was gone along with his toothbrush.

Had he used the second bathroom so he wouldn't wake them up?

"I'll talk to my parents today. I'm sure they would rather have me under Big Tag's security system than out here, and it's more practical." But she would miss this place. She would miss walking by the river and watching the horses and cows. She would miss sitting with her guys around the firepit.

"Awesome. I'm glad you agree and hope you don't freak out when I tell you there's a helicopter on the way," she explained.

Harlow went still with shock. "What? Where the hell… Did you ask Julian to borrow his chopper?"

"No," Ruby replied. "I went someplace closer to you.

Remember when I told you I'm friends with a movie star?"

"Vanessa Malone. Yes. She was your neighbor when you were a kid. Didn't she marry a guy from McKay-Taggart? He was her bodyguard, right?" Sometimes it was hard to keep up with all the clients who married bodyguards. It was like a perk. They should partner with a wedding planner. Get a bodyguard, start planning the wedding.

"Nope. She was assigned him as a Dom during her training period at The Club, but he was a spy for Julian. It's a whole big story, but the long and short of it is, they're married and Michael's brother runs a big-ass ranch fairly close to where you are. He's sending their helicopter to bring you to Dallas. I thought it would be fitting to make your dad drive Niall's Jeep back."

It sounded like a lot. "You're sure this is necessary?"

After a moment, Ruby responded. "I have a weird feeling."

She'd learned to trust her partner's instincts. "They can land in the field north of the house. Any kind of ETA?"

Niall walked back in, a frown on his face. He immediately turned and went to the closet, opening it and disappearing inside.

He looked super serious.

"It should be any time now." Harlow could practically see Ruby wincing as she said the words. "I'm sorry. I kind of wanted you to not be able to say no."

"Because you have a feeling." Harlow felt a chill go down her spine. "We'll be packed up and ready. Can you call my folks and tell them what's happening? If I get on the line, they'll want me to wait."

Adrenaline started to pulse through her. Ruby had a sixth sense about when things were about to go wrong. The last time she'd told Ruby to ignore that sense, they'd hired Daisy O'Donnell and gotten themselves into this mess. She was going to listen to her bestie on how to get out of it.

What was going on with Niall? And where the hell was Jensen? Probably taking a walk or something, but he should leave a damn note. It wasn't like they were on vacation.

"Will do." Ruby paused for a moment. "I'll have the chopper take you right to the MT building, and Big Tag can move you from there to Sanctum. I kind of won't breathe until I know you're there.

I'm sorry. I'm not trying to be your dad."

"It's okay. I'm not even mad at my dad anymore. Tell them everything and have them meet us at Sanctum tonight. Tell Dad I'll order his favorite burger from Top and convince Mom it's the veggie burger." She wasn't going to be angry anymore. Her family loved her, and they would work this all out. Being at Sanctum meant she could have her family and friends over and still be safe. It was a good thing. Niall walked out of the closet, and there was a grim look to his eyes. Her stomach sank. "I'll see you soon."

"See you soon." Ruby hung up.

"What is it?" She asked the question, but she was afraid she already knew the answer. He wouldn't, though. He wouldn't do this to her twice. He wouldn't do this to her after last night. He just…wouldn't.

"He either left on foot or he went with Jack," Niall said, his voice tight.

She wanted to throw up. He left her. Again. He made the choice for her without discussing or talking about it. Something cold hit her. She put the phone down and went over the last twelve hours in her brain, and now she could see what he'd been doing.

One last night. One long good-bye.

He wasn't leaving because he didn't love her. He did love her in as much as he could love anyone. But there was something deeply broken in Jensen. He was being a martyr, but that didn't excuse the fact that she wasn't worth talking to. Wasn't worth letting in on the plots and plans.

Niall was ranting, but then he hadn't been in this place before. Oh, she knew Jensen had pulled some shit on him over the years, but it hit different after spending days in bed with someone. Even if they didn't have sex together, their relationship had hit an intimacy plateau.

Would Niall want her if Jensen wasn't involved? Would they even work? Or would they always miss the part of them that walked away?

She stood there listening to Niall's anger, and all she could feel was sorrow.

And a little panic. Ruby had a feeling that she needed to be in Dallas. Did she need to be in Dallas because someone was coming for them? Or because Jensen was making a mistake. One that could cost him his life.

Ruby said something had changed. That the hit was going down today. Would they take Jensen out if they didn't know where he'd hidden the information? "What would happen if Jensen went with Jack?"

Niall stopped, and his face flushed. "What? I mean I'm assuming he went with Jack and everything he said last night about listening to the lawyer this morning was complete bullshit."

Harlow nodded. She shoved down her heartache because there was a mystery to be solved and logic to be followed. It was good because she knew this time when her heart broke, it might not come back together again. She'd been stupid to open it. But she wasn't thinking about that now. "All right. He goes with Jack when Jack left this morning. He needed roughly four hours to get back to Dallas, and he'll want to shower and shave before checking in, so if he was planning to get to meet with his boss before he went to the meeting at the club to go over security for the Hamilton visit, he would have left around six a.m. It's nine now, so he should be about an hour outside of Dallas. He would go with Jack so Jack can potentially put him in protective custody."

"Leaving us with no protection at all," Niall pointed out, his jaw tight. "He left us here like sitting fucking ducks."

She understood his rage, but she couldn't handle it right now. "Before they'll protect him, he has to show his cards, and that means stopping by his place and getting the data he has on Hamilton. They won't give him crap until they have it in their hands. It's precisely why my parents wanted Uncle Lucas with him. If he surrenders it without an agreement in place, they don't owe him anything."

"Harlow, it doesn't matter now. He made his choice. If he wants to go to fucking jail, then we did everything we could," Niall spat back bitterly.

It was hard to deal with his anger and keep shoving down her pain, but she forced herself to do it. Jensen had blown them all up. He probably thought they would be fine without him, that they could move on through life like he had never been there at all, but there was a reason nothing worked before there had been three of them. She picked up the small suitcase her sister brought her days ago and rushed to pack up as she talked through the problem. It was a mechanical process. Pick up clothes. Shove them in. Let her brain work while her hands did. "Ruby said the hit is on. For today."

Niall stopped. "He left us here when they're coming for us? He found out and didn't even warn us?"

She didn't think he would do that. In fact, she knew that wasn't what happened. It didn't make her feel better. She believed Jensen was trying to "save" them. He would walk into the fire and destroy everything they built because he didn't think he deserved any of it, but he wouldn't leave them behind to die. "He doesn't know. Ruby found out because she's been monitoring the Dark Web. She's got hundreds of connections. Scary connections. If she says this hit is happening, then it is and I'm worried… The only thing that changed between yesterday when they were still hoping to find us and today is Jack and my parents showing up here. My dads have a woman who runs their office, and she would die before she gave up info on them. She would also probably murder anyone who asked. Mom wouldn't tell her agent, and she damn straight wouldn't bring her friends in."

"That whole company of Taggarts know where we are," Niall pointed out.

Harlow shook her head. "The first thing they do at orientation is put the fear of Big Tag in those men. And only Big Tag and Charlotte know. There are a couple of hackers who could get into their system, but they have safeguards. They would know. It's why he's going to kick my dad's ass. Did you call anyone?"

Niall's head shook, but then he picked up his own bag and started shoving things in. "No. Who the hell would I call? Everyone I care about was here. I didn't even call my business after we got here. All I cared about was protecting you and Jensen."

"I know, babe. I'm sorry. I had to ask because that leaves one possibility, and it's nothing I want to even contemplate."

"You think Jack told someone?" Niall paled. "Oh, shit. You think Jack is working for Hamilton."

She barely managed to not roll her eyes. This was not the time nor the place for bratty behavior. Niall didn't know Jack the way she did, so she had to forgive him for what might seem like a logical leap. "No. Jack wouldn't, but he has a whole team he reports to. If he called in, he would have asked for the department that would liaise with the prosecutor. So that's the FBI and the DOJ, and I don't know how many people are involved, but I do know Hamilton bragged a lot about having people on the inside. Bribing officials is something he was excellent at, and the government doesn't pay well enough to stop some people from taking it. It would be easy to pass along Jensen's address in Dallas."

"They're not coming after us. They're going after Jensen. And he has no idea." Niall's eyes closed, and when they opened again there was real fear in them. "We have to call Jack. Jensen doesn't have a phone."

She picked up the sat phone, praying it still worked. "Ruby said he wasn't picking up." It went straight to voice mail. She threw the phone on the bed. "Ruby left him some texts, but Jack can be stubborn. I know exactly how he thinks, and he won't give Jensen a single reason to rethink his position. Not once he's called it in."

"So he'll use Jensen to make his case no matter what."

"I doubt that. I would bet he tried to convince him he should talk to us but he wouldn't. Once the path is set, Jack won't look back. He's a good man but he's very much about his job. Not simply because he's ambitious. Because he believes that what he's doing is right. I would bet anything Jensen convinced him this was for the best and that he's protecting us. So don't expect him to listen to pleas."

There was a sound in the distance.

"We should get out of here." Niall pulled his shirt overhead as Harlow started to get dressed, too. "I'll drive us to the motel your parents are at and we'll figure out what to do from there. I need to get you someplace safe even if we don't think they're coming here. Then I'll deal with Jensen."

That didn't sound like he was going to give the guy a hug. But then he was still reeling. Her Master—if he was still her Master—had never been put in a situation like this. But she had. "Niall, I'm going to ask you to let me take the lead in this. I know your instinct is to protect me…"

He held up a hand. "But you know what you're doing and most of my military career was arresting drunk cadets and making sure no one got out of hand. I never once dealt with a criminal organization.

Harlow, I'm reacting poorly. I'm not taking your feelings into account and I'm sorry, baby. Can we talk while we're in the Jeep?"

That sound was getting closer. She pulled out the other bag. The one Ruby had brought her. While her sister had ensured she had makeup and clothes, Ruby had brought her other accessories. She pulled out the guns and ensured they were loaded and ready. She handed Niall one. "I don't think we'll have much privacy since we're not taking your Jeep. Ruby sent a helo."

Niall's head swiveled as he turned toward the sound. "A helicopter?"

Harlow shrugged as he took the pistol and placed it in his bag after checking it himself. "She worries, and she's into big gestures. Seriously, save a girl's life one time and she never lets you forget she's grateful. As to my feelings… They have to wait. I know I can't move forward with him after this, but I also can't leave him to fate."

"You're going to save him." It wasn't a question. It was merely a statement.

She nodded. "And then we can be done."

"We?" His jaw firmed. "Harlow, I'm never going to be done with you. I know what Jensen did is dumb as shit, and I will follow your lead on how you want to deal with it, but don't think I'm going to let you push me away. We are not a packaged deal. Our agreement was to love you together if you let us. And if you don't then we'll still love you. I will still love you and want to be with you."

He was shaking her walls, and she couldn't have it. Still, she also couldn't tell him no. She moved into his space. "I love you, too, Sir, but I don't know that we can pretend like nothing happened and move on. You lied to me. I understand why you did it, but this is bringing it all back."

He reached out a hand as the sound of the chopper closed in. "You can trust me. I'll do whatever it takes. If you need time I'll give it to you, but I won't be far away. I'll be waiting for you."

She felt the ground thud as the chopper landed in the big yard. Could she trust anyone after this? She squeezed his hand. "We should go."

He picked up their bags and let her go first.

She hoped they got there in time.

Chapter Seventeen

Niall stood back while the blades of the chopper slowed and a young man slid from the pilot's seat. He wore jeans and a T-shirt along with a headset he slid down around his neck. He had dark hair and looked to be roughly sixteen, though he probably wouldn't be flying a helicopter if he was. He smiled and Niall knew this kid was going to bug the shit out of him because he was cocky and giving Harlow a long once-over.

He nearly glanced to his side so he and Jensen could exchange a look that let him know they would protect their girl from overly eager cowboys.

Jensen wasn't there. He wouldn't be there again because he'd walked away without even bothering to leave them a fucking note.

He was so angry, and he had to tamp it down because they were in a crisis.

"Hello," the pilot said with a wave as he strode toward them. He wore cowboy boots and an aw-shucks smile that would likely melt the heart of most women. "Harlow Dawson? My name's Jasper Malone. My auntie sent me to pick you up, and she did not mention that you would turn out to be so gorgeous. Damn, girl. Do you work with my Aunt Vanessa? Ruby is the one who called, but you look more like you should be in Hollywood. Is this your personal assistant?"

"I'm her Dom," Niall said and put all of his will into that one word.

"Hey, new friends," Harlow said and then frowned the guy's way. "Although he's not really new since I met him a couple of times when he was literally a baby trying to climb the bookshelves. I think Ruby babysat him at one point."

"That would likely be one of my younger siblings since I'm not a kid. Ruby's only a couple of years older than me," Jasper pointed out.

"Ten. She's ten years older," Harlow countered. "Niall, this is the heir to Malone Oil. He's also barely eighteen years old, so you can stop with the caveman-possessive thing."

"Well, I would if these cocky assholes would stop showing up looking at you like you're the last cupcake at the buffet." He huffed but realized he'd kind of outed them. "But I promise next time I'll use the word boyfriend."

He was fumbling, and if he wasn't careful he was going to lose her. It would be so easy for her to toss them both out, but he had no intention of allowing Jensen's fuck-up to ruin his relationship with Harlow.

Jasper seemed perfectly non-plussed. "Nah, man. I can play around the word 'boyfriend,' but Dom is a term I'm forced to take seriously. It's a family thing. One of these days they're going to let me into that Hideout place and I'll figure it all out myself. I would go to The Club, but I could run into my momma there. Let's just say there are rooms in our house that me and my siblings know not to enter if we don't want too much information. Now Ruby made it sound like this was an emergency."

Harlow nodded. "We need to get to Dallas. How long will it take?"

Jasper shrugged. "Depends. Dallas is a big place. Ruby said something about getting to my Uncle Mike's building. I've done that in less than an hour before."

"You have a license to fly that thing? Did you steal it?" Niall was still having a hard time with the kid who looked like he should be in high school racing them to Dallas in a small tin can with blades that could kill them.

Jasper grinned. "Buddy, I've been flying since I was fourteen.

This baby was my birthday present. Let's say I had some parental encouragement."

"So your dad is super wealthy and likes to play with toys?" Niall replied as they started to walk toward the chopper.

Jasper snorted. "Nah, my daddy gets air sick if you mention a helo. He can barely handle the corporate jet. My momma took up flying. She would be out here if she wasn't in London dealing with some kind of business problem. Let me tell you, I prefer flying and working the ranch to dealing with all the oil business stuff. They want me to go to…business school. Hey, girl, you have a fun business going with Ruby. You need a pilot? I come with my own chopper, and I know how to use it, if you know what I mean."

Harlow picked up the headset on the passenger seat. "I think we're more a car-driven business, but thanks. And we're not going to the MT building. We need to go straight to a friend's apartment building. Do you have a way for me to climb down without you parking this beast?"

Jasper hopped in his seat, and that left Niall on the back bench. He stored their gear and pulled his headset off the side of Harlow's seat. The minute he put it on, the blades started up, and he could hear Jasper talking over the headset.

"I have a ladder. I can probably put you down on top of a building," Jasper explained as he pushed buttons and flicked switches. "I mean if the building is big and sound enough. Of course, people tend to freak out if they're not used to it."

"Harlow, I know you mean well, but I'm worried. This sounds dangerous," Niall pointed out. He thought she'd given him the gun as a precaution, but now he realized she meant to use hers. He wasn't about to lose her to some wild scheme to save Jensen. "We should have that Big Tag guy handle this."

"Ian's already informed," Harlow said, and even over the tinny sound of the headset he could hear how tight her voice was. "But no one can get in touch with Jensen or Jack. Jensen doesn't have a phone, and Jack turned his off or he's ignoring us because he doesn't want to think about what he's doing. Niall, this is my area of expertise. I'm doing this my way. You're welcome to come with me or I'll have Jasper here drop me off and then he can take you to the McKay-Taggart building and I'll fill you in later."

Well, he knew when he'd been put in his place. That wasn't fair. She was right. She was the one who did shit like this on a regular basis. "I'll come with you. I'm not leaving you."

She sighed as the helo took off. "It might be better if you did. Niall, I don't know what I'm going into. It could get dangerous, or we could be making a complete mountain out of a molehill."

"I'm going with you. I'll follow all of your instructions, but I won't let you go alone."

The helo banked left hard, and he was almost certain that fucker was trying to show off. Or make him hurl.

"I could go with you," Jasper offered. "I know a lot about danger."

"You know a lot about punching cows and trying to avoid boardrooms," Harlow quipped. "He's ex-military. I assure you he can handle himself."

Jasper seemed to slip the chopper into light speed. "Then I'll hang out until you need a pickup. I think this is going to be fun. My uncle's boss is always a hoot, and he's going to love bailing me out of jail for buzzing downtown buildings."

"Uhm, this is illegal?" Niall asked.

"Oh, absolutely. I'm apparently going to be violating the flight plan I filed about twenty minutes ago, but it's fine," Jasper assured him. "I'll tell whatever honey they send to yell at me that I got lost. Dallas is a big place, and honestly, it was laid out by a drunk asshole. Everyone knows that. So it's perfectly normal for me to mistake one building for another."

"A high-rise office building versus a three-story, shitty apartment building?" Niall asked as they raced over ranchland. He noticed one of the cows looking up with an aggrieved huff, probably because they were ruining a perfectly nice morning. Of course, that's what Jensen had done. They should still be in bed, all cuddled up and happy. "I assume we're heading to Jensen's. I only know it's three stories and crappy because he talked about it. I've never been. Do we even have an address?"

"Ruby has it. She's sending me all the details. She found it on the Dark Web," Harlow pointed out.

They were coming for Jensen. They knew where he lived. They would try to steal his information, and if he was there, they would take him out.

As angry as he was at his best friend, he also couldn't imagine a world without him. He might never be as close to Jensen Wiley as he had been the last few days, but he didn't want the man dead.

"It's going to be okay." Harlow turned her head so she could see him. She gave him a weak smile. "They might not get there before we do. Big Tag is sending someone to check it out. Take a deep breath. We're probably panicking for nothing, but I would rather be wrong and make the most awkward scene of all time than be right and late."

He held her gaze for a moment and nodded. "We'll do what we have to."

"Now wait a minute," Jasper said. "Who is this other guy? Sweet darling, are you into all that crazy three-way stuff? Because I've heard that can be fun."

He was going to kill the kid.

Harlow sighed and turned back around. "Pay attention to your flying. And we are not a threesome."

Not anymore. Niall knew the words she didn't say. They had been. They'd been moving toward something so special and right. Nothing would ever feel as good as knowing his best friend was there.

The betrayal weighed heavy on his heart as they sped toward Dallas.

He had no idea what they looked like at the end of this. He only knew they would never be the same.

* * * *

Jensen slid out of the SUV and looked at the craptastic apartment building he'd lived in for the last couple of months. It was a dump. It was more motel than upscale downtown condo. Located on the edge of an industrial district, it was somewhat quiet and cheap, and he was pretty sure most of the people who lived here were involved in some kind of crime.

It wasn't a place for Harlow.

"So the hard drive is in your apartment?" Jack asked, glancing at his watch. He'd spent a lot of the drive on the phone talking to his boss, and it looked like he didn't want to be late for the meeting they set up.

"I have it in a hidden compartment," he replied. "I can go up and get it if you want to stay here."

Jack's cell trilled again, and he sighed. "Ruby. I think they know you're gone."

It was morning, and they would be awake by now. No question. She would have rolled over and sighed and rubbed up against Niall, who would kiss her and call her princess. She wasn't. Harlow wasn't a royal princess with high-maintenance needs. She was a warrior princess.

Did she reach for him and think he'd gone for a walk or to make coffee? How long was it before she realized he was gone?

"I think it's best we don't talk to them until the deal is done," Jensen said. If he heard her voice, he might not be able to do it. If Niall tried to talk him out of it, he might listen because this was the last thing he wanted.

Jack refused the call. "She's going to kick my ass. She's sent about a hundred texts, but I'm sure it's all crap about how I'm ruining everything. I cannot win with that woman."

"Do you want to win with her?" Jensen was curious how much he'd fucked up Jack's life.

Jack's expression shuttered. Like he'd shown too much. He slid his cell in his pants pocket and then the smooth cowboy lawman was back. "She's a friend of my cousin's. I assure you Harlow is going to be pissed at me, so why don't we go and make sure this whole thing is worth it. I don't want to have blown apart my family life for nothing. What floor are you on?"

"The third. I'm the last unit on the left." It wasn't like there was a doorman or anything. There wasn't a lobby, either. It was all apartments with stairs and open walkways.

Jack's cell trilled again, and he groaned. He brought it out with a long sigh. "It's the office. I need to take it. I'll be here. Hurry. We need to be downtown in twenty minutes." He put the phone to his ear. "Hey, Lori. Yeah, we're back in Dallas. You got any updates on the Dark Web search? Nothing?" He nodded to Jensen. "Hurry. I want to get you somewhere safe, but it seems we're okay for now. I've got someone tracking Hamilton. He's not scheduled to fly into

Dallas until tonight."

He would be long gone by then. He'd gotten so close. He knew the Jensen he'd been months back would mourn the loss of his revenge. Now, as he walked around to the back of the building, all he could feel was the pain of losing her. Of Niall never trusting him again. He would be alone for the rest of his life, and it was his own fault.

He should have left with her in LA. He should have made the choice to have a future rather than trying to avenge the past. They could be married by now.

Instead, she would marry Niall, and they would have a beautiful life and he would pay for his sins.

Out of the corner of his eye he saw a car darting into the parking lot. Someone was in a hurry, but that wasn't unusual. They were probably trying to hit their dealer's house before heading to work. Traffic was usually terrible this time of day.

He jogged up the stairs and pulled out his key. Where would they live? He hadn't been to Niall's place and had only heard that Harlow had a pretty condo in a nice part of town.

He'd missed so much. He wished he hadn't, wished he'd been part of their daily lives so he would have more memories.

This was stupid. He was being stupid.

Jensen stopped two doors from his apartment as the truth hit him.

And there's the beautiful, damaged one who needs a shit ton of therapy because of all the damage. That one is the dangerous one because she'll make split-second decisions based on the trauma she survived and not what's best for the three of them. She'll martyr herself because that's all she knows to do. Because she thinks maybe she doesn't deserve good things like love and protection, like no one should risk for her.

Niall had been right. Chase hadn't been talking about Harlow. He'd been comparing Jensen to his wife. Natalie Dawson had been the one to make bad choices based on trauma. Her trauma had been… He couldn't even imagine it, and yet she was whole and happy and a good mom and a great partner to her husbands.

Could he do that? Could he learn to shove down what the world had tried to teach him and believe that he was worthy of love?

A little panic threatened. It seemed so simple. He was doing this to save her. He was making this decision because he was absolutely certain she wouldn't allow him to leave without her, and neither would Niall.

Would he be okay with her doing the same? If she was in trouble and she decided it was too dangerous for him, would he nod and accept it and move on with his life? Fuck no. He wouldn't because he loved her and he owed her everything he had, his love, his protection, his advice, his time, his effort. He owed it to both of them to be part of the team, and yet he'd made a unilateral decision that affected them all with zero input from them.

No, his internal voice argued. They had made themselves clear. Just because he wanted to pretend they hadn't had this discussion didn't mean Harlow and Niall hadn't put their beliefs out there. They thought they should stay together because they were in love. Harlow had assets that could help them stay safe, and yet he hadn't even taken the time to explore the options that might keep them together. He'd simply jumped headlong into… Yep, he'd jumped headlong into martyrdom, like her father had said. And for the reasons her father said. It was easier to let her go than to become the man she needed, to face all the things he needed to in order to be her husband and Niall's true partner.

His chest felt too tight and he could hear a helicopter in the distance, but that wasn't unusual. What was unusual was the emotion he felt welling up and threatening to drown him.

He'd made a mistake. Such a big mistake, and he'd brought Jack into it.

Jensen forced himself to stop and take a long breath. He still had a shot. He could grab the drive and tell Jack he wanted to change the meeting place from the FBI building to the McKay-Taggart building. He could walk in, explain what he was doing, and that his girlfriend would pay for an attorney.

Wow, that hurt, but he was going to have to suck it up and find a way to pay her back in sexual favors or carrying heavy stuff for her. Maybe if he married her and treated her like a queen for forty or fifty years, she would consider the debt paid.

He wasn't even sure how he could repay Niall. He'd done this to him twice now. His best friend was used to getting left behind because Jensen couldn't handle his damn feelings.

He had to find a way to control this…grief? Was it grief? Was it guilt? Was it a childhood spent worrying that everything would fall apart, so he huffed and puffed until it did and he could stop worrying because the worst had already happened?

It was a pattern from childhood and one he had to break. Now that he was standing here looking at the life revenge had built, he knew he was making the worst mistake of his life and he couldn't even call them.

Could he find a ride back to Bonnet and pretend like he'd gone into town? The thought drifted through his brain, but they were up by now and they would know. Harlow would figure it out quickly.

He had to talk to her.

Ruby. Ruby had given her a phone. Ruby would kick his ass but would likely let him call her and start the groveling process.

He would grovel. He would kiss her toes and carry her handbag and be her lapdog everywhere but the dungeon floor.

It was like a weight got lifted off his chest. Like he could suddenly breathe freely, and he hadn't realized how bad it had been before.

He didn't have to live this way. He didn't have to make this decision on his own. He would be upset, feel so small, if either of them had done this to him and he couldn't… He couldn't do this to them. Jack would be pissed, but he was going to talk to them. He would still take down Hamilton, and maybe the best way was for him to go alone into witness protection. But maybe they could find another way. Maybe they could get out of this together.

Maybe she would spit in his face, kick him in the balls, and send him away.

What mattered was that he tried his damnedest to keep them all together.

With new purpose he started walking toward the apartment he'd survived in for the last several months. He wouldn't call it home. Home was where they were.

The helicopter was getting loud, and he wondered if there was some kind of police activity going. He couldn't worry about that right now. All that mattered was getting inside his apartment and getting what he needed. Even though it sounded like the fucker was about to buzz the building. If that was a news chopper, they were going to get into some serious trouble because he could see the way the trees in the front grounds were whipping from the gusts the blades made. He rushed to get to his door to avoid that wind.

He had his hand on the knob when he realized it wasn't locked.

A chill that had not a thing to do with the wind snaked down his spine.

He had a security system but it was attached to his phone, which he'd dumped so they couldn't track him. It wasn't an expensive one, just a system that would have alerted him to someone going in. It would be easy to turn it off if one knew what one was doing, and he knew damn well Hamilton would have someone who knew how to shut off a system.

What he wouldn't have is someone who knew where Jensen hid the data. It wasn't on his laptop or his gaming system. It was hidden in the wall behind carefully smoothed out wallpaper. No one would be able to see it. So if they came, they might still be here.

He was starting to move back, the wind whipping around him, when the door came open and Phil stood there, a pistol in his hands.

"I think you should come in, Jensen. It's time we had a talk. Where's the fed?" Phil asked.

Jensen put his hands up, letting Phil know he wasn't holding a weapon. Now he kind of hoped it was some kind of police helo flying over the building. Not that they would be here for him. How did Phil know about Jack? "What are you talking about?"

He practically had to shout the question. The noise was that loud, and then it began to lessen. The helicopter was moving away. Whatever it needed to do seemed to be finished.

Phil's head gestured to the apartment. "Get the fuck inside. This place is a hellhole, but someone might still call the cops. And I'm talking about Special Agent Jack O'Malley. Little fucker tricked me. I never suspected he was a fed."

His stomach threatened to turn, but he moved into the doorway because it wasn't like there was anywhere to run. There was one path out, and he didn't think Phil would miss with those odds. There was nothing to do but hope Jack figured out something was wrong. Hands held high, he moved from the light into the gloom of his apartment. It was cramped and nondescript, with nothing of himself in the crappy furniture or neutral colors.

"I don't know what you're talking about. The only Jack I know is Jack Cameron, the bartender."

Phil snorted. "Sure. Hey, Billy, go check the parking lot. If you see the fed, kill him."

Jensen turned to try to get to the door. He could shout for Jack to run, anything to warn him.

He heard a cracking sound and then felt the bite of a dart hitting his skin, and then he wasn't thinking about anything but how his every muscle seemed to seize. He fell to the ground because his legs wouldn't hold him anymore. His head hit the carpet, and he shook and shook, the pain overwhelming him, and he thought for a moment his heart was going to stop and all he could think of was the last thing he would have done for the woman he loved was leaving her. Harlow might never find out what happened to him. She might never know the truth. That he wanted to change, wanted to be who she needed him to be.

After a moment the fire in his muscles ceased but the shaking didn't.

"What the hell was that noise above us?" a deep voice asked. "It sounded like a helicopter."

Jensen knew that voice, and if his muscles would move, he would be on his feet ready to attack the bastard.

Cliff Hamilton stood above him.

"I don't know. The traffic is bad today," Phil said with a sneer as he looked down at Jensen. He'd mistaken the gun in his hand. It was a taser, the darts connecting the two of them so Phil could send another shockwave through Jensen at any time. "It's probably the local radio station. They're always reporting on the crappy traffic. They're gone now and like I told you, I made sure the surrounding units are empty during the day. No one cares what we do here."

Hamilton stared down at him with deep-set eyes, a frown on his face. "I want that fed dead. It was part of my deal. I need to present my friends with a body. If I don't, they can bring hell down on my head."

Shit. They had someone inside the FBI. It explained how they figured out where he lived and that he was on his way in. Jack had called and talked to several people on his team, getting things ready for the meeting that was supposed to occur this morning. But Hamilton would know all about it and be done with him and on his way out of town before they had a chance to miss Jack.

"So this is the asshole who's been following me?" Hamilton was a big guy, at least six foot five, with a dark beard and steely eyes. He might have been handsome if his depravity didn't show on his face. "What the hell did I do to him?"

He didn't even know.

"He probably can't tell you. This thing is modified somewhat from its original state. It gives it a little kick," Phil said with a chuckle.

Hamilton looked his way. "Then how the fuck is he supposed to tell me where I can find what he was about to hand over to the feds if he can't talk?"

That seemed to flummox Phil, and Jensen knew he had a shot at buying some time. He had to pretend to not be able to talk.

He wasn't pretending right now, though. He was still shaking, his gut churning. His knees knocked together, and he couldn't control the way his hands clenched and unclenched.

"Uhm, I thought… He can be dangerous. Didn't your contact tell you he used to be a soldier or something?" Phil asked.

"Yeah, he was an MP. Now that I think about it I believe she said I killed someone close to him." Hamilton knelt down. "Is that what I did, you asshole? I took out your girlfriend or something?"

He didn't even fucking know. All this time he'd made this man the center of his world, and he didn't even remember Tommy. He likely hadn't even done it himself. He'd ordered someone to do it. It was all useless. So fucking useless, and now he was going to die here and it was useless, too.

He was useless.

The only thing he'd ever been halfway good at was being Niall's friend and Tommy's brother. He could have been good at loving Harlow if he'd been able to see past his guilt and fear.

It was fear. He was afraid of loving her. Of losing her. Of not being worthy of her.

Hamilton reached out and pulled his head up. "You and me are going to have a talk and you're going to tell me where you put that hard drive. Then I'll kill you. If you think that's not a good deal for you, well, let me show you what I can do while you're alive."

He stood up, a gleam in his eyes, and then he brought his foot back and kicked Jensen squarely in the stomach.

All the air left his lungs and before he could breathe, Hamilton kicked him again. And again.

Jensen groaned and hoped the end came soon.

Chapter Eighteen

Harlow dropped down on the lawn in the greenest patch she could find since she hadn't expected the building to have a slanted roof. Jasper had claimed he could get low enough that the drop wouldn't be too bad. She'd been willing to chance it, but Niall had thrown a Dom hissy fit, and since she really could roll off the fucker, she'd given in.

She looked up and Niall was climbing down. He got to the last rung and carefully jumped.

Jasper immediately took off since he'd already heard some radio chatter about a rogue chopper, and he'd explained he was too pretty to go to jail, so he was heading for his uncle's office where he would update Big Tag on what was going on.

Niall winced as he straightened up but didn't complain. Not about pain. "You should have let me go first. I would have caught you."

She glanced around, her SIG in hand. Everything looked quiet and calm now that the chopper was off. She looked at the numbers. They would have to move to the other side. "I couldn't be sure they don't have someone on lookout. I didn't want you to get shot while you were trying to catch me. I knew you would want to."

He frowned her way. "Well the next time we have to jump out of a chopper, I'd like the chance to spare your knees."

He was a beautiful man. Could she trust him? She damn straight couldn't trust the asshole she'd come to save. "We should move around to the front."

She started for what seemed to be the parking lot, moving past the laundry room. This wasn't like her condo. There were no inside amenities. If Jensen wanted to do a load of laundry and it was raining, he would have to wait. She glanced inside but no one was there.

"Tell me again why we're not calling the cops." Niall's voice had gone quiet, and he moved behind her.

"Because it would cause a hell of a tangle, and we can't be sure they won't arrest Jensen and put him in a cell alongside whoever is trying to kill him." She moved slowly, listening for anything that would let her know they weren't alone. The apartment was set back from the street, and they were in a rundown part of the city. There was a convenience store across the street ahead, but the stores around it were all closed down and abandoned.

All of this could have been avoided if her asshole cousin answered his phone or read his texts.

"Traffic was awful," a deep voice was saying. "Look, can we tell my boss I got here in plenty of time? You said he just went upstairs, right? Big Tag doesn't care that there was a three-car wreck on I30. He'll expect my ass to fly here, and he can be mean. I lost his damn niece. He's never going to forget that. I'm in the dog-house."

Landon Vail. He was a McKay-Taggart bodyguard. She breathed a deep sigh of relief and moved around the building.

"What's happening? Where's Jensen?" She wasted no time.

Jack's eyes widened when he saw her. He looked up as though he could still see the chopper. "Damn it. Ruby. Ruby sent a damn chopper to pick your ass up and make my life hell." He pulled his cell phone. "Guess I should have answered her."

"Yeah, you should have," Harlow said with a frown. "She wasn't flirting with you, asshole. She was trying to tell you that the hit is on for today."

Landon raised a hand. "Yeah, I'm supposed to tell you that, too. I was just getting to the pertinent information."

"After you covered your ass," Niall added.

Landon sighed. "It was traffic, and no one sent a chopper for me. Look, I'm here as Jensen's bodyguard."

Jack's eyes rolled. "I think I can handle it. He doesn't need a bodyguard."

Landon's eyes narrowed. "Big Tag says he does, so if you want to fire me, shoot me because that's the only way I'm not glued to this dude. Apparently there's a hit on him, and it's supposed to go down today. Also, my boss thinks that this Hamilton guy might already be on the move."

Jack's head shook. "No. My intel puts him still in LA until this afternoon."

"You have a leak," Harlow pointed out. "Otherwise, how would they have known you were moving him? We need to put hands on him. I can't believe you let him walk up there alone."

Jack flushed slightly. "I was on the damn phone and then this guy came flying in like a bat out of hell. Look, you might follow the big guy's orders, but I work for the FBI, and Big Tag isn't a god there." His jaw dropped as he stared at his cell. "Fuck me."

"He's on the third floor according to Ruby's intel," Niall stated. "I'll go up and bring him down."

Landon moved in. "Not without me you won't. I'm serious. Big Tag's niece wiggled her way out of a bathroom window and got kidnapped on my watch. And then she got her ass kidnapped from where the kidnappers held her. The first kidnappers. There were two. Now I was not responsible for the secondary kidnapping…"

She held a hand out. "I don't need to know. Niall and I will go get Jensen and once he's safely at the MT building, we'll let you guys handle it."

Jack's head shook. "We're going downtown to my building."

"No." On this she would not be moved. "You might work for the FBI, but someone there is obviously working for Hamilton. There is zero chance all of this is coincidence. Who did you call last night? Did you tell someone you thought you would be bringing him in today?"

"More importantly, did you tell someone where his data was?" Niall asked.

"I talked to several people. People I trust. People I've worked with for years now," Jack replied.

"Then give me a logical reason why the hit suddenly had a target date, and it was the very morning you were bringing Jensen back to Dallas." She wasn't letting Jack off the hook. He was loyal, but he had to see logic. "I'm not joking with you, Jack. You are going to take him to Big Tag and you can have whatever meeting you want in that building, but you aren't bringing him in until you figure out how this information got out. You're lucky they weren't waiting for him. How long has he been up there?"

"He was walking up the stairs when I got here," Landon explained. "I saw him disappear around the corner, but Jack said it was okay."

A pit opened in Harlow's gut. She stared at her cousin. "I swear if he's dead, I'll take you out myself."

Jack seemed to suddenly take the threat seriously. "I didn't… I thought Ruby was calling to tell me I was a bastard for taking Jensen in. He wouldn't let me leave him, damn it. Whose idea do you think this was? It sure as hell wasn't mine since somewhere out there my papa is mad as hell at me and likely ready to sic my momma on me. What am I supposed to do? Knock him out and leave his ass behind? I have a killer to bring in."

She wasn't truly angry about that. "I don't care that you brought him here. Jensen is a big boy, and he made his choices. He wants to go into witness protection for the rest of his life, more power to him. He'll get a whole new life, and I won't be around to bug him anymore."

"I don't think that's what he meant," Jack argued.

She didn't care. "What I'm angry about is the fact that you ignored every attempt to contact you. Ruby has been trying to warn you all morning, and you ignored her like she's some chick with a crush you don't want to deal with."

"Believe me, I know she doesn't have a damn crush on me," Jack shot back. "That woman can't stand me which is why I avoided her, but I do understand. I'm sorry, Harlow."

"I don't need an apology. I need Jensen alive and whole and on his way to someplace safe, which will not be the FBI building until you figure out where your leak is," she announced. "I know you can't imagine anyone would take Hamilton's piles of cash over their deep belief in our justice system…"

Jack held a hand up. "I get it. I fucked up, and for some stupid reasons that I need to work on. I'll go get him. You stay here."

She was done talking to Jack. She started for the stairs. "Landon, we're going up. Watch for anyone coming in or going out."

Landon moved behind her. "I'll take a spot on the stairs while you grab him."

She strode down the path toward the stairs at the west side of the building that would lead her to Jensen's apartment. Naturally it was as far away as possible, and she wondered if he chose it for the privacy. It certainly wasn't for comfort, as the place looked like it was going to fall apart. The walkway was lined with overgrown bushes that would have been nice if anyone gave a damn. They gave the place privacy, but in a creepy way.

She rounded the corner and felt a hand on her arm as someone moved from said creepy bushes, and she realized that her instincts were right on time. A big guy with disheveled hair and kind of wild eyes pulled her against him.

"Drop the gun, bitch," he snarled. He had his own gun shoved against her side.

Niall immediately dropped the gun and had his hands up. "Hey, no problems here, buddy. Why don't you let the girl go?"

Fuck. They were here. She noticed neither Landon nor Jack had rounded the corner. Smart boys. So they would be trying to find a way to get behind them. She wasn't sure that was possible with the overgrown greenery. "Where's Jensen?"

"I said drop the gun," he reiterated, trying to get as close as he could, likely making himself a smaller target.

She did as he asked and let the gun fall to the grass. And eased her hand into her pocket, feeling for the knife she'd put there. She didn't need a gun to take this asshole out, but if she could get some information from him, she would.

She took a deep breath and let the adrenaline flow over her. In a good way. She'd been trained to stay calm in dangerous times.

Your mind is the most important weapon you have, Harlow. Staying calm means you can make decisions other people can't in the same circumstances. You wait and bide your time, and then you make your move and no one will see it coming.

Damn it. She was trained by her dad. Oh, her papa had been there, too, but it had been Chase Dawson who sparred with her, who questioned her until all of this was habit. Staying calm. Breathing. Waiting for the right time.

"Where is Jensen?" She let a tremble hit her voice. Like she was scared and ready to cry. She needed to get as much information as she could. "Please, I want to see my boyfriend."

"Your boyfriend is in serious trouble," the man said. "My boss wants a word with him, and I think maybe he'll talk faster if I take you up there. Maybe if he sees how we're going to treat you, he'll tell us what we want to know."

Niall's face went a florid red, but she watched as he clenched and unclenched his fists, his eyes on her. She gave him a wink. He was trying. He wasn't following his caveman instinct to protect his woman and screwing everything up. He was doing what she asked him to. Staying calm and letting her take the lead.

"I don't...please don't hurt me. I can't...you're going to..." Thank the universe he couldn't see her face because she was really better with making her voice sound all subby and sad. Everyone told her she could sound scared but still look like she was going to cut a bitch. "How many of you are going to...hurt me?"

She didn't say what she meant. How many of you motherfuckers plan on gang raping a girl? She wanted a number.

He chuckled as though all of this was funny. He thought he had them right where he wanted them. Did this asshole even know there were two more of them or had he simply waited in the bushes and done no recon? "Well, darlin', there are only three of us right now, but maybe we'll take you with us. There's always a place for another whore. My boss is going to think you're real pretty."

His boss might think she looked real familiar if he paid any attention. After all, she'd been arrested at one of his company's houses.

"I think you should take me," Niall offered. He was obviously trying not to panic.

Her Master was having a shitty, shitty day.

"What the hell do I want with a fed?" the asshole asked.

So he thought Niall was Jack. Nice.

"Hey, Harlow, are you going to play with him some more or can we get this train moving?" Jack asked as he walked in behind Niall. Landon followed, his gun trained on her attacker.

The man behind her stiffened, but she was already moving. She stabbed him in the arm, the one that was holding the gun, and he immediately dropped it. She then brought her other arm up and back, hitting the fucker in his solar plexus like her dad taught her. Her attacker let out a low moan and stumbled back. But not so far back that Harlow couldn't do the other thing her father taught her.

You've heard the phrase never kick a man while he's down, baby girl? Well, you kick him while he's up or down, and you get him right in the nads.

The man whimpered and fell to the ground.

Harlow picked up her gun and stood over the asshole. She pointed it right at his head. "How many men are up there?"

She believed him, but it was good to verify.

He held his hands up. "Three. It's me and the boss and Phil. The boss didn't want a big group because he had to move real quick, and the person he has at the FBI didn't want a mess made. We're supposed to get the data he stole and get out. If he showed up we were supposed to disappear the asshole, but we couldn't find the drive."

She was confused about a couple of things. There was a scream going on inside her to get upstairs, but she had to find out as much as she could before she went in. Jensen wouldn't give it up, and they knew Jack was out here. They would need to take him out, too, and that was a problem. "You were willing to kill an FBI agent? That's heat you don't want."

"Someone in the bureau doesn't like that kid. We've known who he was for weeks. We have shit on him that will make his disappearance be something the FBI will want to hide. They've been planning this for a while," the man said.

She looked back at Jack, whose expression had shuttered. This part was his mission. She had to go finish hers. "Take care of him. I'm going to get Jensen. I'm not playing, Jack. Am I going to have a problem?"

She'd known the minute she realized Hamilton was here that she would likely be causing local law enforcement a shit ton of paperwork because they wouldn't go down easy, and if they got the cops involved they would defer to the FBI, and she couldn't trust any of them except Jack. So taking them all out was the likeliest scenario. If she tried to bring Hamilton in for questioning, he could get the upper hand and take Jensen hostage.

Jack shook his head. "I'm keeping this one alive, and if he ever wants to see the light of day again, he'll tell everyone the truth. I'd like a couple of moments alone with him. Landon, go with them. Make sure Niall doesn't hurt himself, and stay out of Harlow's way."

Harlow took off, jogging up the stairs. Halfway down the walkway she clung to the side and slowed down, not wanting to make a sound or make the place shake since this was a flimsy building. She put a hand out, and Niall paced his steps to meet hers.

She looked back and took him in. He was grim but determined to watch her back and to get Jensen out of this.

She heard the sound of a taser being flipped on. It was an unmistakable sound. This particular wisdom hadn't come from her dad. It had been Big Tag who taught her how to use and evade and recover from a taser.

She would bet Jensen hadn't gotten hit by one before.

A low groan floated to her ears.

She moved closer, stopping before the front window. The drapes were closed but they didn't mask the sound of fists hitting flesh.

Landon brought up the rear but moved past Niall. He whispered her way. "I'll go first. They're expecting a man. We got two, and it sounds like Jensen's on the floor. Do you want me to shoot to incapacitate?"

She shook her head. "Take 'em all out. Jack has what he needs, and it sounds like Hamilton doesn't, so he's not going to shoot Jensen quickly. Don't play, Landon."

Landon nodded.

And then they moved in.

"My man is about to walk in with your fed friend and then we'll have a good time with him, too," a deep voice was saying. "Hurting you doesn't seem to work, so let's see how long it takes hurting another asshole. You look like the kind of pussy who can't stand to see someone hurt."

"Yeah, he always stopped people getting rough with the girls," another voice said. "He was weak. I'll be glad he's gone so we can start running the clubs like they should be."

"Fuuuuuck…yyyoyou," came Jensen's reply. She could hear his teeth chatter.

Niall reached out. "Be careful. I love you."

She nodded. But didn't say the words. She was too focused, every bit of her attention on the job ahead. A cool professionalism had come over her, and nothing else could touch her right now. She wished she'd left Niall behind but it would have hurt him.

Landon knocked. "Yo, boss, took out the fed. What you want me to do with the body?"

He did a decent impression of the man she'd taken down. Landon was going to be excellent at his job one day.

The door opened and the man from the club frowned in the doorway. "You're not…"

Landon shot him and moved out of the way for Harlow. She pushed past Phil and entered the small space Jensen had called home for months. Hamilton stood over Jensen's body, his eyes wide with shock. Jensen was on the ground, his body still seizing from who knew how many encounters with electricity.

Hamilton dropped the taser and went for his gun and Harlow shot him.

In the end it was that easy.

When you shoot, make sure he doesn't get up. You take aim and fire, and don't wait for him to give you an excuse or tell you how wrong you are. Take him out.

Hamilton fell to the floor as Harlow shot him again. Two to the chest. She thought she could avoid the head shot or it might look like a pro had done it or the mob. Then again…

The truth is usually best. Or some approximation of it. Don't let your cover get too complicated.

Her dad was in her head a lot today.

Niall rushed in, dropping to his knees by Jensen. "Damn, man. What did they do to you?"

"Go easy with the darts. They can hurt coming out. And turn that fucking thing off so it doesn't accidently get him again," Harlow said, standing over them, watching Niall helping Jensen. Jensen had tears running down his cheeks, but she couldn't bring herself to drop to her knees and hold him.

He'd left her. This was what she had for him now.

"Yeah, hey, could you tell Big Tag…no, don't get Big Tag…" Landon sighed into his phone. "Hey, boss, yeah, we're going to need a cleaner. Or maybe a friendly police contact." He paused. "Nah, he's alive. He just won't be using a TENS unit anytime soon. All the friendlies are alive, but I did kill a bald dude who looks like he belongs on the back of a bike as the old version of one of the *Sons of Anarchy* guys. Yes, he was an asshole. You told me I was only allowed to kill assholes…"

She stared down at the men she'd loved and realized how easy it would be to fall right back into their arms again. It had been the safest place. Well, it had seemed like the safest place. Like many things in Jensen's life, it had been a lie.

"Harlow, I think he should go to the hospital," Niall said quietly.

"We'll get him looked at," she heard herself say.

"Well, he was tasing a guy and not in a fun way. Yeah, it was one of her dudes. That's how I knew he was an asshole." Landon put a hand over the microphone of his cell. "He's sending someone. He's going to talk to our DPD contacts, and then he'll put the call into the FBI. I'm going to take the phone down and let him talk to Jack."

Was she going to stand here? If she did for too long, she might break down. He almost died. He'd been tortured.

Jensen was looking up at her with agony in his eyes. He managed to reach a shaking hand up. "Har…har…low…"

The impulse was right there. To take his hand and comfort him and stay with him when he went to the hospital. She wanted to smooth things over for him. And he would take it all. He would take everything she had to give him and then next time he decided something was "better" for her than he was, Jensen would leave. It was what he did.

She took a step back. "Make sure he tells you where the data is. I don't want the feds to get it first. I want a copy made before we turn it over." She turned to Landon. "Here, I'll fill Ian in. I'm sure Jack's busy."

"Harlow," Niall called out as she started to step outside with the phone. "He needs you."

But Jensen didn't, and he'd proved it over and over again.

"He'll live and he has you," she said quietly. "I'll make sure the ambulance knows where to pick him up." She put the phone to her ear. "Hey, Ian, Landon did a great job, but Jack has some real problems."

She walked out, letting professionalism hold back the storm of emotion that threatened.

She wasn't going to give him one more second of her tears.

* * * *

Niall sat in the small room in the emergency department, staring down at his cell. Still nothing.

"She's not calling you back, man. You should go after her." Jensen looked beyond tired, but then he'd had like thousands of volts of electricity run through his system or something. He'd been hooked up to EKGs and had his blood taken and reflexes tested. He'd also talked to the Dallas Police and a man who introduced himself as Jack's boss.

They had been here for hours, and not one word from Harlow.

Was she done with him, too?

"I'm not sending you home in an Uber." He was pissed at Jensen, but he couldn't abandon him. Though now he worried Harlow would think he was choosing Jensen over her.

His gut was in knots, but he wasn't sure what he should do.

"I can call someone." Jensen looked past tired. He'd aged in the hours since he'd gotten out of their bed and made the choice to leave them.

"Who?" Niall was unaware he'd made a bunch of friends while he was seeking his revenge on the man who'd killed his brother.

Who was dead now because Harlow put a bullet in him.

Would Jensen hold that against her?

Why was he even thinking that way? She'd made herself plain. If he had a shot with her—and that felt like a big if all of the sudden—he would have to give up Jensen.

His only family.

Jensen sat back, moving his hand like the IV there bugged him. "Well, I guess I would call an Uber."

"And where would you go?" His friend wasn't thinking straight. "Your place? It's being combed over by the police and the FBI. Do you honestly want to go back there?"

Jensen's last act before the ambulance had shown up had been to crawl to his kitchen, to find the place behind his refrigerator where he'd slipped the drive. It was covered with wallpaper and had taken him a moment to locate since his hand had still been shaking, but he'd passed it off to Landon to take to Harlow.

"It's all I have," Jensen admitted. "I can't even sleep in my car. It's still impounded. I'll figure out how to get that out."

"I already got it out for you."

Niall turned, and one of the Dawson brothers stood in the doorway.

Well, his luck was holding, since that was Chase Dawson come to tell them to stay the fuck away from his daughter. Behind him was Ben. He could tell the difference because Chase's expression was utterly impassive, and Ben looked sympathetic.

Chase stepped inside. He wore a button-down and slacks with loafers that likely cost more than Niall made in a month. "I had your vehicle brought down here. It's waiting when you're ready to leave. You should know that Ian has smoothed everything over with the police and the FBI… Well, we're not sure what they're doing at this point, but they don't want anything else to do with you. They're satisfied they can take down the rest of the organization."

Yes, that was a man who looked like he'd gotten everything he wanted.

"Are you doing okay?" Ben was in a T-shirt and jeans and sneakers, casual to his twin's chic.

"Where's Harlow?" Jensen asked, ignoring the question.

A brow rose over Chase's eyes. "She's with her mom. I'm fairly certain at this point her sister and Ruby and Gigi have joined them. I think they were opening a bottle of wine when I left. She had a rough day."

"She spent some time talking to the cops. They were practically high-fiving her," Ben admitted. "We managed to get to the station about halfway through her interview."

Jensen's eyes were steady on Chase. "Is she safe? They let her go?"

"From being prosecuted for taking out Hamilton?" Chase waved that off. "Like I said we have contacts, too. And obviously they let her go. How else would she be with her mom? I assure you they're not opening wine down at the station."

Ben sighed. "Give the kid a break. He had a rough day. They said that taser they used on him was amped up beyond anything they've seen. The cops were worried about his heart function after all that electricity."

"They should be more worried about his brain." Chase took up a place at the end of Jensen's bed, looking him over like he was a subject to study. "You know if it had been Harlow, she could have taken it. She knows what a taser feels like. I didn't do it. It's precisely why I let her train with Big Tag. I couldn't tase my baby girl any more than I could send assassins out after her."

"What?" Niall stood.

Chase waved him off. "They weren't real, but she would have flunked the course if she'd gotten tagged. Huh, tagged by Tag. That's what he should call it. Anyway, I hoped Big Tag would scare the shit out of her and she would go back to college and get her master's in history or something and be safe."

"She was never going back. She didn't love getting her undergrad," Ben pointed out. "You can't treat her like Greer."

"I know that. Now. She took to that training like a duck to water. A violent, aggressive, perfectly competent at taking out the bad guys duck," Chase said with a sigh. "I have to deal with it. Anyway, don't worry about Harlow. She'll be fine. Jasper got off with a warning from the FAA. I think that was because they sent out a young woman who he took to lunch and probably is in bed with now. Youth. That kid should be happy he didn't kill anyone today."

"He's a handful," Ben agreed. "I'm glad we only had girls. So much more reasonable."

Chase snorted.

Niall stood, done with the brothers' banter. "But Harlow did kill someone, and she's not unaffected by it. I want to talk to her."

One of Chase's big shoulders shrugged. "Then you should call her."

"You know she's not answering her phone," Niall replied.

Ben sent him a sympathetic look. "I think she needs some time."

"Like years," Chase added.

Niall shook his head. "If I give her time, I'll lose her."

Chase frowned and gestured to Jensen. "I don't think she's taking him back. Are you planning on dumping your best friend for a girl you've known for a couple of months?"

"If I have to," Niall said.

"Yes," Jensen said at the same time.

"Well, isn't that interesting." Chase looked at his twin. "You were right. He's going to martyr himself, and the other one is going to be too timid."

Niall knew which one he was. "I'm not timid. I thought we were solid, Harlow and I. We said I love you even after this asshole dumped us."

"I didn't dump you," Jensen said with some fire back in his tone. He'd been lifeless for hours, dull and without any of the bravado he'd come to expect from his friend. "I was protecting you."

"You say potato he says abandonment," Chase snarked. "It all boils down to the same thing. Asshole here has decided twice to protect my daughter by leaving her behind to clean up all of his messes."

"Hey, I thought we were being gentle about this," Ben complained.

"I am," Chase affirmed. "I left my gun at home. That's me being gentle."

"I didn't mean for her to clean up my mess. I meant to do that myself." Jensen sounded stronger. "I meant to clean it up so she didn't have to be touched by it. I was going to give Jack what I had on Hamilton and offer to testify."

"Without the lawyer we so generously provided you with," Chase pointed out. "Did you think Lucas left his home for funsies?"

"Well, I kind of thought he left so he could fuck with his son." Niall wasn't going to let them run all over Jensen. They didn't have clean hands in this either. Especially Chase. "You're the one who pushed her boundaries time and time again. I need you to understand that if I'm her man, I'm going to have a problem with that, Mr. Dawson."

Chase's eyes narrowed. "Then it's a good thing you're not her man since you're here with him and not her."

"Chase," Ben began.

The man was intimidating, but Niall'd had a day. He got into his potential future father-in-law's space. "I do not intend to let her go. I owe Jensen, and I know that hurts her right now, but she's a logical, kind woman and she needed some space. She's not going to have it for long because I intend to convince her to marry me, and when I do, I'm going to trust her. I'm going to support her. And I'm going to call her father out when he fails to do the same."

Chase's face fell. "Damn it. Fine. Ben, I owe you twenty."

Ben snorted as he sank down to the seat Niall had vacated. "I told you he wasn't going to play dead."

"Well, he's been quiet up to this point," Chase shot back.

He wasn't going to be quiet forever. He liked to lay back and wait to see if he was needed rather than inserting himself into every situation, but it was clear Chase needed more. "I love your daughter, and if she'll have me it won't matter that you don't like me. What will matter is her happiness, and she can't have that if you're constantly fighting her. She loves you. She also worries you think she's an incompetent moron rather than the brave warrior princess she is."

"And now I like him." Chase sighed again, a long-suffering sound. "All right. My brother here seems to think our daughter can't be happy without at least one of you."

"Both," Ben corrected. "You know I said both."

"We can't pick one?" Chase asked.

Ben stared at him.

Chase's shoulders came down, and he seemed to give in. "Fine. But it's obvious to me they're going about this all wrong. And killing that asshole isn't going to bother Harlow. She's had to save more than one young woman from his criminal organization. Trust me. She'll sleep like a baby when it comes to that."

"But she's going to be upset that she's not with the men she loves." Ben sounded like he'd been thinking about the situation. "She's angry with Jensen for leaving her again."

"I thought I was protecting her," Jensen said.

"You should still do that. I can offer you a ticket to Europe since the whole witness protection thing isn't going to work out for you,"

Chase offered.

Jensen's gaze focused, and he flushed slightly. "I was trying to keep her safe. I might have done it in a stupid way, but I love her. I love her so much I chose her over my revenge. I know that sounds dumb, and I wish I had made different choices, but I'm here now. I know you won't believe me but I made the decision to call her after I turned over what Jack needed. I was going to ask Niall and Harlow to come to Dallas and be with me when the feds interviewed me. I was going to beg forgiveness. You were right. I didn't think I was worthy of her. Hell, I don't think I deserve the support and friendship Niall has given me, but I want to try. I want to change and be good for them."

Chase sobered. "Changing for someone else… It's a starting place."

Ben nodded. "A good intention, but it won't work until you decide to change for you. Another person can make you want to change, but in the end you have to love yourself enough to do it for you."

Chase stood at the foot of Jensen's bed and stared him down. "So this is how it's going to go. Your car is outside. When we spring you from this place, you're going to The Club. There's a hotel there, and you have a room for however long you need it. You're going to work as a dungeon monitor but only after you pass all of our tests. I'm going to warn you. I will be strict. It's part time, so I suggest you find another job, too."

"I'll ask some friends around town," Niall promised. Something was happening, and he was starting to think it was good. "I might be able to get him a job at a gym."

"He can work at yours," Ben suggested.

"I don't want to make Harlow uncomfortable," Niall replied.

Chase seemed to think about that for a moment. "What are you willing to risk to give her what she needs?"

An easy question to answer. "Anything."

"Then it's time to top her," Ben explained. "She doesn't have to accept Jensen right away, but keeping him in your life is important. Seeing him and understanding that he's not leaving this time will go a long way to fixing the situation."

"You're going to help us?" Jensen asked.

That was wrong. "They want to help her, and our gorgeous princess is stubborn. She's capable of burning her own house down when she gets mad, but what she needs is to meet the brick wall. My brick wall. The one that doesn't move or shake when she's upset or loses her cool. The one that won't crumble or fall. I'm not letting her spend a single night without me."

Ben gave him a thumbs-up. "That's how to roll, Niall. If you let her sleep on it, she'll tell you she wants a break and she'll overthink things and let her fear and pride keep you apart. Jensen is a different story. She does need a break from you. She needs you to show her you can change, that your priorities are different this time, and that means loving her from afar for a while. You want her happy?"

Jensen nodded. "So much I was willing to give her up."

"How about you? You want to be happy, Wiley? Do you deserve to be happy?" Chase asked, and there was no sarcasm in his tone this time. He was serious and open, and this was the father Harlow loved.

"I don't know," Jensen replied with quiet honesty. "I know I want to be happy, but I'm not sure I deserve it."

"Then we'll work on that," Chase said. "Niall, you're going with Ben. I'll take Jensen to The Club, and I expect you both to be there in a couple of days. We have a group that plays basketball twice a week."

"We're playing basketball?" Jensen asked and then nodded. "Yes, we can play basketball. Niall, are you okay with this? I left you, too. I left you alone to take care of her and I just… I've been trying to leave you on your own for years now. I don't want to. You and Harlow are everything to me."

He let go of his anger. It was a surprisingly easy thing to do since he'd figured out a long time ago that he did deserve happiness. There was only one way for him. Sharing Harlow with his best friend. "I'm okay with getting our girl back and making her happy. And somehow I don't think it's just going to be basketball, man."

Ben stood and put a hand on his shoulder. "You, Niall, are a smart man. Now let's talk about how you're going to break into my daughter's condo and be waiting for her when she gets home from her extended session with the girls to complain about men. It's why we're here. If wc stayed it would turn on us."

"I thought we should go to a bar or something, but Ben thought we should do some charity work." Chase was right back to snarky. It seemed to be his true language.

But Niall had seen the real man lurking under his rage and sarcasm. He'd seen the man who loved his daughter and would open his home and heart to the people she loved.

He was going to be a hell of a father-in-law.

"I'm ready," Niall said and reached a hand out to his best friend. "I'll see you tomorrow."

Jensen took his hand, squeezing it tight. "You love her enough for both of us tonight."

"Did not need to hear that," Chase said under his breath.

Niall snorted. He wasn't taking anything back. "Will do."

He followed Ben out, ready to start the fight of his life.

Chapter Nineteen

Harlow sat in Ruby's car, staring up at her building.

This was not how she'd expected to end the evening.

"Where did your dads go? How are you not worried about them disappearing?" Ruby sat in the driver's seat of her SUV, her hands on the steering wheel.

She'd been a rock this afternoon and long into the evening. Ruby waited at the police station where she'd given her statement.

Then Ruby had taken her to her parents' place where her mom and Greer and Gigi had been waiting with food and wine and willing ears.

Not that she'd used those. Everyone had tried to get her to talk about her feelings, but she couldn't. She couldn't be the dumbass girl who cried over the guy who'd left her twice. The first was reasonable. She hadn't known what he could do. The second time she'd been very informed and still let the asshole into her bed.

"I suspect they went to tell Jensen and Niall to stay away from me." She'd briefly talked to her fathers. Dad had been pissed she hadn't called him in, and Papa had actually agreed with him but they'd dropped it pretty quickly. They'd hugged her and told her they loved her, and Dad told her how proud he was that she'd followed all her training and dropped the asshole with two to the chest.

"I thought Niall wasn't the bad guy here," Ruby prodded gently.

Her mom had looked worried when she left with Ruby, but Harlow promised to be back for breakfast in the morning and everyone had given her some space. It looked like her bestie was ready to push her.

"I know. He didn't leave me, but I'm also not sure that it can work. They've been friends for a long time. Honestly, they're practically brothers, and while Niall might be mad at Jensen right now, he will get over it." She'd thought about it all afternoon. Ever since the moment she looked down and Niall was on the ground beside Jensen, holding his hand, following his instincts when she couldn't give in to hers.

Ruby was quiet for a moment. "You haven't forgiven him for spying on you for Jensen?"

She should have gotten out of the car faster. Harlow sighed and sat back. "I think I have. It wasn't like he stalked me. He moved into my circle and hung out and tried to help me when he could. But that kind of makes my point. He moved his whole life when Jensen asked him to."

"He seems like he loves it here," Ruby replied. "I would be surprised if he doesn't try to keep his membership at The Hideout. Are you going to ask the board to expel him?"

"No." But how was she going to see him every weekend? She tended to spend most Friday and Saturday nights at The Hideout. Thursday nights, too. Sundays they usually had brunch at someone's house, and all of the members were invited. Niall usually showed up and wolfed down pancakes and bacon and laughed with everyone. "I don't think he should get kicked out. He's a good Dom, and I think he needs the club."

Ruby's eyes narrowed. "So you're going to pull away and leave it to him."

Ruby knew her well. "I thought I should take some time off."

It made sense. She needed to focus on herself and why she made terrible choices. She needed to focus on the business and her open cases and building a life without them.

"So you don't want one without the other?" Ruby asked the harsh question, though her tone was sympathetic.

"It's not like that. I do want him, but I don't think it can work. I did for a second. I even told Niall I loved him. I do. But I saw him with Jensen."

"You wanted him to pick you? Instead of going with Jensen to the hospital?"

"Of course not. I don't want him to have to choose. Jensen is the only family he has left, and I can't take him away. No matter how pissed I am at Jensen."

"You aren't pissed at Jensen," Ruby argued. "Look, your mom and sister and cousin are all treating you with kid gloves, but I'm your friend."

Oh, was this about to go bad? She wasn't sure why. It wasn't like Ruby was close to either guy. "What are you trying to say?"

"I don't think you're letting yourself feel what you actually feel. You ran on pure adrenaline this afternoon, and it felt way better than realizing Jensen made the same mistake again. You aren't angry at Jensen."

She nodded because this was something she would wholly admit to. "Jensen is being Jensen. I'm the one who should have known. I should have known when he slept with us last night. I thought he was all in, but he was saying good-bye, and I stupidly didn't see it."

Ruby groaned. "That's not what I'm talking about either. Look, I know you're mad. I know you want to blame yourself because you, bestie, are a control freak, and if you are the one at fault then you can make sure it won't happen again. If it's all your fault, then there's no need to talk to either of them. You don't have to open yourself to them because it was your fault, and you certainly can't trust yourself to not make poor choices. But Harlow, it's not a poor choice to love someone. Even if it all goes bad. Do you have any idea what I would give to have the love you've been given? And I think that's part of the problem."

Ruby was shaking her walls a little. She wasn't wrong. Her best friend had pretty much summed up her thought process, but she was still confused. She wasn't mad at Ruby. Ruby loved her and was trying to help her. Harlow just wasn't sure how. "What do you mean? Say it because this is starting to feel like a therapy session, and don't think my mom hasn't already begged me to let her make an appointment for me."

Ruby sat back as a light rain started, gently falling on the windshield and making the rest of the world seem gauzy. "You know about my mom, right?"

Ruby's mom had been distant, from what she understood. She'd loved her, but after Ruby's dad had walked, she'd shut down. She gave Ruby the necessities. Roof over her head, food on the table, what she needed for school. But Sonja Lockwood's real comfort was alcohol, and she got mean when she drank. Which was most of the time. "Yes. I know you're still not close."

Ruby sighed, a weary sound. "Not close. She moved to Houston, and I only found out when my Christmas card was returned. I don't know what I would have done without Vanessa Malone. I don't think I would have gone to college. I often tell the universe thank you for sending me into her sister's house the night we met. But that's ancient history. What I'm trying to say is I worry that because you've never had a family member flake on you, you're being harder on yourself and them than you should be."

"Because my parents love me?"

"Because love feels like something that should be easy."

She was forgetting a few things. "I assure you being Chase Dawson's daughter isn't easy."

"So you have to put up with a father who adores you so much he loses his head from time to time. I know it's annoying. I'm not being sarcastic. It is annoying, but you've never questioned if he loved you. If you're lovable at all. Not really. I mean we all do, but it can be harder when you have evidence to support that you aren't," Ruby explained.

Like a mom who told her she wrecked her life. Like a dad who walked out. "You're saying I'm taking the love I've been given for granted?"

Ruby's head shook. "I'm not saying that. I'm saying Jensen was the first time you truly got your heart broken, and I know how hard it was for you to trust him again. You were willing to risk everything for him."

Her heart ached. "I was."

"And the one thing he couldn't risk was you," Ruby pointed out.

"He didn't ask me."

"Because from what I can tell Jensen has rarely been in control of his life. Think about it, Harlow. He was parentified. He was poor. He had all of the responsibility and none of the control. Everything was on him, and he was a kid," Ruby said. "I don't love what he did to you, but I understand some of the forces that led him to make the decisions he did. When everything is on you, you learn to make decisions rapidly and without input. I know I did it until I was a teenager and met Vanessa and Michael and learned that family doesn't have to share blood. I'm better now. I learned how to trust people. And before you say you can't love without trust, I assure you I still love my mom and I know I can't trust her. I know she doesn't love me, but I…I guess I still hope she'll show up one day."

Harlow reached out and put a hand on Ruby's. "I hope so, too, but I don't know that I'm doing what you think I'm doing. Niall can't be happy without Jensen in his life."

Ruby flipped her hand over and held it. "I am going to ask you a couple of questions, and I need you to be honest with me. Do you love Niall? It's okay if you don't. It's okay if this whole thing was fun and sexy and exciting and you really only loved Jensen. But you have to be honest."

"I love Niall. I love him so much it fucking hurts." No hesitation there. She was trying to be honest with herself.

"Okay, and you don't think you can ever forgive Jensen?"

"I don't…" Honesty. "I'm so mad at him."

Ruby took a long breath. "What's under the anger?"

Tears filled her eyes. "Sorrow. I'm so sad that he didn't trust me. Fear. I don't know I'll ever love anyone the way I loved them. But it can't work. I can't take Niall away from his only family."

"And how is that any different than what Jensen did to you?"

Fuck. Harlow sat back, breaking the connection because damn it, she was right. "I didn't talk to him. I stood there and looked at them and made the decision to spare Niall."

"Nope. Who were you sparing, sweetie? Who did you want to save from heartache?"

The tears spilled over. "Me." She had looked at them together and realized Niall would have to make the choice between them, and she wasn't sure what he would do. She'd made the decision to spare Niall the problem of choosing. But she was saving herself the heartache of potentially not being chosen. Even when he'd told her he chose her. "I love him, and I'm scared he'll regret choosing me. And I worry that it won't work without Jensen."

"Does he have to break all contact with Jensen to be welcome in your life?"

Put like that it sounded awful. "Of course not."

Ruby was relentless. "Could he still maintain a relationship with Jensen that doesn't include you?"

She would never dictate her boyfriend's friendships. "Yes."

"Then shouldn't he be the one to decide what he wants? Like you wanted to be the one when Jensen left?"

What had she done? She'd looked down and been jealous that Niall could still feel for Jensen when she was frozen. Jealous he could be the better person. Worried he wouldn't understand that she couldn't be. She still loved Jensen and watching him lie there… It damn near broke her, but she was trapped in a place where she couldn't try again. She wasn't sure she ever could. But would she demand he leave Niall's life, too? Did she even want that? Or did she want to put Niall in exactly the place he'd been in before? Watching over someone because the person who asked was too afraid to try?

"Harlow, lay it out to him," Ruby advised. "Tell him what you're feeling. Please don't lock all of this up inside. Regret is a toxin in your veins, and I don't want that for you. If you don't feel like he'll hear you out, then he's not the right man for you."

Harlow brushed away tears. She knew exactly what Niall would do. "He'll listen to everything I want to say, and he'll hold me and kiss me and tell me he loves me and chooses me. But what if it… What if I need them both?"

"Then you find a way to make it work," Ruby said with obvious relief that she was finally talking instead of making sarcastic comments and drinking too much wine.

Harlow suspected that she would have gotten this whole conversation with her mom in the morning if Ruby hadn't pushed her. Or Greer. Or Gigi. So many people who wouldn't leave her alone. "I don't know if I can trust Jensen."

"Would you consider it if he worked on himself?" Ruby asked.

She knew her bestie. "What do you know?"

"I know your dad isn't going to tell Jensen to fuck off," Ruby revealed. "I might have listened to your dad and your papa in their office. You know the one without windows, but the lack of windows weirdly makes it easier for sound to bounce around to certain places. Like the air duct in the bathroom next door."

Ruby would have made an excellent spy. "And what were they talking about?"

"Your dad called The Club and rented an apartment for Jensen. He and your papa are going to offer him a chance. He works at The Club and he goes to therapy, and they don't force him to leave the city," Ruby replied.

"But why?" She could believe it of her papa. It sounded like him. Her dad… She kind of thought Chase Dawson would lead the charge to shove Jensen out.

"Because he loves you and if you love Jensen, then your dad is going to try to make sure Jensen has what he needs to be good for you," Ruby replied. "Because I think in some ways your dad sees himself as the you."

Oh, so many tears now. "Mom struggled in the beginning. Because she loved them but didn't think she was worthy. And he was brave when it was hard for him. He was brave because he knew he wouldn't ever love anyone the way he loved my mom. I'm not being brave."

"And that's okay. You need some time, but don't shut and lock doors you might need to open later," Ruby advised. "Your relationship with Niall started out as friendship. I don't think that's how it went with Jensen though, right?"

"We pretty much fell in bed the first night, and it was all passion and fighting and fucking." Ruby's words were forcing her to examine the situation. She was right. Harlow had been running on adrenaline for hours. She needed to sleep and think. "We didn't work on a friendship, but that was what was great about the last week. I liked spending time with him. I liked how when I wanted to be alone, they had each other. It felt natural to be with them in a way it didn't before."

"So take time before you make decisions. Not with Niall. I think you know what you want with him, and if you only want him if Jensen comes with him, then you need to let him go."

Harlow shook her head and reached for her cell. "I want him. I love him. No matter what happens with Jensen, I want to be with him if he wants me. Would you mind taking me to his place if he's there?"

She dialed his number while Ruby said yes and took the car out of park.

"Hello, Harlow," Niall said. "Are you all right? Are you still at your mom's?"

Just hearing his voice made the tears fall faster. "I'm so sorry I was cold to you."

"Princess, you were processing. It's all right. I love you. I'm waiting for you," he assured her.

"Then I can come over? I want to talk."

"You could go to my place but I kind of already broke into yours. I wasn't letting you sleep alone tonight," he replied.

She hung up and thanked her friend and ran through the rain for the lobby. Need ran through her. Need to see him, to assure herself he was okay. He would tell her if Jensen was all right.

When the elevator opened on her floor, he was standing there. He opened his arms.

And she was safe again.

* * * *

Jensen stood in the big lobby of the building he was staying in. The Club was part office building, part BDSM club, and part luxury hotel/condos. It was absolutely unlike any place he'd ever been in.

This was Harlow's world and yet he could still see her laughing and having fun in his rundown childhood home. He could see her sitting by the river with her feet in the water, sipping an iced tea.

This might be her world, the one she grew up in, but she wasn't some spoiled rotten princess who couldn't appreciate anything without a designer label. Harlow could be happy in any number of places.

He hoped she could be happy with Niall. He prayed for that.

It had been three days since he'd moved from his hospital room to the gorgeous one bedroom with a balcony and a glorious view of Dallas. It was stunning, but all he could do as he sat out there at night was think about her.

Niall had called and promised she was doing well. Niall told him they were moving between his crappy loft and Harlow's place while he was getting back into the groove of working. They were planning on going to The Hideout this weekend.

He wished them all the good things in the world.

Maybe one day she would be able to look at him again. Maybe one day they could be friends.

Fuck, he missed her. He missed her and missed Niall and missed the him he might have been if he hadn't walked out that door. If he'd realized what he wanted before he and Jack had gotten to Dallas.

If…

His brand-spanking-new therapist had told him to write all the if onlys down so they could move on to actual real plans that would work to achieve what Jensen wanted.

But what he wanted was her and he didn't…

Yep. There it was. That damn intrusive voice that told him he was nothing. He was poor white trash and he wouldn't come to anything. He was lucky the military had taken him because the only other place people thought he belonged was jail. He let his brother die.

Identify the voice. Listen to it for a moment if you feel the need. And then reply.

Leo Meyer had him set up protocols for dealing with intrusive thoughts. It involved a lot of talking to himself. And meditation. Which he was weirdly good at. And yoga, which he was not good at.

Yet.

You try. You might fail sometimes, but you get up and you keep moving. You might have come from poverty, but money doesn't make a person who they are. Choices do, and you're going to make good ones. He went through the mental affirmations until he got to the one that hurt. It made him ache, but Leo told him something he'd immediately recognized as truth. He'd told him healing couldn't occur until the pain was acknowledged and accepted. So Jensen stood there in the middle of the lush lobby fighting back tears as he forced himself to accept the heartbreak. *I loved my brother. I did what I could. I will miss him every single fucking day, but I did not kill him. I was busy ensuring he had a future. I made the right choices when it came to Tommy right up until I decided to devote my life to revenge, and that is over now and my brother would be proud.*

Take that, intrusive voice.

"Take this." Chase Dawson was suddenly in front of him offering him a water bottle. "You gotta stay hydrated. I know we're old dudes, but Taggart is still nasty when it comes to checking a guy."

He took a long breath and hoped he wasn't tearing up because he didn't want to break down in front of Harlow's dad. He took the bottle. "Thanks. I should have brought my own, but I was in a hurry. I had a session with Leo."

"And now you can kick his ass at four on four," Chase said with a nod. "You're going to be our ringer, Jensen. You and the other one. And before you tell me you don't know how to play basketball, it doesn't matter. Your knees don't creak. Trust me, you got this. Everyone else is old. Body check Taggart a couple of times and he'll slow down. And, kid, it's okay to get emotional. If you need to break down on the court, no one will think twice. Just try to do it after we're up by ten or so. Then go to town."

Embarrassment flooded him. "Sorry. I didn't mean to be that obvious."

Chase stared at him for a moment. "Yeah, it's hard at first. When Leo cracks you open and convinces you it's okay to be vulnerable and shit and that emotion is like the whole meaning of human existence, so it doesn't make us better men to avoid it. That's a hard lesson, but it gets easier."

Maybe he didn't need embarrassment either. "Why are you helping me? I'm so grateful, but I don't understand. Niall and Harlow are together. He'll take care of her. He'll love her. He's the best man I know."

Chase frowned at him. "And you're the bad guy?"

"See, that is a loaded question because my intentions were good, and I even had this last-minute revelation that I was being a self-sacrificing moron for absolutely no reason. So all this new info in my brain tells me I'm actually not the bad guy," he replied. "But I think Harlow sees me that way, so I would expect you do, too."

He'd wondered that first night if it hadn't all been a slow play to murder him. He'd still gotten in the car and let Chase drive to The Club and give him his schedule. Work and therapy and working out and back to The Club.

He was supposed to start classes next week to get his certification as a personal trainer, but he kind of wanted to study some business, too. Niall could use someone who could help him run the business part of the gym.

"You are not the bad guy," Chase said with a sigh as though this took a part of his soul to say. "You're a dumbass, but then we all are. Look, it might have been pointed out to me that you didn't have a father figure. That you had to be the father figure. Well, lucky for you, I had a great dad. Oh, he was my older brother, but he was solid. Still is. So consider this my official taking you under my wing. I'm a sarcastic asshole but if I care about you, I'll go to the ends of the earth. Look, this love thing is hard when you didn't get a lot of it as a kid. It's also hard if you got a lot of love and never had to worry about anyone leaving. You and Harlow are on opposite ends of hard, but I suspect my daughter is going to come around and be the brave, glorious woman she is eventually. Ah, there's my proof right now. Don't fuck this up."

His jaw nearly dropped as Harlow walked through the revolving door, Niall following her. She was in a dress looking like she brought the damn sun with her. Everything felt more light, more beautiful, with her in the lobby.

She laughed at something Niall said and slid her sunglasses off. Niall was dressed in basketball shorts and a tank, carrying his gym bag. He saw Jensen before Harlow did and put a hand on Harlow's arm. He leaned over and whispered something in her ear.

She pulled back and shook her head.

She didn't want to see him. "I should go. Where are we meeting?"

"You should be patient and trust her," Chase said under his breath.

Harlow turned and started walking right up to them. She hugged her dad. "Hey. You're still doing this? I would have thought you guys would have moved to like checkers or something."

Her dad laughed. "We're not that old yet. Well, Taggart is."

"Fuck you," the big blond guy said as he walked past them.

"Wiley, if you think I'm going easy on you because you had a couple thousand volts through your system a few days ago, you're wrong. Old, my ass. I am timeless."

Chase flashed a grin as Taggart disappeared behind the door leading to the courtyard. "See, you want to put him on his ass now, right?"

"You are a terrible influence," Harlow said with a shake of her head. She turned to him and her light dimmed slightly. "How are you, Jensen?"

She was so pretty. He wanted to take her hand and tell her everything. But patience was the key. "I'm okay. The shaking has stopped, and I haven't tripped over my own feet since yesterday. I'm having sessions with your Uncle Leo, and they're going well. How about you?"

"Niall is keeping me busy," she replied. "But today I'm here to support my mom and my auntie. They lead a survivor's group. It's the one they belonged to years ago, and now they help facilitate. They're having a tea today to celebrate their volunteers. I'm going to be in serving mode."

He remembered how nice her serving mode could be, but he tamped that right down since her dad seemed to have a six sense about him. "That sounds great. Niall? Are you ready for this?"

Niall gave him a big smile and slapped him on the back. "I'm here so the olds don't take you out, brother."

No. Niall was here to support him. Those tears were right there again. "Thank you."

Harlow kissed Niall on the cheek and started to walk toward the banquet hall. "Don't tear an ACL, please. I know they're all old, but they're mean and well trained. Do not underestimate them. Hey, lunch after? My mom is serving tea cakes and shit. I need a burger and a beer."

He waited for Niall to tell her yes and then realized everyone was looking at him.

"No?" Harlow asked. A brow rose over her eyes. "Niall thought you might like a burger. They serve a lot of froufrou food here."

"Yes." He nearly tripped trying to get the word out. "Yeah, I would love a burger. I would love to have lunch with you. With you and Niall. That would be great."

Chase snorted. "So awkward. I'm going to go to the locker room and make fun of my brother."

Harlow walked back as her dad left. "It's only lunch."

He nodded. "Only lunch."

"Do you want it to be more?" She managed to make the question a challenge.

"I want it to be forever, but baby, I'm willing to work. Your dad is right about a lot of things. Not the sniper stuff. He's extremely invested in not getting sniped, and the actual statistics don't hold up, but that's not the point."

She was smiling. Like she used to. Like he amused her. "I think it's a perfect point, and you should bring it up with Dad on the basketball court because it will totally throw him off."

"I think I'm on his team. But I'll hold it for a good time," Jensen promised. "My real point is I'm trying. And it's for you but it's for me, too. I think I might like being happy for once. Like this asshole who is obviously euphoric."

Niall shrugged. "How could I not be? I got my warrior princess."

"Then it's just lunch, but Jensen, you should know that lunch can be a starting point," she said.

"We take it slow this time," Jensen offered. "I know sometimes you think we're a flash fire, but I'm going to be good for you. So friends for now?"

She held a hand out. "Friends for now." She sighed. "It won't take long if you keep looking at me like that, Jensen. Niall, I love you. Take down my dads for me."

She turned and walked away, and Jensen and Niall watched her.

"I don't think we should take down her dads," Niall said. "She's kidding about that. Her mom would be pissed if one of them ended up in a brace or something."

Oh, he thought they were about to see a whole bunch of braces. "She doesn't hate me."

Niall turned to him. "No. She loves you and I love you, and let's take a deep breath and try to find something normal. I happen to know that you're going to be invited to play at The Hideout this weekend. Don't expect sex. Just ease in and get a lay of the land and if she decides she wants a second top…"

"I'll be there."

He had a sudden surge of real hope.

She loved him. He loved her. He loved Niall.

All he had to do was love himself, too, and it would all work out.

"Let's play some basketball," Jensen said. "Although apparently it's also therapy, so you should be ready for that."

"I'm ready for anything, brother," Niall replied.

Jensen was ready for his future to start.

Epilogue

One Year Later

Harlow stood in front of the mirror and watched her mom. Natalie Dawson looked gorgeous in her mother-of-the-bride dress, but she was obviously more concerned with her daughter's. It wasn't like her mom hadn't seen her in this dress before, but she cried every single time.

"You look so beautiful," her mom said, putting a tissue to her eyes.

She felt beautiful in the stunning sheath dress. She was fairly certain her grooms were going to lose their minds.

"She does," Greer said with a smile. "Exactly as beautiful as our mom was on her wedding day. I told the photographer there are some specific shots we want."

Greer and Gigi and Ruby were her bridal gang, and they had been with her every step of the way. One of the things they'd decided to use as inspiration was her parents' wedding. They were going to do a couple of shots mirroring her favorite pics of her parents, but with her friends as stand-ins.

"Gabe is in the tuxedo I picked for him," Gigi promised. "I had to fight to get him in it, but I swear he's a young Julian Lodge. Getting Jack to stand in for…well, older Jack…was the real issue. Now that was a struggle."

Jack had been through the ringer, but somehow she thought Ruby had a hand in getting that Special Agent in a tux. But that was another story for another day. Love seemed to be in the air for all of her friends. The members of The Hideout were all settling down, and she was here for it. She'd started calling the last year mating season.

"It's going to be wonderful," she said, checking herself over one more time and thinking about how she'd woken up this morning. To men who snuck into her parents' house and slept with her even though she'd tried to play the bad luck card. She hadn't tried hard. She'd missed them even after a couple of hours. Jensen had promised they would be gone long before dawn.

And then she'd had to wake them up to kick them out so her dad didn't find out how much Taggart was teaching her soon-to-be husbands about getting around security systems.

"It is," her mom said and kissed her on her cheek. "We've been to a lot of weddings lately, but this is the best. I'm going to make sure everything is ready, and your dad isn't talking to the pastor again."

"About the three sniper positions he located? I clocked those babies the minute I walked in." What could she say? She was her father's daughter. But both of them, which is why she was able to find a church she could get married in with windows and everything. If Dad had his way, they would be doing this in a bunker with security on every door. "Seriously. It was the best of my options, Mom. The one I first wanted had twenty, and I didn't think Dad could handle it."

"You are so sweet to think of him, baby. I can't tell you how much I appreciate you being accommodating," her mom said as she brushed away tears. "I'll be back in a couple of minutes. You relax and get ready. We're almost there."

Her mom left and Ruby walked in looking gorgeous in her bridesmaid dress, and a bit irritated.

Ruby pointed a finger her way. "You are a menace."

She was. And she was perfectly comfy being that. "Yes, but why? It could be many reasons."

Ruby stared at her. "You invited Lucy Flanders. You barely know Lucy Flanders."

Oh, then the fun had started. There were certain feuds within the spy kids' group, and it was always super fun to watch them blow up.

"I totally know that whole family. I spent several summers in Bliss with Aunt Georgia. Gigi did, too."

Gigi gave her a thumbs-up. "Gotta love Bliss."

"Then you also know that Kala Taggart loses her damn mind when the woman walks in the room," Ruby accused.

Gigi giggled. "It was funny. There was a lot of talk of finding holy water and how Lucifer isn't allowed in a church. It's the perfect amount of drama because her mom won't actually let her try an exorcism. I don't think she would know how to do that, but I could be wrong. Big Tag likes his kids prepared for anything."

An exorcism at her wedding would be something to talk about forever. She had to laugh. "I invited her because I knew she would be in town and we're friendly. The drama is merely a nice side effect."

The last year of her life had been nicely drama free. Oh, not outside of her relationship. Her family and friends were stock full of spectacularly juicy drama. The spy kids delivered on that. And her friends and family didn't disappoint either, but her own life had become a well of peace.

Jensen had transformed into a man she could count on. He'd put in all the effort since that day when he left her. He was an excellent partner. He worked with her and Ruby part time. Sometimes he simply answered the phones and made sure their books were properly kept. Sometimes he went undercover with her. He was good in the field, and she liked having him watch her back. He was pretty uncomfortable flirting for information though. He usually ended up explaining that he had a girlfriend. Jensen helped at the gym, too. He'd recently enrolled in community college and was planning to study business. He went to therapy twice a week without fail.

That first lunch had become a series of them. A month of lunches and Saturdays playing together led to dinners and dates, and after six months they'd all moved into her condo together. They were happy there for now, but someday they would look for a house.

Their relationship was as adrenaline free as it could be, and it worked. They'd taken the incendiary fire that burned between them and now it was a well-tended hearth that would keep them warm for the rest of their lives.

Through it all Niall had been their quiet strength.

She had no idea what she would do without those men.

Ruby laughed and moved to pour herself a glass of champagne. "Then I will cease playing peacekeeper. Besides, Kala won't disrupt the ceremony. Any shit she pulls will be at the reception, and we're all hoping for some crazy shit. That open bar is going to lead to some poor choices, bestie."

"Yeah, but sometimes poor choices lead to something great." Harlow wouldn't take back any of her poor choices. They led her to the exact right place.

"I hope so," Ruby said quietly and took a drink.

"I'm happy with all my bad choices," Gigi countered with a grin. And then winced. "Oh, but you should know that Daisy Carter might have accidently knocked over one of the pillar candles when she tripped on… I mean I think it was air, but it might have been thick air."

Harlow felt her jaw drop. "What?"

Gigi put up her hands, waving off the danger. "It was a very small fire. Her husband apparently cased the place and knew where the fire extinguisher was. He was good at that. Like he's had to do that before."

Harlow could only imagine the heroics Nate Carter performed to save his wife from herself.

Damn, but she was happy for them. She was happy for everyone.

There was a knock on the door and then her dads were there. They looked absolutely dapper in their matching tuxedoes, but she could still tell them apart.

Even when they both got teary.

"Papa," she said, moving to him and giving him a hug. "You look amazing."

"Not as amazing as you, sweetheart," he whispered.

She turned to her dad, giving him a vibrant smile. "Only three sniper positions."

He chuckled and wrapped his arms around her. "I appreciate that, baby girl. You should know I might have paid Taggart to put a guard on each of them. Though he's already hit me with three lasers, and I'm pretty sure he brought water guns for the reception. I love that asshole. Keeps things fun."

It was good to know everyone was going to enjoy her wedding.

She was going to enjoy her marriage. For the rest of her life.

"It's time," her mom said from the doorway.

Greer stepped up and kissed her on the cheek. "See you when you're Mrs. Wiley-Jensen."

Her dad frowned. "I think they should be Dawsons."

They were actually talking about it. She didn't want to hyphenate her name, and she kind of was attached to Dawson. Her Uncle Lucas had given up his last name and changed it to O'Malley to match his partners. "We'll see about it. Hey, I'm just lucky I found the nicest most tolerant pastor in the world."

She was sure her parents' generous donation had a little to do with it, but she was getting the wedding she'd never even thought to dream of.

She followed them out of the bridal suite into the atrium. There was only the slightest hint of smoke left, and someone had reset those candles.

There was nothing so broken it couldn't be salvaged in some way. Sometimes in truly spectacular ways.

She looked down the aisle at those two glorious men who stood there waiting for her. The music started and she felt her heart race. Not out of fear or cold feet.

This was happening. It was finally happening.

Gigi went down the aisle, with Gabe resting a hand possessively on her arm as he led her away.

Ruby and Jack were next, and then Greer and Travis Taggart, who'd oddly become one of Jensen's best friends.

Then it was her turn.

"Are you sure?" her dad asked out of the side of his mouth. "There's still time to run."

"She's not leaving," Papa said with a smile. "She knows what she wants."

Her dad offered his arm. "Well, they've grown on me. But Greer is going to be married to her career."

Papa huffed, an amused sound. "Sure, she is. Let's go. I've been looking forward to this since the day you were born."

She threaded her arms through theirs.

Jensen and Niall looked up at the same time, and their smiles lit up the whole church.

"You've been trying to marry her off since she was born?" Dad returned. "And I'm the asshole dad?"

"I wasn't trying to marry her off. I was looking forward to her wedding," Papa argued.

"Not what I heard. I heard I'm the good one," Dad continued.

They could argue all the way down the aisle. It would be fitting.

"Hush. I love you both. Now get me down this aisle," she said with a smile.

Her dad took a long breath. "Just because you're getting married, you should know you'll always be our girl."

"Always," her papa agreed.

Always. And always theirs.

The music changed, the wedding march beginning, and Harlow started the walk into her happily ever after.

Olivia Barnes-Fleetwood, Tanner McNamara-O'Malley and Kade McNamara-O'Malley continue the legacy in *The Temporary Siren*, coming in 2026.

Author's Note

I'm often asked by generous readers how they can help get the word out about a book they enjoyed. There are so many ways to help an author you like. Leave a review. If your e-reader allows you to lend a book to a friend, please share it. Go to Goodreads and connect with others. Recommend the books you love because stories are meant to be shared. Thank you so much for reading this book and for supporting all the authors you love!

Brooke's Bliss

Nights in Bliss, Colorado, Book 15
By Lexi Blake writing as Sophie Oak

Brooke Harper thought she would make it big in New York City, but she knew her heart would always be back in her hometown of Bliss, Colorado. She'd intended to come home as the big-shot fashion designer she'd always wanted to be, but her dream job turned into a nightmare, and now she's crawling home to lick her wounds. When she meets up with two hot cowboys one night at Hell on Wheels, she decides they're just what she needs to get her groove back.

Bailey Kent hasn't stopped thinking about Brooke since he met her years before when he first visited Bliss. She's his dream woman, and now she's within reach. She responds so beautifully not only to him, but to his brother. They've shared women all their lives, but both know Brooke is the one. There's only one problem. She's his muse, but she sees him as a way station, not the destination on this journey she's taking.

Only one problem? Shane Kent knows his brother sometimes doesn't see the bigger picture. Bay's head and heart are wrapped up in his art, and it's Shane's job to remember the reality of whatever situation they're in, and this time it's big trouble. Their last job took them to a ranch that might have been selling more than cattle. Shane witnessed something criminal and they ran, but their old crew is looking for them and he's worried they'll find Brooke, too. And then there's the fact that they once hit on her sister-in-law and her brothers hate them…

It'll take a miracle to bring these three together, so it's a good thing Bliss is known for them.

The Accidental Siren

Texas Sirens: Legacy, Book 1
By Lexi Blake writing as Sophie Oak
Now Available

Joshua Barnes-Fleetwood is the prince of Willow Fork, Texas, but not all is right with his world. He's the heir to a multimillion-dollar company, has a family he adores, and his best friend at his side. He can't figure out what is missing until Nicole takes a job at Christa's Café. The pretty waitress is a mystery he needs to solve. He's never been so attracted to a woman, and after one night in her company, he's sure she can handle his needs. Unfortunately, he's also sure she's lying to him.

Jared "Grim" Burch found a home with the Barnes-Fleetwood family when he desperately needed one. With support from his newfound family, Grim beat all the odds and became a veterinarian. In Willow Fork, however, there are still people who are suspicious of him and his past. When he sees Nicole, he knows she's the perfect woman for him and Josh, but he wonders if he has the right to bring her into his sometimes dangerous circle.

For Nicole Mason, Willow Fork is nothing more than a pit stop. Once she can save up the money to fix her car, she'll do what she's been doing for the last several years. Run. Framed for her husband's murder, she can never stop looking over her shoulder. There's always someone on her trail, and she can't let them bring her back to the real killer. Getting to know Josh and Grim makes her dream of the life they could have together. If only she could trust them with her secrets.

When their past catches up to them all, they'll find out that even a small town can be big trouble.

* * * *

Josh stopped as they reached the truck, and he realized Nicole wasn't as close as she'd been before.

It was almost one in the morning, but The Barn was still rocking behind them. Neon lights split the darkness, and the thump of music formed a soundtrack.

They'd danced and talked and had a couple of drinks, but not so much he couldn't try to seduce the gorgeous woman. She'd had two margaritas and then switched to water. He and Grim had done the same but with beers. He didn't want a drunken hookup with her.

But he did want her. Like crazy want her. Like he hadn't felt in a long time. He knew damn well it was too soon, but he would make it work.

Except she looked worried now.

"Hey, you okay?" He stopped, giving her some space.

"She's worried, and probably rightfully so." Grim leaned against the truck with a sigh. "Nicole, nothing has to happen. We can take you home and drop you off. All I ask is you let me see you safely home. We probably should have sent you with Olivia."

Their sister had left half an hour before with her friends. She'd offered Nicole a ride, but the gorgeous dark-haired woman had wanted to stay.

Had she changed her mind?

It could be damn hard to be a woman in the world. "Do you have a friend you can call?"

She grimaced. "I have the number to a cab."

Josh snorted. "No, you have the number to Gwen Stapleton, who is surely asleep by this point. And honestly, she shouldn't be driving, much less pretending to be an Uber." He needed to make her comfortable. The night had been even more amazing than he'd thought it could be. Nicole hadn't preferred one over the other. She'd spent time dancing with both of them, and when she'd gotten looks, she'd simply ignored them all. When she'd been slow dancing with Grim and Josh had moved in behind her, she hadn't seemed surprised. She'd matched her movements to theirs, and he'd known this could work.

But not if she was afraid of them. Hanging out in a public place was one thing. Being alone with them was another.

"Darlin', if you're worried, we can walk right back in there and find someone to drive you home that you feel more comfortable with," Grim offered.

She bit her bottom lip, and then her head was shaking. "Who would that be? The only people I know in this town are Christa and the other waitresses, but I don't know them well enough to ask them to pick me up."

"I know Christa," Josh assured her. "She's my momma's best friend, and she will come get you. I would be all right with Christa taking you home."

"Our concern is that you get there safely. That's all," Grim assured her.

One hand went to her hip, and her sass was back. "Oh, really? So you two weren't going to try anything?"

Josh held his hands up as though to show he was harmless. "Nothing at all, if you tell me no."

Her lips formed a straight line. "And if I'm not capable of telling you no tonight?"

His cock kind of jumped in his jeans. That was what he'd been looking for. "You know what we want, right?"

She nodded slowly. "You both want me. You want to take turns."

"Not at all. There won't be any turn taking. Both of us will be with you the whole way," he vowed.

About Lexi Blake

New York Times bestselling author Lexi Blake lives in North Texas with her husband and three kids. Since starting her publishing journey in 2010, she's sold over three million copies of her books. She began writing at a young age, concentrating on plays and journalism. It wasn't until she started writing romance that she found success. She likes to find humor in the strangest places and believes in happy endings.

Connect with Lexi online:

Facebook: Lexi-Blake
Twitter: authorlexiblake
Website: www.LexiBlake.net
Instagram: authorlexiblake

Sign up for Lexi's free newsletter at www.LexiBlake.net.

www.ingramcontent.com/pod-product-compliance
Lightning Source LLC
Chambersburg PA
CBHW030538310726
48979CB00010B/1948/J
9781963890310